"Do y̲... about...

It wasn't what Lau... just popped out.

"Not really. I'm sure God has better things to do than to handle my petty problems. Especially when I'm capable of handling them all by myself."

"Oh, right. Your idea of handling this is rushing off to St. Louis, locking Ashleigh in a tower like Rapunzel."

"Put that way, it does sound a bit rough. But she's my little girl."

"And she needs reminding of that. Gently, from a loving father. Do you want company?"

"Maybe I do. I'm out of my depth here. Maybe you can stop me from saying anything I'll regret."

"I can try. But I won't make any promises. I've already seen you in action, Sheriff Jordan, and I can't imagine you're easy to stop in any situation."

He tipped his hat up with one finger. "Some day we'll have to test that theory."

Books by Lynn Bulock

Love Inspired

Silhouette Romance

LYNN BULOCK

lives in Thousand Oaks, California, with her husband and two sons, a dog and a cat. She has been telling stories since she could talk and writing them down since fourth grade. She is the author of nine contemporary romance novels.

The Prodigal's Return

Lynn Bulock

Love Inspired®

Published by Steeple Hill Books™

STEEPLE HILL BOOKS

Steeple
Hill™

ISBN 0-373-87151-1

THE PRODIGAL'S RETURN

Copyright © 2001 by Lynn M. Bulock

All rights reserved. Except for use in any review, the reproduction
or utilization of this work in whole or in part in any form by any
electronic, mechanical or other means, now known or hereafter
invented, including xerography, photocopying and recording, or in
any information storage or retrieval system, is forbidden without
the written permission of the editorial office, Steeple Hill Books,
300 East 42nd Street, New York, NY 10017 U.S.A.

All characters in this book have no existence outside the imagination of
the author and have no relation whatsoever to anyone bearing the same
name or names. They are not even distantly inspired by any individual
known or unknown to the author, and all incidents are pure invention.

This edition published by arrangement with Steeple Hill Books.

® and TM are trademarks of Steeple Hill Books, used under license.
Trademarks indicated with ® are registered in the United States Patent
and Trademark Office, the Canadian Trade Marks Office and in other
countries.

Visit us at www.steeplehill.com

Printed in U.S.A.

Do not be anxious about anything,
but in everything by prayer and petition, with
thanksgiving, present your requests to God. And the
peace of God, which transcends all understanding,
will guard your hearts and minds in Christ Jesus.
—*Philippians* 4: 6-7

To Joe, always,
and
To my "other mother," Louise Bulock:
I don't think I could have
done this one without you.

Chapter One

❧

"Ring, already," Laurel Harrison told her silent phone. It was only nine in the morning in her cheery yellow kitchen in California, but that didn't matter.

What mattered was that it was already eleven in Missouri. This was the information age, wasn't it? So where was her information? She wanted the news from home and she wanted it now. Or maybe even ten minutes ago. That fit with her L.A. lifestyle.

She took a sip of coffee and made a face no one saw. Her latte had gotten cold. She'd already stuck it in the microwave once, so that wasn't an option. She stood in the middle of her beautiful kitchen and tapped one foot, thinking.

Going to the freezer in the built-in, side-by-side refrigerator, she found the bag of coffee ice cubes. She knew without even wondering that no one else in her family kept ice cubes made of decaf espresso in the freezer. It just wasn't the kind of thing one did in Missouri. And right this moment it seemed a little odd to her, too.

Shrugging off her discomfort, she took the bag of ice cubes over to the mini-bar between the family room and kitchen. Other houses in the neighborhood had a full-fledged wine bar there, or a cocktail island. Laurel had a coffee bar to rival those of the professionals. She poured her cooling drink and a generous portion of the ice cubes into the blender, put on the lid, and turned the appliance on.

As she poured the frozen concoction out of the blender a moment later, she looked up at the framed poster over the mini-bar. It was from the theater release of what had been Sam's last movie. Somehow it seemed fitting that she needed to dust the glass.

"This just isn't home anymore, Sam," she said softly. Not for her, anyway. When Sam was alive this had been home. This morning it didn't feel like anything but a house. Her elegant surroundings looked almost foreign to her.

A wave of desire to go home, really home, to

Friedens, Missouri, washed over her. Granted, it hadn't been home in almost seventeen years. But without Sam, Southern California didn't feel like where she belonged anymore.

If Jeremy walked in on her while she was in this mood, he'd groan. They'd already had this discussion a few times in the past year, and each time Laurel's feelings got stronger. Without Sam here, California didn't feel like the place to raise a teenager. But Jeremy's main argument against the move was that they probably didn't even have skateboards in Missouri.

Not that she could argue with him much. They hadn't seen many skateboards when they'd gone back to Friedens for her dad's wedding. Was that really only six weeks ago? Laurel marveled at how her life had changed again in that amount of time.

When she'd gone back to California after the wedding, she'd managed to convince herself that maybe she did belong here, after all. Maybe Jeremy's argument that he should go to high school here, with his friends at Westlake, made sense, and she could postpone moving until he was in college.

Instead, God trailed his fingers through her well-ordered life and stirred things up. In the course of half a day, her new direction was clear and obvious. Did the Holy Spirit make person-to-person telephone calls? Until this week, Laurel would have said no. Now she was pretty confident the answer was yes.

Deciding to do something practical while she waited for the phone to ring, Laurel got a clean cotton towel from the kitchen and dusted the poster frame and glass. The small date down in the corner, from two years earlier, still didn't look right. It was hard to believe Sam had been gone for 18 months, too sick to work on screenplays for half a year before that.

If she needed a reminder, there was his computer. It sat silent these days, except for Jeremy's e-mail and video games. She and Jeremy were the lone occupants of this house that was far too big and grand for just the two of them.

Usually mornings found her sitting at the breakfast bar making lists over a cup of coffee. Her silly coffee was her one indulgence. She wanted a really good cup of coffee to start the day, and Sam had always made sure she had one. Now it was up to her, along with everything else. And with each passing moment she grew more convinced as the adult in charge that "home" didn't need to be Southern California.

When the phone rang she dropped her towel in surprise, even though she'd been waiting for it, listening for it, for over an hour. Her fingers hesitated over the handset of the cordless phone. Answering it would end her suspense, and she wasn't sure she wanted that.

She should have flown to St. Louis to be in Friedens for her father's surgery. But nobody won an argument with Hank Collins, even when he was arguing from a hospital bed, so in the end she sat in California and waited for the call. Everyone had assured her that her dad would be even more upset if she came all the way home again so soon after her trip to his wedding.

So here she was, in a standoff with her own telephone. It rang again. No sense in assuming that it was Claire. It could be anybody. She picked it up. "Hello."

"It's me." The sound of her sister's voice made Laurel search for her chair with her free hand behind her. She suddenly felt too weak to stand and listen to the news. Not that there was anything in Claire's tone that said the news was going to be bad. It was just that hearing her voice made Laurel realize just how long she'd been waiting, almost holding her breath.

"Tell me it all went fine." Her slightly panicky voice bounced off the pale yellow kitchen walls, the pristine tile and sparkling glass.

"It really did. I can't imagine how many people were praying us through this one," Claire said. She sounded almost as shaky as Laurel felt.

The conversation passed by in a blur, and before Laurel knew it she was holding a quiet phone in her hand again. She realized she hadn't told Claire she'd finally made the decision to move back to Friedens. That was probably for the best. Claire would just say she was overreacting to Dad's surgery.

Maybe she was, partly. Laurel was pretty sure this decision to move was brought on by much more than her dad's health.

It took her a moment to realize that she needed to hang up the phone. Doing so, she breathed the first of several silent prayers of thanks that her dad was okay.

Her lanky teenager stumbled into the kitchen a moment later. "Was that Aunt Claire or Aunt Carrie?"

He pushed a shock of brown hair out of his face. Laurel could see concern in those brown eyes that looked so much like his father's.

"It was Aunt Claire. And everything is fine. Grandpa made it through the surgery and is in recovery already."

A smile lit up his face. Laurel treasured it. Jeremy smiling that broadly wasn't something she saw every day. There were a lot of challenges to raising a fourteen-year-old boy alone, and one of the biggest was putting up with his adolescent moods.

Before she could give him any more details, or even a hug, the phone rang again. Jeremy picked it up, talking to the person on the other end just long enough that Laurel began to think it was one of his friends. Just when she'd turned to get herself a cool drink of water, Jeremy handed her the phone.

"It's Grandpa Sam."

Laurel realized that she should have called her father-in-law once she got off the phone with Claire. No one there in Friedens would have thought to tell the older gentleman how Hank's surgery had gone, though he'd be interested.

"Hello, Mr. Sam." Nobody aside from Jeremy called the elder Sam Harrison anything but "Mr. Sam." "I guess you're calling about Dad?"

Sam's voice on the phone was gruff. "Not exactly. I hope he's doing real well. The shorter time I have to deal with that idiot deputy he put in charge, the better."

"Oh?" His tone told her there was a story here, and Laurel knew he didn't need much urging to keep telling it, whatever it was. Mr. Sam was never at a loss for words.

"The fool sure isn't the same caliber of law officer as your father. Do you know what he had the nerve to tell me this morning?'' He didn't even pause for breath to let her guess. ''He said that if he caught me breaking even the slightest traffic law in Lurlene, even failure to signal a turn, he was going to take my keys. Ban me from driving within the city limits of Friedens. Can you imagine that?''

''I hardly think that's legal.'' Even when the individual in question was eighty-two and his car was an aqua vintage Cadillac that was a city block long, that didn't strike Laurel as right. ''Maybe you can lay low for a little while and he'll forget about you.''

There was a harrumph from Mr. Sam's end of the phone. ''Maybe. You haven't met Tripp yet, have you? He's a pretty persistent guy. And up until today I would have said he had good sense, too.''

''Having good sense'' was the older gentleman's highest compliment. It was also one that was instantly withdrawn when someone crossed him. ''Do you think a call from me would help?'' Laurel asked.

''Not likely. I mean, what could you do? You're two thousand miles away.''

''I could be a lot closer.'' The words came out in a rush. ''I'm really regretting not being there for my dad and my sisters. How would you feel about a houseguest for a while?''

There was a pause. "One houseguest?"

"No, you know it would be two."

Mr. Sam cleared his throat. "As long as it would be the two of you, I think I could stand it for a while. Maybe that would keep me from tangling with Tripp again. Your father won't be back at work for a while, will he?"

"Afraid not. Although if I know Dad, he won't stay down a moment longer than necessary."

"Good. Maybe if you two come out and keep me company, I can find a way to keep my car keys." They made small talk for a few moments, and then Mr. Sam hung up, conscious that he was spending money on long distance in the middle of the day.

Each call seemed to strengthen Laurel's resolve that going home was the right thing to do. Talking to Mr. Sam wasn't as disturbing as getting bad news about her father, but it was close. She worried about Sam's father, living alone in a large house, driving his huge car and getting into who-knows-how-much trouble around town. He'd been cantankerous as a younger man and hadn't aged gracefully.

How long would Jeremy have his grandfathers around? Laurel knew she was doing him a disservice by living as far away from them as she did. Mr. Sam didn't hold with new things like e-mail.

Even when Sam had gotten his father a computer before he'd gotten terribly sick, Mr. Sam hadn't take to the new means of communication. And though money wasn't a problem for him in any way, he still didn't pick up the phone and call long distance very often.

Not that her father was much better. He'd taken to the computer a little, out of necessity. Even a police department the size of Friedens's did a lot of work on the computer these days. So naturally his new familiarity with it all spilled over into Hank's personal life. Marrying Gloria had helped him overcome his long distance phobia a little, too. Laurel knew she'd heard from him more in the past two months than she had in previous years.

With this sudden health problem, that communication felt like a blessing. She felt secure knowing that if things went terribly wrong, she wouldn't agonize over what she hadn't said. She'd healed whatever wounds she had with her father many years before, and now told him she loved him at every opportunity. That was one of the many legacies Sam had left her. She wasn't shy anymore about telling anyone close to her that she loved them. Time was too short for that.

Now that she didn't have to sit around and wait on a phone call, Laurel got busy around the house. Today she was especially glad she'd never given in to Sam's argument that they needed household help. Even when Sam had been well and working from home, there wasn't much to clean up after three people. Most days about an hour took care of all the housework she needed to do. Another hour spent doing laundry, and maybe as much time running errands left her with a lot of time on her hands.

She liked being home where Jeremy could find her when he needed her. That was becoming less frequent every day, of course. Independent teenage boys wouldn't admit they needed a mother for anything less than broken bones, dramatic blood flow or money. Fortunately the traumatic two out of the three weren't a daily occurrence, even with Jeremy's wild skateboarding.

An hour later Laurel was out of chores. She didn't plan to leave the house to run errands today, just in case Claire or Carrie called back. She was still full of nervous energy, and searching for a way to tell Jeremy that his summer was going to be far different from what he'd planned.

Maybe she'd go into the storage room and sort things out to decide what suitcases they'd need for an extended visit to Friedens. She wanted to look at all of them, including some that hadn't gotten a workout since Sam's days on location, when he'd watched directors shoot his screenplays.

She headed for the desk in the hall where the cordless phone sat. Or, at least, where it should have been. Jeremy was forever borrowing the handset and losing it in his bedroom. She pushed the button that activated the pager in the handset and cocked her head to listen. Was there a muffled beeping coming from some pile of dirty laundry in Jeremy's room? It was hard to tell.

Before she could activate the pager again, the phone rang. "Rats." Nothing aggravated her more than a ringing phone that she couldn't answer. "Jeremy, you have my phone," she called. It was still ringing.

She went to Jeremy's room, looking around for the telephone handset as she went. "Jeremy Samuel, answer that phone. It might be one of your aunts again."

By the time she got into his room, Jeremy had rescued the telephone from whatever corner it had landed in, and was talking to someone. "Yeah, hold on. Wait a minute, my mom wants to talk to me."

He looked up at her. "It's for me. Todd."

He went back to his conversation and what she heard next pushed Laurel over the fence she'd been sitting on.

"Yeah. I'm back. I know, but we're in the Dark

Ages here. No caller ID, no extension in my room. No chance of my own phone line in this lifetime.''

He sounded so aggravated. Laurel looked down at Jeremy's rangy form splayed across the floor, and saw a child who was being raised in an environment that was so foreign to her own memories of growing up that it felt like another planet.

If she had ever dared speak that way to her father, or even in her father's presence, she couldn't imagine the consequences. Jeremy knew there were no consequences, but Laurel wasn't so sure that was a wonderful thing. Was this really the life she wanted for her son, while they faced his teen years? Was it the life she wanted for herself? The answer to the question was easy, and made her turn on her heels and leave the room to do some serious thinking.

''Poor Jeremy,'' she murmured in the hallway. ''You'll never know how this one day changed your whole life.''

California was not the place for her to raise this young man. And today was the day to take steps to ensure she didn't have to raise him here any longer.

It was hot in his office. Tripp Jordan wasn't used to experiencing summers like this yet. Back in the detective room of the station house in St. Louis, the windows were always closed. There was temperature-controlled air all the time, summer or winter. Of course, it was often too hot in the winter and too cool in the summer, but it didn't bring you into contact with nature, for sure.

Here there were all kinds of distractions. Not the least of which was the knowledge that he was now officially in charge here and wasn't ready for it. He'd been in charge all week, but it hadn't sunk in until this morning, when he'd faced the fact that Hank was in surgery and wouldn't be back for weeks.

He still felt out of place in Hank's office. His chair didn't sit right and the desk was too low at one corner. Plus there was the temperature problem in here—it was hot. And the coffee wasn't strong enough. Or maybe it was just that Verna made *good* coffee. He was still used to the sludge at St. Louis police stations. Real coffee, made lovingly by hand by his fifty-something secretary with her tight perm and plastic-rimmed glasses, was a new experience. The woman reminded him of his aunts, who looked sweet and old-fashioned but had every situation well in hand. And he'd always felt uncomfortable around them, too.

No matter how many faults he found with Friedens or his office in the tiny police station, he still wasn't sorry he'd taken the job. So maybe he hadn't been prepared for the changes of the past week, but being Hank's deputy had been great so far.

When the town had been looking for a deputy, Tripp had jumped at Hank's offer to take the job. The city council had liked him, the interviews had gone smoothly—and Tripp had gotten out of St. Louis, where it had felt as if the walls were closing in on him.

Once he had been hired on in Friedens, he rented a great apartment over a vacant downtown store, where the odds and ends of furniture he'd collected over the years looked dwarfed. He'd gotten settled in, and had even gotten used to seeing himself back in uniform after eight years in suits and ties.

He didn't miss the tie, but he still missed the hat: the sharp fedora that was the trademark of the "hat squad" of St. Louis homicide. Deputies around here didn't wear any kind of hat. Even the sheriff's hat that he'd been issued when he took over for Hank was a poor substitute for that fedora.

He was running his hand around the brim, trying to break it in some, when Verna ushered in his first visitor of the day. His initial guess when he saw the woman was that she was the town's version of the welcoming committee, bringing him brownies.

Although she looked old and delicate enough to be Verna's mother, she dispelled his notion that she was a grandmotherly type in a hurry. The sweet-looking older lady in front of him proceeded to scald his ears with a scathing diatribe on the unsafe driving habits of some of her fellow senior citizens. She claimed to be a representative of the Women's Club—and the PTO, although Tripp thought that she could have given birth to the school board members he'd seen. This lady hadn't had anybody in the school system in decades.

Still, she was persistent. Tripp felt himself breaking out in a sweat just listening to her. Trying to get a word in edgewise was almost impossible. Might as well wait until Mrs. Whoever-she-was wound down on her own.

He nodded and made appropriate sympathetic noises for about ten minutes. Then he'd had enough and tried to break in. After three attempts he was successful. "So let me summarize this. You believe that I ought to be writing some tickets downtown?"

The old harridan's nostrils flared. "Not just tickets. Citations. That Sam Harrison ought to go to jail. He's parked in my flower bed twice this month. That old heap of his is a menace, even standing still."

"Well, Mrs...." Tripp looked down at the desk, hoping he'd jotted down something when Verna ushered the lady into his office. "Mrs. Becker—"

"That's Baker," she corrected in a frosty tone.

"Mrs. Baker." He had to learn to decipher his own handwriting better. "Sorry about that. I'll go track down Sam Harrison and have a talk with him. If he's as dangerous as you say, I'll take appropriate action."

Mrs. Baker sniffed. "You won't have to go far. That awful car is parked two doors down from here right now. In front of a fire hydrant."

Tripp stood up and put on his hat. "Then I'll get right on it. Can I escort you out, ma'am?"

"I'm not that feeble, and you're not a Boy Scout. Although you look like one in that hat."

Tripp didn't say anything else. He couldn't, for fear of further offending an old lady on his first official day as sheriff.

It was going to be a long couple of weeks before Hank got back. How long did uncomplicated bypass surgery take to heal? He hoped it was uncomplicated. He didn't know how many days of this he could take.

Chapter Two

"You're kidding, right? Jeremy, tell me she's kidding." Gina Evans was in danger of spilling her café au lait all over Laurel's kitchen table.

"Hey, Gina, you tell *me* she's kidding. Then we'll both think so." Jeremy's voice was hopeful.

His expression told Laurel that her son was sure she'd gone around the bend, to even suggest something as strange as moving back to Missouri. And her best friend agreed with him.

Laurel leaned against the door frame of the kitchen. That way she could stand in the family room, not invading Jeremy's personal space, but still be in command of the situation. With a teenager, that was important. Especially when the teenager reached the point that Jeremy already had, at fourteen, of being taller than she was.

"Afraid not. Why would I kid about something this major?" She reached out to ruffle his hair, and Jeremy pulled away.

That part hurt, but Laurel had to remind herself that it was only natural. Jeremy wasn't her little boy anymore. He was a young man, and this was going to come as a shock to him, no matter what.

His voice conveyed that shock and anger. "Help me out here, Gina. Make her see how crazy this is."

The brunette shrugged and took a sip of coffee. "As much as I'd hate to see your mom move, it's not so crazy. I could get her a small fortune for this house. She could probably buy the biggest mansion in that little town you guys are from—"

"It's Friedens—and Mom, what would I do back there? You may miss it, but I sure don't. I've never lived there, remember?" His brown eyes glowed with emotion.

"All too well."

Gina watched them both, as if observing a game of ping pong. Wisely, she was saying nothing.

Jeremy kept glaring. "What's that supposed to mean?"

"It means that you've grown up in a different place both physically and emotionally. And I remember it every time you answer me in that tone of voice, every time you nag for the latest electronic gadget. You remind me each time you try to talk me into letting you sleep in on Sunday morning because you've stayed up too late in a chat room or with one of your buddies doing skateboard tricks out on that ramp you set up on the driveway.''

"Like none of that would happen in Missouri?" Jeremy huffed. ''Well, I know the skateboard part wouldn't happen, because I didn't see another skater the whole time we were there for Grandpa's wedding. Not one.''

Laurel suspected Jeremy might be right, but she replied, ''There have to be some there. I can't imagine even a place as backward as Friedens, Missouri, being totally devoid of skateboarders. And if it is, you'll start a new trend by being the coolest guy in town.''

The light went out of Jeremy's face. ''So you're serious about this?''

Laurel nodded. ''I am. Jer, I miss my family. I feel really rotten that I wasn't there when my dad and my sisters needed me this week. And I want to go back and help Grandpa Sam with stuff. Besides, I think it would be great if I could give you a lot more freedom than I'm ever going to be comfortable giving you here.''

That got his attention. Gina nodded while he wasn't watching her, to give Laurel encouragement that she might be on the right track.

"What kind of freedom?" Jeremy asked.

Laurel tried to frame her thoughts, so that she could be honest and still appeal to her son. "A whole bunch of kinds, really. The freedom to wander around town without me worrying what kind of trouble you could get into every moment. The freedom to have lots of people you could go talk to about a problem if you didn't want to talk to me."

"Like who?"

His voice held challenge, but there was also interest. Laurel felt that maybe he was considering the idea. "Like your uncle Ben or either of your grandpas, or even that pastor at Grandpa Hank's church that you thought was so cool."

"The one that made the jokes at the wedding? He *was* pretty cool. I could probably even stand listening to him, if only I didn't have to get up before daylight to do it."

Laurel reached out and took his hands. She was amazed at how they dwarfed hers. Jeremy wasn't anywhere near grown-up in intellect, but his body was making man-size leaps into maturity. She was in awe every day that this was the child to whom she had given birth. Fourteen years didn't seem like nearly enough time for this kind of transformation.

"So you'd give it a shot? For me?" she asked.

"I guess. Are you going to let Gina sell our house right away?"

"No. We'll go out and stay with Grandpa Sam. Don't roll your eyes when I say this, but I'm going to have to pray a while first about any decision as big as selling the house." She could see her son fighting a grin, and the urge to roll his eyes. "Hey, so you have an old-fashioned mother who prefers to take all decisions, no matter how large or small, to the Lord."

Now Jeremy's normal, rather impish grin was back. "Actually, I like that part. That way I can pray at the same time, and see if God might be on my side this time and move us back here."

"Don't hold your breath on that one, sport. Not right away, for sure."

She let go of his hands, and Jeremy straightened. He dashed the brown hair out of his face.

"So how much time do I have?"

Somehow he reminded her of the valiant hero facing the firing squad. She was sure that was the image he wanted to project.

She did some quick mental calculating. "I can't

very well just pack up tomorrow. If I take a week, will it give you enough time to tell your friends, and skate all your favorite places a few times?''

"How about ten days. I have a lot of friends. And a lot of favorite places." He sounded wistful. For a moment Laurel wondered if she really was doing the right thing.

As if to answer her, the telephone rang, and she looked for the handset to the cordless. Of course it wasn't there.

Jeremy shrugged. "Not my problem this time. I haven't used the phone since I was on the computer last night with Bill playing games..." His voice trailed off. "Which means it's probably there, huh? I'll go get it."

He headed off in search of the phone and Laurel sat back down with Gina. "So what do you think? Am I as crazy as Jeremy believes I am?"

"Don't ask me. I'm in trouble either way I answer. If I tell you you're making a crazy impulsive decision, you'll argue with me. And if I tell you it sounds great and to go for it, I'm losing my best friend."

"I guess it's hardly fair to ask you to take sides," Laurel conceded. "But tell me more about selling this house. I never thought I'd say this, but I think it's time."

*   *   *

Friedens—Ten days later

Every new day as acting sheriff brought Tripp more challenges. He was near the two week mark now. At least he wasn't bored. The temperature in the office didn't bother him as much anymore. He'd gotten used to drinking decent coffee on a regular basis. Now that he was in the office as sheriff, instead of out patrolling as a deputy, he had developed more of a rapport with Verna. She didn't intimidate him as much, although he did still feel as if he were being inspected.

Mrs. Baker and a few of her friends seemed to stop by daily with something that got under their skin. Sometimes he could hear Verna out in the main office pacifying them. On those days he considered whether Verna needed a raise. But sometimes the Old Ladies Brigade couldn't be stopped that easily. Tripp told himself he had to stop referring to them that way even in his own mind, or he'd slip and end up saying it out loud. Even if he were only talking to Verna it wouldn't be a good idea: she was probably related to half the brigade.

Over the past couple of days, they appeared to be on a rampage. Their problems were so petty. They ranged from kids still shooting off leftover bottle rockets from the Fourth of July, to threatening dogs, to parking tickets he'd missed.

After years of solving real problems in big city homicide, Tripp now kept telling himself that Lillian Baker and her friends should be a piece of cake. He was having a hard time holding his temper in check when their complaints turned out to be so minor that they weren't worth his time to investigate.

Didn't they ever have any real crime here? He knew that Hank had broken up a methamphetamine ring, because Tripp had worked some of the busts himself. It was the only major crime he could recall since living in Friedens. No murders, no other drug rings or even major burglaries. If somebody had a gun, they were probably hunting animals in season, and had a legal permit. Even the local merchants didn't report much shoplifting.

Tripp could hear Lillian Baker out there again, talking something over with Verna. His department secretary and part-time dispatcher was beginning to grow on him. She had the patience of a saint, and more common sense than most people he could name. She knew when to pay attention to the complaints of Lillian and the crew, and when to soft-pedal them as well. So far she hadn't been wrong. And since Hank was still recuperating from his surgery and couldn't come in to lend a hand for quite a while yet, Verna's good judgment was a precious commodity.

Tripp considered himself to have pretty good judgment himself, where crime and criminals were concerned. It was just that he was used to the kind of slime who shot each other on whims, dealt street drugs to their own grandmothers if necessary, and in general valued life very little. The primarily honest, fundamentally sane people of Friedens were a new experience for him. It did take a little getting used to.

Today Mrs. Baker seemed to be in the outer office by herself. He could hear her voice, sharp with complaint. Maybe it was time to go out there and give Verna a break. His coffee cup was nearly empty anyway, so he could stroll out and see what the problem was this time.

"About time you got out here," Lillian Baker said with a sniff.

Prickles of aggravation made him want to run a finger under his collar. Who did she think she was? He tried not to sputter as he answered her. "Do you have a real problem this time, Mrs. Baker? I am not rescuing any stray animals or taking any reports of burnt bottle rockets." He tried to look as stern as possible. Not that it had any effect on the silver-haired lady in front of him. Nothing phased her.

"No, this time it's not anything minor. This time I think we have a federal offense on our hands." She sounded triumphant.

She had his attention. "Tell me more."

"I didn't get my mail this morning. And what I had in the box didn't go out, either. That old boat of Sam Harrison's is parked right in front of my house, blocking the mailbox. Dorothy couldn't get anywhere near the box. Obstructing the mail— that's a federal offense, isn't it?" Her bright eyes glittered with intensity.

"It probably is." Not the kind of federal offense he was hoping for to liven up his morning, but in the long run it was easier to deal with than bank robbery. "And you're right in coming in to report this. I told Mr. Harrison weeks ago that I didn't want to see that car anywhere near downtown." He turned to Verna. "I'm sure I should know the answer to this already, but do we have a boot? A car immobilizer?"

"I didn't think you meant the kind to wear when it rains." Verna's tone was more humorous than sharp. "Sorry to disappoint you, but we've never really had the need for one. And before you ask, there's no city tow truck, either."

"Not like working for the city of St. Louis. There I could get a car towed in twenty minutes flat, every time."

Verna shook her head, making iron-gray perm ringlets bounce. "I didn't say there wasn't a tow truck in the city—just that the city didn't own one. Max down at the Gas 'n' Go would be more than happy to send his son down with their tow truck. They've been serving the sheriff that way for years.''

Tripp was learning something about small-town politics by now. ''Is that why the city-owned cars fill up at the Gas 'n' Go instead of having our own pump?''

Verna smiled. ''Now you're getting it. Should I call down there and have him meet you in front of Miz Baker's house?''

''Please do.'' He turned to Lillian Baker who stood in front of his desk, tapping a foot on the worn linoleum. ''Would you like to be driven home in the sheriff's car?''

Mrs. Baker recoiled. ''I couldn't possibly. What would the neighbors think?''

''They'll be fine. I'll let you ride in the front, and I promise I won't turn on the lights or the siren. If anybody asks, you can tell them it was your reward for reporting a serious crime.''

It was the first time Tripp had seen any member of the Old Ladies Brigade smile.

An hour later Mrs. Baker had gotten her ride home in the sheriff's car, and Tripp was done getting Sam Harrison's aqua horror out of the Bakers' flower bed. The car was probably a classic, and Tripp expected he should be congratulating Mr.

Sam for keeping it running this long. If only the older man didn't have the habit of leaving it in such inconvenient, not to mention illegal, places. Mr. Sam hadn't been exactly receptive to Tripp's last warning: this parking job was evidence of that. *Fine.* Let him get the heap back from behind the Gas 'n' Go.

How much did one charge for a towing job and parking ticket in Friedens? Tripp had no idea. It just hadn't come up since he'd got here. The few parking offenses he dealt with had been downtown meter violations, and most of those were ridiculously small fees if you stopped in at the sheriff's office and paid them the same day.

The system here really made the guys who ran the towing business in St. Louis look like pirates. One of his old buddies had told him on the phone just last week that the highest legal tow fees were approaching $500 with storage.

He ought to point that out to Mr. Harrison when the grumpy old guy came by the sheriff's department later today, as Tripp expected he would. Maybe then, he'd appreciate the fifty dollars or so that Tripp was sure he'd work out with Max for the use of the tow truck and his "storage" lot in back of the station.

Right now, he didn't feel like dealing with Sam Harrison. For the first time, Tripp felt like taking a cue from Hank and stopping in at the Town Hall restaurant for a cup of coffee and a chat with the unofficial city leaders who seemed to spend most of their mornings there. He got back in the car and told Verna over the radio what he was doing. She sounded as if she approved. This day was just full of first-time experiences.

Two cups of coffee and buckets of information later, Tripp strolled up the sidewalk to the office. He was beginning to get the hang of this sheriff thing. Maybe he'd look through the case files to see what he could work on before Hank got back. If things kept going this well, he might get a commendation from his boss for doing such a great job as acting sheriff.

With that fine thought in his head, he walked into the office. There was a stranger in the front room, and she wasn't happy. She wasn't somebody he'd met in Friedens before. No, he'd remember a woman this well dressed. Those nails she was drumming on the counter were professionally done in pale pink. The tailored summer pantsuit she wore hadn't come straight off the rack, judging from the way it fit her slender form to perfection.

Even seeing just the back of her, Tripp could tell that the most recent cut and style of that lush cinnamon mane had cost more than his uniform. What was Ms. Society doing in Friedens, in his office? She wasn't a stranger to Verna, at least, because the two of them were deep in conversation.

"Tripp can straighten it all out, honey" Verna was telling her.

"I'm sure." Her voice was cultured and frosty. "*Acting* Sheriff Jordan is just the man I want to see."

"Then this is your lucky day, ma'am." It was fun to watch her startle and whirl to face him. Her look of surprise would have been gratifying—if Tripp hadn't been so busy keeping his jaw from dropping at the beauty in her face combined with the force of her gaze. Those flashing hazel eyes could have done him in at twenty paces. It might be her lucky day, but in an instant Tripp stopped feeling as if it was his. This woman felt like trouble.

"Mr. Jordan—"

He didn't have time to correct her before she went on.

"Kindly tell me what's going on here. Lurlene is gone, and I only left her twenty minutes at the most. I just know you're behind this."

"Gone? As in missing?" Tripp's mind was spinning. What did this gorgeous woman have against him, and why was she so sure that he was responsible for her missing friend or relation?

"Gone. As in missing."

She wasn't tall enough to confront him effectively, but Tripp felt like backing up, anyway, as she came toward him. "And I know nobody took her legally, because the car keys were in my pocket the whole time."

"So do you need to report an abduction, Ms...." Tripp fished for a name.

"Abduction? Of course not." Her eyes narrowed and one perfect fingernail poked the middle of his chest. "You have no idea who I am, or what I'm talking about, do you."

She had him there. Tripp shook his head, hoping she'd move away from him. Just that tiny touch of one finger on his chest was having the strangest effect on him.

"Should I know who you are?" There wasn't anybody of celebrity status he hadn't met in town. And nobody had any movie star relatives that he knew of.

"Don't you remember me from the wedding?"

Tripp had attended only one wedding in recent memory, and it had been Hank's. A vague thought was growing in the back of his mind, and it could only mean trouble. His memory of the wedding guests he'd been introduced to was spotty. He hadn't stayed for the reception because he knew Hank would be happier if someone was minding business at the sheriff's office. Besides, Tripp didn't like wedding receptions that much, anyway. Too fussy and fancy and mostly feminine. It was beginning to dawn on Tripp that he probably should have gone to this wedding reception for a few moments.

"Don't tell me you're—" he began, only to have the woman draw herself up to full height. Her glare answered his question before her words did.

"I'm Laurel Collins Harrison. And I want Lurlene back in the next ten minutes or you have some real explaining to do, mister." There was no mistaking her tone. It was a declaration of war.

Now he knew he was in deep trouble.

Chapter Three

Her father didn't usually hire idiots. He tended toward men who were made from the same mold he was: canny and circumspect. Surely Tripp Jordan must have struck Hank the same way—but he wasn't doing much for Laurel. He looked like a grounded fish the way his mouth opened and shut while he tried to answer her. No, that mouth was much more attractive than a fish's. But still, he just didn't strike her as up to her father's caliber.

Someone had pointed him out briefly at the wedding, but she hadn't gone over to say hello. Since he hadn't bothered to come to the reception, she'd never had a conversation with him. And so far, this one wasn't going all that well.

"Laurel? As in Hank's daughter? That's the Collins part, right?"

Maybe he really *was* dense as a doorknob. "Right. And the Harrison part is as in Sam. Which is where Lurlene comes in."

"I can't answer for Lurlene, whoever she is. When I towed that car, it was empty. There was nobody named Lurlene in it. She must have gotten out to look for you before we got there. Or maybe she just doesn't like officers of the law. Mr. Sam sure doesn't."

She shook her head. "What have you been doing for the eight months since Daddy hired you? Don't you know anybody around here yet?"

He stood a little taller and puffed his chest out, to look threatening. It wasn't working. She probably knew every trick in law enforcement, which meant there was little he could do to intimidate her.

"I know plenty of people. Just not this Lurlene."

Verna coughed discreetly. "Lurlene is Mr. Sam's old Cadillac, Tripp."

It was a comfort to Laurel to see relief in the man's eyes. At least he really had been concerned when he thought he'd lost a person.

As fast as the relief had come into his expression, it faded to be replaced by aggravation.

"You really had me going, Mrs. Harrison. I

thought Lurlene was a person. How am I supposed to know you're talking about that rattletrap car?''

Laurel tried not to roll her eyes. She was definitely picking up bad habits from Jeremy. ''Go out on the street and ask any five people who live in Friedens. I'll bet you any money you'd care to wager that four out of five can tell you who Lurlene is.''

His brow knit. The expression didn't do anything to make him look brighter. That was a shame. Laurel really wanted to give this man the benefit of the doubt. Her dad had said nice things about him. And Hank didn't say nice things about too many people.

Tripp seemed to relax a little, then shrugged. ''Maybe they could. But I can tell you one thing about that car that nobody else can. I have every right to tow it, because I told Mr. Sam over a week ago that I didn't want to see it illegally parked within the city limits. Not ever again. And look how much attention he paid to that.''

''I don't think you can legally take away an old man's right to drive if he's got a valid license.''

''I never said I was taking away his right to drive. Just reminding him he doesn't have a right to commit illegal acts, because nobody's got that right. And that parking job was definitely an illegal act.'' He looked stern.

Now Laurel was the one who felt slightly foolish. "What if he wasn't the one who parked it?"

Tripp shook his head. "Don't tell me you're going to own up to this?"

"Guilty. But am I going to have to go home and tell Mr. Sam that he let me have his car for half an hour, and I got her towed away?"

"Maybe not. Do you have fifty dollars on you?"

"Fifty dollars? That's outrageous! Is the Gas 'n' Go actually charging the city for towing now?"

His double take was satisfying. "How do you know what the towing arrangement is? I thought you said you didn't even live here."

"I may not live here, but I talk to my dad plenty. And Max has never charged the city for towing. Especially not for cars that live right here in Friedens. Lurlene is nearly a landmark. But we've had that discussion already and it didn't impress you, did it." This man got under her hide like a burr!

"Still, I'm going to have to fine you."

Was she imagining things, or was there a sparkle in his eyes?

"We can put it in the sheriff's department's retirement fund if you like, or give it to some kind of charity. And whether you tell Sam or not is up to you."

"I still say that's outrageous. And now you're

probably going to tell me you don't take credit cards.''

His grin was positively feral. ''You know so much about this department. Has Hank ever taken plastic for anything?''

''Not even from bail bondsmen.'' Laurel sighed. ''At least tell me an out-of-state check is good. I have a valid California driver's license to go with it.''

''You better. I'd hate to cite you twice in one day.''

The man was brighter than she'd thought. But he was definitely the most aggravating individual she'd met since coming home. Laurel wondered where her father's head had been when he hired this one.

Still, when Tripp wasn't being absolutely aggravating, he was good looking. Of course, her father would never have noticed that. Laurel was surprised she noticed it herself. When was the last time a man had teased her senses the way Tripp did? Not in a very long while, that was for sure. She suspected she'd consider him somewhat less attractive once she wrote that check for towing. It was hard to flirt with a man while you paid him to return your car.

She was a looker. Tripp tried not to stare too hard at Hank's daughter while he drove her over to the Gas 'n' Go to get Mr. Sam's car. She was beautiful in ways that didn't usually attract him. Too polished, too put-together. If he didn't know she was Friedens born and bred, he'd tag her as a spoiled princess. She had that air about her some-how.

He wasn't much of a fashion expert, but having a teenage daughter, even one he didn't see every day, had taught him plenty about trends and prices. Laurel's handbag would have paid her traffic fine five times over. Even the matching leather cover to her checkbook would have covered the damage, with change to spare.

He tried to keep his eyes on the road as much as possible. It just wouldn't do to commit any traf-fic infractions himself, while he was driving this woman somewhere. If he did, he knew Hank would hear about it so fast it would make Tripp's head spin.

His head was already spinning just from being close to Laurel. She looked good and smelled even better. He had no idea what perfume she was wear-ing—not that he intended to ask. Given her general air of wealth and privilege, it was going to be something that cost more per ounce than he was capable of comprehending.

Still, he took a deep breath, enjoying the blend

of citrus and rose and something much more exotic that filled the squad car.

"This is the second time today I've had a lady in the front seat of the car. A new record," he said, trying to make small talk.

"Better than the back seat, like a suspect, anyway." When she smiled, she looked younger and less elegant.

"True. Although if you hadn't had that checkbook, maybe you'd be riding in the back seat by now."

"From what little I've seen of you so far, Acting Sheriff Jordan, I imagine I would. You'd be the last one to cut me any slack because of who I am."

"Would you expect me to?"

"No." Her voice still held a note of laughter. "Nobody else in town ever has. Dad stopped paying any of us allowance after we turned sixteen, and just paid our traffic tickets, instead. He said it wasn't any more expensive. At least, until Carrie came along."

"You, I expect, were the calm one." Where had that come from? And why did he want to know so badly?

"To a point. I never hit that teenage rebellion stage. At least, not until I came home from my first semester at junior college and announced I wanted to marry one of the professors."

"I cannot even imagine what Hank said about that."

"And you don't want to. It was probably two years after the wedding before my dad and Sam had a civil conversation. Of course, by then we had moved out to California and the distance alone was driving Dad crazy."

"It's hard to be apart from your family."

She turned to look at him, her expression growing thoughtful. "You sound like you know something about that."

"I do. I've got a thirteen-year-old daughter back in St. Louis. She lives with her grandmother, and I only see her about twice a month."

Her expression held sympathy, but not pity. Tripp's opinion of this woman was improving the more time they spent together.

"That's not very often. Especially at that age. I'm sorry."

"It's the way life works— And we're here." Tripp tried not to sound sharp. But the last thing he wanted right now was sympathy from Hank's daughter.

"Well, okay. Thanks."

She didn't seem to know what else to say. That was a switch. Laurel Harrison didn't look like the type to be short on words too often.

She started to slide out the passenger side, then

turned. "Do you need to come in and tell Max to give me the car?"

"No. Just show him that receipt Verna made up. He said that was good enough for him. Of course, that was when he thought Sam would be carrying it himself. But I think he'll recognize you."

"He'd better. His younger brother took me to the junior prom."

"Then I suppose you can work things out by yourself. And keep that car legally parked now, you hear?"

"Don't worry. I can't afford another ticket. Or another tow job. I'm supposed to be keeping Mr. Sam out of trouble, not getting myself in trouble."

She closed the car door and walked toward the gas station with as much dignity as if she were walking down a fashion runway. Tripp had to admit, he was enjoying the view of her retreat.

As she disappeared, Tripp tried to figure out what it was that intrigued him so. Maybe it was the fact she was so different from most of the women he knew. Everything about her was quiet, understated, but terribly expensive.

He pulled away from the Gas 'n' Go, still musing on their differences. Laurel's family could keep a Cadillac for decades, while he couldn't hold on to anything for long. Even the important stuff, like his wife, his daughter and his home, had slipped away from him. Of course, not all of that was his fault alone. It took two to make or break a marriage, and Rose Simms Jordan had done her share of both. How had he ever expected that sweet girl, born worrier that she was, to handle being married to a cop?

She'd been a basket case from day one, panicky if he was ten minutes late, calling the station house a dozen times a shift. Once Ashleigh was born, the situation got even worse. Tripp was almost grateful when the day came that Rose claimed she couldn't handle another day worrying about him, and went back to her mother. Being the practical sort, Pearl Simms took her back.

Of course, he'd always expected that Rose would grow up and come to her senses, and that they'd get back together. Marriage was a forever thing, wasn't it? He'd always thought so before his fell apart. Instead, she seemed quite content to live with her mother and daughter in a safe, quiet household where she didn't fret every moment about Tripp Jordan and the possibility of his getting shot, stabbed or mangled.

Ashleigh grew from a preschooler to a young lady, while her parents became more and more distant. Even after that divorce Rose had insisted on, when his daughter was nine, they were still friendly for Ashleigh's sake. Their daughter never saw them squabble, and Tripp could say that he'd never said a bad word about Rose in front of the child. If Rose had ever put him down in front of Ash, it had never gotten back to him. Things probably would have drifted along like that for another decade, if it weren't for Rose's health.

Why had she spent all her time worrying about everybody else, and not enough about herself? Tripp still asked himself that question on a regular basis. If they had still been living together, would he have picked up on the fact that she was having more frequent and increasingly severe headaches? Probably not. She had always been good at hiding her own discomfort and focusing on him.

There wasn't even any record of her having been to a doctor before the morning she collapsed at work. And both Rose's mother and Ashleigh agreed that Rose had never complained. The doctors called it a "cerebral accident." Whatever it was, it destroyed the person that Tripp remembered as Rose. Someone else lingered, unresponsive for a week. There was a lot of talk about brain death and lack of quality of life, and Tripp was very thankful at that moment that he was not the one legally responsible for making the decision that Pearl ended up making.

Maybe after that he should have insisted Ashleigh come live with him. But he couldn't tear the child away from the only stability she knew, even if it no longer included her mother. Rose's mom was already helping raise his daughter. As much as he wanted Ashleigh with him, her sense of security was more important.

He knew firsthand what an unstable home life did to a kid. Besides, he didn't know anything about raising a girl. Especially not now, in the thorny teenage years. Just keeping her from throwing a major sulk or a full-blown teary scene in their limited time together was nearly impossible. What would he do with her twenty-four hours a day, seven days a week? They'd both be wrecks.

It wasn't nearly as easy now that he was in Friedens and she was in St. Louis. It took more of an effort to connect with his daughter each time they got together. Still, they did connect, even though it wasn't always easy. And he'd take a bullet to the heart before he'd give up his bond with Ash.

Tripp was almost to the office when he noticed something unusual. At least, it was unusual for Friedens. There was a kid on a skateboard messing around on the stairs of the public library.

Something about the rangy, skinny kid struck a chord in Tripp. He'd been that kind of kid, daring the world to knock the chip off his shoulder. Those shoulders were bowed in for protection, and the kid wasn't used to his growing body just yet. What was he—maybe fourteen or fifteen? It wasn't an age Tripp would wish on anybody, that was certain.

There weren't any No Skateboarding signs posted in Friedens, so he couldn't just stop the car and tell the kid he was breaking the law. The young man was no novice at what he was doing; that was evident in the way he sized up the metal rail on the staircase for a trick. If he knew how to slide down a metal stair rail on that thing, he also knew enough to argue that if there wasn't a sign posted, he wasn't doing anything illegal.

Tripp didn't have it in for the kid. He just wanted to talk to him, find out where had he come from, and what he was doing in Friedens. It wasn't exactly a hangout for city kids in search of entertainment.

Tripp knew he was attracting attention by traveling this slowly down the street. Everybody for three blocks would slow down with him, leery of doing something to get a ticket from the acting sheriff. So he sped up a little and cruised on past. He'd go park the car and come back on foot. All the better to talk to the unknown young man, anyway. No sense in giving the kid a reason to dislike him right off the bat. And as Tripp remembered from the city well enough, skateboarders didn't need another reason to dislike or distrust an officer of the law.

Laurel felt like a guilty teenager sneaking in after curfew. She pulled Lurlene into the garage and looked for any evidence that might tell Sam about the car's little adventure. She didn't see anything. She retrieved her packages from the trunk and crossed the distance from the detached garage to the old Victorian house.

"I'm home. Anybody here?" The house felt empty. There was no music playing. Mr. Sam would have had big band or jazz playing on the console stereo that was almost as big as Lurlene. Jeremy would have found an alternative rock station for his radio, or put on a CD. No, there was no sound in here aside from the hum of the air conditioner.

Laurel peeked in each room on the first floor of the house as she passed by. Nobody in the parlor, which she expected. The dining room sat in empty majesty, heavy mahogany furniture as ostentatious as a dowager in a hat. Only when she got to the kitchen in the back were there any signs of life.

Even then it was just Mr. Sam's old cat Buster, curled up on the middle of the kitchen table. That alerted her as nothing else did that no one was home. Mr. Sam loved that cat, but not enough to tolerate his presence on the kitchen table. She looked again, and saw a sheet of yellow legal pad under the cat's wide rump. He made a grumble of discontent when she eased the paper out from under him to read what was written there.

"Out of milk. Gone to get some. Back by three." It wasn't signed, but with handwriting that bad, Mr. Sam didn't need to sign his notes.

Laurel looked at her watch. It was past four now. Where were the guys? Pulling the car keys out of her purse, she headed for the front door again. Visions of Mr. Sam falling ill on the way home from the store crowded into her worried mind, tumbling on top of images of Jeremy getting in trouble or hurt in town somewhere.

"Lord, protect them both," she said out loud. "At least, until I can find them and fuss at them if they're all right."

She knew it wasn't the world's sanest prayer. But it was one that she knew mothers had been saying for hundreds of years.

She was going to have to call Gina when she got home, or e-mail her, to share this latest news with a sympathetic soul. Laurel headed for the car so she could find Jeremy and his grandfather before her imagination ran away with her.

Chapter Four

An hour later, Laurel was still talking to God. This time it was under her breath, asking for patience, as she argued with Mr. Sam aloud. That eventual phone call to Gina was getting longer by the minute as she had more reason to vent. "I know you're used to living alone and not being accountable for your time. And honestly, Sam, I'm not trying to rein you in."

"Then what's this business of being sure I had heat stroke just because I was ten minutes late?" The older man's tufts of white hair stood up at right angles to his scalp.

"You were more than ten minutes late. And I was worried about you." Laurel didn't add, *just like I'd be worried about Jeremy,* although she wanted to. For that matter, she was still a little concerned about Jeremy. He should have been home by now as well. But pointing that out wouldn't sit well with Mr. Sam. If she told him how much she kept tabs on Jeremy, he would be sure she was equating his behavior with that of her child. And they were already arguing over who was responsible for whom, and how much.

Laurel took a deep breath, and let it out slowly. "I guess it boils down to the fact that we both need to get used to having another adult around, Sam. You aren't used to letting anybody know what's going on in your life. And I'm only used to keeping track of a forgetful teenager."

"Speaking of my grandson, where is he?" Sam peered around the kitchen. "At least I left you a note about where I was going to be."

"That you did. And I appreciate that part." What she didn't appreciate was his obvious attempt to shift the attention to Jeremy. Besides, it was aggravating when Mr. Sam was right about something. Laurel was beginning to think she'd been on her own too long to live under the same roof with anybody but Jeremy.

Sam lifted his glass. "Maybe once we finish this cold lemonade, we ought to go out scouting for him. I'd even let you drive. You seemed to do a good job before."

Laurel felt a pang of guilt at that one. It was on the tip of her tongue to confess her afternoon's problems to Mr. Sam and get it off her chest. Instead, she got up from the table and put her nearly empty glass next to the sink. From that position, she could see Sam's old answering machine. He'd grudgingly accepted the thing as a gift from them years ago. Even then, he'd only taken the machine when they assured him it was their own used model, that they were upgrading. Mr. Sam had never been into modern conveniences, as evidenced by the car he drove and the house he'd never renovated or moved out of. This archaic model seemed to suit Mr. Sam just fine. And right now, the message light was blinking.

"We may not need to go out after him. Maybe Jer got smart enough to call home and tell me what's going on." She punched the button on the machine, listening for the message.

It wasn't Jeremy's uncertain tenor that greeted her. Instead, it was a confident baritone, one that she'd already become too familiar with.

"This is Sheriff Jordan calling for Mrs. Smithee. We have your son Allen down here at the police department visiting us for a short time and would like you to call or come and retrieve him as soon as possible. Thank you."

Allen Smithee? Jeremy had told Jordan that his

name was Allen Smithee? Jeremy was going to be grounded for life once she bailed him out.

"Now you know that sheriff isn't going to understand Jeremy's joke," Sam said behind her with a chuckle. "Bet that Tripp is going to be pretty put-out when you tell him what's going on."

"Not as put-out as my son is going to be when I get through with him. Mind if I take the keys back?"

Sam waved at the kitchen table where his key ring still sat. "Go right ahead. I'm not getting involved in this one for love or money. That's one of the wonders of grandparenting."

"Right. Somebody else handles the mess." Laurel tried not to sound too sour. One phone call to her friend Gina was never going to be enough to explain all of this.

Sam put a hand on her shoulder. "Don't be too hard on the boy, Laurel. It's the kind of thing his father would have done, and that's a source of entertainment for me."

"I'm glad somebody's enjoying this. I don't think it's very cute." She tried not to clench her jaw. Her first thought was absolute aggravation at her smart-aleck son. Her second thought dismayed her even more, because she wanted to go look in the front hall mirror.

Before she faced Tripp Jordan again today, she

wanted to make sure her hair was combed and that she had fresh lipstick on. And her own little flash of vanity was even more upsetting than the prospect of dealing with a smirking fourteen-year-old.

Tripp looked confused when she came into his office. "Didn't expect to see you here again today."

"That's because you didn't understand Jeremy's practical joke. If you knew anything about Hollywood, script writing and the movie business, you would have, but no one expects you to."

This time he didn't look quite as dense with his brow furrowed. Laurel gave thanks that he didn't immediately look angry, either.

"Who is Jeremy, and what are we talking about?" Tripp stood up, making his chair squeal as the unoiled wheels rolled across the tile floor.

"Jeremy is my son. He's fourteen, about six feet tall, and is usually seen on or near a skateboard. And right now I suspect he's answering to the name Allen Smithee instead of Jeremy Harrison."

So far Tripp wasn't looking as if he understood any of this. "Why would he do that? He gave me the right phone number, obviously, or you wouldn't be here."

"Calling himself Allen Smithee was probably his first thought when you asked him what his name was. A Southern California police officer would probably have told him, 'Nice try kid, give me your real name,' and the joke would have been over.''

Tripp shook his head as if to clear out cobwebs. He looked as if he were seconds from running a hand through his dark hair in exasperation. ''I still don't get it. You want to explain this whole thing in terms that even a Missourian can understand?''

Laurel took a deep breath. ''It's a private joke for anybody involved in movies. Since about the 1930s, anybody who produced a picture, or directed it, or wrote the script and later decided they didn't want their name in the credits because the movie turned out too awful for words used the same fake name.''

Realization dawned on Tripp's handsome face. ''And I'll bet that name is Allen Smithee, right?''

''Correct. Jeremy's dad threatened more than once to use the Allen Smithee clause on something he wrote, but he never carried through with it.''

''So Sam, Jr. was a screenwriter?''

''For fifteen years. And Jeremy learned some of the ins and outs of the movie business from his dad.''

''So I've been had.''

''I'm afraid so. Please tell me you won't press charges.''

She didn't expect the laugh that came from Tripp.

"I should, just to teach him a lesson. But since I pulled him in on basically bogus charges myself just to get him off the street, it serves me right."

Laurel didn't know whether to laugh or cry. "Bogus? You mean Friedens doesn't have a law against skateboarding? And you brought him in, anyway?"

"It's not on the books yet. Not specifically. But only because we haven't had anybody skateboarding around town. I suppose that we could stretch some of the trespassing or loitering statutes we use for the teens cruising in cars on Friday nights. It just hasn't come up until now."

"Now I don't know who to be madder at, you or Jeremy. For him to have his first full day in Friedens end this way wasn't what I had in mind."

Now Tripp looked annoyed. "But of course you approve of him misleading an officer of the law?"

"No, I certainly don't." Why did this man get under her skin at every turn? Or maybe she was just letting him in. "You have to know that, given my background. But like I explained before—"

"I know, if I were more up on the movie business, I would have known. Guess I missed that day at the academy."

He was beginning to sound angry now, and Laurel felt herself backing down just a little from her protective motherly stance. She breathed deeply, trying to make herself calm down. "I'm sorry, honestly. I didn't mean to come off defending my son's behavior when he was in the wrong. And he is clearly in the wrong here, Tripp. No one should expect you to recognize the false name he gave you. What can I do to get him out of whatever cell he's in?"

Tripp shook his head. A hint of his one-sided grin was back. "He's not in a cell. He's in the break room, having a cold soda. And probably sweating because I let him know I called his mother. But I didn't lock him up."

He came around the desk, and Laurel was suddenly close enough to smell the spicy sharpness of his cologne. Her heart pounded alarmingly in her chest at his nearness. And her tongue stuck to the roof of her mouth when she tried to speak. "Thank you. For not locking him up. It's the last thing he needs right now."

"On top of moving across the country and suddenly finding himself in strange territory? You're probably right. Fourteen with no friends during summer vacation isn't exactly the greatest combination."

He was getting under her skin again. "Now you

make me sound like a bad parent. I'm just trying to balance his needs and my own.''

Tripp raised his hands. "Whoa. I'm not accusing you of anything. Just pointing out that I might understand the young man's behavior. Maybe I'm not totally the enemy."

"I never said you were. But I didn't expect you to be handing out parenting advice. How much experience do you have, really?"

"Not nearly enough, since her mother moved in with Ash's grandmother when Ash was four. And then…she passed away." Before Laurel could say anything, he reached into a back pocket and pulled out a worn black leather wallet. "This is Ashleigh. She's thirteen and lives with her grandmother in St. Louis."

Now she felt foolish. "I'm sorry. For assuming what I did— She's beautiful." She was, too, in that betwixt-and-between way that girls of a certain age had. Not a child, not a woman—and she probably drove her father crazy every moment they were together.

Her compliment seemed to smooth Tripp's ruffled feathers. "Thank you. I think she's rather lovely. And when she's not trying to talk me out of money or my sanity, she's almost beautiful," Tripp said. Suddenly, Laurel felt more empathy for the man than she had at any time in their short acquaintance. "Teenagers are something else, aren't they?" she said. "And raising one of the opposite sex by yourself is no picnic. Maybe we can actually help each other out some."

Tripp looked startled. "Maybe we can. Although I may be helping you more than you can help me, because Ash only gets here every other weekend or so. And summertime seems to mess up my visitation. There're sleep-overs, vacation trips with her girlfriends' families—you name it."

He sounded wistful, and Laurel felt for him. Jeremy was growing up before her eyes. It couldn't be much different for Tripp. She was lucky because she could spend so much time with Jeremy. But here was a father who only saw his daughter a few days a month, and it wasn't going to get much better as Ashleigh navigated the choppy waters of adolescence.

"I think we'd better go in and see Jeremy now," she said quietly. Changing the subject kept her from doing something foolish, like reaching out to this man. He was still an aggravating guy trying to replace her father in a job he probably wasn't cut out to do. There was no sense in getting attached to him or feeling sorry for him. Even if she did stay in Friedens for good, Tripp Jordan would be back to being her father's deputy in a few weeks. And Laurel knew that her father's rules for his daughters definitely included one that said, No socializing with law enforcement officers.

Laurel knew that her dad still groused when Carrie brought anybody home, even for a meal, that worked with her in public safety. The thought of what he'd say if word got to him that Laurel had gone so far as to fraternize with his acting sheriff made her shiver. It was definitely time to go see Jeremy.

The woman was full of surprises. Tripp didn't know quite what to make of her. Every time he thought he had Laurel Harrison even part way figured out, she threw him another curve, so to speak. Not that he noticed her real curves too much. *Right.* He couldn't even say that in his head and be truthful. He'd already noticed her curves and her angles and just about everything else physical about her.

How someone so different from Rose could attract him, and in a day's time, was amazing. This woman was polished, put together and opinionated. He liked sweet, soft women who might actually worry about him, or worry about hurting his feelings—didn't he? And if he could predict anything about Laurel from the interaction they'd had, he'd be willing to bet she wasn't going to worry about hurting his feelings.

She couldn't be all bad, though. She seemed to be doing an excellent job raising Jeremy by herself. And she'd noticed right off what a fine-looking young lady Ashleigh was. Those were both points in her favor. Jeremy obviously cared a great deal about what she thought of him. More, perhaps, than Tripp himself had cared at fourteen what his mother felt about his behavior. He could remember a few encounters with his mother at a station house at that age, and he was sure he never had the contrite look on his face this kid had when Laurel walked in the break room.

Jeremy looked up from his cold drink when they entered. Tripp wished there'd been a camera handy to capture the look on the young man's face.

"Tripp, this is my son Jeremy Samuel Harrison. Otherwise known as Allen Smithee."

Jeremy almost winced when his mother said that. Tripp fought back a grin, not wanting to give the kid any satisfaction.

"Your mom explained your little joke. Which, by the way, could be a misdemeanor if I wanted to make it one. Falsifying your identity during an arrest is not funny." He tried to sound as stern as possible, to let the kid sweat a little.

It was working. Jeremy looked down at the table. "I'm sorry. It just came out, you know?"

That sent his mother into action. "No, Jeremy,

he doesn't know. Which is the whole point. Maybe that stunt would have been funny in California." Laurel sat across from her son and got his attention by taking his hands in hers. "But here it is definitely breaking the law. Your grandpa Hank is going to go ballistic on this one."

The kid grew even paler. "I didn't think about that part."

"That much is obvious. There seem to be several things you didn't think about. What are we going to do about all of them?"

Jeremy shrugged his thin, bony shoulders. He looked close to tears. Tripp felt like cutting him a little slack and was opening his mouth to do just that, when Verna came through the break room door.

"Sheriff, I hate to bother you, but you have an urgent phone call."

Now? "I can't think of anything so urgent that it couldn't wait a few more minutes."

Verna held her ground. "Well, apparently Ashleigh's grandmother can think of something that urgent because she told me she wanted you on the phone—now."

It was the only thing she could have said that would get him out of the break room. He pushed past his surprised secretary and headed for the phone on her desk.

"Pearl? You there?"

"I sure am." Rose's mom sounded tired.

Panic rose in a wave around him again. "Is she okay?" he blurted out, certain there was horrible news.

"Physically, your darling daughter is fine, I guess. For now there's not a scratch on her." Pearl sounded shaken. "But she can't spend another night under my roof, Tripp. This time I need you to come get her."

"Why? What did she do?"

"It's more what she *wants* to do. Or what she hasn't done yet, but will. All those trips to the library to keep up with her summer reading list from school? And about half the visits at those girl-friends' houses?" Her voice was rising sharply. "Those were just excuses. She's been seeing that Richards boy down the street."

"Ashleigh's too young to date." The minute the words were out of his mouth, Tripp realized how foolish they sounded. He might think Ash was too young, and he knew Rose's mom thought the same way, but that hadn't stopped Ash so far. His pronouncement wasn't going to stop her now, either.

"That's not all." Pearl sounded grim. "That Richards boy is eighteen. Just graduated high school in June. And our Miss Ashleigh is head over heels in puppy love with him. You've got to do something, Jay. The sooner the better.''

"I'll be there by dinnertime.'' Tripp hung up the phone and headed back to the break room. How was he going to explain this to Laurel? Suddenly Jeremy's little misdemeanor didn't look like much. Not when stacked up against the attempted murder charge Tripp was going to face himself if he saw that Richards kid.

This was turning into the worst day he could remember, and it wasn't over yet.

Chapter Five

Laurel had just about given up on Tripp, when he walked back in the break room. She remembered from experience that urgent calls could take much longer than expected. Still, this one was taking a lot longer than she would have thought possible.

When he came back in, she could tell that something had happened. He looked worn and angry. The mouth she'd found appealing when it was grinning at her was pressed into a firm line. His eyes darkened to a smolder and his fists clenched and unclenched.

"Looks like we need to leave you to your business," she said. "Whatever happened just now is more important than this."

Surprise clouded his face. "How could you tell

that? We haven't even known each other a day. And most of my buddies say I'm the best poker player they know.''

Laurel shrugged. "Parents make lousy poker players. Verna said it was a call about your daughter. And I'm the mother of a teenage boy, remember? I can recognize the look of another distraught parent even when he's trying to hide it.'' She knew that statement would get her an eye roll from Jeremy, but she didn't care. Right now, Tripp looked miserable, and she wanted to help if she could.

"Glad to know my reputation at the card table is intact, anyway.'' He looked at Jeremy as if he was trying to decide something. "Could you give me a minute alone with your mom? Take your skateboard from Miss Verna and head home to your grandpa's with it. Straight home, would you?''

Jeremy stood up, wide-eyed. "Yes, sir. Does that mean you're not going to charge me, after all?''

There was a long silence from the sheriff. "Not this time.''

For a moment Laurel had thought Tripp would ask Jeremy what he should be charged with. Whatever had happened with his daughter, it was taking his whole concentration.

"And Jeremy?''

His question stopped her son at the door. He turned to face them, looking incredibly young and less cocky than she'd seen him in a very long time.

"Yes, sir?"

"A plain 'yes' would be okay. This isn't military school, although if your Grandpa Collins catches wind of your goings-on, you could be headed for one. I just wanted to tell you I wouldn't keep your mom long. Thanks for lending her to me."

Jeremy grinned. "I'd say any time, but I wouldn't mean it. Do you think we're even, if I lend her to you for a little while?"

There was a ghost of a smile on Tripp's face. "Depends on the advice she gives me."

Jeremy looked at her. "This better be good, Mom. You don't want me to have a juvenile record, do you?"

"No, but if you do, you won't be able to blame me. Now go tell Grandpa Sam I'll be along soon." She made shooing motions, and he left quickly, slamming doors behind him as only a teenage male in a hurry to leave can do.

She motioned to Tripp. "This looks like one we both need to sit down for. Let's get the worst out of the way first. Ashleigh's alive and well, I hope."

He nodded. "Not a scratch on her according to Pearl, her grandmother."

"Okay. That's good. That lets out the worst possibilities." She knew problems were different for girls' parents. Even in this modern world, troubles with female teens involved more broken hearts than broken bones. "Is she still there with Pearl? No running away?"

"Still there. Under lock and key, if I have anything to say about it." He looked grim.

"I recognize that look," Laurel told him. "As the oldest of three daughters I saw it often when any of us brought home somebody Daddy didn't approve of. She's seeing a boy, isn't she."

He seemed to explode with emotion. "Yes! And she's too young to even consider it. She's just thirteen. What business does she have dating? And how did Pearl let this happen?"

"You can't shadow a thirteen-year-old every minute. At least, not if you want to keep what little sanity you possess, or leave her with any dignity. I assume she didn't go to her grandmother and actually ask if it was okay to start dating."

"You've got that right. Pearl thought she was at the library. Or at a friend's house." He looked pained when he met Laurel's gaze. "The worst part of it is that I'm pretty sure I could have done something if I'd been there."

"Maybe you could have, maybe not. I assume it's not too late to do plenty now, though. If she's

still there with Pearl, Ashleigh hasn't eloped with
this kid—whoever he is—or made any other dras-
tic commitments."

"Of course not." Tripp looked like a raging bull
again. "She *is* only thirteen. Even Ashleigh remembers that most of the time."

"How old is the boy? Do you know him?"

"Only by reputation, and it isn't good. He's
eighteen. Way too old to be hanging around my
daughter."

"I haven't seen pictures of Ashleigh. Is it obvious that she's only thirteen?"

Tripp's head snapped sharply in Laurel's direction. "What are you implying about my little
girl?"

Whoa. She breathed a silent prayer for help.
Suddenly she felt she was in way over her head.
"Hey, I remember being a teenager. The last thing
most girls want is to look their age, whatever it is.
Is it possible that this boy doesn't have a clue how
young she is?"

Tripp paused and stopped frowning for the first
time since he'd walked back in the room. "It's
possible. I hate to give him any credit at all. That
would make it harder to wring his scrawny neck
when I catch him tonight."

That sure sounded like her father twenty years
ago. Laurel searched for the right words. What did

her mom always say at this point, to calm Hank down? She'd had plenty of practice, and none of the three girls had ever lost a boyfriend.

"Do you want to pray about this?" It wasn't what she'd intended to ask, but it just popped out.

"Not really. I'm sure God has better things to do than to handle my petty problems. Especially when I'm capable of handling them all by myself."

"Oh, right. Your idea of handling this is rushing off to St. Louis, locking Ashleigh in a tower like Rapunzel and making a fool of yourself by threatening some kid who probably doesn't have a clue how he's upset you."

Tripp's smile was wan. "Put that way, it does sound a bit rough. But she's my little girl."

"And she needs reminding of that. Gently, from a loving father who obviously wants the best for her and expects the best from her. Just like our heavenly father does for us, Tripp. Sure you won't reconsider a quick prayer before you go off?"

He stood up, looking tired. "Say one for me. You seem to have much more confidence in God than I do. But thanks for the reminder, anyway."

"Any time. Who's going to mind the store while you're away?"

Tripp shrugged. "I figure Verna and the two patrol officers we've got on duty can handle things. If they can't, I'm not going to be out of radio contact or more than an hour away at any time. And I don't expect to stay in St. Louis long.''

"Do you want company? Mr. Sam and Jeremy could manage without me for a few hours.'' Where had that offer come from? This man brought out the most amazing reactions in her.

Tripp shook his head. "I can't ask you to do that.''

"You didn't. I invited myself. If you want me.''

"Maybe I do. I'm out of my depth here. If nothing else, maybe you can translate what Pearl and Ashleigh are saying into language a street cop can understand. And maybe you can stop the street cop from saying anything he'll instantly and permanently regret.''

"I can try. But I won't make any promises. I've already seen you in action, Sheriff Jordan, and I can't imagine you're easy to stop in any situation.''

He tipped his hat up with one finger in a gesture that made her shiver. "Someday we'll have to test that theory.''

An hour later, Laurel was sure she'd finally lost her mind. What on earth had possessed her to ask if she could go along on this little jaunt? There hadn't been time to call Gina. Her friend definitely would have talked her out of this venture.

Instead, she was here with Tripp who was still

grim and mostly silent while he navigated the SUV that was his personal vehicle down the highway toward St. Louis.

So far this had been a slightly odd and awkward trip. First, he had followed her to Mr. Sam's, where she had dropped off the car and told her family what she was doing. There hadn't been time to change clothes or shoes, which she regretted. She'd hurried back outside, as Mr. Sam and Jeremy exchanged surprised glances, and had gotten into Tripp's vehicle.

Now they were on their way in silence, and Laurel was telling herself that she was more than a little unhinged for doing this. She searched her mind for conversation topics that might bring Tripp out of his shell a little. None came to mind.

She didn't have much experience with law enforcement officers who weren't related to her. Hank had always made sure of that. Of course, he hadn't been any happier when she'd brought Sam home. But then, what father would be thrilled by his nineteen-year-old daughter bringing home one of the professors from the junior college she attended? Especially one who was thirty-four, and had the itch to move to California and become a screenwriter.

Next to all that turmoil, Ashleigh's dating an eighteen-year-old sounded fairly tame. Although,

five years at her age was as much of a gap as
fifteen years had been for Sam and Laurel.

At least they had both been adults by the time
they broke the news to her folks that they were in
love. At the time, she had felt like an adult. But
the older Jeremy got, the less sure she was that
nineteen had been old enough to get married and
move across the country. Still, things had worked
out between them.

In the midst of her musing, Laurel was aware of
a hand on her arm. It was Tripp's hand, warm from
the steering wheel, and insistent.

"I asked if you wanted to stop for anything?"

She felt herself blushing. "You probably asked
several times, didn't you. I tend to go off into my
own airspace once in a while."

He shrugged. "I figured it must be a California
thing."

"Not really. I was a daydreamer in Missouri,
too. It's just a little more socially acceptable out
there."

That made him chuckle. "Yeah, well, it doesn't
answer my question. Are you hungry or thirsty or
anything? Because once we get past the next two
highway exits, I'm not stopping until we get to St.
Louis."

"It's kind of you to offer, but I'm fine. And I

know you want to get to Pearl's and see your daughter.''

"I do and I don't. What do I say to her? If I yell at her like I want to, she won't want to come home with me. But I don't want to give her any choice. I can't let her stay at Pearl's and mess up her life.''

He still stared straight ahead at the traffic on the highway. Both hands were back on the wheel, and Laurel could see where his knuckles were turning white from his intense grip.

"I still think that praying about this whole situation together might be a good idea. How about if I just said something out loud, and if you agree with me, you can say, 'Amen'? Will that work?''

There was a long pause, and then Tripp nodded. "Okay. I'll give you that much. But if I don't agree, don't hold your breath waiting on that 'Amen,' either.''

That seemed to be Tripp. Bold, blunt and just a bit contentious. Laurel wondered what that bold spirit could do for good under the right circumstances. It was an awesome thought.

"Okay, here goes. Let me gather my thoughts a little." Laurel tried to concentrate on this girl she hadn't met yet, and the girl's father, whom she knew so little. It was difficult, with trucks rumbling past, and this man who so confused her sitting so close.

Another deep breath, then she closed her eyes. *"Dear Lord, you hold us all in the palm of your hand. Even with your perfect example, it is so hard to be a parent. We know that you have a plan for each and every one of your children, Ashleigh included. Help her to see evidence of that plan in her life, and help her father find the right words to lovingly guide her in the right direction."*

"Amen."

Tripp's answer was so soft, Laurel almost didn't hear it. When she looked over, his hands didn't seem to be gripping the wheel quite as tightly. It comforted her a little. Maybe now he'd slow down to within five miles of the speed limit. She should have put something about peace and calm in that prayer.

"We should have brought Jeremy."

Laurel's pronouncement startled Tripp so much that he almost swerved in his haste to look at her.

Maybe he hadn't really heard her right. "We should have what?"

"Brought Jeremy along. As company for Ashleigh on the way back."

"Oh, yeah, that's just what I want. Here, honey, I want to get you away from this environment where you're hanging out with boys. Oh, and guess what I brought for you on the way home?''

"Ouch. I didn't think of it that way. But neither would Jeremy. He's not exactly a smooth operator around girls yet.''

"Just things with wheels, huh?'' Tripp tried to hide the snarl in his voice. Laurel didn't deserve him snapping at her the entire trip, even when her ideas weren't the greatest.

"Mostly just skateboards, at this point. Although, he is showing some interest in helping Mr. Sam retool Lurlene. Those older cars have much simpler workings, according to his grandfather.''

"He's right. To understand the new ones, you have to have a degree in computer science. I miss the days when I could do more than change my own oil.''

"I'll bet you were the kind of teenager that always had your head under the hood of a car, weren't you.''

He could hear the smile in her voice. "You got that right. Usually I was under that hood doing something that would get me into trouble, like making whatever I was driving a little faster, a little harder to catch…'' He felt absolutely nostalgic. "How about your husband? Did he inherit his father's love for old vehicles?''

"Not really. But then, by the time we met he

had worked that all out of his system, if it was ever there.''

''Oh? I thought all young men went through a decade or so when they tinkered with cars continually. Everybody I knew did. And I remember your dad saying you got married young.''

''I was young. Nineteen.'' She sounded a little far away, and Tripp wondered what she was thinking. Had he unintentionally messed up here? It wouldn't surprise him if he had. Around this woman he wasn't any smoother than a teenager himself.

''Is that all dad said about my marriage?''

Now, that sounded like an odd question. What was behind it? ''Pretty much. We haven't had a lot of time to talk about things like that. He said you married young, and he and your mom didn't exactly take to Sam right away.''

''That's an understatement if I ever heard one. My mother came around some before she died. But even after Jeremy was born, Dad wasn't so sure about Sam.''

There was something in her words that he still found puzzling.

''Tripp, if you're just being kind, and Dad said what he really thought about Sam, you don't have to be chivalrous on my account.''

''You don't know me well enough yet to know

I'm never that chivalrous. Did Sam have a record or something? It's about all I can imagine Hank holding against him."

"No, Sam had never been arrested. He just wasn't the man my father had in mind. He was a professor at the junior college, and when we met he didn't have tenure or much money, or much of anything except a desire to dump the job he had and go to California."

Tripp felt he might have more in common with his boss than he'd realized. When they got settled down and back to Friedens, he would have to ask Hank how he had handled the situation with Sam without killing his future son-in-law. "So Hank was upset that he was losing his little girl."

"That was part of it. The other part of it is that Sam was closer, by several years, to Daddy's age than mine."

Tripp did some quick mental math. When she'd said Sam was an assistant professor, he just assumed he was a very young assistant. "Whoa. I know your dad is over sixty, though not by much. So you were dating a man who was, what, over thirty?"

"Thirty-four. And he didn't lie to my parents about it, either."

Wow. He was really going to have to have that talk with Hank. His admiration for his boss grew by the moment. "I guess that's one point in his favor. But I have to admit, I would have been as upset as your dad."

"No doubt. You're already upset, and your daughter and this boy she's allegedly been seeing are both teenagers."

"Just barely," he reminded her, starting to feel prickly again. "She's only been one for a matter of months, and the boy is way too close to being an adult for my taste. Does your observation mean you don't see as much wrong with this as I do?"

Out of the corner of his eye he could see her shaking her head.

"Not my call to make. I know that when I was nineteen the age difference between us mattered much more to my parents than to me. Or to Sam. But we *were* both adults, and your daughter is far from that point."

"At least we agree on something."

Tripp pulled off the highway and started working his way through the grid of south St. Louis streets that made up his old familiar neighborhood—brick row houses and small apartment buildings interspersed with bungalows with stone steps and porches. Kids rode bikes on the street, the bravest and most foolish ones swerving into the path of cars. If it hadn't been for Laurel, he would have stopped and yelled at the kids. Tripp swore as he maneuvered quickly to avoid one of them.

He could hear Laurel's intake of breath.

"If you're going to take your daughter home," she admonished, "you don't want to use language like that near her."

His temples were pounding. "I don't. I also don't want to hit a kid on a bike. I'm human, Laurel, and most of the places I've found myself in as an adult are filled with people who swear."

"Not in Friedens. Not like that."

He tried not to sigh. "You're right. Verna has a swear jar just for such occasions, and I'm the main contributor." He didn't add that Hank wasn't far behind him, because that obviously wasn't the image Laurel had of her dad.

There wasn't any more time to argue about this, anyway. They were at Pearl's front door. Tripp parked at the curb and turned off the ignition. Now more than ever, he missed his hat. His real hat, the sharp gray fedora that sat in his closet in Friedens gathering dust.

In that hat he could face down anybody, including Pearl and his argumentative daughter. The sheriff's hat just didn't give him the same feeling of authority.

Maybe because he didn't feel like a sheriff. He'd always felt like a detective, always been comfortable in the job. Even as Hank's deputy he liked the territory. But now he was on unfamiliar ground in so many ways. The job didn't fit, the hat didn't fit—and he had no idea what to say to his daughter.

He thought back to the prayer Laurel had said a few minutes earlier. Maybe it wasn't such a bad idea, after all. He was definitely struggling with what he would say to his daughter when he got inside. This could be one of the most important conversations of his life, and he felt ill-prepared to do it alone.

"Amen," he said again under his breath as he stood on the hot asphalt outside Pearl's house. In this situation he needed all the help he could get.

Chapter Six

$\sim$

He didn't come around and open her door, but that didn't surprise Laurel. Tripp Jordan had too much on his mind right now to worry about manners. She suspected that under normal circumstances he might have remembered something like that. But these weren't normal circumstances for either of them.

She felt tremendously out of place here. Why had she ever agreed to help a near stranger with something this emotionally charged? Little flickers of nervous fear played in her stomach as they went up the concrete walk to Pearl's house. Standing on the front porch and watching Tripp ring the doorbell, Laurel tried to calm herself by taking in details of the place.

If nothing else, Gina would want a full description of the house, when Laurel finally called California tonight. Her friend's eye for detail in housing wouldn't be satisfied until she knew exactly where and in what kind of place these people lived. Gina always said it helped her picture the person involved more than anything else.

The front of Pearl's porch was stone, and big pots of geraniums topped the half columns that rose waist-high. Pearl must be a pretty good gardener, because there were still flowers blooming in pots in St. Louis in August. That was an accomplishment.

There was a metal glider swing under one window on the porch. Laurel could imagine sitting there when the temperature cooled down a little in the evenings. She wondered if Ashleigh and her friends ever did that. Was being thirteen so radically different now from when she was that age? She knew that in some ways it was, but in others there still had to be the same worries and concerns about hair and clothes and who one was or wasn't.

The door opening startled her out of her thoughts.

"You made record time," the woman that she assumed was Pearl Simms said.

She was a compact, friendly-looking soul with gray hair. Laurel liked her on sight.

"Who's your friend?"

She could see Tripp's shoulders stiffen a little. He opened his mouth, then closed it. Laurel got the feeling that he had almost told Ashleigh's grandmother that this wasn't a friend he was bringing. But then how would he explain her to Pearl?

He shrugged and motioned for Laurel to go into the cool living room before him. "Moral support, I guess. Pearl, this is Hank's daughter, Laurel Harrison. She's got a fourteen-year-old son and she offered to come with me. Mostly, I believe, because she was afraid I might hurt somebody if left to my own devices."

"You? Now, where would she ever get that idea, Jay? Just because you're armed and dangerous most of the time, and have a temper like a Rottweiler…"

Laurel noticed that Pearl was smiling as she said that. But it was a wry smile. Laurel made a mental note to ask one of them why she'd called him 'Jay.'

"I'm almost sorry I told you about that Richards boy. Thought about sending him some kind of message to get out of town if he knew what was good for him."

"This isn't the Wild West. I won't go after him, much as I'd like to." Tripp sighed. "Now where's

Ashleigh? Or is she even speaking to anybody at this point?''

"Just barely. Why don't I get you two settled here in the living room with something cold to drink after that drive? Then I can go upstairs and tell her you're here."

Pearl motioned toward overstuffed furniture lining the living room walls. The room was a mix of pink, rose and cream prints, with rose walls that made Tripp look like the proverbial bull in the china shop. He sank down in a red chair that looked like the most "masculine" piece of furniture available, while Laurel took a corner of the cabbage rose-printed couch.

Sitting on something other than an auto seat felt great. She hadn't realized just how tense she'd been until given a chance to relax. Laurel rolled her shoulders to work out the kinks, while Pearl moved through an oak dining room with a bay window. The woman stopped in a doorway that Laurel assumed was to the kitchen, and turned.

"Iced tea or lemonade? I don't keep much soda in the house."

"Tea is fine," Laurel said. "And I agree with you on the soda ban. Of course, if I kept much of it around, it would be gone in a flash with a four-teen-year-old boy."

"As is everything else, I imagine." Pearl went

into the kitchen, and Laurel resumed looking around the living room.

It was the kind of house that would fetch an unbelievable amount of money in California. Gina would absolutely drool over something like this. It was a classic bungalow with dark woodwork that hadn't ever been subjected to paint, and lots of nooks and built-in cabinets, still exuding the charm of the beginning of the last century.

"I know, it's old," Tripp said, obviously misinterpreting her long looks. "But Pearl keeps it up beautifully. And I come back when I can, to help paint the trim or do other chores that require getting on a ladder. Last thing I want is a slightly round lady over seventy getting on a ladder."

"I heard that, Jay," Pearl called from the kitchen. Tripp winced. "And I'll have you know that I'm still perfectly capable of getting on a ladder. Or even on the roof, if I had the mind."

His eyes widened at being caught, and Laurel suppressed a giggle. She was glad somebody else was dealing with a feisty older person for a change. It was on the tip of her tongue to suggest that they should introduce Pearl to Mr. Sam and sit back to watch what happened. But she thought the better of it when she looked at Tripp again. He was glaring out the lace-curtained window. No need to provoke him any more.

Pearl came in with a tray of tall drinks. There were even mint springs poking over the rims of the iced tea glasses. "Here we go. That blue one is Ashleigh's. I'll go invite her down to join the rest of us." She set down the tray on the marble coffee table and went up the front staircase.

Laurel could hear her knocking on a door, and muffled answers in response. Then Pearl came down the stairs.

"She'll be out in a minute. Has to fix her face, I imagine." She sat down on the other end of the sofa and picked up a glass of iced tea for herself. "So, Laurel, how's your father doing? I remember Jay saying that he had had surgery recently."

"He's doing real well, Mrs. Simms. Not well enough to come back to work in the next couple of weeks. But the doctors are happy with his progress. And he's home, at least, and starting to exercise a little. And drive his wife nuts, I think."

Pearl smiled. "That's probably a good sign. A man well enough to be aggravating must be on the road to recovery— And here's our girl."

Laurel could see a figure descending the stairs. Ashleigh took her time, sauntering down in typical recalcitrant-teenager fashion. Chunky thong sandals appeared first, with tiny feet and long legs that seemed to stretch on forever. She looked girlish enough that Laurel almost expected an adhesive bandage on one of those knees.

Her denim shorts were short and cuffed even shorter, a fact not lost on her father, judging by his disapproving expression. Her nail polish was a wild blue with glitter flecks, and several bead bracelets decorated her left arm. Her shirt was a man's plain white T-shirt that swallowed her, even rolled up at the sleeves. Laurel wondered if Ashleigh had borrowed it from Tripp the last time she was visiting him. Somehow, that one small detail made her want to reach out to the girl whose sullen expression mirrored her father's.

Eyes like Tripp's hazel ones glared out of a delicate face, lashes ringed with mascara that was too thick and too dark. It looked recently applied. The slight dark smears around the girl's eyes made Laurel think that Ashleigh had cried off one batch, washed her face, and started over just to greet her father. Looking at the girl, Laurel began to feel that she was very glad Jeremy was a boy. She knew how to deal with his straight-forward problems.

"Hey there." Tripp's greeting was incredibly soft and gentle. Laurel was surprised, after all the ranting he'd done driving up here. Maybe he could still see the little girl under the fashion statement. She hoped so, for Ashleigh's sake.

Ashleigh crossed the room until she reached an

overstuffed chair upholstered in a print that matched the couch. "'Lo." She ruined the image of sullen maturity that she'd projected coming down the stairs by flinging herself in the chair, throwing one leg immediately over the arm. The pose was a reminder to Laurel that this was still a young woman in that iffy ground between childhood and adulthood.

Tripp looked a bit hurt. Laurel suspected that it hadn't been that long ago that his every entrance was greeted with little-girl enthusiasm, hugs around the neck and bouncing. Now the gremlins had come and stolen his "baby," leaving this sullen teen in her place. Laurel felt like welcoming him to the universal parents' club.

And Ashleigh was only thirteen. They had a long way to go.

What did he say now? Tripp sat in Pearl's living room feeling a sweat break out on the back of his neck. How and when had his baby girl turned into this woman-child? And why hadn't he been more aware of the metamorphosis? He wanted to rage and storm, but that would only make Ashleigh tearful or stormy herself. And neither response would help this situation.

He'd already made her cry. That much was evident by the awful, smeared eye makeup that made

her look like a raccoon. He felt awful, because he
knew she was going to cry again. That would be
all his fault, too, and he never knew how to handle
crying women. At least that was one thing in Laurel's favor. In the course of one day he'd written
her a ticket and nearly arrested her son, and she
hadn't turned on the waterworks once.

Now if she could just help him in the situation
at hand. He looked around at the room full of
women, and all he could think about was how out
of his depth he felt. Give him bank robbers or psy-
chopathic murderers any day. He would have felt
even more ill at ease if Laurel's prayer hadn't been
hovering in his consciousness. What had she asked
for? Gentleness, and the right words. He hoped
God had both for him, because he had neither on
his own.

"So, who are you, anyway?" His daughter's
rude question was directed at Laurel.

Suddenly he wasn't worried about making her
cry anymore. After a statement like that, he almost
wanted to make her cry, or at least be contrite.

"You don't look like anybody that belongs in
that hick town my dad's working in," she continued.

"Ashleigh!"

She sat up straight at the sharpness of his voice.
Laurel checked any further outburst from him

with a simple look. It told him to back off, that she was a grown-up and could handle this herself. And all without a single word. That done, she turned to Ashleigh to answer her.

"I ought to take that as a compliment. I'm sort of from Friedens, but I've been living in California for more years than you've been alive. My name's Laurel Harrison, and you and I have something in common," she said to Ashleigh.

"Like what?"

There was an air of disbelief about his daughter, as if she couldn't imagine what she and Laurel could share. Looking at the two of them, it was a little hard for him to imagine, too.

"We've both done time as the sheriff's daughter. My dad was elected sheriff the first time when I was ten. So I know what it feels like to walk around a 'hick town,' as you call it, and feel like everybody's looking at you."

Ashleigh seemed to regard her with new interest. "Yeah? Did you get in trouble with your dad a lot?"

"I was the oldest of three girls. I didn't get in trouble that often because my dad was usually bailing my kid sister out of some scrape or another. Now, with your dad it's another story. He's already given me a ticket for illegal parking and I've only been back in town two days."

Ashleigh shook her head. "And I thought he was rough on *me*. Ease up, will you, Dad?"

He started to snap at her, but held back because he realized something. In allying the females against him on this minor point, Laurel had brought back the ghost of his child-like daughter. Ashleigh wasn't looking at him from her lofty new teenage perspective right now. She was part of a small conspiracy against the sheriff. And that, in his eyes, was far better than having her feel all alone and at odds with her dad.

"Hey, what do you want? I'm the law in that town while Laurel's dad recovers from his surgery. What do you think he would say if I went easy on all the lawbreakers while he was away? Heck, if nothing else, we'd go broke."

That got to Laurel, whose eyes flashed an encouraging message at him. Clearly, he was ahead in the verbal game for a moment. With Laurel and his daughter, though, it might be the only time all night that he'd be one up on them. Better to use his advantage while he had it.

"So your grandma told me how you've been spending your summer vacation," he said as calmly as possible to Ashleigh. "Sounds like we have some serious talking to do."

She looked down at the floor, and the leg that was still flung over the arm of the chair swung again like a pendulum. "I guess. I still don't see why everybody is so upset."

Another look from Laurel checked the explosion Tripp wanted to let go. Bringing her along on this outing had been a great idea. He wished he could take credit for it, instead of having Laurel and her faith to thank. It was hard to admit that being led by simple faith might work better than using logic and rules. Those rules worked in law enforcement—why didn't they work as well in the other thorny problems of life? For now, he'd try to do things the way he knew Laurel was counting on.

It took two deep, slow breaths for him to settle down enough not to yell. "We're upset because we're worried about you, Ash. You haven't been keeping to the house rules around here. You've been making decisions for yourself that I don't think you're old enough to make yet. And because of the choices you've made, we need to come to a different arrangement with your grandma on where you live for a while."

There. He hadn't yelled once. And he hadn't brought up that Richards kid's name, either. Of course, his pulse rate was still as high as if he had been on the range shooting his weapon, but that was probably to be expected. The point in his favor was that while his daughter still looked pouty and unhappy, she wasn't crying. Maybe there was something to be said for this faith stuff, after all.

They were walking out the door toward Tripp's SUV, when Laurel saw the first problem facing them. Where did everybody sit going home? Coming up, it had been natural for her to sit in the front seat. There were only two of them in the vehicle. Now what did she do? Automatically offer Ashleigh the front seat, and perhaps upset Tripp? If she asked which seat he wanted her to take, it would put him in a bind. She whispered a fast prayer for guidance and racked her brain for ideas.

Nothing came right away. Ashleigh was still struggling in the entryway of Pearl's house, insisting on lugging a duffel bag too heavy for her to carry. Tripp had a suitcase he swore was filled with rocks, and there were still two cardboard boxes on the porch.

Looking at the boxes again gave Laurel some inspiration. "Hey, Ashleigh, do you want me to get one of these?" she called out.

Ash smiled and looked around her duffel bag. "I think you're still company, Laurel. And company shouldn't carry boxes. But if you want to carry something, take that smaller one. It's full of CDs, and I know that if Dad takes it he'll 'accidentally' drop it, because he doesn't like my music.''

Tripp gave a short bark of laughter. ''Knows me pretty well, doesn't she?''

''She ought to, as much alike as the two of you are'' Laurel could hear Pearl mutter. Her comment made Laurel hide a grin so that Tripp wouldn't ask what was going on. There was no need to add fuel to the fire right now.

Laurel stopped on the porch and took the box. That gave Tripp and his daughter enough time to get to the car, open the back hatch for the duffel bag and some other necessities of Ashleigh's life, and get things relatively settled in the back of the SUV. If she dallied just a little longer, maybe father and daughter would sort out the seating arrangement before she got there.

Ashleigh saved everybody an awkward situation by bounding over to the passenger side. ''I get the front seat. Okay?''

''If it's all right with Laurel,'' Tripp said. ''Since she is still company and all.''

''Go ahead.'' Laurel put the box in the still-open back of the SUV. ''Maybe that way I can sleep on the way back.''

Ashleigh laughed. ''You must be used to some pretty rough driving if you can sleep while my dad drives.''

"Sheriff's daughter, remember? I think it comes with the territory."

Ashleigh actually giggled as she boosted herself up into the high front seat. "Almost forgot that part. Do you have any good stories you can tell on the way home?"

"Only about my dad. I haven't known yours long enough to have any stories on him except the ones I've already told you about my ticket."

"Hey, maybe we can swap."

Ashleigh closed her door, and Laurel could hear Tripp blustering from the front porch where he'd gone to retrieve the last box.

"Oh, no. No ganging up on the poor defenseless sheriff."

The picture of Tripp being poor or defenseless made her want to giggle with Ashleigh. It just didn't seem possible.

The ride back to Friedens was much less tense and seemed quicker than the trip there. Ashleigh fiddled with the car radio, earning her a growl or two from her father. And as promised, Laurel traded little bits of information with Ashleigh, over Tripp's constant protests.

"How am I supposed to keep my mind on the road if I'm busy monitoring this conversation?" he grumbled.

"So don't monitor. Drive instead, and trust us to be…discreet."

"Like that'll happen."

"I promise, I won't tell anything on Daddy that's too embarrassing. That way Ashleigh won't feel any need to reciprocate. But I would like to know what the deal is with your various names."

"Not yet. I don't share that information on the first date."

Ashleigh hooted with laughter. "First date? Is that what this is, Dad? If so, what are you going to do for an encore?"

"That didn't come out right." Even in the darkened car Laurel could guess that the back of Tripp's neck was turning red. She could almost feel the glow from where she sat. "First…whatever. Meeting. Day spent mostly together. This whole experience defies description."

"I think I understand." Laurel wasn't sure she really did understand whatever was going on, but she wanted to try to put Tripp at ease. His statement about this being a "first date" might have been a slip, but it surprised her, too. And she'd be at a loss on what to call today.

Laurel's head was spinning. How would she describe this day to Gina on the phone, without using the words "first date," as Tripp had? It had started out as a confrontation, then moved on to alternately helping each other out and aggravating each other silly. To her that sounded like most of the elements of a first date rolled into one very long day. In the darkened back seat, Laurel was feeling glad this day was nearly over.

Chapter Seven

Laurel didn't know what to expect when they got back to Friedens. When the SUV stopped in front of Mr. Sam's house, she thought Tripp would just leave the motor running and tell her goodbye, and maybe thanks for the company. But Ashleigh put a stop to that plan right away.

"Oh, no. You and Grandma won't let my friends get away with just dropping me off on the street. You make them stop the car, and somebody walks me to the door. Just like you won't let me go out if somebody honks a horn."

Tripp cut the engine and turned around toward the back seat. "She's right on that score. And if it's proper behavior for a thirteen-year-old's friends, then it's proper behavior for us to show her, as well. So who's walking Laurel to the door?''

Laurel could almost hear the eye rolling that went with the sigh from Ashleigh.

''Honestly. She's your friend, Dad. Not that I don't want her to be my friend, too. We need to trade more sheriff stories.''

''Not tonight. There have been enough stories between the two of you. Shall we?''

His expression made Laurel feel a little fluttery. In the streetlight's dim glow, Tripp looked bemused. ''You don't have to. But then, if you don't walk me to the door we're setting a bad example.'' Laurel felt as if she were just running on. '''Bye, Ashleigh. It was nice meeting you. I'll see you again around town. A lot, I hope.''

''Me, too.''

Laurel got out of the car by herself, stepping down on the curb. She closed the heavy door behind her, wondering if she'd remembered to bring a key. She wasn't yet used to picking one up when she left Sam's house. She'd been independent for too long to get used to a new routine right away.

She fumbled in her purse, and was glad to feel the outlines of Mr. Sam's spare house key. It was hard to miss—attached to a key chain that she hoped was a fake rabbit's foot.

Tripp walked around the car and stood next to

her. "Seriously, I appreciate your help tonight. I know we don't agree on everything about my daughter. I don't think we'll ever agree on much, given what I've seen so far today. But it was good to have another point of view."

They reached the front door quickly. A moth batted around the lone yellow bulb in the porch light. The front curtains were drawn. Someplace in the back of the house, Jeremy and his grandfather were probably watching television together. If she knew them, it would be a show with lots of screeching tires and loud male behavior. Or a ball game.

"I'm glad I came. If nothing else, it made me thankful for having a teenage boy. He may be quite a handful in his own way, but I remember being thirteen too well to want to relive it on a daily basis from a daughter's perspective."

"That's fine with me. As long as I can call you to find out what that perspective is." Tripp looked serious. "I can, can't I? Call you, I mean?"

"Sure. Anytime." Why couldn't she take her eyes off him? He was still the same aggravating, blustering man that had towed her car away this morning. Was anything so different after spending a day in his company?

Yes, it was. Tripp was still annoying in his own way, but she understood more about him now.

She'd seen a concerned father, a trustworthy officer and a very appealing man when he showed her glimpses of his personality. She felt as if she had to say something light to defuse the moment.

"If I'm not here, I'll be out joyriding in Lurlene."

"Not likely. You know where I keep the tow truck now." A hint of teasing had returned to his voice, and somehow it made Laurel more comfortable.

Maybe the feeling of comfort was why she let down her guard for a moment. Paying attention to getting the key in the lock, she didn't see Tripp leaning toward her until he was so close that she couldn't have pushed him away.

Not that she would have. The kiss he placed on her lips was warm and electric, just brief enough to be surprising, just long enough to make her want more than she got. Her senses were reeling when he pulled away.

In a husky voice close to her ear, he said, "And Laurel? My name's Jesse. As in Jesse James Jordan. That's why Pearl calls me Jay."

"Oh. And the 'Tripp' part?"

"For triple-J. It was as far from Jesse James as I could get. Which is important when you're in law enforcement."

She was still tongue-tied. "I guess so. Good night."

His smile was slow and warm, and made her tingle even more than his kiss had. "Good night."

She stumbled into the house, her face glowing. Laurel stood in the front hall and fanned herself for a few moments before she found Mr. Sam and Jeremy sharing a bowl of popcorn and a loud discussion over who to root for in a Los Angeles Dodgers–St. Louis Cardinals game tied in the ninth inning.

She was happy the room was dim and that they couldn't see much of her expression. "Are you guys enjoying this?" she asked.

"The game or the argument?" Sam picked up Buster, who was getting close to the popcorn bowl. "Personally, I'm having a great time with both. And cats don't eat popcorn, so move on, Buster."

"This is great. But Grandpa's team is going to lose even if they are the home team." Jeremy took another handful of popcorn.

"Nah, McGwire still has an at-bat at the bottom of the inning. You guys are history," Sam retorted.

Laurel felt as if she glowed like a beacon where Tripp…or did she call him Jesse now…had kissed her. "Well, I'm going to go upstairs and read for a while. See you two in the morning."

They mumbled good-night, and Laurel went to

her bedroom. She opened the windows wide and turned on the box fan in one corner. She knew better than to try to convince Mr. Sam that they needed the air-conditioning.

After years of California weather, Missouri felt uncomfortable to her. Had the summers of her childhood here been this warm and humid, even after dark? She expected so—but that was then, when she was a kid with scabby knees and no knowledge that other places existed that didn't feel in August like somebody's sauna.

They were going to have to get Mr. Sam to agree to at least some modern conveniences. Like a portable telephone for example. There were two telephones in the house, one in the kitchen and one in a rounded niche in the upstairs hallway. To call Gina, she would have to drag a chair into the hall and sit there while she told her everything that had happened. It felt awfully exposed, but she knew the guys would be watching their ball game for some time to come.

While Gina's phone rang, she did a quick mental calculation. It was only eight in the evening in California. Maybe that explained why Gina wasn't home. Laurel puzzled over what kind of message to leave. What did she tell her best friend? That she had met the most amazing man when he towed away her car? No, better just to ask Gina to call her when she got a chance.

She finished her brief message, changed into her nightgown and stretched out on the bed with her book. Maybe if she lay very still and got interested in the story she was reading, she could convince herself there was a cool breeze blowing in the room.

In the morning, Laurel woke up to the fan blowing cooler air across her body. She had an uncomfortable kink in one arm where she'd rolled over on top of her book after she'd fallen asleep. She felt as if she'd gotten up on the wrong side of the bed, except that she hadn't even put her feet on the floor yet.

Stretching while sitting on the edge of the bed got some of the knots out of her tired body. Then she padded over to the closet to get her lightweight robe.

It was strange staying in this room without Sam. She'd done it several times since he died, but it never got any easier. There were still reminders in this house of her husband's boyhood and young adulthood. Even though he'd moved out to go to college over thirty years before, it still felt as if the room were being saved for him. She wondered if there would be a room like that in her house when Jeremy was grown-up.

Of course, she would need to buy a house in Missouri. And today that didn't sound as appealing as it had for two weeks. She was a little grumpy and out of sorts this morning, and she missed California. Why did she have to long for mountains today?

Laurel knew she was still doing the right thing by staying here in Missouri. When she'd been in California, she'd been terribly homesick for Friedens and the people in the town.

It just wasn't fair that now that she was here she missed so many things about her adopted state. Even the house that had felt strange to her just days ago now looked pretty good. Especially compared to waking up in this virtual shrine to her late husband.

These feelings, plus the unbearable weather, were going to do her in today.

While she went downstairs to make coffee, she tried to remember all the good things about living in Friedens. She came up with some, but wasn't sure if there were enough to get her out of her grouchy mood.

A good cup of coffee, was one of the things she missed most of all. Looking around Mr. Sam's kitchen, she didn't see any way to produce what she thought of as good coffee. She missed the whir of a grinder grinding dark beans, and the hiss of steam from her espresso machine. Here, people who drank coffee made it from out of a metal can with a grocery store logo and brewed it in an inexpensive plastic drip coffeemaker.

She did the best she could with what was at hand, but Laurel wasn't very satisfied with the result. Sipping the pallid stuff at Mr. Sam's kitchen table, she looked out on the backyard. She sighed. There was no hummingbird feeder here, and there were no mountains in the distance.

When the phone rang it startled her. This call would obviously be for Mr. Sam, because it was still before six in California. Nobody she knew would call this early.

"Harrison residence," she said briskly into the phone.

"Laurel? You don't sound like you, honey."

Gina's voice was the most welcome sound she could imagine. "What are you doing up at this hour. I mean, it's early enough here. It's the crack of dawn there."

"I know. I've got a closing later today and I'm nervous about this one. I woke up wanting a cup of your good coffee, and I was intrigued by your message."

"I woke up wanting a cup of my good coffee, too." Laurel felt glum. "I wish we both had one."

"At least, I can trot down the street to grab a decent espresso. You'd have to get work as a *barista* to ensure quality, I suspect."

Laurel sighed. "It's worse than that. Nobody here would even recognize the word *barista*. I'd have to open a store, espresso maker and all."

Suddenly, it was as if God touched her lightly on the shoulder. Maybe this chance conversation would be the answer to several problems all at once. "Gina, how busy do you feel like being for the next couple of days?"

Her friend giggled on the other end of the line. "You know me. I hate sitting still. Tell me what you have in mind."

Tucking her feet up under her still holding her cooling cup of weak coffee, Laurel began to spin out a plan that sounded outrageous even to her. But it just might be a way to get a decent cup of coffee in Friedens, Missouri.

"Okay, what else could go wrong today?" Tripp knew as soon as he asked Verna the question that he'd regret the answer. He'd had Ashleigh with him for barely two days, and nothing had worked out the way he'd expected.

She moped constantly, and everything she

owned was still packed in boxes and suitcases. It was as if she truly believed that if she sulked hard enough or pouted long enough, her father and grandmother would give in and let her go back to St. Louis.

Tripp couldn't remember an occasion when he and Pearl hadn't stood firm on something major. But being a teenager, Ashleigh could probably remember that one time, somewhere in the distant past, when he and Pearl had dropped the ball. That would now be the standard. Never mind that order had reigned for years.

Ashleigh was the kind of kid who expected the unexpected. Or maybe it was just her age. Tripp remembered being a teen, and he hadn't ever wanted past behavior to be an indicator of what the future held. Certainly not his own behavior at that age, when he was convinced that he could always do better, or be faster, or get caught less.

His mother's behavior had always been constant; raising a son alone had made her strict. It was all she could do, married to a man like his dad. He'd show up once in a while, sometimes even work a few weeks and give her money. Occasionally the time without hearing from his dad would stretch into over a year. Those were the times Tripp remembered seeing his mother cry a lot.

He was fifteen before he understood the mail his mother got from the state Department of Corrections. He was never sure if knowing his father was in jail was a blessing or a curse. At least they knew where he was at those times. No more or less money came in than when he had been "missing," so it wasn't a greater hardship. And in the neighborhood Tripp grew up in, a relative in jail wasn't even much of a stigma.

How had he gotten into this blue mood of musing, anyway? he wondered now. Tripp put down his coffee mug and surveyed his office. Verna had given him no answer to his question, preferring to go back to her desk and get to work, instead. She could sense his moods by now, and probably knew this wasn't a day to hang around and chat.

"I'm going to go check on Ashleigh and pick up the mail," Tripp said.

"Tell her hello," Verna said. She told him that every time, which was at least twice a day. Ashleigh was at that awkward stage; too old for a sitter, too young to be left totally alone. That was why leaving her with Pearl would have been best, but Ashleigh had done away with that option. So Tripp looked in on her often, or called, and most days they had lunch together as well. He hoped that soon she'd make some friends around here and he'd have to keep track of her in a wider area.

It wasn't much more than a block between the department and his building. He picked up the mail scattered below the door slot, and went up the stairs with it. There was more for Ashleigh than there was for him. He recognized Pearl's handwriting on one envelope, and girlish scrawls on several others—from her friends, he assumed.

Ashleigh wasn't in the living room when he opened the door. His home still looked like he missed Rose. There wasn't nearly as much color in his life without her. He could manage the important stuff, like laundry and making sure there were always groceries in the refrigerator. But that was about it. He'd lived in this apartment for nearly a year, and only one picture hung on the walls—Ashleigh's eighth-grade graduation picture. And even that was put up with tape, still in its greeting card holder.

He didn't even have to look into his bedroom to know that it could use a feminine touch, too. Though, everything was clean and in relative order, and there were vacuum cleaner tracks on the carpet.

But the whole place had the charm of a military barracks. He had hoped Ashleigh coming to stay with him would change that. So far it hadn't. She'd complained a little about his lack of style, but hadn't added her own yet.

Maybe she'd soon feel like she belonged, and would begin to hang up her posters and put her clothes in the closet. When she asked for a bedspread, Tripp would know she was moving in. That was one of those feminine things that made a house a home, wasn't it? He thought so, because his bed was still covered with nothing but a set of sheets and a navy blue blanket that had seen better days. He made the bed every morning, but there was none of that fussy stuff, like a bed spread, that women put on top of it.

Music was coming from Ashleigh's bedroom. That was a good sign, because it meant she had actually unpacked her CDs and boom box. He knocked on the door.

"What is it?"

She didn't sound as sullen as she had yesterday. Maybe they were making progress. "Mail call. And I thought I'd find out if you wanted to go to the café for lunch today."

"Do they have grilled cheese sandwiches? Remember, I don't eat things with faces."

When had that come up? The last time he checked, her favorite foods had been chicken nuggets and pepperoni pizza. Those definitely involved "faces." He decided it was better not to mention that, and searched his memory of the menu at the Town Hall.

"I believe they have grilled cheese. And I know they have pancakes and omelettes as well. Or do eggs have faces?"

Ashleigh wrinkled her nose. "Dad! Now you're just teasing me."

He hadn't been, but didn't know how to respond. "Sorry." It never hurt to apologize to a woman. "Would you like to sit around and open our mail together before we go to lunch?"

"Sure. Most of it, anyway. I want to save the one from Sarah for when I'm alone."

That seemed fair. Tripp eased his frame onto the hardwood floor of Ashleigh's bedroom, thinking that a throw rug would be a nice touch in here. Maybe he could ask Laurel to help him out. It would give him a chance to see her again without arresting her or anybody in her family. That would be a change.

He sorted through the envelopes. "This one's junk. These two are bills. This one, however, looks promising." It was addressed to him and didn't have a window in the envelope—always a good sign. If it didn't say *Occupant* or *Resident* and wasn't obviously a bill, it was unique in Tripp's mail. However, when Tripp unfolded the business letter—which turned out to be from Gloria—and began to read it, his mood changed abruptly. It seemed her company, Martin Property, had sold this building out from under him.

He stifled language that Laurel had said he shouldn't use in front of Ash. Maybe it wasn't all bad. Maybe selling the building didn't mean what it would in St. Louis: an instant rent increase or even eviction.

So far Friedens had been different. And he couldn't imagine Gloria letting him down in such a spectacular fashion. He read on, feeling a little more relief with each sentence. The new owners, a company he'd never heard of called Wings & Wheels, Inc., promised no rent increase or tenant eviction. In fact, according to Gloria, the new owner was delighted to have a stable tenant.

All this outfit wanted, apparently, was to turn the bottom floor of the building into a retail store again. That didn't thrill him, but it could be worse. He could have moved his daughter to Friedens just in time for them to be put out on the street.

"Any good news?" Tripp asked.

Ash leaned over his shoulder. "Grandma misses me. That's good news, isn't it?"

"Of course. Maybe we can call her after lunch. And my good news is that we get to stay here another month."

"Fantastic." Ashleigh bounced back onto the bed. "Do you think that restaurant down the block uses beef fat for their French fries? I could eat some fries with my grilled cheese. But not if they use nasty old beef fat.''

Another challenge, and it was barely noon. ''We'll see. Find some shoes and let's head out.'' Maybe somebody at the Town Hall would know who the mysterious Wings & Wheels tycoon was. Somebody there usually knew everything worth telling in this town.

Chapter Eight

He hadn't thought he'd see Laurel in the Town Hall. Tripp expected that she'd eat lunch at home with Mr. Sam and Jeremy. Maybe even fix them something nutritious, and California like a good old-fashioned sprout sandwich with a side of tofu.

So seeing her eating a bacon cheeseburger was a surprise. The smile she gave Tripp in greeting was a relief. He still wasn't sure if he'd offended her with that kiss goodnight. If she'd been offended then, it had definitely faded by now, judging from the warmth of that smile. She waved them over to the booth. How could anybody still look that elegant while eating a drippy cheeseburger? Yet Laurel could pull it off.

"Hey, come on over. If you aren't politically opposed to my lunch, that is."

"And as long as I sit as far away from it as possible, I'm okay," Ashleigh assured her.

"So you won't be reminded that it had a face?" Laurel crinkled up her nose.

"So I won't be reminded how good the bacon smells. I don't like killing animals for food, but I sure miss the smell of bacon."

His daughter's comment took Tripp by surprise. He watched her slide into the vacant side of the booth, leaving him to sit on the outside, directly across from Laurel.

They ordered quickly from a waitress who didn't look much older than Ashleigh. His daughter probably didn't approve of Tripp's choice of grilled ham and cheese, but he hoped the salad he ordered alongside his sandwich would mollify her.

Ashleigh sighed as the waitress left. "I was counting on you to back me up here, Laurel. But you let me down."

She shrugged, looking at her cheeseburger. "I know, Ash. I'm usually with you on the vegetarian issue, but about once a month I go real carnivorous. I don't know what that's about, but I tend to listen to my body on those occasions, even though it's probably a reminder of my animal nature. Did you ever notice that before Adam and Eve left the garden, the Bible doesn't talk about people eating other animals? Just plants and fruit from trees.''

''Whoa. Never caught on to that before. Of course, I don't read the Bible much.''

Tripp nearly did a double take on that one, too. As far as he knew, Ashleigh had *never* read the Bible, period. He wasn't even sure that she owned one. But he sensed now was not the time to bring that up.

Laurel grimaced. ''Jeremy's the same way. I can't get him real interested, even in one of those teen study editions. I figure if I leave enough of them around in the coffee house, maybe I can snag him and a few others, as well.''

Tripp's ears perked up. ''Coffee house? What coffee house?''

''I made a decision to open a business. You're looking at the owner of Friedens' newest retail establishment.''

Tripp felt the back of his neck prickle. ''Don't tell me you're Wings & Wheels?''

''Guilty as charged. It's actually Sam's corporation, left over from some of his screenwriting projects that went to charity. I was a corporate officer and took it over after he died. Yesterday my friend Gina convinced me that a coffee house in Friedens, Missouri, was enough of a charity project to interest the corporation.''

"Hooray for Gina. Remind me to thank her in person next time I see her."

"Not likely to happen soon. She lives in California."

"That's probably healthier for her. So you're the one that bought my building and will turn my life upside down." His appetite was fading fast.

"Yes, I bought the building. Didn't know it was your building until after I'd bought it. Gloria didn't fill me in on that part right away—just that it had a good, stable tenant upstairs. And I promise we won't make much noise. I intend to have a clientele with an eleven o'clock curfew, maximum."

"And that's supposed to calm me down?" Tripp was aware he sounded like a grumpy old man. "I went into that building thinking the bottom floor would be vacant for good. Maybe something like an antique store or a quilt supplies shop would go in."

"Sorry. There's already an abundance of antique stores in town. And you should see my one attempt at fancy sewing. It wasn't pretty."

Ashleigh stifled a giggle. "You should hear what Grandma Pearl said about my pillow from consumer ed class. She liked my cookies, though. Of course they were the kind you didn't have to bake. Just stir up melted stuff like peanut butter and chocolate chips."

"I could go for some of those some time. Think you could make a batch for me?"

"Sure. I've got the recipe someplace. It's probably in my backpack with the rest of the school stuff I haven't taken out of there."

Was Tripp hearing correctly? His daughter was offering to *unpack* something?

His temper cooled down a little. Having a coffee house under his apartment was still a lousy idea. But if a byproduct of Laurel's crazy scheme was getting his daughter interested in something in Friedens, maybe it wouldn't be all bad. At least, it would be something to ease his troubled mind when Laurel's clientele got on his nerves.

"So tell me about who this coffee house is going to serve. Since you said they'd have a curfew, I have to gather it isn't the same crowd that hangs out at the Town Hall."

"Not exactly. I have to admit that at least half my desire to have a coffee house is fueled by my own selfish need for a good cup of cappuccino. Gina's arranging for my equipment to be shipped, and it's store quality."

Tripp hoped he wasn't gaping. "You're kidding. You didn't have to go out and buy stuff to start a coffee house? Where did you put all that stuff in California?"

"Well, let's just say our house had an interesting

wall between the family room and the kitchen.'' Laurel looked sheepish. ''But I have an ulterior motive in terms of whom I hope to attract to the place. I've noticed there's precious little to do in Friedens if you're under twenty-one.''

''If you haven't noticed, there isn't much to do if you're *over* twenty-one and don't want to hang out someplace with beer and pool tables.'' Tripp was aware that he sounded even older and grumpier than before.

''Right. But the teens don't even have an option like that. I figured a coffee house could be fun. And if I work with the pastor from my dad's church, he can show me how to do Christian youth outreach the right way, while I'm serving up coffee.''

''Lost sheep and lattes, huh?''

''That's awful, Tripp. Or should I call you Je—''

He didn't even let her finish. '' 'Tripp' works just fine. Or 'Sheriff.' Or even 'Deputy.' Out on the street, I don't go by anything else.''

She must have caught the guarded look in his eye.

''Got it. Sheriff Jordan it is. Will I get used to saying 'Deputy Jordan' in a few weeks, when Dad goes back on duty?''

''I hope so. Because you're probably the only

person looking forward to his return more than I am, believe me.''

''I don't know. I think Mr. Sam is counting the days.''

''Only because your dad apparently has a soft spot for old guys with block-long convertibles. Can't you do anything to keep him off the street?''

''Not a thing. He's licensed, he's legal and he hasn't hit anything yet. I do believe it would absolutely kill him to give up driving that car, and I'm not about to be the one to deprive him of the one pleasure he has left in life.''

Tripp shook his head. ''Suit yourself. I just hope you're not with him when the inevitable happens.''

Laurel had a stubborn glitter in her eyes. ''Maybe it's not inevitable and it won't happen.''

The argument was defused by the arrival of Tripp's and Ashleigh's lunch. Tripp was glad to see the food. He didn't feel like squabbling any more with Laurel.

They ate in silence for a few minutes. ''So what are you calling this coffee house?'' he finally asked her.

''I'm playing with a couple of ideas. Nothing definite yet. And I've got my sisters working on it, as well. Not that I expect to get much from Carrie. Now Claire might come up with a name. But like I told Jeremy, if I keep praying about it while I paint walls and get the place ready to open, something will come to me.''

"Really? You're that trusting that a name for a venture like this, where you're investing thousands of dollars, will just pop into your head?'' It didn't sound practical.

"I truly believe that it will.''

The glow to Laurel's expression scared him even more than thinking about her as his landlady. Tripp tried to find enough appetite to dig into his salad.

The first thing Laurel had done at the coffee house was have a phone installed. That way she could paint walls and talk to her sisters at the same time. It seemed as if she talked to them on the phone much more than she ever saw them. Carrie was always working odd shifts. Claire's family and her work with The Caring Closet kept her busy, and she was involved in something with her husband Ben's business, as well.

While Laurel painted, she also made calls to Gina. Though the painting made her feel that she was on track, talking to Gina comforted her in a far different way.

"So tell me again about this guy that took over for your dad. He still sounds like Andy Taylor or something.''

Laurel almost told her friend that Tripp was a far better kisser than the sheriff of Mayberry had probably ever been. But then Gina would have demanded a full explanation, and she wasn't ready to give her that yet. So she went for an easier answer.

"Hardly. He's got a much quicker temper than any jovial television lawman. And Friedens is hardly Mayberry, despite what you think about my entire home state."

Gina laughed on the other end. "You almost made me upset my iced chai. And I'm sorry, but anyplace that is the way you've described that little town comes close enough to Mayberry to make me know I'm happier here, thank you."

"Well, I'm still happier in Missouri. I think...." Laurel dipped the roller into the pan again, readying another width of wall to be covered with paint the color of café au lait.

"Oh? Do I detect a little uncertainty?" Gina got to the heart of the matter, as usual.

"Just a touch. I wish I felt a clear guidance on this whole issue. I thought I did, or I wouldn't have started it—but now I'm not as positive."

"What does your family think of this whole adventure?"

"That's a good question. I have to admit I

haven't asked their opinions—just told them I was doing it.''

"Just jumped on in, huh? Gee, Laurel, it's like you were used to living two thousand miles away from them or something.''

Gina's teasing made her smile. "Okay, I see the point. Maybe I do need to work myself into the family again. Get used to answering to somebody, and having others to bounce opinions off. I know what Gloria thinks of this idea. But then, it was her building I bought, so of course she'd be happy about it.''

"And your dad?''

"I just assumed that if Gloria was happy with it, then he would be, too. Maybe talking to him about this whole issue would be best.''

"Maybe it would. I'm sure he has a definite opinion.''

Laurel knew Gina had heard too many stories about the whole Collins crew to be polite or tactful anymore. "That is true. So I get to solicit that opinion from a guy just recovering from major surgery. Won't that be fun?''

"Oh, lighten up. It could be a diversion for both of you.''

"It could. Or it could be the shot heard 'round the world. Hard to tell with my father. But you're right about my asking for his opinion. Even your timing is excellent. Early morning there means midday here, and Dad should be up and as ornery as he's going to be.''

''Sounds delightful. Call or e-mail me to let me know what they say.''

Gina said goodbye, and Laurel could hear papers rattling in the background before she finished hanging up the phone. Leave it to Gina to be doing at least two things at once.

Of course, Laurel was doing much the same— painting walls and talking to her friend on the phone. She finished another swath with her roller and then decided that when she used up the paint in the pan she'd take Gina's good advice and go talk to her father. After all, she had come back to Missouri to be near her family. And their opinion was important to her.

Hank looked as if he was recovering nicely. Of course, that meant that Gloria looked frazzled and out of sorts—the result of having a man hanging around the house.

''If he gets any healthier and starts rearranging the kitchen, I'm making him go back to work,'' she said to Laurel. ''Do you have time for a cup of coffee?''

''Don't bother,'' Hank groused. ''It's that de-caffeinated stuff they said I should drink at the hospital. Tastes like dishwater. Besides, I hear you're starting your own business because you don't like Missouri coffee.''

Laurel wasn't sure if he was teasing or gently complaining about being left out of the decision. With her dad, either was possible. ''Not just because I don't like Missouri coffee. And if you'll come visit me at the coffee house when it opens, I'll make sure to have a pot of decaf ready just for you.''

Hank snorted. ''You're just too kind. It's a conspiracy between those doctors and my family, I swear. You'll probably rat on me if I ask for anything stronger, won't you.''

''Never. Because I know you wouldn't do that to me and put me in an awkward position.'' Laurel decided to tease him back. He wasn't sick enough to be treated with kid gloves anymore.

''I'm just too honest for my own good. Is that why you didn't ask me what I thought of this crazy business venture to begin with?''

His eyes were twinkling, so Laurel didn't take things too personally. ''I think my friend Gina in California had that part right. I'm so used to living two thousand miles from anybody that I just go ahead and make my own decisions.'' Suddenly she really wanted to know what he thought. ''So do you really think it's that crazy?''

"I was surprised when Gloria told me she was selling you the building. Can you afford that?"

"If I stretched, Dad, I could afford two. Sam may have been many things you didn't approve of, but he was a good provider. We'll never have to worry about money."

"That's good to know. And Laurel, honey, you have to realize by now that it wasn't that I didn't approve of your husband. I just didn't like that he took you away. We'd been a close family, living right here in Friedens. I always figured it would stay that way and that I'd have all my kids and grandkids around forever."

Laurel breathed a silent prayer of thanks. She'd come over to talk about the coffee house venture, but had gotten something much more important out of her father. This was a discussion that should have happened years ago.

"You could have said that a while back."

Hank nodded. "Like when Sam was still alive? Guess this heart surgery has put everything closer to the surface for me. I'm not hesitant to say what I think anymore. Never know if you're going to get another chance."

Laurel felt herself tearing up. "Aw, Dad. I didn't come over here to cry at your kitchen table."

"Oh, go ahead," Gloria piped up from the

counter. "Everybody else has so far. I've gone through more boxes of tissues in the past month than I normally use in a year."

"And some of them have been for me," said Hank. He reached out and covered Laurel's hand with his. His hand was gnarled and familiar, with a couple of new scars where IV lines and other needles had made their marks.

That final gesture of caring from her father let loose the tears Laurel had held in until now. "I'll take you up on that tissue offer," she said to Gloria. "Dad, what am I going to do?"

"What do you want to do? It's not likely you'll take anybody else's advice if it conflicts with what you feel in your heart. You never have before."

Laurel laughed a little through her tears. "Yeah, I wonder where I get that from."

"Both your parents. And my charming new bride seems to be as opinionated as any other member of the Collins family."

"Which is why I fit right in," Gloria said, putting the box of tissues next to Laurel's elbow. "And *I* don't think your coffee house idea is so crazy. It'll give you something to do. Plus, the kids need somewhere to hang out. There wasn't a place for teenagers to do anything fun and trouble-free even when my son Mike was that age—and Friedens hasn't changed much since."

"Tripp thinks I'm crazy," Laurel blurted. It surprised her how much she cared what her father's deputy thought of her behavior.

"Ah, he's more conservative than I am, and that's saying something." Her father patted her hand again. "He'll come around to your way of thinking, once the place is all fixed up. At least, he will if it won't be too difficult to keep the peace there. You're not planning on having loud rock music at all hours, or building Jeremy a skate ramp in the back parking lot, are you?"

"I might have said something to Jeremy about some small apparatus in the parking lot. No ramps. It'd be too hard to keep track of safety issues. And the music will be loud Christian rock, no matter when it plays. Late hours will not be encouraged."

"Then you'll probably be okay. Give Tripp a little credit, Laurel. He's a good guy. I wouldn't have hired him if I hadn't seen a lot of potential there."

"Oh, he's got plenty of potential." Laurel sniffled a last time with her tissue. "I just hope he won't drive me absolutely mad before this coffee house opens."

"You'll probably have more problems with the building inspector than with Tripp."

Gloria sounded as if she was trying to be reassuring. Laurel wasn't sure doing battle with the building inspector would be all that much worse than doing battle with Tripp.

"At least we can probably get you an 'in' with the fire marshal through Mike and your sister Carrie. But only if you offer her free coffee every day for about a month."

"Great. I haven't even opened yet and I'm already running a tab for my sister." Laurel chuckled.

"Hey, this was your idea. And I'm the one that's supposed to be giving you encouragement, right?"

"Right." She stood up and hugged her father gently so she wouldn't hurt his incision. "And in your own special way you're doing just that. Thanks, Dad."

"Anytime. Think my doctor would complain if I came over to help you paint?"

"Yes," Gloria and Laurel chorused.

"You're still doing physical therapy exercises just to cough the right way. There is no way you're lifting anything like a paint roller," Gloria reminded him.

He shrugged. "Hey, you can't blame a guy for trying."

Gloria walked over to where he sat and kissed him on the forehead. It made Laurel smile to see the gesture between the two of them. Her dad was going to be all right. And he had a loving companion to make sure of it.

"Well, just keep trying dear," Gloria said to him. "I'm sure eventually you'll get away with something. Just not this time."

Chapter Nine

Laurel sat at Mr. Sam's kitchen table the next morning, toying with her breakfast. She didn't even bother to make coffee at the house anymore. Sam preferred to drink his own brew at his own pace. If she went into the coffee house and made a pot there while she worked, things were more peaceful.

She could hardly wait until all her equipment came and she could start making coffee for customers. She already had big signs in the windows advertising her opening. But going into business was more work than she thought.

That one year of junior college so many years ago might not be enough in the long run, she mused. Maybe once she got settled in here a little more she should check out the local junior college and see what business courses it offered. And she'd need more computer skills if she was going to keep inventory and tax records.

Too bad the junior college didn't have a course on understanding sheriffs. That probably fell somewhere in the "abnormal psychology" category. Laurel wondered if she was qualified to teach that one: she had experience with one sheriff, and was now gaining more with another. But her father was easier to understand so far. Tripp was still a puzzle.

Now that she knew his name was Jesse, "Tripp" didn't roll off her tongue the way it had before. He looked more like a Jesse, somehow. For a moment she slipped into a daydream where she whispered his name, softly and close to his ear. She could almost feel the way his dark hair would tickle her lips. Just the thought made her blush. Why was this man so compelling to her? And what was she going to do about it?

She was still mulling over those questions later at the coffee house, while she worked through a pot of Kona and a list of the things she needed to acquire that could probably be scavenged out of basements, garages, yard sales and auctions.

Almost everybody she knew had one set of mismatched flatware they'd be willing to part with for next to nothing. If she collected several of those,

she'd have enough spoons to last her for a while.
And she could always use those odd chairs that
seemed to accumulate in family garages. Coffee
mugs of all shapes and sizes cost next to nothing
at most garage sales.

The heavy-duty dishwasher she'd need was going to be an expense, but when you factored in all
the used things she was taking off folks' hands, the
cost of operating went down dramatically.

She was more nervous about the youth ministry
part of the coffee house venture than the business
management. In California, her ministry work had
mostly consisted of teaching Sunday school to people a whole lot shorter than she was. She loved the
teens, but always let the "professionals" in the
youth group handle them.

Still, here she seemed to be surrounded by teenagers and loved it. Surely this was a nudge from
the Lord that she was moving in the right direction.
What was it that Claire had said when she told her
all about this? *"God doesn't call the equipped, he
equips the called."* Maybe this was Laurel's
chance to get equipped for something different.

There was a tapping on the front window glass.
Laurel looked over, and there was Tripp banging
on her window with a quarter. She started to motion for him to just come in, then remembered the
front door was locked. Both sheriffs of her ac-

quaintance would have a fit if she were in there with all the doors unlocked. Once she was open for business, it would be different. But alone, she knew better.

She hustled to the front, pulling keys out of her pocket.

"Hey. This is extremely embarrassing, but I think I want to be your first customer."

"Why is it embarrassing?" Laurel asked, as she let Tripp into the store.

"Because I'm probably your biggest detractor so far. I know I've complained about everything that you're proposing to do with this place. But I can smell that pot of coffee up in my apartment, and it's marvelous. And, of course, I am totally out of anything that even resembles coffee."

Laurel motioned toward the pot. "Go ahead and fill up. Do you have time to sit at my one lone table and enjoy a first cup? It's definitely on the house, by the way. I don't have all my licenses yet. I don't think selling it would even be legal."

"Suit yourself. As long as you'd do the same for anybody who asked. I don't want police privilege."

It warmed her heart to see his honesty. The more she was around Tripp, the more she had to revise her first opinion of him. He was canny and fair, reminding her, more than she wanted to admit, of her father. And he looked pretty good in that uniform, even hatless, standing in her kitchen area pouring coffee.

She knew he set great store by his hats. Even her dad had mentioned Tripp's hats. "You miss them, don't you."

He looked across the room at her, puzzled.

"Your 'real' hats from your homicide days."

"That is just uncanny. Yes, I do. I know I must have said so, probably more than once. But that was what I was thinking right now. That it felt odd to be ready for work and bareheaded." He crossed the distance between them and set down his mug. "Nobody else does that with me—knows what I'm thinking, or even cares. How come you do?"

His eyes bored into her, making it hard for her to answer. "I don't know, exactly. It's not like I'm studying you on purpose."

"Or that you particularly like me, either—"

He was closer now, and his voice was husky. It sent a thrill of warning up her spine.

"—although you have to like me a little. At least you didn't slap me silly when I kissed you the other day."

"No need to. I enjoyed it, too. Of course, it probably violates the rules we've set up for our offspring on first dates. But it was a very odd first date."

"That it was. Think we could follow it up with a more normal second one? Or would that be tempting fate with the two of us?"

"What are you doing Sunday? My favorite country church out past Labadie is having their annual picnic. We could take as many of our motley crew as wanted to go."

Tripp's brow wrinkled. "Not exactly what I had in mind, but why not? I need to get involved in more community stuff around here, anyway. What time do you want me to pick you up?"

"Eleven. There's dinner on the grounds, and Ashleigh can probably find enough to eat among the side dishes and various goodies that she won't have to confront anything with a face. Personally, I intend to make a fool of myself over fried chicken. Theirs is the best, and I haven't had it in years."

"Great. I'll see you then." He picked up his coffee and headed toward the door. "Now don't think all this friendliness means I won't cite you for noise levels if your clientele is rowdy after you've opened."

"I wouldn't dream of it. And Tripp? Wear a hat Sunday. I want to see one of your favorites."

That seemed to put him off balance, somehow, and he almost spilled his coffee as he headed out. But he nodded and left, and Laurel was smiling as she went back to her lists. An unusual man, and an even more unusual relationship she was crafting. Only God knew where this was going, for sure, because she certainly didn't.

A country church picnic wasn't Tripp's idea of the perfect date. He figured they'd maybe go into St. Louis, or at least Washington, to a fancy restaurant—have an evening alone where he wasn't reminded of being acting sheriff and neither he nor Laurel had to be anybody's parent. Leave it to her to find the polar opposite of what he expected.

Of course, Ashleigh wanted to go when he told her about it. So Tripp expected that the outing would include Jeremy, and probably Mr. Sam, as well. At least he could count on the old man to leave that tomcat at home. What little he knew about church picnics told him they excluded cats. For a change, Tripp was glad Buster wasn't a big old yellow dog.

When he drove up to Mr. Sam's, Laurel and Jeremy were the only ones sitting on the front porch. He leaned out the car window and asked, "Mr. Sam's not coming? I hope he isn't feeling poorly."

Laurel shook her head as she came over. "Not this time. He just doesn't care to go to this particular picnic. Want to scoot into the back with Jer-

emy so I can tell your dad how to drive?'' she
asked Ashleigh.

"Definitely. Anybody that can tell him how to
drive is welcome to the front seat.''

Ashleigh got out of the front and slid deftly into
the back seat, motioning to Jeremy. "Hey. How
are you doing?''

Tripp knew that neither he nor Laurel had introduced the teens to each other, but with that radar
kids of a certain age had, they had found each other
anyway. And apparently at least grudgingly approved of each other. "Okay," Jeremy said. "How
about you?''

Ashleigh shrugged wordlessly, but Jeremy
seemed to understand the gesture. Maybe it was
teen code. Before Tripp could say anything more
to either of them Laurel was in the front seat,
claiming his attention.

Laurel looked cool and comfortable in a flow-
ered sundress with a light jacket.

"I even wore a hat to keep yours company.''
She modeled hers, a chic straw number trimmed
with a hot pink ribbon. It made him feel almost
underdressed in his white shirt, light gray trousers
and gray felt fedora.

Maybe he had misunderstood. "This is a picnic.
Like, outside, right?" he asked.

"Sure. But it's a *church* picnic. If we hustle

we'll still catch most of the service. Head out to I-44 and go past Labadie, and I'll give you directions after that.''

''Okay.'' He was a little confused by the ''church'' part. And the way she just slid into his car and started telling him what to do. Some date. But then again, this was Laurel. Did he really expect normalcy where she was concerned? It hadn't happened in the past and it wasn't likely to happen now.

They found the church on Laurel's first try. That impressed Tripp because he was pretty sure from what she'd said that she hadn't been there for a couple of years. Several old gentlemen were directing parking in a fenced pasture borrowed for the occasion. Today neat rows of trucks, SUVs and cars filled it, instead of cows or horses.

There was already a good crowd heading over to an old stone church. Tripp listened to the bells ringing in the steeple, wondering how he was supposed to act in this church. He hadn't been inside many since Rose died. After that he'd just lost the will to sit and talk to God on a regular basis.

Granted, he still believed in God. Still read his Bible when he felt the need, still prayed on the rare occasion. But he just didn't do anything on a daily basis with God. After all, Rose had—and look where that had gotten her.

That probably wasn't fair to Ashleigh. He knew that Pearl set a better example than he did in that regard. His daughter's religious education was being neglected, he knew. That part almost nagged him back into a proper relationship with God—one that included going to church on a regular basis and talking about his faith more. Making it a part of his life, the way Laurel did.

As a teenager, having a mother who prayed for him was the one thing that Jesse James Jordan could testify had probably kept him out of jail. True, Ashleigh wasn't anywhere near as wild or as angry as he'd been as a teen. But without that strong foundation, how would she grow up?

All this went through his mind as he made his way from the car to the doors of the church, Laurel, Jeremy and Ashleigh in tow. It wasn't a long enough trip for all his thoughts.

Laurel didn't mean to spend most of the service watching Tripp and Ashleigh. This country church was one of her havens. She usually spent her limited time here praying, just soaking up the atmosphere. She felt so close to God in this place, more than in any other church she'd attended on a much more regular basis.

There seemed to be less in the way, between herself and her Lord here. It wasn't a fancy place, just an old stone building with a roof that obviously leaked, given the water stains. The windows weren't stained glass, and the bottom panel of each window was flung open because the church had stopped being used on a daily basis long before air-conditioning came along.

Still, people came for special events such as this picnic, and then it became a beautiful place. Fresh flowers lovingly tended in backyards and gardens graced the altar in vases. The minister seemed as glad as Laurel was to be here in this place doing what he was doing today.

That was apparently a new concept for Ashleigh. The girl watched the minister intently. She didn't seem familiar with any of the hymns, even though they were old-fashioned favorites that most of Laurel's Sunday school classes probably would have recognized.

When at times there was laughter, and even applause at one point after the small choir finished a beautiful number, Ashleigh looked concerned, almost worried. This didn't seem to be what she was used to in church, if she was used to any at all.

By the time they were leaving the sanctuary and shaking the hand of the minister, Laurel was brimming with questions for Tripp all about his faith experiences and Ashleigh's as well. She might not have the right time to answer them all day. Which meant she was going to come near to bursting with suspense, if she didn't watch it. Of course, she would probably come near to bursting, anyway, later when they sat down for fried chicken. Why not twice in one day?

It wouldn't do anybody any good if she gave vent to her questions. Tripp would probably be angry and defensive. And Laurel sensed a yearning in him, too, as if he were coming to some spiritual decision. Better not press any issue that steered him away from that resolve. Whatever he was struggling with, he had to deal with on his own.

Laurel hurried out of church, instead, to buy tickets for the dinner.

"Are we under five hundred?" Jeremy asked, making Tripp and Ashleigh look confused.

"Just barely," Laurel told him. "In the four-eighties. And yes, they do start calling tables to sit down to dinner with the number one, and work their way forward from there."

Tripp raised an eyebrow. "Are you telling me that there are four hundred and eighty-odd people ahead of us for fried chicken? Every chicken in the county will have died by the time we get there."

"It won't be as long as you think. Besides, I have things to do for a while, anyway. I need to stop by the bazaar tables and see what's going on."

As usual there was a whole table of beautiful potted plants and flowers. Laurel chose two pots of English ivy and further confused Tripp by asking if he had any tools in the car, like a trowel or a shovel.

"I do, but are you going to plant those here?" He looked down at the ivy she held in both hands.

"Of course. Want me to go with you to get the trowel?"

"It's a shovel, and I'll find it myself, thank you."

"Great. I'll get the kids something cold to drink, and meet you right back here."

He was back with the shovel before they'd taken more than one deep swallow of cold lemonade. "I got you one, too. Freshly squeezed and shaken with ice." She handed him the plastic cup in exchange for the shovel. Jeremy and Ashleigh each had a pot of ivy by this time, and followed her as she led them to the back of the churchyard.

Tripp still looked perplexed, and Laurel mentally smacked her forehead. "I forget sometimes that you aren't from around here. And that I've only known you a few weeks. Sam is buried in this cemetery, and we're going to plant these on the Harrison family plot."

"Dad said he wanted to be back here because it was peaceful." Jeremy spoke back over his shoulder, still managing to move forward without stumbling in the ruts on what passed for a path into the cemetery. "Not in some weird smoggy place in Los Angeles, even if he wasn't going to know he was there anyway."

Jeremy moved ahead of the grown-ups, and Ashleigh caught up with him. "This is peaceful. I can see why your dad said that." She turned around and looked at her father. "How come Mama isn't buried out in the country someplace quiet like this?"

"Because when your mom died, none of us had ever lived closer to any green space than Forest Park. And although it is peaceful, they discourage burying people there. Especially near the zoo." Ashleigh stuck her tongue out at him and turned around to follow Jeremy.

Laurel lagged a little. "Didn't mean to bring up a sore subject. Sorry about that."

"Not your fault, exactly. I'm almost glad to hear her talk about her mother. She doesn't usually say anything. Is Jeremy that way?"

"Not anymore. For a while after Sam died, he was angry and sullen most of the time. Of course, he was also a boy just a little younger than Ashleigh is now, and they're not known for being talkative in the best of situations. But he's coming around."

"That's good. Ashleigh was nine. I know she remembers her mom and misses her."

"Do you? Miss her still? I have no doubt *you* remember her." That was evident from the look Tripp got sometimes when they were together.

"I think so. Her name was Rose, by the way. She did have an identity other than Pearl's daughter and Ashleigh's mother. Although by the time she died, I'd reduced her to those roles most of the time in my mind."

They reached the Harrison's plot, which was edged in tennis-ball sized stones. Jeremy and Ashleigh were pulling a few stray weeds and discussing the best place to put the ivy.

"Do you want to dig, or hand me the shovel?" Laurel asked Tripp.

"Hand you the shovel. As odd as this day has been so far, somehow wielding a shovel in there would just make it too odd to continue. Although I look forward to anything that gets us onto another topic of conversation."

"Fine. Then go up the path in the direction we came. Find the chalkboard on the side of the white, screened building on top of the hill and see what's written on it. You can motivate us all to work faster if you do that. It's the numbers they're serving for dinner."

Tripp looked grateful. "Now, that I can handle. I'll be back in a few minutes."

Laurel had no doubt that he would be back. But she also knew he'd probably try to time his reappearance with their finishing up their planting and being ready to move on. She supposed that was understandable. This was a pretty odd "date."

She handed Jeremy the shovel. "You seem to have picked out the right place. Let's start digging."

Chapter Ten

Eating fried chicken seemed to suit Tripp better than the rest of the day's activities. He and Jeremy had an impressive pile of bones mounting up between them. Laurel found herself marveling at how much the two of them could actually eat.

After a while, even Ashleigh forgot to be terribly disgusted by the violence done to chickens and just watched in amazement. She and Laurel were done with dinner and eyeing the trays full of homemade desserts being brought around by the ladies of the church. Jeremy was reaching for a fifth or sixth piece of chicken, and Tripp was still eating right along with him.

"Don't you two ever get full?" Laurel finally asked. "I mean, I know that it takes quite a bit to fill Jeremy up, but you stopped growing a while back, Sheriff Jordan.''

"While we're here and I'm out of uniform, I might even answer to 'Jesse,''' he told her. "It's been such an unusual day all around, I might as well add to it."

"It's nice to see you doing something unusual or unexpected for a change. I don't think he does enough of that kind of thing, do you?" she asked Ashleigh.

Ashleigh shook her head in answer to Laurel's question. "Almost never." She turned to her dad. "Grandma Pearl says you're more hidebound than she is. What does that mean?"

Tripp nearly choked on his chicken. Laurel thought she was going to have to reach across the table and pound him on the back. He took a long drink of iced tea before he answered.

"It means your grandma has too much time on her hands." He took another swig of tea. "No, honestly, Ash, it means that I'm more set in my ways than a seventy-year-old lady. And if I'm truthful about things, she's probably right."

"I'll say. She was at least considering letting me ride places with people under twenty-one who had their driver's license. And I could talk on the phone for more than twenty minutes at a time." Ashleigh eyed Jeremy's plate. "If you eat any more chicken, it better be a wing. I don't want to think that two different chickens died just to feed you."

"Hey, I'm a growing boy. Even Mom says so." Jeremy grinned. "And I don't care much for wings. They're all bone or fat. I'm probably ready for pie, anyway."

Ashleigh gaped at him. "You have room for pie? How?"

Laurel laughed. "The same way your father does. Only in his case it seems to be German chocolate cake." She'd love to know how these trim guys did it, even as active as they were. The male metabolism must be one of God's little miracles.

"Are you going to need a nap, and am I going to have to drive home?" she asked Tripp.

"I doubt it. I won't nap all that long after dinner. Just a little while, under one of those trees in the back."

Jeremy looked smug. "Yeah, well, it won't be peaceful enough there for a nap soon. You haven't seen the band."

Tripp raised an eyebrow. "Band? Is this kid for real?"

"He certainly is. There's usually a quartet or more. That covered pavilion down there becomes a dance floor, and they alternate square dances with more regular dance music. Or as regular as you

can get when most of your band is an accordion,
a fiddle and a big old bass taller than the guy playing it. There are usually guys on guitar and drums
that play when it suits them. It varies from year to
year.''

"So do you dance?"

His question surprised her. "I haven't in quite a
while. But for you, I'd make an exception."

"Great. It'll get me away from this chicken before I eat enough to founder." Tripp pushed back
from the table, and everybody else followed suit.

"There is no way I am going to dance to that
geeky music. Can we go play more carnival
games?" Jeremy asked.

"Be my guest. Keep Ashleigh with you, and
give her any stuffed animals you win that are bigger than Buster. If you do that, I'll even pay for
the games." Laurel fished around in her purse for
enough money to keep him busy for an hour or
more. With carnival tickets at fifty cents each, it
wouldn't take a lot of money.

The kids scooted off in the direction of the hoop
shoot and the duck pond. Laurel and Tripp wandered toward the dance floor, where the band was
tuning up. A man testing a fiddle stood in one corner, plucking strings and judging pitch. He'd been
at every one of these picnics Laurel could remember attending, looking like one of those dolls with

a dried apple for a head, a battered cowboy hat perched on top of wizened features.

"Looks like we're just in time." Tripp surveyed the crowd. "I'm glad this isn't my county. I can relax a little and not wonder what happens if any of this crowd gets out of hand."

Laurel looked around at her fellow picnic attendees. The mean age seemed to be about sixty-five. "Like that's going to happen."

His expression was serious. "You can never tell. Even at a church picnic, somebody can take exception to what someone else says, or how they're bumped into on a dance floor."

"I guess. You'd know more about it than I would."

The band launched into a countrified waltz and Tripp held out his hand. Laurel took it, feeling a thrill at contact with him again. He was a surprisingly smooth dancer. She hadn't given any thought to the side of his personality that might go dancing or dining, or any of the normal things people did on dates. At least, she thought that was what they still did. It had been forever since the dating scene had been part of her life.

For a moment she had to concentrate on movement. It had been years since she'd danced, either alone or with somebody else. It hadn't been that frequent an occurrence when Sam was alive, because he just wasn't a dancer. He had many fine qualities to make up for it—but he'd never been much of a dancer. Tripp, on the other hand, seemed to have a natural flair for it. They fell into a natural rhythm together quickly.

Laurel knew she must have a fairly silly smile on her face. Here she was, in the arms of a handsome man in public—and enjoying every moment of it. Tripp seemed to be enjoying it, too. His usual sharp expression had softened under the brim of that fedora. He looked happy, maybe even content. Neither expression was one she was used to seeing on his face, and it gave Laurel a pang of regret.

This was a good man. He deserved more moments of happiness than life seemed to give him. She couldn't help reaching up and brushing fingertips softly across his cheek. "I like the smile," she told him. "It really goes with the hat."

His brow furrowed. "Does it? I don't remember wearing the two together for quite some time."

"That's a shame, because it's a very nice hat and an even nicer smile." Was she flirting with this man? Maybe so. It felt right.

"It's kind of you to say that. So tell me what today is all about. I've never visited a cemetery on a date before. I hope it's not a message about where this relationship is going."

Laurel laughed softly. "Just the opposite, I

think. I feel comfortable letting you in to my life some. And that means my whole life, multifaceted and odd as it seems to be. As long as I'm back in Missouri to stay for a while, I want to do the things that were a part of my life when I lived here. And that means attending church picnics—even the one at the church where Sam is buried.''

"Okay. I think I can live with that. What else is high on your list of things to do in Missouri?''

"Mostly boring stuff, like getting Jeremy registered for school and going to restaurant supply stores for things for the coffee house. You're lucky enough to share what is probably my one leisure day this week.''

Tripp shook his head. "Lady, you've got some stamina. I have to keep on that kind of schedule with my job, and I can't say I always love it. But you seem to keep up this kind of twenty-four-hour activity in life, no matter what. How do you do it?''

Laurel shrugged. The movement made her aware of his warm hand at the small of her back while he guided her around the dance floor. It felt good, as if it belonged there. But it was distracting, and she had to think about his question for a moment before answering. "I just do, I guess. It isn't something I think about much until somebody makes me. I've always been pretty busy just running a house and being Jeremy's mom."

"Haven't you worked outside the home?"

She shook her head. "Not for money, and not for ages. When Sam was younger and a struggling screenwriter, yes. But once he had a couple of hits, I didn't need to. And with even one child, there's so much stuff to do. Then, once his dad got sick, I did even more of the parenting things. And the household things, like paying the bills and keeping everything going, have always fallen to me. It was too difficult to guess when Sam was going to be home or when he'd be off on location with a movie. Prayer helps a lot. It keeps me connected to God, and the source of my energy."

"Trust you to turn anything into a religious discussion." Tripp sounded a little edgy but he was still smiling.

"Trust you not to see everything as a part of the whole fabric of life. Faith isn't something you can just pick up on Sunday, or when it suits you, and then lay it down for the rest of your busy week. If you do, it makes for a much harder week."

Tripp shook his head. The gesture made one errant curl escape his hat brim. Seeing the dark lock made Laurel want to run her finger inside the brim of that hat where it met his forehead. It made her wish the music would go on forever and that Tripp would forget their serious discussion to lean down and kiss her.

"So life would be easier if I gave it more faith, hmm?" he asked softly. "Just how do I go about doing that?"

His look was intense. Deep eyes searched her face, and Laurel had to moisten her lips with her tongue before she could answer. "For you, I have no idea. I know what it took for me, what it takes every day. I have to surrender it all to Jesus, to admit from the moment I get up to the moment I go to bed that this is His day and I'm letting him manage it. That's hardest to do where Jeremy is concerned. I want to keep that particular part of my life to manage myself."

"You are the parent, after all. Isn't it giving up responsibility to think somebody else is going to be responsible for raising your child, even when that somebody else is your God?"

The music had stopped, and they were still in each other's arms near the edge of the dance floor. Laurel hoped another slow number would start up again. Right now, she needed the time to talk to Tripp without breaking the flow. Miraculously, the band launched into another waltz, and their dance continued to flow around this intense conversation. If that in itself wasn't proof of the power of prayer, she wasn't sure what would be.

She felt buoyed up by that thought. "For me, at least, it's the only thing I can do. To try and raise Jeremy by myself, without God's guidance, would be the irresponsible thing. He's verging on manhood, Tripp. If I haven't taught him how to make the right decisions, and how to walk with the Lord by himself at this point, I don't think any other parenting I try to do will be very effective."

"You sound like my mother. She always told me she wasn't the only one raising me, that she could only pray for me and give me back to God. I thought when I was fourteen it meant she was washing her hands of me. Only when I got older and had my own child did I even begin to comprehend what she meant."

His mouth thinned into a narrow line. "My mom never knew I understood. She died before I could tell her that. She was gone before Rose was. Maybe that's one of the reasons I have trouble keeping as much faith in God as you seem to have. Everybody I've known who had that kind of faith seems to have died too young. Maybe this stubborn streak is my insurance for staying alive."

"Is it working? Do you really feel all that alive?" The question was blunt, but at the same time she knew it was the right thing to ask him just now.

"Not nearly as alive as I want to be," Tripp

admitted. "I spend too much time working and worrying. Don't get me wrong, I love my job. I'll love it again even more when your dad comes back to take over his part. But between the job and Ashleigh, I don't get much time to be at rest."

"To do things just like this." The second number was ending, and this time Laurel stepped reluctantly out of his arms. It was time to end the dance.

"Exactly. Do you think you could help me learn?" It was more serious than any other question he'd asked her.

Laurel felt her heart jump in response. "I can try, Jesse. I can most certainly try."

"Good." He leaned down and brushed his lips against hers, softly. It was the kind of kiss that wouldn't even embarrass their watching teenagers, if they were indeed watching. But it still thrilled Laurel down to her toes. "I think we have a lot to try together. In the meantime, I just want to hear you say that one more time."

"What, that I can try?" She tried not to let her puzzlement show.

"No. Just my name."

"Jesse? I'll say it as many times as you like." She lifted up on tiptoe and whispered near his ear. "Jesse. Jesse James Jordan. The most stubborn man I've ever met."

"Too stubborn to love?" His question was quick and sincere.

Another shock of excitement rushed through her. "I doubt it. After growing up in my family, I believe a person would have to be made of stone to be too stubborn to love. Give me some more time to work on it."

"Definitely." He seemed oblivious to the fact that they were at a church picnic, standing near the edge of a crowded dance floor. "Take all the time you like, because I'm going to need quite a bit of it myself to get used to this situation."

Tripp leaned toward her and kissed her. This time the kiss was soft and warm, slower than any before and incredibly sweet. And it didn't surprise her in the least when it was broken up by a stuffed animal bopping her on the head.

"Oops. Didn't mean to interrupt anything like that," Ashleigh said with a giggle. "Look what Jeremy won me. I think it's a boa constrictor. Neat, huh?"

"Delightful," her father said to her. "What do you say we take it back to town?"

Laurel felt like Cinderella at midnight. The clock was surely chiming on her magical time with Jesse. In the car going home, he would go back to being Sheriff Jordan. The closer they got to Friedens, she knew the more they'd lose of this person in the gray fedora who had just kissed her so sweetly. It was a shame because she would miss that man. Now how did she find a way to make him show up in Tripp's everyday life?

It had to be the hat. He hadn't worn it in so long that the band had shrunk, cutting off circulation to his brain. What on earth had he been doing, pouring out his heart to Laurel Harrison? And in public, no less?

He'd actually been listening as she basically witnessed to him. And for a few moments there, that witness had sounded very, very good. Almost as good as she looked to him on the dance floor.

She was so different from any woman he'd ever known. Different in good ways, and in ways that gave him great pause. But undoubtedly different in so many ways from Rose, or Pearl, or his mother.

She was so vibrant and so alive. A little bit spacey and free-spirited. Too trusting for his own personal taste. And more reliant on the Lord than he could ever be. But there was such a glow of life around her that pulled him like a moth to a front porch light. It was time to pull back and not get scorched.

That was what happened to moths that flew too close, wasn't it? They went down in flames and got swept away in the morning. Well, he had way too much to do right now to go down in flames. It was time to turn away from the glow that was Laurel, no matter how tempting she seemed.

Today had probably been a bad idea. He was too full of fried chicken, and had made an absolute fool of himself at that picnic. Now they were two-thirds of the way home, and nobody had said a word in the car for miles. The music on the radio was one of Ashleigh's annoying stations, and she wasn't even listening. She and Jeremy had both fallen asleep in the back seat; he could see them in the rearview mirror.

Ash had that silly stuffed snake in one arm, and she looked about ten years old with the toy clasped to her. Its ridiculous red felt tongue flipped in the breeze from the partially open back window, as if to taunt him.

Tripp went back to watching the road and silently berating himself for his foolish behavior. How could he possibly have asked Laurel if she could learn to love him? He didn't even *want* anybody else to love him. That was too dangerous, too tangled for him at this point in his life.

He was thankful that Laurel hadn't said anything on the way home, either. Maybe she was regretting today as much as he was. Maybe she really missed Sam more than she let on, and was relieved that Tripp was pulling back. She probably had enough to worry about right now, without adding relationship woes.

Tripp had never before been so glad to see the Harrison house. "Well, thanks for the picnic," he said, trying not to sound as brusque as he felt. He didn't even turn off the engine. "I hope you have a nice evening. Feels like it could actually rain and cool down some, doesn't it?"

Laurel was gathering her things in the seat around her, massaging one temple with two fingers. "I think you're right. The weather has to be what's giving me this incredible headache."

At least she was tactful. Tripp knew he was most likely the cause of that throbbing that made her look dazed. She was every bit as stunned by the afternoon as he was, and looking for a way out, just the way he was.

She leaned over the seat back and jostled Jeremy awake. "Come on, guy. We're home. Let's go find Grandpa Sam and Buster. See what inning that Cardinals game is in."

"They aren't even playing the Dodgers. Why bother?" Jeremy groused like a much younger kid, sliding out of the back seat. "Thanks for the ride, Sheriff Jordan."

"Thanks for the snake, Jeremy," Ashleigh added. "Should I name him after you?"

"No way. Anybody can see that's a girl snake.

Look at the fake eyelashes. Bye.'' With that parting comment, Jeremy was out and up the walk heading for his grandfather's front door.

''Yes, Sheriff Jordan, thank you for the ride home. I'm sure we'll see you again soon.'' Laurel sounded hurt and distant.

She followed Jeremy up the walk to the porch. Tripp watched them go into the house, and then headed for home. By now he felt even more confused than he had been on the dance floor. And he was getting a headache to match Laurel's. It must be the hat.

Chapter Eleven

It didn't rain on Sunday night, and Laurel's headache didn't go away, either. She woke up Monday morning still feeling muzzy and sleep-deprived, with a pounding that could only mean a sinus headache.

She was beginning to think she'd made a really dumb decision coming back here. What did God want her to do in this place, anyway? Half the time she had no idea.

As she lay in bed trying to figure out how to proceed for the day, the phone in the hall rang. It was early enough that Jeremy was still sound asleep, so there was no hope of his answering it.

Laurel couldn't stand hearing the phone ring without picking it up. She supposed it was still a leftover from her teenage days when the phone never stopped ringing and every call was important to one or another of them. With three girls, a father who ran the sheriff's department, and a mother who did more volunteer work than two normal women put together, they had actually worn out several of the old black plastic telephones during her childhood.

So when the phone rang a third time and Mr. Sam still hadn't picked it up, Laurel got out of bed and padded barefoot down the hall to grab the receiver. She didn't even get her whole formal "Harrison residence" greeting finished before Gina interrupted her.

"Hey, it's me. You can stop being polite," she joked.

"You don't know how much of a relief that is this morning. I'm not in a very polite mood. What are you doing up at the crack of dawn there again?" Laurel asked her friend.

"Real estate, of course. Buying stuff, selling stuff, just wheeling and dealing all over the place. Which is why I called you at this awful hour."

"It's not so awful here. After seven, I'm sure." Laurel tried to rearrange her tousled hair and talk on the phone at the same time. She hoped it looked better than it felt.

"Do you need to run a deal by somebody who

has absolutely no understanding of the business?''
Laurel's question wasn't the joke that it seemed.
Gina often explained to Laurel the workings of a
transaction and the problems she was having. That
way, Gina explained, when she put it in plain language that anyone could understand, she could find
the flaws in her own work.

"No, and I don't even need a prayer partner
right this moment. For a change."

Laurel could hear Gina taking a sip of something
and she could imagine a frothy latte in her friend's
favorite mug. For a moment she felt terribly jealous.

"That reminds me," said Gina, "did all the
equipment get there okay?"

"They're supposed to come out this afternoon
and uncrate the espresso machine and several other
pieces. It shipped just beautifully, thanks." Gina
had some expertise with moving companies, and
she had told Laurel the right ones to use to get her
precious coffee equipment to Missouri. So far everything had come through without even a scratch.

"But then, the stuff that's already in Missouri
isn't my primary concern right now. The stuff
that's in California interests me more."

"Don't tell me we had a burglary," Laurel said,
suddenly worried. "I just changed all the password
settings on the security system before I left."

"No, no burglaries. Calm down. But the changed settings were what I called about, in a roundabout way. What would you think of somebody looking at your house, if I can find a way in that doesn't set off enough alarms for Fort Knox?"

"What do you mean, 'looking' at my house? Like, to appraise or something?" They'd talked about the fact that it was likely to go on the market when Laurel got enough time to deal with real estate in two states.

"Not exactly. I'm showing the world's pickiest client around Westlake. He *almost* likes everything I've shown him, but there's inevitably something wrong with every place. You know the old song and dance. One is too big, the other one is too small. Sometimes he likes the neighborhood, but not the houses that are for sale. Other times he likes a house, but dislikes the neighborhood. I'm at my wit's end with this guy."

"You've said that before. And those are usually the people that make you happiest when you've found them a house."

"This is true. I will be overjoyed if this guy buys a house from me. When we did a scouting trip around new neighborhoods last night, nothing that had a For Sale sign in the front yard did anything for him. Naturally."

There was a sigh on Gina's end of the phone,

then she went on. "Anyway, I finally had Mr. Picky just ride with me and look at the outsides of houses from the passenger seat. And fifteen minutes after we started doing that, he fell in love—"

Somehow Laurel knew where this was leading. It made a pool of uneasiness form in the pit of her stomach. "Don't tell me."

"Yes! When he found out there was even the barest possibility that your house could be for sale, he wanted me to call you at that moment and see if he could go inside and look around."

"But my house isn't for sale," Laurel reminded her. "And I'm not positive it's going to be anytime soon."

"Really? I thought you were thrilled about being back in Missouri. That you were opening your dream business and settling down in the bosom of your family."

"Depends on the time of day. And the company I'm keeping."

"Sheriff acting up on you again?"

"Yeah, he is. Or I'm acting up on him. I'm not sure which it is, really. Yesterday was wonderful and awful at the same time. Do you mind if I spend your money telling you all about it?"

"Go ahead. I'll take it out of my commission when I sell your house," Gina said.

Laurel knew her savvy friend was joking. So she didn't mind bending Gina's ear for twenty minutes, telling her about Sunday.

"So what do you think?" Laurel asked, once she'd given Gina the whole story.

"I think he's a guy. A very human, normal guy. And like most guys, he shies away from commitment. Some people get buyers' remorse when they've signed a contract on a house. I see that all the time. A lot of guys get relationship remorse the same way, when the wrong words come out of their mouths."

"You think that's it?" Laurel shifted her position on Sam's hard wooden hall floor. She was going to have to install a cordless phone. Or at least place a small easy chair in the hallway so she wouldn't have to sit on the floor. It was probably never a problem for Mr. Sam. He was seldom on the phone more than a minute or two.

"I'm not a trained psychologist or anything. But you have to be pretty knowledgeable about people to sell real estate. And this guy just sounds like he ran away with himself a little."

"I hope you're right. I never thought I'd say this again, but I would almost like to give this whole relationship thing a chance again."

"Whoa. That is something different, coming

from you. Does this mean I can show Mr. Picky your house, after all?''

Laurel shifted on the hard floor again, and finally stood up to ease the kinks out of her protesting muscles. ''Sure, go ahead. It isn't the right house for just Jeremy and me, even if we came back tomorrow. Which we won't. Let me give you the new security code so nothing will buzz, beep or yell at you when you open the doors.''

''Fantastic. Now, of course, this means he'll probably hate the inside on sight, but at least I've tried everything.'' Gina sounded tired. ''Okay, I've got my pencil and paper. Give me the numbers.''

Later, while she sipped a latte and pored over figures at the coffee house, Laurel mulled over what to tell Jeremy, and when. She knew he would be upset at the prospect of selling the house. Even the promise that they'd find something in the same general area so he'd still be going to Westlake High with his friends if they moved back wouldn't make him totally happy.

Right this moment, she wasn't even sure what would make *her* happy. After a lifetime of independence in California, coming back home to Missouri wasn't what she'd fantasized about. Her family had their own lives to live, and she didn't see any of her sisters all that much. Jeremy wasn't hanging out with his cousins the way she'd planned because Kyle was too young and Trent had daily football practice that wore him out.

The idea of the coffee house was exciting, and Laurel really felt it was the right thing to do. But would Friedens support it? What if six months from now she had to come to terms with being a colossal failure?

She sighed and leaned back in her creaky wooden chair. She felt so disconnected. California wasn't home anymore, but it was what she was used to. Missouri wasn't home, either, and she felt out of place here. When would things feel better?

The wondering started a silent prayer, and soon she was talking to God aloud. There was nobody else here to wonder if she was a little strange. She might as well do what felt natural. *"I am so confused,"* she told her Father. *"If this isn't what You want me to do, what is it? And what about Tripp? Are we supposed to be together in some way? I think I love him. I wouldn't be surprised if he loves me in his own strange way. I know I love his daughter. She needs a mother, Lord. And I wouldn't mind another child at all."*

There was no immediate answer. Laurel wasn't used to one anyway. Just pouring out all her problems like this made them seem easier to deal with and made her feel less like she was bearing the whole weight of the world on her shoulders.

She looked across the room and noticed that her "thought for the day" calendar was about four days behind. She walked over to the counter where it sat and pulled off the out-of-date sheets. *One day at a time,* the message seemed to be. *That's all you can do, anyway. Just take it all one day at a time.*

It was pretty good advice. Today's tasks could fit on her plate without overwhelming her. She could sweep the floor and make sure there were enough donated and scrounged supplies to get on with the youth gathering Pastor Ron wanted to hold here for midweek services, instead of doing things at the chapel as usual. Maybe she could even talk Jeremy into coming in and helping by hanging up some of the posters he'd brought. It might be a good way to broach the subject of the move in the least threatening environment. One day, and one task, at a time.

This was positively the last straw. Tripp looked at the block-long Cadillac parked in front of the Town Hall. Neither meter had money in it. Here it was, the busiest time of day for the café, right during the lunch rush, and this monstrosity took up two of their parking spaces! And Sam Harrison wasn't even inside the café where Tripp could call the matter to his attention.

It was too far away from the coffee house for

Laurel to have parked here. She mostly walked downtown to get to the place, anyway. Only when she had something heavy to transport did she use Sam's car. This had to be Mr. Sam's work.

Maybe Tripp was just unhappy that he didn't have an excuse to talk to Laurel right now. He tried to figure out if that was part of the aggravation he felt, or if all of it was directed toward the cantankerous older driver of the gleaming chrome-and-aqua monstrosity in front of him.

Hard to tell. Right now, anybody with the last name of Harrison wasn't high on his gift list. The car drove him to distraction. Mr. Sam's ignoring every traffic law ever written made him want to yell. It wasn't the most serious problem he faced as acting sheriff, but it had to be the most frustrating.

Sam's parking violations were more annoying than Jeremy's continuing skateboard tricks on the public library staircase. He was ready to wring the kid's scrawny neck if he caught him using the handrail for a slide one more time. Lillian Baker would soon have a conniption over all her reports on the Harrison males' illegal activities.

If he heard one more "Laurel says this" or "Laurel thinks that" from his daughter, he was going to gag. It was great that Ashleigh had a role model. And Laurel made a good one. But given the fact that he was trying to find as much fault as possible with the woman—just to keep from falling in love with her—his daughter's attachment was problematic.

Right now, he had to stop worrying about the Harrison clan in general, and find one member in particular—or tow this car away.

Just as he was ready to call Verna and have her get Mel and the truck to do the deed, Mr. Sam came out of the bank.

"*Now* what's wrong? I've only been in there long enough to make one deposit and see that cute little teller's wedding pictures," the old man groused.

"Yeah, well, it was long enough for both your meters to run out. If you put money in them to begin with."

Mr. Sam stood up straight, giving Tripp a great view of a shock of white hair. "Of course I put money in them. You really don't think much of me as a driver, do you, Mr. Jordan."

"Is it too much to ask that you at least call me 'Deputy'? I know your opinion on my replacing Hank and I'm willing to let that part slide. But plain old 'mister' doesn't sit right with me."

Harrison scowled. "What you've done so far to earn any title is beyond me. Somebody could have been in there robbing the bank for all you cared.

But no, you had to get all heated up about a couple of nickels for the parking meters. If I put a quarter in each of them, will you be satisfied?''

"Mr. Sam, I won't be satisfied until you hand me the keys to that junker, or the receipt that shows you sold it to the dump and stopped driving it," Tripp told him. That bit about bank robbery pushed him over the edge of civility.

"You should live so long." Sam Harrison glared at him. "Now, if you'll step aside, I'll move the car so you'll stop getting so exercised."

"If you move it now, I'm going to have to write you a ticket. At least put a nickel in both of those meters first, to prove you mean well." It probably wasn't worth egging the old guy on, but Tripp was on a roll.

"Of all the—" Harrison reached into his pants pocket. "I don't even have any nickels. I'm going to have to put dimes in both of them. I hope you're happy. And me on a fixed income."

Tripp didn't laugh. He even managed not to smile as he stepped aside for Harrison to feed his meters and get into the car. If that old man was on a fixed income, it was fixed so high that it would make Tripp's pension look like chump change. And right now, after dealing with him, Tripp felt old enough to collect that pension and get out of town while he still had a chance.

There wasn't any reason to wonder why Hank was recovering from heart surgery. The characters in this town would do in the most patient of men. Tripp shook his head, watching Mr. Sam pull out with a squeal of brakes and head down the street as close to the speed limit as was possible, just to get Tripp's goat.

Tripp was going to have to send Hank a get well card. Maybe even flowers. His boss couldn't get back too soon for him.

When he walked into the office, Verna looked up from her desk and clucked. "You must have run into Mr. Sam and Lurlene. It's the only thing I can think of that would make you look that sour. If you don't watch it, you're going to get ulcers."

"Thanks, Verna. I needed that vote of confidence. Any calls while I was gone?"

"Ashleigh called twice, but it's been more than forty-five minutes since the last call."

He walked into his office and dialed his home phone number. It kept ringing until the machine picked up.

"I'm gone again," he said to Verna, walking back to the front door. "Nobody's answering there."

"This just isn't your day, is it, Tripp." Verna sighed as he headed out. "She's probably taking a shower or listening to music loud enough that she can't hear you. My grandson wears those head-phones—''

He closed the door on whatever she was saying next, and strode down the sidewalk. He quickly covered the distance home and climbed the stairs two at a time. Ash not answering the phone just gave him a bad feeling. That feeling didn't improve when he called upstairs and nobody answered.

The door was locked. Tripp fumbled for his house key and opened it, knowing he was going to find an empty apartment. Sure enough, once inside he saw that the notepad he'd instructed Ash to use when she couldn't get hold of him was lying neatly on the kitchen table next to a sharpened pencil. Nothing was written on the pad—not even doodles.

He was muttering under his breath now. She'd been so good for quite a while. Why did she pick today to wander around town without letting him know? The child would be grounded, once he found her.

He dialed Pearl's number quickly, and she picked up on the second ring. They didn't exchange too many pleasantries before he asked if Ashleigh had called.

''No, she hasn't. And I haven't called her today, either. Why, is something wrong?''

"Not yet," he said to Pearl. No sense worrying her if he didn't need to.

"Good. She's been doing so well, I figured it was about time for a slip-up."

After that comment, he wasn't going to let her have the satisfaction of telling him she told him so. Tripp said a quick goodbye. Verna was right about the ulcers. If there were too many more days like this in his future, he was going to have to buy stock in some antacid company.

The first place he looked on the way out was the coffee house. He could see Laurel through the window, but she was alone. His pulse was quickening by now. Where was that kid? Maybe she was with Jeremy somewhere. He went back to the front of the sheriff's department for his vehicle, scanning all the businesses in between, but with no luck. It was all he could do to keep himself from turning on the lights and siren the moment he got into the car.

A quick cruise of downtown didn't net him anything in the way of sightings of either Jeremy or his missing daughter. Tripp hated to think what his blood pressure was doing by now. On impulse, he pulled up back in front of the apartment building, parking in a fire lane. What was he going to do, give himself a ticket? If he'd held off on Mr. Sam today, he could be generous to himself.

The apartment was still empty. There were no messages on the machine except his own—the one telling Ashleigh from the department that she was in trouble. This time when he went downstairs he went into the coffee house. Laurel looked up and smiled when he came through the door.

"You really ought to keep this door locked," he grumbled.

"I know. Dad says so, too, but I can't lock it all the time in broad daylight. I feel caged that way."

"I'm looking for Ashleigh," he said, trying to sound calm. "You haven't seen her, have you?"

"Sure have. She was down here about an hour ago. Said she'd tried to get you at the office. All she wanted was to go to the library, so I told her to have a nice time and that I'd tell you if you checked up on her."

Now he was ready to explode. "You what? Don't you know that she's supposed to talk to me before she goes anywhere? Or, at least, leave a message with Verna, or on the notepad at home? What makes you think you can countermand that?"

"She was only going to the library. I didn't think that was on the list of forbidden territories." Half Laurel's mouth was quirked upward in a smile.

Tripp was still trying to keep from yelling at this irresponsible woman. "Well, it is. Anyplace is on that list, if she doesn't talk to me first. Period. That kid is grounded but good."

He was into his car and halfway to the library before he realized he hadn't even said hello or goodbye to Laurel. But given her major lack of judgment regarding his daughter, he couldn't say his lack of manners bothered him. If she thought she was getting an apology this time, the woman was wrong.

Chapter Twelve

Laurel looked around the coffee house on Wednesday night. She didn't feel ready for this. Pastor Ron would be here any minute. She was so thankful that he'd agreed to come and help her out this first time. Suddenly she felt as if she'd bitten off more than she could chew with this project.

The coffee house looked good. It was inviting and there were more than enough mismatched tables and chairs sitting around for the kids to use. She still didn't have all her licenses to open as a real business, but everyone in the city government had assured her that running a church-sponsored youth group event, where no money changed hands, wouldn't be a problem.

Still, she was so nervous. What if nobody came

aside from Pastor Ron and Jeremy? What if a bunch of kids came, and nobody had a good time? It was hard to entertain teenagers.

The bell over the front door jingled, and Laurel turned to see who was walking in. It was Jeremy, and he had both of his cousins with him.

"Guys, I'm thrilled to see you. Can I get you something from the coffee bar?"

"Not yet, Aunt Laurel." Trent waved his hand. "And Mom said to make sure anything you gave the squirt was decaf."

Kyle scowled up at him, and Laurel butted in before a fight could get started. "Don't worry, that's all I'm serving this late at night. I figured it wouldn't be as cool for you older people, but the parents would probably thank me. Anybody else coming that you know of?" She tried to sound casual.

"Sure. Probably the whole youth group. And the girls always bring friends to anything so they have somebody to whisper secrets to." Kyle rolled his eyes, letting his aunt know what he thought of that behavior.

"Great. So you didn't have to twist their arms to get them here?" she asked Jeremy, indicating his cousins.

"Nah. They made sure I would come. It isn't exactly tops on my list of places to be. I mean, not as many times as I've already scrubbed the floors and cleaned the blackboard.'' He turned to Trent. ''She keeps changing all the specials, and she's nowhere near opening. I think what I'm doing breaks the child labor laws or something.''

Laurel's exasperation rose. ''Jeremy Samuel, you know that isn't true. You haven't been in here more than four hours altogether so far. And I promised you a trip to the skate store in St. Louis with a padded budget just for what you've done in that little bit of time.''

''Right. I know you mean it, but when are you going to be able to do that anytime soon? Besides, you know it's not going to be nearly as cool as the stores at home.''

Laurel took note that California was still ''at home'' as far as Jeremy was concerned. Her lack of discussion regarding the house sale was coming back to haunt her.

Not that anything was happening there for sure. But now she'd waited so long to discuss a sore subject that Jeremy would be furious when she brought it up. None of this was working the way she'd planned.

Before she could say anything else, the bell over the door rang again. Pastor Ron came in, saying hello to everybody. And Ashleigh Jordan slipped in behind him.

"I thought you were grounded for life," Laurel said. "What made your father change his mind?"

Ashleigh shrugged in a noncommittal fashion. "It's a church thing, isn't it? Even my dad isn't that mean."

Before she could say anything else to Ashleigh, or anyone else, Laurel was swamped with the sudden influx of noisy teenagers pouring into the coffee house. How could eight bodies make that much noise in this big a space? And how could each of them have a different question to ask or exotic coffee drink she'd never heard of to see if she could fix? She was the Coffee Queen, wasn't she? Gina always said so. Nobody really made tangerine-flavored syrup for cappuccinos, did they? And if they did, why hadn't she found it by now?

It took close to an hour to sort out all the drink requests and music discussions and put a CD on the player for more than two songs. By eight-fifteen Laurel was sitting on a wooden stool watching Pastor Ron work magic with the high-schoolers. The middle-schoolers had finished what little coffee drinking they were going to do and had settled down to the business of beating each other at board games or table versions of soccer and hockey. Laurel was glad someone had suggested she get things such as the battered foosball table in one corner. Kyle and one of the girls were having a blast, while their friends chose sides to root for. There was even some actual serious discussion going on amid the banter.

Sitting around with cups of cappuccino had made the high school group feel sophisticated, apparently. They were challenging Ron on points of scripture and asking for answers to questions Laurel didn't remember being ready to ask at fifteen.

Ashleigh didn't seem to be ready, either. She sat on a wooden stool identical to Laurel's, at the edge of the high school group. She hadn't said a word, and was using a spoon to chase around the foam in her cappuccino, letting it drop back into the cup with a soft, liquid plop. She didn't look bored—more like she was wistful or ready to ask something, but just didn't have the nerve yet.

Bless Pastor Ron, because he picked up on that somehow and turned slowly to her in the wide circle of kids around him.

"What do you think about this, Ashleigh? You've been awfully quiet and you seem like you have something to add."

She shook her head and her dark hair cascaded over her face. "Uh-uh. Not a thing."

"No opinion, or just don't know these kids well enough to voice it?" Ron leaned forward in the captain's chair he'd grabbed for his own during this discussion.

Ashleigh was nearly in tears when she dashed her hair out of her face. Laurel wanted to hug her. But she stayed right in her seat and didn't move because there was something happening and she needed to let it happen.

"It's not just the kids. They're talking about all these things I don't get. They're using words I don't understand. I always thought I was cool and knew a whole lot because I was from the city and they were from this little place where nothing happens." The tears were coming in earnest now, and Laurel could see Jeremy nodding along with her.

This was touching him in ways she couldn't hope to. Laurel held her breath.

"Nobody said you weren't any of those things, Ashleigh." The affirmation came from Heather, the quietest girl in the room.

It was the first full sentence Laurel had heard from the girl all night.

"Yeah, but don't you *get* it?" said Ashleigh. "None of that matters! You are all talking about how long you've known Jesus. About walking with the Lord and doing this or that, or how you've been tested, or what you said to a friend when they were doubting something." Ashleigh's shoulders were shaking now. "I don't even know if I know Jesus the way you do. I just want what you've got."

Without another word, Heather got up from

where she was sitting and put a slender arm around
Ashleigh's shoulder. Jeremy had risen when the
girl did, and he was by Ashleigh's side in a moment. There was quiet in the room for a bit, then
the trio went over to a separate table together and
started talking quietly. The rest of the high school
group went on, in soft tones, with the discussion
they'd been having before.

Laurel noticed that almost all the older kids
looked at the trio at the table occasionally. They
tried to catch Heather's eye once in a while, without any luck. The three heads were bent together,
and soon hands were joined while they discussed
something softly.

Pastor Ron seemed to know before Heather
looked up that he was being summoned. He held
his hand up to Trent, who was expounding on
something, and softly said, "Hold that thought."
Looking even more like a mountain man with a
clergy collar than usual, he came over to the table
and bent over the young girl.

Breathless and silent, no longer aware of anything else in the room, Laurel watched Ashleigh as
she struggled with the simplicity of what Ron was
telling her. She could hear bits of his words, re-
peating for Ashleigh a prayer that it seemed Laurel
had known all her life, "And I ask you, Lord Jesus,

to come into my heart...,'' and heard Ashleigh's soft repetition of those beautiful words.

Laurel herself was crying without realizing it, until a tear dropped onto one of her hands. *Thank you, Father. Now I know why I'm doing this. If nothing else of worth ever happens in this place, it's all worthwhile if one child knows you.* And judging from the glow on Ashleigh's face, one child did, in a way that she hadn't until tonight.

Tripp fidgeted through another interminable explanation of one of the four or five thousand line-item entries in the city budget that the town council was going over in this work session. He was sure they would get to the police part of the budget sometime this century. After all, they had ninety-nine more years to go, didn't they?

This was driving him insane. He wanted to ditch this meeting and go home to see if Ash was behaving herself. The quick call to the apartment just before the meeting started had been unhelpful. She was apparently following his instructions to the letter—but not until he had a telephone in his hand and was listening to her new message on the answering machine was Tripp aware of the flaw in his plan.

''*Hi,*'' Ashleigh's voice said. ''You've reached the Jordan home, but no one can answer your call.

My father can't come to the phone right now, and
I'm not allowed to talk because I'm grounded. So
if this isn't Dad checking up on me, please leave
a message and he'll call you back later. I won't
call you back because, like I said, I'm grounded,
and it includes the phone. 'Bye.''

So, was Ashleigh sitting there listening to the
message playing? Or was the message playing in
an empty apartment? He had no way of knowing
that, and no way, until this budget hearing was
over, of finding out. He looked back at the docu-
ments in front of him. They were three line-items
closer to parking meters. This could take a while.

Another hour passed before anybody wanted to
talk to him. Then they asked three questions—two
totally unnecessary and one that made sense. Then
they thanked him for his time, and he was out.
Tripp's head was spinning. How on earth did Hank
do this? And the man actually enjoyed it. There
had to be a knack to this sheriff business that he
just wasn't getting.

Now, at least, he could get home and see what
his darling daughter was up to. Maybe everything
would be just perfect there, which would help erase
the discomfort of the past two hours of boredom.
Maybe he'd even let her off the leash far enough
to get on the telephone with some of her friends
in St. Louis, if she'd been good.

Raising a daughter wasn't as easy as he'd thought. But then, right now, nothing in life seemed to be. He didn't get it. He was a decent guy and he followed all the rules. He did just what he was supposed to virtually every minute of every day, but still nobody cut him a break. Could it be that Laurel was actually right about something? That he had to let loose of his feelings and emotions, instead of gripping the rule book so tightly?

There was so much about the woman that drew him in and intrigued him. But there was just as much that pushed him away—like the fact that she thought it was perfectly all right to let Ashleigh report to her. So what if it was a perfectly innocent trip to the library? It didn't matter that he would have approved of the three-block walk and actually been happy she was spending her time there. What did matter was that he hadn't been consulted.

He parked the SUV in the back lot. There were several cars behind the building, and he wondered what was going on. Laurel hadn't gotten that coffee house open already, after all, had she? He seemed to remember Ashleigh mentioning something about a youth group thing down there that she was missing due to his "extreme cruelty," but that didn't mean people with cars, did it? Something was up, anyway. He could hear the music wafting out to the parking lot.

He mused on whether that was undoing part of Ash's grounding. If she wasn't supposed to enjoy her CDs while she was grounded, how did enjoying the neighbors' music fit in? He went up the stairs and paused at the door. It was quiet in the apartment, but then, it was supposed to be. There wasn't much that Ash was allowed to be doing to make noise.

He unlocked the door, and was treated to the sight of his daughter sitting on the couch, hands in her lap, obviously waiting for him to come home.

"Dad!"

She sprung up from where she sat, bouncing in a way that looked more like the Ash he knew and loved than the proper person sitting on the couch had.

She grabbed his hand and dragged him over to sit where she had been a moment before. Tripp felt misgivings even before her small hands pushed him down to land on the couch.

"Now don't get mad..." she began with one of those phrases that every parent hates.

"Ash, never start a conversation like that with me." He didn't care if he sounded snappish. The kid had obviously done something he wouldn't approve of, or she wouldn't say that.

"Okay. I won't again, ever, I promise. But I've got two things to tell you, and one of them is just so awesome, but first I have to tell you the other one…"

She was breathless with something, either excitement or fear; he couldn't tell which. Tripp wanted to shout at her to get to the point, but he wasn't sure if he wanted to hear either thing that she had to tell him.

"Okay. Go ahead. What's the first thing that *isn't* so awesome?" He was using one of his best suspect-interviewing tones of voice, and it cut through her overexcitedness.

She sat down in the chair at right angles to the couch. "Okay. I know I'm supposed to be grounded."

"No, you *are* grounded. There's no 'supposed to be' about it."

"When you came home for dinner, I asked if you meant church stuff, too, and you asked, 'What did you think?' And remember, I said I thought church stuff should be okay and you said, 'Think again.'"

She stopped talking, and Tripp looked at her. She didn't look as sure of herself, but she was still up to something. "I remember that part so far. What do you have to tell me, Ash?"

"Well, I thought again. And you hadn't said I absolutely couldn't go to church stuff—you just said, 'Think again,' and I knew you were in that meeting, so I went down to the youth group thing Laurel had downstairs.''

"You what?'' Tripp's first impulse was to raise his voice. But even a moderate tone of voice made her lean back into the safety of her chair. "Please tell me Laurel didn't let you stay. She knew you were grounded."

"She didn't ask me to *leave*. And it was church stuff.''

"If the apartment wasn't on fire, you didn't need to leave it, Ashleigh Marie.'' His jaw was clenched so hard, it was difficult to spit out the words.

"I know what I did was wrong. That was why I wanted to tell you that part first.''

"Good, because there isn't going to be any second. This discussion is over. I'm so disappointed in you, I don't know what to say. And I'm even more disappointed in Laurel Harrison for not kicking you out of there the moment you went down.''

Ashleigh opened her mouth again, and Tripp held up a hand. "Not one more word, Ash. Let me be perfectly clear. You are still grounded. And that means no talking on the phone unless you're calling 911 or me. No leaving the apartment unless it's on fire or I say you can go someplace. Which I won't, for a very long time. Nod 'yes' if you understand that.''

She nodded, eyes filling with tears, and for a

moment Tripp almost felt sorry for her. But this wasn't a time to back down on anything. "Great. Now I'm going downstairs to read Laurel the riot act for letting you stay there. When I get back here, I expect you to be in bed. Lights out, no music, nothing. Understood?"

"Sure." She didn't look up from the floorboards, and her agreement was more of a sigh than anything else.

He left her sitting in the chair and went quickly downstairs. Naturally, in the less than fifteen minutes he'd been upstairs with Ashleigh, all signs of life had disappeared from the coffee house. He rattled the front door, but for a change it really was locked.

He had to find Laurel Harrison while he was still this angry. They had plenty to settle, and this time it would be settled his way.

He headed toward Mr. Sam's house, hoping Laurel was at home by now. The two of them were going to have a very interesting discussion, probably their last one ever. And right now that suited him just fine.

Chapter Thirteen

The Harrisons' street was dark. There were porch lights on at some of the houses, but there weren't as many streetlights as there were in the downtown business section. Tripp peered at the uneven puddles of light his headlights threw on the rutted street.

As he stepped on the accelerator again to get the last half block to the Harrisons' house, something darted out in front of the car. Swearing softly, he jammed on the brakes. It might have been a squirrel or a rabbit dashing across the street, but with his luck there'd be headlines in the Friedens paper tomorrow about the acting sheriff hitting somebody's puppy.

Whatever it was made it across the street, and

Tripp started up again. Why didn't he just give up and keep antacids in the pocket of this uniform? He needed a double dose this week alone. There was the Harrisons' house up ahead, and he started to pull up to the curb near Lurlene. In the process, he stopped short. Sam had left the front driver's side door of his horrible car wide open. It blocked nearly a lane of the wide street. Tripp was incredibly lucky that he hadn't torn the thing straight off the hinges.

This was the limit. Tripp had no more patience for anything. He ground the vehicle into reverse and pulled it back away from the Cadillac. He slammed the door to the cruiser as hard as he wanted to slam the one on the convertible. Of course, if he closed that one, nobody would believe what he'd seen.

For the first time in months, Tripp wanted a partner. That way one of them could go get Harrison, while the other one stood guard to make sure the next driver down the street didn't have a wreck.

Since he was alone, that wasn't an option. He mounted the porch steps three at a time. If there was a doorbell, he didn't see it. Of course, Mr. Sam hadn't bothered with his front porch light. It felt good to pound on the solid front door with his fist. Maybe that would get the old man's attention.

''What do you want! And it's not like you have

to knock the door down," Mr. Sam complained, when he finally answered the door.

"If I did, it would be the second time in five minutes I took the door off something you owned," Tripp fumed. "I came over here to find Laurel, but before I do, it looks like I have to stop and cite you for about six different violations. When I get done with you, there are going to be so many points on your driver's license, you won't get it back before your hundredth birthday."

"I have no idea what you're talking about. I've been sitting in the back room watching the Cardinals game. Haven't been anywhere near the car in hours."

"Yeah, well, I don't believe that one. I nearly tore the front door off that heap on my way in here because it was wide open halfway out in the street. And you haven't said where Laurel is, either."

"That's because I don't know. Jeremy came home with his cousins a while back, and I haven't seen his mother. But you can rest assured that even if I had, I wouldn't tell the likes of you. So I'd suggest you either write your phony ticket or get off my front porch."

Tripp was so mad he was starting to see spots. "Fine. I'll write my tickets. *Plural.* And while I'm doing it, you come out here and close this car door."

Mr. Sam shook his head. "I keep telling you, I don't know what you're talking about..." He looked over his shoulder into the darkened hallway. "Unless Jeremy was doing something with the car while he was out front with that skateboard. He came in, though, to answer the phone."

Mr. Sam peered around Tripp into the darkness. "Well, that rascal. I'm sorry for doubting you, Sheriff Jordan."

"You'll be even sorrier when I finish writing the tickets." Tripp was already on the way back to the cruiser to get his book. "And I still don't believe you don't know where Laurel is."

Their argument on the front porch was interrupted by Jeremy coming out of the house in a hurry. "Grandpa! Where's Mom? I have to talk to her right now! That was Gina on the phone, and she thinks she's selling our house to some guy. Mom wouldn't do that without telling me. Where is she?"

"That's everybody's question," Tripp told him. "It sounds like she's got explaining to do all over when we find her. But so do you?"

Mr. Sam grabbed Jeremy's arm to stop his wild flight from the house. "Hold on, now. I don't know where your mom is. And you have some explaining to do too. Did you leave my car door that way?"

Jeremy stopped in his tracks. "Uh, yeah. I was trying to jump it on my skateboard. Then the phone rang, and nobody was getting it. Why, is there a problem?"

There was never a convenient piece of wallboard to put your fist through in frustration when you needed one. Tripp couldn't think of any way to defuse this much frustration.

"Look, you two. Close the car door before somebody rips it off. Which won't be a problem an hour from now because I'm coming back to impound that vehicle the minute I find Laurel. I don't care who made a public nuisance out of it in the middle of the street—I'm finding a way to bring it in tonight. This is just the last straw."

Both the Harrisons were silent, looking at him open-mouthed.

Tripp looked at Jeremy. "Were you in on what happened with Ashleigh at the coffee house?"

"Sure. Did she tell you?" Jeremy perked up, which Tripp thought was a strange response.

"She told me plenty. And if she wasn't grounded for life before, she is now. Along with your mother, if that were legal."

"Which it isn't. Even I know that much." The kid stuck his chin out defiantly. "And if you don't, you're a worse replacement for Grandpa Hank than I thought you were."

That stung, coming from a kid who didn't even shave yet. "Yeah, well, I know one thing. Your mom *could* sell that house in California without telling you anything. And she probably would, too. So get used to seeing me on a regular basis when I arrest you for trying to jump over things with that skateboard."

He left them on the porch to return to the cruiser. He still needed to find Laurel, and fast. This was turning into a night like no other since he'd taken over for Hank Collins. All he needed now was livestock wandering down Main Street, or a drunken brawl at the pool hall, to make his life complete.

Once back in the cruiser, he pulled away and parked about three blocks from Mr. Sam's house, where he could relax a bit. Then he did something that was out of character for him—but this had hardly been a regular kind of night. He got out his phone and called Hank, at home, at nearly ten o'clock at night.

"Tripp? Something wrong?" Hank sounded more surprised by the call than Tripp had thought he would be.

"A little bit of everything. Most of it is personal, and nothing I can't handle in time. But I need a little help. I'm looking for Laurel, and she's not at the coffee house and she's not at Sam's. You got any good ideas where I might find her?''

''Not an idea, a straight fact. She's sitting here at my kitchen table,'' Hank replied.

''Then handcuff her to the chair or something, because I want to talk to her and I need her in one place. Do *not* let that woman leave, understand?''

''Understood. I'm sure you'll explain more when you get over here.''

''Which will be three minutes, tops,'' Tripp said, and hung up. He might break a few traffic laws doing it, but he'd get to Hank's in record time.

''Did he say what he wanted?'' Laurel asked her father.

''Not exactly. But he sounded serious. Do you think he wasn't happy with what went on with his daughter?''

''How could he not be? Unless she wasn't telling me the whole truth when she said she had permission to come. If that's the case, we're all in deep trouble. That man does live by the letter of the law.''

''It's why he's good at his job.'' Hank sat back down. ''You'd at least agree with me on that, now, wouldn't you?''

''I would, by now. If you'd asked me when I first got here, I wouldn't have had the same opinion. But I can actually see why you hired him, Dad.''

"Well, I'm so glad you approve of my decision.'' Hank made a face. "Now ask me if I approve of yours.''

"Which one? The one to move back to Friedens, open a coffee house, or date your deputy?''

"A little bit of all of them, I guess. Laurel, do you ever stop to think about anybody else's opinion?''

"About as often as you do,'' she countered, earning a slight wince from Hank.

"Okay. I had that coming. And don't misunderstand, I'm glad to have you back if you really want to be here. But if you're just here out of guilt, or some odd notion I don't have much time left or something…''

"Not at all. I want to be here, most of the time. California hasn't felt right since Sam's been gone. I love the weather, and the scenery. But the whole atmosphere isn't comfortable for me.'' She cupped her chin in one hand. "Think there's any way we could get me a mountain or two, and some cool nights, though? This humidity is about to kill me.''

Hank shook his head. "These kids who've always had air-conditioning. Don't get me started on that.''

"I won't. We could be here all night just talking about that, and I think I hear your deputy outside."

Somebody was sure slamming car doors and thumping around. In a few seconds Tripp was at the back door. He must have wanted in badly to come around back, instead of waiting at the front.

"What do you think you're doing with my daughter?" he said as he strode into the kitchen. "Did you even ask her if she had permission to come down there tonight? Because you *knew* she was grounded."

"Of course I asked. And she said—"

"I'm not even sure I should listen to this. You're an adult. You should have known better than to believe whatever she said."

Laurel sprang up. "Now, wait a minute. That does us both a disservice. I believe kids should be trusted to tell the truth, so that's what I expect out of them—"

"Right. When they're not out providing false names to police officers," Tripp fumed. "And if your standards are so high, why didn't you tell Jeremy you were selling the house?"

She felt as if she'd crashed into a brick wall. "What did you say?"

"Which time? I want to figure out which statement finally got your attention." Tripp was standing over her now, and he seemed menacing. "If it was the last one, I wanted to know why you didn't come right out and tell your own kid you are selling the house and moving. He seems to think that is what's happening after talking to your friend Gina. And I'm surprised, given the stuff you've been preaching to me, that you don't practice nearly as much honesty or trust.''

She felt numb. ''That isn't the way it was. He's got it wrong. I haven't signed anything yet. Gina and I have talked about it, maybe. But nothing has happened. And how do you know all this, anyway?''

''We had an interesting discussion when I was at Mr. Sam's to try and find you. Speaking of which, now that I've done so, we have to sort through a couple of things quickly so I can go back and impound his car like I promised.''

''You can't do that! Dad, tell him he can't do that,'' Laurel said to her father, who'd been watching this whole exchange, still holding onto the kitchen doorknob.

''I won't tell him any such thing until I hear a whole bunch more from both of you. And I want you sitting down and using civil tones in my house, got it?''

Her father's voice had the same effect on both of them. Chairs were pulled away from the table, and everyone sat. Quietly. When Hank was sitting between the two of them as they faced each other, he put both hands on the tabletop. "Now, one at a time and slowly. No name-calling or other obnoxious behavior. I care about both of you, and I'll have you remember I'm an old man with a heart condition."

Laurel could see a scowl on Tripp's face to match her own. "You're not old…" she said, only to hear Tripp echo the same thing.

"See. Something you agree on. Now let's find a few more things. Tripp, you start with a little bit about why you nearly arrested Sam or impounded Lurlene or whatever happened. I have to think my grandson was involved somehow," Hank said. He leaned back in his chair to listen, and Laurel was reminded of an Old Testament judge.

"I'm still mad at you," Tripp said to Laurel. "But now I'm madder at myself. Why didn't any of you clunk me over the head tonight to get me to listen to the important parts of the story?"

"Did you give anybody a chance? I can imagine you didn't give Ashleigh one. And she was just floating on clouds when she left the coffee house. That was part of the reason I wanted to come over here right after the youth group meeting."

Laurel turned to her dad, and Tripp hoped that

Ash would still look at him twenty-five years from now the way she was looking at Hank.

"That still means a lot to me. Thanks." Hank sounded a touch choked up.

But then, there'd been a lot of hot and angry words exchanged at his table over the past hour. Hank had even contributed a few.

But Tripp still felt as if he'd contributed most of them himself. "I've really been out of control the past couple hours. Laurel, tell me what I can do to right the many wrongs I've created tonight."

"It's going to take a while for me, Tripp, but I'm a grown-up. I can handle it. First, I'd say you need to go home and talk to Ashleigh. Then, if you want to call or come over and speak with Jeremy, you're welcome."

"Okay. I may do that, depending on how late I'm up with Ashleigh. And I never thought I'd say this, but please tell Mr. Harrison that I won't be coming to tow away his car. At least, not tonight. I make no promises for the future."

"I understand that. And thank you for listening tonight. I feel better about some of the things that have happened lately, after hearing you out."

Laurel looked extremely solemn. He could tell that one of the things she didn't feel better about was any hopes for a relationship with him. But

then, given his asinine behavior in the past week
or so, who could blame her?

She got up from the table, and went behind her
dad to give him a quick hug. "I have to get going.
Sounds like I have some ruffled feathers to smooth
out. I hate to ask you this, but could you give me
a ride home? I had Pastor Ron drop me off, and I
was going to have Gloria take me home, but I'm
sure she's given up and gone to bed. And I know
Mr. Sam has, so it's no use calling him."

"Sure. It's the least I can do." He looked at his
boss. "You want my resignation now, or can it
wait?"

"Why would I want your resignation? Everybody's entitled to a few errors in judgment. Be
thankful yours have only involved words and family members." Hank got to his feet slowly. "And
don't count on me to mediate one of these again.
My neck is so stiff from watching you two back
and forth, I feel like I've seen a match at Wimble-
don."

"Guess we did go on. I'll talk to you tomorrow
sometime, then, okay?"

Hank nodded. "You do that. And I don't want
to hear any more talk of resignations."

Tripp nodded and followed Laurel to the front
door. "Good night, Dad," she called as she let

them out. He could hear Hank calling back to her before the door shut.

"We wore him out. I feel bad about that part," she said, going down the front walk. "But I'm glad he was willing to talk with us. I can't imagine how that whole exchange would have developed without a mediator."

"Would have lasted about two minutes, like all my interactions tonight with people who are important to me. And I would have screwed up just as effectively." It was the truth, and Tripp had no problem admitting it. "I notice you're not jumping in to contradict me."

"No, I'm not. But I have to take some responsibility, too. I'm sorry I didn't ask more pointed questions with Ashleigh tonight. But it really sounded as if she had your okay to be there."

"I know. She should have. I feel like an absolutely rotten parent now."

"It will pass. I don't think any permanent damage has been done. Tell her you'll give her a chance to flex her forgiveness muscles as a brand-new Christian."

Laurel sounded as if she was only half teasing. "I almost like that idea." It was a bit scary to admit that to her. Maybe the gap between them, in parenting styles and a host of other things, wasn't as broad as it seemed.

They didn't say much more on the ride over to Mr. Sam's. Laurel insisted he drop her off and head home to Ashleigh. It was a relief to see that Lurlene had been garaged, leaving the street empty. At least there wasn't that obvious reminder of his making a fool of himself.

He went home as fast as possible without breaking any speed laws. There were lights on in the apartment, but Ashleigh wasn't there at the door to greet him when he came in. She was probably in bed.

He went and knocked on her door. "May I come in, Ash? We need to talk, and I need to apologize. Bet you didn't expect that, did you?"

There was silence on the other side of the door. He knocked again. "Ash?"

He could see light on inside her room, so Tripp opened the door, expecting to find his daughter worn out, probably from crying, and fallen asleep on top of the quilt.

Instead, the bedside lamp revealed an empty room. There were open drawers in the dresser, and the closet was ajar. This was not good. Not good at all.

He made a quick pass through the whole place—kitchen, bathroom and his bedroom—but there was no sign of Ashleigh anywhere. He was close to panic now. "What did I do? What on earth did I do?'' His question echoed off the kitchen's tile walls. There was a folded piece of paper on the table. Somehow he'd missed it before.

As he was unfolding it, the phone rang. Still unfolding with one hand, he picked up the phone.

''Tripp?'' It was Laurel and she sounded distressed. ''I've got trouble here. Sam and Jeremy are gone. They're in the car, and I'm really worried because they took Buster with them. I can't even find a litter box. It looks like everybody's run away.''

He was trying to force out words to answer her but he couldn't, and the penciled words on Ashleigh's note kept blurring before his eyes. ''Trouble doesn't end there, Laurel. Call Gloria and wake her up, and have her bring you to their house. I'll meet you there in ten minutes. Ashleigh is with them, and they're all on their way to St. Louis to Pearl's.''

Chapter Fourteen

Of course, there was no answer at Pearl's, either. Tripp was pacing Hank and Gloria's kitchen. "They really haven't been gone long enough to call my buddies on the St. Louis force and send a car to Pearl's," he muttered. "And that would only scare them all, if Pearl has just bedded down the whole crew with blankets on the sofas and turned off the ringer on the phone. Which she could have done."

"I'm glad this is a tile floor. You'd have worn through carpet by now," Gloria told him. "Can you think and sit at the same time, or is pacing a universal law enforcement guy thing?"

"I can stop pacing. But I can't sit," he told her. "Even Laurel isn't sitting down."

"That's only because I've already been through enough tonight that I feel drained. If I sit down, I'll stay there for good."

She sounded grim, and there were dark smudges of fatigue under her eyes. Tripp felt a pang of guilt for having helped put them there.

"So *now* will you let me resign?" he asked Hank. "It's the only way I can do this. Then I'd be free to take Laurel and head towards St. Louis to figure out what's going on."

"You are not resigning. But you *are* going to St. Louis as soon as I'm sure you're stable enough to drive," Hank said to him. "I've actually got things worked out in such a way that even Gloria approves."

Tripp looked over at Gloria, who was pouting a little.

"Approves is a bit strong," she said. "Letting you do this is about as much as I'll agree to. He's rigged up this elaborate communications system so that he can manage everything you've been doing without going out on the street. Of course, he had to get Verna out of bed to do it. And have Fire & Rescue loan him two officers."

"Let me guess. Mike and Carrie," Laurel put in. "It's the only way I can imagine that both of you would be okay with this goofy plan."

Hank looked over at Tripp. "She's pretty good

at this. Sure you won't have a spot on the squad when you get back?"

"The thought gives me the chills. I have enough to worry about just having her in town," Tripp said. "So let's get out of here before I think of forty more reasons why this is a lousy idea. Can I take the cruiser so I'll stay in better radio contact?"

"I wouldn't have it any other way. Be careful out there. You've got some people who are very important to me depending on you."

Hank's eyes glittered a little, and Tripp pretended not to notice. If he paid attention to that, he'd lose his own slender resolve. All he could do was nod and motion toward Laurel.

Pearl's house was dark when they got there. Laurel was sure they'd broken land speed records on the way to St. Louis, but no one had stopped them. "So is the quiet a good sign or a bad one?"

"We'll know in a minute. It would be just as dark if they were all in there asleep as it would be if they were here and gone. I'm betting on here and gone, though, because I don't see that boat of Sam's anywhere. Pearl doesn't have a big enough garage to store it and her car at once."

Laurel's heart sank. She hadn't thought of that part. As they were going up the front walk to check on things, she saw a tall, slender figure detach itself from the shadows on a near-by porch and come toward them. "Tripp?" she said quietly.

He spun around from the doorway. "Who is it?"

The figure on the sidewalk stopped with raised palms. "Whoa, Detective Jordan? It's me, Lyle."

Laurel could hear Tripp moan softly.

"That's all I need right now—the Richards kid."

"Can I come up there? Or are you still mad at me? I've got a message from Ashleigh. At least, I sort of do."

"If that's the case, come on up here," Tripp said. "We'll call a truce."

In the dim light on the front porch, Laurel could see a young man with pale hair, who didn't look the eighteen years that she knew he was. "First of all, I want to apologize for things this summer. Honest, I had no idea how old Ashleigh was. She said she was in high school, and I figured I hadn't seen her around at school just because I go to the ROTC magnet academy, and she must have been going to Roosevelt."

Laurel could feel Tripp stiffen beside her.

"Okay, apology accepted," he said. "Have you seen her tonight? You must have, or you wouldn't know I was angry with you."

"Oh, I knew that a couple of weeks ago from Mrs. Simms. She didn't waste any time telling me off, once she'd sent Ashleigh down to where you were. But yeah, I saw Ashleigh tonight."

"Who was with her?" Laurel asked. She was anxious for news of her family, as well.

"A pretty different bunch of people, if you don't mind me saying. But the old guy had a very cool car. I don't think Mrs. Simms was going to go with them until she saw that car, man."

"So they're gone?" Tripp sounded even more tired than before.

"They didn't stay long," Lyle said. "I talked to Ash out on the porch, while they were loading some stuff into the trunk of that car. Not a lot of stuff, but definitely some suitcases. There would have been more room for stuff if they'd let me keep the cat for them like I wanted to. But the old guy said Buster didn't take to strangers much. Which I thought was odd, because that cat was all over me."

Laurel tried to hide a smile. Buster was one of the best judges of character she knew, but she wasn't about to tell Tripp that right now. "So they all left…Pearl and Mr. Sam and Jeremy and Ashleigh—and they had the cat with them."

"Yeah. Been gone over two hours, I'd guess. They hardly got here before they took off again.

Ashleigh had just about enough time to tell me how happy she was, and then they split."

"Happy? She wasn't crying her eyes out or anything?" Tripp asked, sagging against the porch wall.

"No, man, it wasn't like that. She was telling me about this awesome thing she had happen to her today...I guess it's yesterday now, about knowing Jesus and stuff. She's not running away, exactly. It's more like they're running to something. Or someplace. She's just keeping the guys company, and they wanted to pick up Pearl to keep things legal, I guess."

Now it was Laurel who felt lightheaded and wanted the support of the wall behind her. "They're driving to California, aren't they. It's just the kind of crazy thing I can imagine Sam doing for Jeremy."

"They didn't say where they were going—just that they had to get started before anybody knew they were gone, or you'd arrest them," Lyle said to Tripp. "Are you going to? Arrest them? I don't want to get Ashleigh in trouble. Not when she seemed so happy."

"We'll see about arresting them, once I find them." Tripp sounded very tired. "I just want to find them first. Did they say anything else?"

"Not much. Mrs. Simms and the old guy were

talking about highways. I didn't think there was a Route 66 anymore. Is there still, or was that a fifties thing?"

"It's not official anymore. But it would make sense as their route if Sam sees this as some kind of farewell trip for Lurlene."

Lyle's brow wrinkled. "I thought Mrs. Simms's name was Pearl."

"It is. Lurlene is that cool old car," Laurel replied.

"Man, that is even cooler. To have a car named Lurlene. I hope you find them okay. But maybe not too soon."

"Son, right now it couldn't be soon enough," Tripp said, echoing Laurel's unspoken sentiments. "Now I'm going to go in here and see if I can't find anything that tells me whether or not they're really on old Route 66 heading for Los Angeles or not. And you can go home and go to bed."

"Will do. Say hi to Ashleigh for me when you see her."

Laurel was surprised that Tripp stuck out his hand and shook with Lyle as if that "Richards kid" really were another man that had done him a favor. "Will do. And thanks for the news."

He sighed as the kid went down the steps, and Tripp fumbled with the lock on Pearl's front door.

"Got it. Let's see what we can find," he said to Laurel.

"I don't expect a note. Do you?" she asked him.

"No, but there are a few things I hope I don't find. Like half of Pearl's closet empty, or..." He broke off, swearing softly. "Or that—" he finished, pointing to the kitchen countertop.

Laurel looked toward where he was pointing, and at first what she saw didn't register. Then she realized that she was looking at Mr. Sam's license plates. "We've got a long night ahead of us, don't we."

"We do. And our first stop is going to be the local station house, where I hope they'll do us the favor of running Pearl's registration on the DMV records. I better go out back to the garage, just to make sure first. But it looks like they planned on us following them and they didn't want to make it easy."

A short while later the sergeant on duty who remembered Tripp, kept writing down information as Tripp and Laurel added to their story. "So let me get this straight. We're apparently looking for four people and a cat, and they're in a perfectly legal 1964 Cadillac convertible, except that it now has the plates to another vehicle on it. But you don't want them arrested for stolen plates."

"That about covers it. We just want to find them

as soon as possible. The kids are with their own grandparents and there are no arrest issues there, either. As far as that goes, Pearl has technically shared custody with me for years."

"I can run the plates, and alert Highway Patrol to give us a heads-up if anybody sees them. If you don't want them arrested, that's about all I can do."

"Works for me. I just appreciate your verifying Pearl's license number so we know what to look for. We're in radio and phone contact with the sheriff in Friedens, and you can report through him."

The sergeant stood up. "Will do. Sure you don't want another cup of our wonderful coffee, for old time's sake, Detective? Or should I say 'Deputy' now?"

"For the time being it's still 'Deputy.' I could see it going back to 'Detective' if anybody will have me when this is over. This is probably more mayhem than anybody in Friedens has been involved with the entire time Hank's been sheriff."

"Don't bet on it," Laurel said to him. "I remember worse on his watch. If you want, I can tell you stories while we head toward wherever we're heading."

"Springfield, Missouri. I can't imagine they've gotten much farther than that already." Tripp made his goodbyes to the sergeant, and they headed back to the cruiser.

"I'll bet you're tired of the inside of this thing already," Tripp said, patting the dash.

"I am. And I'm just tired, period. How are you holding up?"

"Poorly. But I have no choice but to keep going."

Laurel thought he looked more tired than she'd ever seen him. As they headed out of the city, down Highway 44, tracing the route of the old Route 66, she silently prayed for her friend and companion. It was a while before she realized that in her mind she'd gone back to calling him Jesse.

Later, she wasn't sure how long she'd slept on the ride. She only knew that she had been sound asleep until the washboard effect of rough pavement under their wheels jounced her awake.

"What's going on? Where are we?" It was dark, and Tripp was leaning over the steering wheel.

"On the side of the highway. I think I dozed off a little. Sorry." He shook his head as if to clear it. "I don't think I can go any farther. Can you drive?"

"Not for a while. I'm hardly alert enough to unfasten my seat belt."

"We make a fine pair, don't we?"

His voice cracked, and Laurel thought he was near tears of desperation.

"I passed up a rest stop a few miles back, and now I'm sorry I did. Noticed a sign for a truck stop on up ahead about four miles. I'm pretty sure I can make that, but then we're quitting for a while."

"Fine." Laurel was so tired she couldn't argue. It worried her to think that the kids could be out there someplace with a driver as tired as she and Tripp were, but she couldn't go any farther either right now. Surely if they'd gotten to that point as well, Mr. Sam would have the good sense to stop someplace.

They made it to the brightly lit parking lot of the truck stop without further incident. Laurel called Hank on the cell phone; just to make sure it still worked.

"Now, you know if I'd heard anything, I'd have called or radioed immediately. And I still will," her father reassured her. "Keep your phone on, get some rest, and know that Gloria and I are praying for you."

"Thanks, Dad." She ended the call and put the phone on the dash.

Rolling the window down to let the cool night air into the car, she went around outside to where Tripp was sitting on the hood. His right fist was methodically thumping the metal, not hard enough to hurt, she knew, but hard enough to keep him awake and vent some frustration. When she stood right in front of him, she could see that there were tears in his eyes.

"I can't do anything else. I've done everything I could, and it's still not enough. Why isn't it enough?"

The pain in his voice seared her. "I don't know. I honestly don't know," she said to him, putting her arms around the wounded man. He took her embrace, almost staggered into it. "It never is enough, though. What we do alone. Tripp, I know you're going to be even more upset when I say this, but we need to pray."

He passed the back of one hand across his face, as if to wipe away the fatigue. "No, you're right. I have nowhere else to turn and nothing else I can do. It's a shame that things had to come to this, before I could admit that—but there it is. Okay, Laurel, help me do this. You helped Ashleigh, now help me."

He took her hands down from his shoulders, and held her fingers in a trembling grip. Then he leaned his head down so they were touching foreheads, giving them as much privacy as one could get in a brightly lit stretch of asphalt such as this.

Laurel didn't know what to say, or how to say it. She just opened her mouth and let the beginning of a prayer come out. *"Heavenly Father, we're lost. We can't find Pearl and Mr. Sam, can't find the kids, and have lost track, almost, of You as well…"*

Tripp's voice was surprisingly strong as he took over. *"Lord, Laurel may or may not be that lost. But You know that I am. It's been years since I've come to you for anything. Years since I've dared to admit that You are God and You are in control. Help me to be able to do that now."*

The only sounds were the traffic noises from the highway, and Laurel was aware of their breathing.

"Lord Jesus, help me surrender all my flawed and broken life to you. Take it all, for what it's worth. And please, if you can, give me back my daughter."

Tripp ran out of words then, and leaned into her even more heavily.

"You all right?" she asked him softly.

"I think so. Can you say 'Amen' to all that?"

"Amen. More than once, Amen. Now what do we do, Jesse?"

He tilted his head back and looked up at the dark sky. "Didn't notice how many stars were out tonight until now. And I don't know about you, but what I'm going to do now is trust in God and go to sleep. I honestly think I can now."

Laurel watched in near amazement as he did just

that. Tripp walked around to the driver's side of the cruiser, got in, reclined the seat and relaxed. She couldn't think of any better testimony to his newfound faith than to join him. Stretching out in the passenger seat, she was sure that she wouldn't be able to doze off.

His fingers curled around hers where their hands lay on the seat. She could feel the faint motion of his body as he slept. She tilted her head back against the head rest, and prayed silently in thanks and praise.

When the phone on the dash shrilled, Tripp sat bolt upright and nearly hit his head on the roof of the cruiser. Laurel was even quicker than he was to snatch the phone and answer it. "Dad?" she asked in a voice that cracked.

Tripp could tell it was Hank on the other end by her expression as she listened. Focusing a little more now, he realized it was daylight. They must have slept for hours. He felt refreshed enough to go on, which seemed to be what God had in store for them, the way Laurel was chattering into the phone.

"No, Dad. That can't be. God just wouldn't let it happen—"

Her voice cracked again, and Tripp's heart went with it. It was all he could do to keep from grabbing the phone and talking to Hank himself. He tried to catch Laurel's eye. Hearing half this conversation was killing him.

"Then where are they? Does anybody know?"

She paused to listen, and Tripp mouthed *tell me*.

"Oh, wait. I just realized Jesse couldn't hear any of what you're saying. He's probably going crazy here. Hold on."

She put the phone down. "Okay. At first it was bad news, but it's gotten better. The police in Springfield found the car. It had been wrecked, and the occupants taken to the hospital."

Tripp's heart quit beating, he was sure of it. "Are they…" He just couldn't say any more.

"Tripp, that's the part where it gets better. There were only two young men in their twenties in the car—local guys. Somebody obviously stole Lurlene from Mr. Sam and made off with her. Now all we have to do is figure out where that happened, and we can find our family."

Chapter Fifteen

꩜

"So, you want to go inside and get some coffee? I bet it's awful," Laurel said, aware of how badly she was trembling.

Tripp laughed. "By your standards it's probably not even coffee. But I could use a couple of cups. And some bacon and eggs and whatever else they'll throw on a plate. I don't remember the last time I ate. Do you?"

"No, but now that you mention food, I'm starving." Laurel could feel her stomach gnawing. "Dad says he'll call the minute he has word. Or the Springfield Police or the Highway Patrol will get hold of us, depending on who has jurisdiction wherever they are."

Tripp smiled. He looked so at ease that Laurel

was astounded. His peace was actually lasting, and it was a wonderful thing.

"Good enough for me. Until we know where to go, we can't go anywhere. Not unless we want to go look at that car wrapped around some tree."

Laurel shivered. "Not me, thanks. That would only remind me that it could have been our families in there, instead. Come on and let's get that breakfast before I change my mind about going into the 24-7 Trucker's Home."

When they got inside, the place was bright and very clean. And the coffee smelled better than she had expected. It might not be as good as what she could have made at the coffee house, but it would be passable.

Having her fingers wrapped around a thick china mug of steaming brew was comforting. After a couple of sips, she excused herself to freshen up. She could only imagine what her hair looked like after sleeping in the car.

The reflection in the mirror was as bad as she had anticipated, and she had little with her with which to repair the damage. She did what she could, then went back to the table, where she found Tripp working on an order of toast, and a cinnamon roll waiting for her at her place.

"How did you know what I wanted? Did I say something without realizing it?"

"No, I just took an educated guess. And it appears that for a change I was able to think like you enough to get it right."

She got another smile from Tripp. The gesture left her slightly shaky and near tears. "You did very well. I'm surprised that you'd even want to try and think like me after the past twenty-four hours."

Tripp put down his piece of toast. "I've been too rough on you. You may not do things the way I would, but there's more than one way of doing things in most situations. And I have to admit that your way has worked more often than not."

He took her hand. His fingers were warm and comforting. She could get used to having this man hold her hand, Laurel thought.

"It really is more like God's way, isn't it. You just managed to show me how to follow it. And I can't thank you enough for that."

"Thank me when we find the family." She took back her fingers. "Until then, you're probably doing a better job with this trust thing than I am. I told you, the parenting act is where I have trouble letting go, remember?"

"All too well. Does it get easier? You've got a few more years of practice than I do in that department."

"It hasn't gotten easy yet. I'll let you know if

it does," she said, concentrating on her coffee so he wouldn't see the tears that sprang up. She felt vulnerable enough around Jesse right now.

The waitress came back with a big plate of eggs, bacon and more toast, and set it in front of Tripp. The moment she put it down, the cell phone sprang to life again. This time Tripp was quicker than Laurel was to get it, although it almost cost him a cup of coffee in his lap. He managed to right the cup with one hand, while answering.

"Great. Hank, that is just great—"

His smile was even broader than before, and Laurel could tell they'd finally found the family and everybody was okay.

"If we're at a place called the 24-7 Trucker's Home, how far do we go before we find that? Only twelve miles, huh? Well, it's good to know an eighty-two-year-old man could only outdrive me by twelve miles. I will. Goodbye."

"The Springfield Police just took a report of a stolen car from a gentleman at a motel right off the highway. I don't know what you're going to do, but I'm going to finish part of these eggs, then get in the car and go find them."

"Somewhere in there I intend to pray," she responded, trying not to sound too stern.

"Oh, *every place* in there I intend to do that," Tripp said. "I'm just still a little self-conscious about doing it in public out loud. But maybe that will grow on me, too.''

Before he could say anything else, a huge, bearded trucker clapped him on the back. ''Congratulations, there, Sheriff. Or whatever we call you. Is this the honeymoon breakfast?''

Laurel nearly spit out her coffee. ''What are you talking about?''

''A bunch of us were in here this morning. We saw you two getting cozy in the parking lot, and figured you'd run out of steam to go any farther after an Arkansas run.'' He paused a moment, expecting her to fill in the blank, but she still had no idea. ''You know, to get married. No blood tests down there, no waiting, no nothing. Lots of folks make that run. And y'all look so happy...''

Laurel felt uncontrollable laughter building up. ''No, that's not quite it. But thanks for the congratulations. We did just get good news.''

''Well, good,'' the trucker said, backing away slowly. The sight of the two of them dissolving into laughter seemed to unnerve him. ''Y'all have a good day, then.''

''Oh, we will,'' Tripp told him. ''We definitely will. It's all good from here on out.''

For a change, Laurel was inclined to agree with him on all points.

* * *

Twenty minutes later they were still laughing over the look on the trucker's face. It wasn't a fancy motel they pulled up in front of. But to Tripp it looked pretty good. Especially when Ashleigh and Pearl, Sam and Jeremy were all sitting on benches outside the registration lobby, waiting for them.

Ashleigh sprang up the moment she recognized his car. He was on the pavement and had her in his arms in a heartbeat. "You scared me to death," he exclaimed. "And I'm so sorry about what I said to you. Don't you ever do this again, please."

"It sounded like a really good idea yesterday," Ashleigh said. "Getting Jeremy back to California and all, and just getting away for a while. But I guess it was pretty dumb, huh?"

"It could have been dangerous," Laurel said, walking up to the group. "I'm so glad nobody was in that car when they made off with it."

Mr. Sam shook his head. "I almost wish I had been. Maybe I could have kept them from destroying it."

"Or maybe you could have been hurt, or worse," Tripp said, unwilling to point out all the possibilities in front of Pearl and the kids.

"You're probably right. For once, I don't mind saying that." Sam chuckled. "I'll bet you weren't sorry to hear about that car biting the dust."

"To tell the truth, I'll miss her," Tripp replied. He would, too, in an odd sort of way. Without Lurlene, there would definitely be less challenge in his daily life.

"You won't miss her long. Pearl says she's got a neighbor who might be able to hook me up with a '69 Impala. Those things had get up and go. And they're almost as big as Lurlene."

Tripp managed not to groan out loud. Considering Mr. Sam in a car the size of the Cadillac, but with speed involved, would make him gray yet. At least he'd have plenty of fodder for his prayer life.

"So how will we all fit in the cruiser to get home? It's going to be a tight squeeze," Pearl pointed out.

"It will work." Laurel was already turning around to sort things out. "Tripp and I can keep the front seat, and put Ash in the middle where there's less leg room. She's the shortest. Then Jeremy and Sam and Pearl can ride in the back. Of course, that means that you three will have to put up with Buster on your laps."

"He's a good traveler. Your biggest challenge is going to be this woman's luggage," Mr. Sam said, gesturing at Pearl. "You'd think we were going on a world cruise, the way she packed that suitcase."

Pearl sniffed. "At least *one* of us was prepared.

I didn't notice anybody complaining when I was sharing my tube of toothpaste last night.''

They all laughed at that. Laurel had Jeremy in as tight a grip as Tripp had had Ashleigh a few moments earlier. "And what do you have to say for yourself? Do you really think I'd sell the house out from under you without telling you?''

"Not really, but..." Jeremy stopped, looking at Tripp.

"But a certain hot-headed sheriff told him otherwise. Which I need to apologize for, as well. I was angry, Jeremy, and my mouth got away from me.'' He offered the kid his hand. "Friends?''

"Sure. As long as you don't arrest Grandpa or Mrs. Simms or anybody.''

"That's an easy bargain to keep this time. I just want to get everybody home. Where's the cat and the luggage?''

It took half an hour to pack up the reluctant Buster, who might not have been quite as good a traveler as Mr. Sam maintained. Tripp wasn't thrilled about driving for five hours with a yowling cat in the car.

Surprisingly, Buster piped down quickly once they were on the road. The only time he started up again was when they stopped the cruiser at the Springfield Police impound lot to pick up the plates from the ruined Cadillac. Once they were back on the road, Buster settled down fast.

"So, what now?" Tripp asked Laurel as they sped down the highway. "I mean, once we get back to Friedens?"

"I'm not quite sure. I need to do a lot of talking to several people. Some of it involves long distance, and some of it involves travel."

"Sure." He tried not to show the anxiety her statement caused him. He'd just found Laurel. Was she really going to be gone that fast?

"Mom? Can we talk first, before you do all that 'talking with other people'?" Jeremy's voice from the back seat was a surprise.

"Sure. But I think that needs to wait until we get home, too. This is a pretty crowded place for serious talks."

"Yeah, but I've gotten used to serious talks in cars. That was the coolest part of riding around with Grandpa Sam and Ash's grandma and stuff. We all talked."

Pearl sniffed. "What else is there to do in a car where there's no tape or CD player, and the radio only gets scratchy AM stations?"

"You tried to get us to sing," Ashleigh reminded her, causing general laughter in the back seat.

"All right, so you reminded me that was only fun when you were four." Pearl sounded put out.

"Anyway, I don't mind talking in front of family if you don't," said Jeremy. "And just about everybody here is family, I think."

"Close enough," Mr. Sam piped up. "And I, for one, wouldn't mind getting closer."

"If you get any closer, we'll be related for sure." Pearl kept coming up with barbs that made Tripp lose concentration.

"Well, none of us is getting any younger, Mrs. Simms. If I'm going to have a chance with a beautiful woman, it may be now or never."

Pearl still had a comeback. "Laurel, why didn't you tell me this man was such a slick customer?"

Laurel shook her head. "Pearl, of all the attributes I'd use for Mr. Sam, that wouldn't be one of them."

"Unless he was trying to talk his way out of a traffic ticket," Tripp added, causing more laughter. "But Jeremy, let's get back to your serious discussion. You were about to say something, I think."

"Yeah. If I could ever finish." The kid sounded fifteen with a vengeance. "What I was trying to say was I like this serious talking. It makes me feel like somebody is listening to me, like I count. And

I like having relatives around to talk to—not just you, Mom. No offense or anything.''

"None taken. Please go on."

Laurel sounded a little choked up in the front seat, and Tripp wished he could reach over Ashleigh to grab her hand. Fortunately, his daughter was perceptive enough to pat the other woman's knee and lean on her shoulder. Good for Ashleigh.

"I know I've been the one saying I want to go back to California the most. And I still miss my friends, and the skate parks and my room and stuff. But going to high school with Trent and Ashleigh would be kind of cool. And like Grandpa Sam said, we're not getting any younger. Especially him and Grandpa Hank. I might miss a lot if we went back to California."

"Now, that insight I could have done without," Sam grumbled.

"So Jeremy, are you saying you're not ready to move back to California? That we could stay here in Missouri, and you wouldn't be so unhappy and sure that I ruined your life?"

"Not most days, anyway. And see, this way when I'm grouchy you'll have something to blame it on."

"Jeremy, you're a teenage boy. What more do I need to blame your moods on? That's one of the bonuses of living this close to your grandfathers.

They can tell you stories about how moody and awful your dad and I were as teenagers.''

"Cool. Ammunition." Jeremy sounded quite pleased with himself. "Anyway, can we stay? If we don't, who's going to keep Ashleigh okay with being the sheriff's kid and everything?''

"You aren't going to have to worry about that much longer. I think your grandpa Hank is coming back to work as soon as possible.''

Ashleigh sighed. ''Like being the deputy's kid is going to be so different at the high school. I'll still be a social outcast.''

"No, Ash, that's not the way it works here. It will be cool, trust me.'' Tripp gave thanks for Laurel again. It was finally time for him to speak up.

"I'm pulling this car over. Anybody who wants to get out and stretch their legs at this burger joint at the exit, feel free to do so.''

Everybody took the hint, including Laurel. But he called her back to the car, while the rest of the crew took turns standing out on the parking lot holding Buster and going into the restaurant. Tripp noticed the kids came out with milk shakes.

"Great. Your dad is going to make me have this cruiser detailed once I get it back to Friedens.''

"I don't think that's what you wanted me here for. To talk about the inside of the cruiser,'' Laurel said.

She had the strangest expression on her face. For a moment he almost lost his nerve to say anything. But everybody was watching expectantly from the parking lot, and like Jeremy said, none of them was getting any younger.

"Laurel, do I have a chance with you? Because I want one. I really hope you decide to stay in Missouri. In Friedens, where I can make up for the past month or so of blunders and false starts and—"

"Tickets? Arrests? Towing my car away?" she added. But she was smiling when she said it. "You have the strangest way with a pickup line I've ever seen. But yes, Jesse, you have a chance with me. Odd as it sounds, I like you and your hidebound, officer-of-the-law ways."

His heart leaped. "Just *like* me?"

"Now you're fishing," she said, running a finger down his nose and letting it rest for just a moment on his lip.

It felt so good that he wanted to nip at her finger, but he didn't, what with the audience they had outside.

"Besides," she added, "if I say I love you, you'll just chalk it up to my airheaded California ways."

"Never. Underneath that tanned exterior, there's a levelheaded Missourian. I've seen it all along."

"Wow. You have almost as clever a way with words as Mr. Sam," she said ruefully. "How can I resist sweet-talk like that?"

He looked deep into her sparkling blue eyes, trying to find the right words. "Don't resist. Just give me a chance to try to do it right. Really trying to win your heart with dates and flowers, and all the things I haven't done so far."

Laurel laughed. "I'm kind of getting used to tickets and rides in cruisers. They're familiar, anyway. Jesse, my dad is going to be so shocked when we come back to town and tell him I'm dating his deputy."

"I think he's seen this coming. Don't know if he likes it—if he doesn't, he can just fire me. But that way he'll lose his handpicked candidate if he doesn't run for sheriff in November, and he'll have to run again himself."

"Which I suspect he's not eager to do. You'd make a good sheriff, Jesse. If you run, promise me one thing."

"What?" Right now he'd promise her almost anything, because he couldn't hold back from kissing her after that promise.

"That you'll go back to being Jesse in public. And wearing that gray fedora. They both suit you much better than 'Deputy Tripp' and his uniform."

"Done," he agreed. "For you, I'd do almost

anything. Laurel, you've given me a life I didn't know I could have. Together we found our families, and I've found my faith. How could I say no to anything you asked?''

''Well, in that case, maybe we should take up the matter of that Impala Mr. Sam wants to buy from Pearl's neighbor...'' She was twirling a strand of that honey hair around one finger, and looking at him through lowered eyelashes.

''*Almost* anything, then. That little bit sounds like official business for Sheriff Jordan, and I think right now he's off-duty.'' And he finally leaned over and kissed her. It was such a wonderful experience, he could almost drown out the applause from the peanut gallery on the parking lot. Almost.

Epilogue

November

It seemed fitting that Jesse hold his final press conference before the election in The Right Place. Laurel looked over to the corner table of her busy coffee house, where one television reporter with a video camera, two apparent radio reporters and several people with notebooks, representing the newspapers in the county, were all talking to the handsome man in the fedora.

He'd kept his promise to wear it, and the banners around town and the bumper stickers all said Jesse J. Jordan for Sheriff. Laurel felt a swell of pride as she looked at him. Pride and love for the man who'd won her heart just the way he'd sworn to.

"So, if you're elected sheriff, what's your first order of business?" one of the radio reporters asked.

"Getting married on Saturday. And if I lose the election, my first order of business will be getting married on Saturday. After that, and a brief honeymoon at an undisclosed location, my second order of business will be convincing the county council to add funds to the sheriff's department budget for Police Explorer Scouts and a teen ride-along program. There have to be things for the young people to do in this county besides visiting my future bride's coffee house. My kids, and their friends, have made sure I understand that."

The reporters were all busily taking notes. Laurel kept smiling. It was all she could do to keep from interrupting the press conference to tell them all how much she loved Jesse. That wouldn't do his campaign for sheriff any good, except maybe with the married women's vote, so she just kept polishing the espresso machine.

She needed to set things up for the after-school rush, anyway. The high school would let out soon, and Trent, Jeremy and Ashleigh and all their friends would crowd in here. It would be noisy and hectic, and she'd love every minute of it.

If she got very lucky, all their parents would be in at least once, along with Hank, who'd drop by for his one daily cup of "real" coffee. She would cap off the afternoon rush by sitting with her two sisters and enjoying a visit.

And the future sheriff would come in at least once, threatening to cite everybody for noise pollution when the music got loud. The teenagers would all groan and beg her to fix him a mocha to sweeten him up, or kiss him to make him forget the noise. And she'd probably agree to both.

Laurel smiled again, thinking about it. This place felt like "the right place" in all the right ways. She was definitely home to stay.

* * * * *

*Watch for Laurel's
sister Carrie's story,
coming soon to
LOVE INSPIRED.*

Dear Reader,

A funny thing happened while I was writing this book about a woman struggling with a move from California to Missouri. I moved! Unlike Laurel, my family moved from Missouri, which has always been home for me, to California, which is a whole new experience. When I began the idea for this book, I had no idea that when I would be writing it, I would be in the process of moving five people and two animals across the country. It's been a fascinating experience.

So far the most fascinating thing about my new locale is that we have mountains. We're near a Christian university campus, and when I want real inspiration I climb to the cross...not just in prayer, but actually putting on my hiking shoes and going up a nearby hill where a twenty-foot wooden cross dominates the landscape.

I hope that you have a way to "climb to the cross" for inspiration in your daily life. It certainly makes a difference in my life, and what gets accomplished when I come back down to reality.

Blessings,

Lynn

I love to hear from readers. You can write me at P.O. Box 2067, Thousand Oaks, CA 91358.

Next Month From Steeple Hill's

Love Inspired

LOVING THY NEIGHBOR

by

Ruth Scofield

When teacher Quincee Davis moves into a new house with her niece and nephews, who should live next door but Judge Hamilton Paxton, the man who suspended her driver's license for thirty days! An attraction soon grows between them, but Hamilton doesn't think he's worthy of her love. Can they create a loving family along with the Lord's help?

**Don't miss
LOVING THY NEIGHBOR
On sale August 2001**

Love Inspired

Visit us at www.steeplehill.com
LILTN

"WHAT DO YOU
WANT FROM ME?"

Roman smiled. "Last time we were here together, we were interrupted a bit prematurely. I thought ye might wish to make up for that." He advanced.

She retreated. "Stay away from me."

Roman canted his head. "Ye've changed, lass, for I remember ye moaning in me arms in this very room."

He had her backed up nearly to the wall. They were mere inches apart.

"What do you want from me?" she asked again.

He wanted *her*. Body and soul, writhing with ecstasy beneath his hands. He stared at her, enraged at himself, at his weakness, and lost in the horrible knowledge that no matter what, he still wanted her and could not hurt her.

Other **AVON ROMANCES**

Coming Soon

And Don't Miss These
ROMANTIC TREASURES
from Avon Books

HIGHLAND WOLF

LOIS GREIMAN

AVON BOOKS ◆ NEW YORK

AVON BOOKS
A division of
The Hearst Corporation
1350 Avenue of the Americas
New York, New York 10019

Copyright © 1997 by Lois Greiman
Published by arrangement with the author
Inside cover author photo by Barbara Ridenous
Visit our website at **http://AvonBooks.com**
Library of Congress Catalog Card Number: 96–97091
ISBN: 0–380–78191–3

First Avon Books Printing: April 1997

AVON TRADEMARK REG. U.S. PAT. OFF. AND IN OTHER COUNTRIES, MARCA REGISTRADA, HECHO EN U.S.A.

Printed in the U.S.A.

RA 10 9 8 7 6 5 4 3 2 1

To Janet Wright, who taught me the intrinsic value of wild flowers and tin roofs, who wasn't too busy for horseback picnics and wild bouts of giggling. Thanks for being there for me, Jan. If every child had a big sister like you, the world would be a kinder place.

Prologue

In the year of our Lord, 1509

"**I** say we storm Firthport and bring me son home." Dugald MacAulay's eyes blazed as he addressed the room at large.

"Do ye ken where he is kept then?" Roman Forbes remained seated, quiet as the wolf for which he was named.

"Nay! I ken na, but I am na so daft that I canna find me own firstborn. And if the Forbeses are too scairt ta go with me, me and mine will go alone."

"Yer other sons." Leith Forbes nodded as he rose to his feet. He was a big man, even more powerful than the day he had become the lord of his clan. "They are a brave pair."

"Aye." Roderic was seated across the trestle table from Roman. The fire in the great hall glowed bright, making his gold hair shimmer so that he looked the antithesis of his dark-haired brother, Leith. "They wouldna be scairt ta go with ye past the border. Nay." He too shook his head. "They wouldna be scairt ta die for their kin. And who can say? Mayhap they wouldna both be kilt. One might survive with but a few wounds. Fiona," he said, turning to the red-haired woman near the fire.

1

"Prepare yer herbs. Brave men go ta die because their brother has been smitten by love."

"Love!" Dugald stormed, his face going red. "David does na love an English wench. 'Tis rather that his wick led him where his head knew better than ta go. Dunna think that I am so daft as ta misunderstand what ye try ta do. Ye would dissuade me from me course, bend me purposes, convince me ta use words when weapons are needed. Ye Forbeses, ye form great alliances, but what good an alliance if ye are ta mild ta fight when a fight is due?"

"Is a fight due, Dugald?" Leith asked, facing his wife's cousin. "Firthport is a far distance and well fortified. Will ye challenge the entire city?"

"Nay!" said MacAulay, gripping the hilt of his sword. "I challenge only Harrington and those that would ally themselves with him. Indeed, I will skewer him ta the wall for the lies he has spewed against me family name."

"Your son did not steal the ring he is said to have taken." Fiona rose slowly from her place near the hearth. She held a babe against her shoulder. Motioning to the child's mother, she passed him over with a hushed word of advice. "We know he does not steal," she said as she approached the men. "But can we know for certain that he does not love?"

"'Tis possible that he has lost his heart ta an Englishwoman," Leith agreed, turning a gentle glance toward his bride of eighteen years. "Such things have been known ta happen. And how would yer David feel if ye kilt the father of the woman who holds his heart?"

"Ahh Gawd," Dugald groaned, scrubbing his face with frustrated vigor. "I canna fight the lot of ye. And I suppose ye are right. 'Tis lucky I be that me David is yet intact and whole, knowing Harrington as I do."

"Ye know him well?" Roman spoke again, assessing information, thinking, planning. His foster parents had not called him home simply for the sake of loneliness. He had been schooled to be a barrister. Diplomacy was his forte. This was just one of many Highland problems he had been asked to resolve. But Fiona and Leith were a formidable pair without his expertise. Few could withstand either their logic or their wisdom.

"Long ago, when Harrington's first wife still lived, he was a friend of sorts ta me auld laird. I was na more than a lad then, but I know him well enough ta say Harrington be a black-hearted devil who would slaughter his own children ta gain his ends. In truth, some say he has done just that," Dugald vowed.

"A necklace is a small price to pay for the life of one's child," Fiona said, settling her warm gaze on Roman. She had called him son long before she had borne her own, long before he had been called the Wolf.

Dugald sighed. "Aye," he said, hefting a small leather pouch. " 'Tis but baubles in a bag, I suppose. Still..." He emptied the drawstring purse into his hand. Gems as bright as hope sparkled against his palm. " 'Twas the necklace auld MacAulay gave ta his bride. It should have been yers long ago, Lady Fiona."

"It belonged with you at MacAulay Hold," Fiona said. "But had it been mine own, I would gladly give it back to you now."

"Yer generosity has na been overrated, lady," Dugald said. "Still, I am loath ta grant Harrington's demands and give it up for the return of my son, who should have never wandered ta Firthport at the outset."

"'Tis a bonny piece," admitted Roderic. "Who will take it ta England?"

"'Tis me own duty and . . ." Dugald began, but Leith raised his hand to stop him.

"Visions of Harrington skewered ta the wall might disturb me sleep."

Dugald opened his mouth as if to speak, but paused and finally chuckled. "Yer saying I should na go."

Leith shrugged. "I am saying there are men with cooler heads in this situation."

Dugald turned his gaze from Laird Leith to Roman. "Did ye, perchance, have someone in mind, Forbes?"

"I know ye think I can do na wrong, brother," Roderic said, drawing everyone's gaze to him. "But I fear I am na the man for this . . ."

Leith cut him off with a snort. "As if I would ask ye ta leave yer Flame when she is due ta bear yer third bairn. 'Twas all I could manage ta coerce ye ta leave her side for a day."

Roderic chuckled. "If I am na ta be the man of men"—he glanced at Roman as if perplexed—"then who might it be? Hawk could go, of course, but he will not return from France for some weeks yet. Colin has traveled ta the north. Arthur—but nay, he's still mending. Graham, merely a lad. Andrew . . ." He shook his head. "It looks as if we'll have ta send one of the women. Roman, saddle a horse, it seems yer mother will be riding . . ."

"Methinks yer wit is thinning with age," Roman said, spearing his uncle with a scowl. But that dire expression only made Roderic laugh.

"Yer the man for the task, Roman, and ye well know it," he said. "But ye should learn ta smile, lest the English think all we Scots be so dour."

"The Wolf does na smile," said Dugald, "but he

is wise, and mayhap he sees little ta cheer him regarding the capture of me son."

"And mayhap he has yet ta meet the woman who will show him this world is na so sober a place," Roderic countered, eyeing Roman closely.

"Am I forgetting, or did yer own gentle lady take a knife ta ye a fortnight afore yer wedding?" Roman asked.

Roderic chuckled, rubbing his chest as if an old wound nagged him. "When ye've seen some age, lad, ye'll learn that the scars but make the memories sweeter."

Leith laughed, drawing Fiona into his embrace. Roman watched them. They were his parents by choice if not by birth. He would not fail them.

"Would ye like me ta go in yer stead, Laird MacAulay?" Roman asked, his tone solemn.

Dugald blew out a quiet breath and speared Roman with his gaze. "Laird Leith advises against going meself, and I suppose he is right. Me temper would only find me trouble. But ye . . ." He paused. "If the Wolf of the Highlands canna bring me son back alive, there is none that can."

Chapter 1

"Betty luv, give me somethin' warm ta remember ya by." The sailor was dressed in typical seafarer's garb. He was young. He held the maid's wrist with a strong hand, though his words were a bit slurred.

The barmaid stood motionless, still holding a pitcher of mulled wine.

Roman Forbes remained immobile, too, silently assessing the drama before him. Watching the girl's face, he thought she might pull away, but instead, she shrugged and stepped closer to the sailor.

"So ya be wantin' somethin' warm?" she asked. Her voice was husky and deep, her neckline just as low, and the sway of her generous hips equally as suggestive.

The sailor's legs fell open as she slid easily between them to seat herself on his lap.

"I'd dearly love to give you somethin' to remember me by," she said. Leaning forward slightly, she granted the room at large a liberal view of her charms. Full, pale breasts threatened to spill over the top of her tightly laced bodice. The sailor swallowed and failed to move his gaze from the soft mounds before him.

"But, I'm a very busy woman, 'andsome," said

6

the maid as she let her knee slip closer to the apex of her captor's legs.

"I'll . . ." The sailor's voice sounded reedy in the sudden silence. "I'll make it worth your while," he said, and managed to pull forth a coin from a pouch at his side. It winked slyly in the light of the tallow candles.

"Ahh," crooned the girl, glancing at the coin. "So ya brought incentive, did ya, luv?" she asked, leaning closer still, and placing a hand on his chest.

"Aye," he answered, "and my money and my . . ." He glanced at his attentive companions and managed a grin, though it was shaky. "My *skills* is good."

"I'm certain they are," said the maid, slipping her hand slowly down his chest. "And will I get that shiny coin just for a bit of . . . warmth?" Her fingers brushed his midsection, where laces secured his hose to his open doublet.

The sailor sucked air through his teeth like a man prepared for ecstasy or agony. Even from Roman's position some yards away, he could see the lad pale at the bold touch of the maid's hand. "You'll have the coin . . . and more," he vowed.

"Then how can I refuse?" She leaned closer still, until her breasts were mere inches from the sailor's face. The lad's eyes popped. The grin was frozen on his lips. Not a man in the Red Fox drew a breath. Then, grasping the top of the sailor's hose, the maid gave them a tug and tilted the contents of the pitcher onto his nether parts.

There was a moment of stunned silence before the sailor launched himself into the air with a yelp. But Betty had already danced away, the promised coin between her fingers.

The pub exploded with laughter.

"Was that warm enough for ya, Jimmy?" yelled one man.

"That's more heat than I've gotten from 'er," yelled another.

"Would ye sit on *my* lap for a coin, Betty luv?"

The sailor slowed his wild hopping long enough to stare at her, his mouth and eyes still round with surprise.

The inn quieted.

The maid smiled, holding the coin aloft. " 'Tis the going rate for a little warmth," she quipped.

Not a body stirred. In the silence, Roman slipped a hand to the needle-sharp dagger stashed in the garter near his knee. He didn't need trouble. Not now. But a man's wounded pride was as good an excuse for trouble as any.

Nevertheless, the sailor finally grimaced and shrugged, his expression sheepish. "The view was well worth the coin," he said, and seated himself again, though a bit gingerly.

Approval emanated from the crowd. There were cheers, a couple of slaps to the lad's shoulders, and more than a few whistles of appreciation for the free entertainment just provided.

Roman relaxed marginally and slipped his blade back into place. So the lass had outsmarted the sailor and escaped repercussions. It was good, for he had no wish to defend the maid and start a brawl against these Englishmen.

His task was simple enough. He had but to deliver the necklace to Lord Harrington and see David MacAulay returned safely home. With luck his mission would be complete long before his friend Hawk returned from France and was sent to England to assist him.

Mayhap there would even be time to stop back here for a mug of ale and one more glance at the bonny Betty. Roman's gaze followed her as she turned toward the taproom door, only a few feet from his table. Her hips swayed dramatically as she moved through the crowd. They were generous hips, set below a tightly cinched waist and wide, spilling breasts. Strange, he usually preferred a trimmer form. But she attracted him. Perhaps it was her saucy demeanor. Or perhaps it was her . . .

"Tits!" said the man from the far side of the table. "God's bones, I'd give half a year's allowance to get my hands on her tits."

Dalbert Harrington—the viscount's only son. Roman had received instructions to meet him here and had disliked him from the moment they had met less than an hour before. It wouldn't take much for his feelings to turn to hatred. But such emotion would hardly aid his cause, he knew, so he nodded as if in agreement and took a sip of whiskey.

"Mayhap 'twould be best if I delivered the goods ta yer father tanight," he said.

Dalbert was silent for a moment. Then he laughed, throwing back his fair head to howl at the smoke-darkened beams of the ceiling. "Christ, man," he said, straightening. "You've just viewed the best tits outside of London and all you can talk about is *goods*? I hadn't heard you Scots were such a stiff lot! Or should I say, such a *limp* lot?" He laughed at his own double entendre, then guzzled down a good portion of his drink before chuckling again. "You should visit me in London, sometime. The whores there would loosen you up."

Roman smiled. He was a diplomat in a foreign land. Level-headed, intelligent, respected. He wouldn't hit the bastard. Yet.

"I appreciate yer offer," he said, keeping his tone even. "But for now I think it best if we discuss the business at hand. I have come, as requested. And because of the delicacy of the situation, I feel it best ta—"

"Delicacy!" rasped Dalbert, suddenly gripping

the table's edge with clawed hands. "Your mongrel friend fucked my sister, then stole her ring!"

Roman remained very still, waiting, willing his own temper into submission. Dalbert Harrington might well have friends among this rough crowd, he thought. Friends that would come to the nobleman's aid if things got out of hand.

But the other customers seemed intent on their own conversation.

"I am truly sorry for the circumstances," Roman said softly, neither denying nor affirming Dalbert's accusations. "As is the lad's father."

"Circumstances! If I had *my* way, *I* would handle the . . . circumstances." Narrowing his eyes, he chuckled and drank again. "But Father's squeamish about castration." Strong words, but Roman sensed that Dalbert was full of bluster. He seemed calmer as he settled back into his chair and took another quaff of ale.

Their gazes met. Roman kept his benign, but beneath the table, he clenched his fist. Nothing would feel better than ramming the Englishman's teeth down his throat. But he dared not air his temper. Not now, not ever.

He lowered his eyes with an effort and shrugged as if the matter were out of his hands. But he wondered, how many Scottish lasses had been raped by Englishmen? How many unwanted bairns had been born to noble asses like this viscount's son? True, the Englishmen's barbarism did not excuse a Scotsman's actions, but if he knew David at all, the lad had not taken the girl against her will. Not David MacAulay. True, he may be a bit cocky and full of himself, but he was not cruel.

"Yer father has made an agreement with the laird of the MacAulays," Roman said, gently settling a leather pouch on the table between them. "I have but come to deliver the requested item."

"Item! More like a damned whore's fee!" Dalbert said with a snort. He finished off his drink and laughed. "Think of it. My father's darling Christine. No better than a whore. No better than . . ." The taproom door swung open again. Betty hurried out, carrying a pitcher in each hand. Dalbert turned his sneer toward the girl. "No better than her!" he said.

Roman glanced at the barmaid. If young Betty had gained Dalbert's disdain, perhaps she was a lass worth . . .

A sharp prick of premonition drew Roman's attention back to the table. He reached out instinctively, but already Dalbert had snatched the pouch and was turning it upside down.

The necklace tumbled out to lie on the rough table like a goddess on a lowly bed of bracken. Glittering light of blue and white sparkled in the room.

"Sweet Jesus!" someone gasped.

"Good God!" Dalbert said, reaching out to touch a midnight blue sapphire.

But Roman scooped the necklace up and whisked it beneath the table before Harrington's fingers touched it. The gems were cool against his palm. He tightened his grip, cursing himself for a careless fool.

"Good God," Dalbert repeated. His tone was breathy. "Father said it was a piece handsome enough to match his mother's ring, but I didn't know . . ." His voice trailed to a halt.

Roman felt a hundred eyes watching him. Damnation! It would be a miracle if he lived out the night now.

He could pull his knife and back toward the exit, or he could turn the gems and the responsibility over to Dalbert Harrington.

The inn was silent again.

"It seems yer father thought this little trinket

might sweeten your sister's dowry," Roman said quietly.

Dalbert laughed. His eyes were bright with excitement. "Any man would be lucky to get it. I mean, *her*," he corrected, and laughed again. "But I have to tell you, Scot, you're in a bad part of town to be carrying around that kind of rocks. Perhaps it would be best if I delivered them to Father myself."

Roman carefully kept his voice steady and his body relaxed. Now was not the time to be making foolish mistakes. "That will na be necessary. I told the MacAulay I'd personally put the gems inta Lord Harrington's hand before escorting the lad back ta his homeland."

"So you don't trust me?" asked Dalbert. His tone was casual, but his eyes were too bright.

He was intoxicated and volatile. Roman forced his muscles to relax a bit more. Careful handling was necessary if he wished to see the light of day once more.

"I made a vow ta a friend, and I am honorbound ta keep it," Roman said. "I'm sure you understand honor."

Though Roman had tried his best to keep sarcasm from his tone, Dalbert gripped his mug in a tight clasp and snarled something unintelligible. Roman considered his hidden blade, then discarded the idea. He couldn't take the risk of cutting this man. If Dalbert attacked, Roman would tilt him off-balance, and . . .

"Now, luvs," said a husky voice. "We don't want no trouble between friends at the Red Fox."

Roman watched Dalbert's features soften slightly as his attention was diverted.

"Well, I surely would not wish to cause you any trouble," said Dalbert. "Who am I to stand in the way of my father's plans? In fact, I'd like to prove there are no hard feelings," he said, and, standing quickly, reached out to wrap an arm about the barmaid's waist.

"So, Betty," he crooned, not taking his gaze from Roman. "How about helping create peace between our country and his. You can even make a little extra coin out of the bargain. You interested in money?"

"Always am, luv," she said, tilting her pretty face toward the Englishman. Her floppy white coif puffed out behind her head.

"Then let's all be friends," Dalbert said, turning to gaze down at her.

"I'm friendly, guvnor, but like I said earlier, I'm a busy woman."

"Surely not too busy to make a little extra coin," he said, squeezing a bit tighter and trailing a finger over her half-bared shoulder.

"Extra coin is always welcome," she agreed. "Still, a girl's got to keep her job. And old Bart is apt to get peeved if I leave the inn before my time's up."

"You said yourself that you don't want any trouble here," Dalbert reminded and traced a finger over her collarbone. She stiffened slightly, but didn't pull away. "I think you should be friendly to our neighbor here." Leaning closer, he kissed the spot where his fingers had just been. "The Scot is feeling friendly, too. In fact, he's been drooling after you all evening. Said he could use a bit of sweet English tart. What do you say?" he asked, not taking his gaze from the maid's bosom. "Are you willing to share some of your bounty with our guest here?"

"I'm all for sharing," said Betty. "So, I'll tell you what, m' lord, I'll get you a couple of free drinks." She tried to slip away, but Dalbert only tightened his grip.

"The Scot here can obviously afford to pay a good price for a night's work," said Dalbert. "In truth, one of those rocks would be worth a king's ransom. Hell, there must a been a hundred stones in there. Who'd miss one? But if he's too stingy to pay, I'll give you twice your usual fee, just to show him there's no hard feelings.

"What do you think, Scot?"

Beneath the table, Roman stashed the necklace in the ceremonial sporran that hung from his waist. It was a silly thing. Adorned with horsehair and silver, it would be cumbersome in a fight. He yearned for his serviceable hill-climbing pouch. But it was too late to worry about his accoutrements now. He rose slowly to his feet. Dalbert Harrington was not only a fool. He was a rich, intoxicated fool, and, therefore, he was dangerous.

"Maybe you don't trust me with the necklace," Harrington said with a leering smile. "But you can trust me on this, Scot. You aren't going to find a more prime piece of flesh than our Betty here. So are you going to take me up on my offer, or am I going to have to return to Father and tell him that you thought yourself too good to deal with the likes of us?"

Roman remained silent, keeping his expression bland, his eyes steady. He had already offended Harrington. He couldn't afford to make matters worse, not with David MacAulay's life on the line. So he raised his brows as if considering the matter. He, too, could play this game.

"What do you say, lass?" he asked the maid softly. "Are you interested in the proposition?"

He watched her raise her chin, watched her eyes fill with speculation and more. "That depends," she said, "on the size of your . . ." She tugged her arm free from Dalbert's grasp and advanced. "Rocks."

A dropped pin could have been heard from thirty yards.

Dalbert chuckled.

"I didn't get a good look at them earlier," she added, stepping away from Harrington. "Care to display them so we all can see?"

Roman knew disdain when he heard it. And he heard it now. But he nodded once in concession to her wit. "We Scots are usually more private about such exhibitions," he said, and let his gaze slip to her bosom before lifting it slowly back to her face. "But I assure you, you wouldna be disappointed."

"I fear I've heard that before, guvnor," she said. Though her cheeks showed a slight stain of pink, she leaned forward, showing her cleavage. "But when it come down ta hard facts, I *was* disappointed."

Their gazes met and held.

"Then you were with the wrong man," he said quietly.

She raised her brows and skimmed slim fingers from her cleavage up her throat. "And you think you could satisfy me?"

"That I promise," he said.

She came closer. Her hips swayed with a life of their own. "Well then, luv," she crooned, leaning in so that her lips were only inches from his. "I'm interested . . ."

This was just a game he played to satisfy Dalbert Harrington, Roman assured himself. But against his will and his better judgment, his breath stopped in his throat. Beneath the weight of his leather sporran, he could feel his own interest roused to life. He was a fool, he admonished himself. But he was also a man, with a man's weaknesses.

Betty leaned closer still. She didn't smell of sweat and spoiled ale, as he had expected. Instead, the aroma of sweet lavender filled his nostrils. He raised his hand, wanting to touch her face. But suddenly she slapped it down.

"I'm interested in your jewels, Scotsman. But only the ones in your pouch, not the ones in your skirt," she said.

Dalbert threw back his head and guffawed. The tension was broken. Others joined in the laughter. Dalbert collapsed into his chair amidst the noise.

The barmaid turned to leave, but Roman caught her hand in a careful grip. She swung back toward him. Their gazes clashed. Her eyes were as blue as the precious jewels he'd just stashed in his sporran.

"Mayhap some other time," Roman said quietly. If he tried, he could manage to feel grateful for her part in dissolving the tension in the room. At least the tautness in his loins was a less dangerous situation. "When we dunna have an audience."

He heard the intake of her breath. "You want company, Scotsman?" she asked. "I'm told Pete Langer's got a herd of fine sheep. You could pick and choose."

On the far side of the room, a furtive figure rose. A finger of apprehension slid up Roman's spine as he turned to watch. Who was he? Someone leaving to plan the theft of his necklace, mayhap? But it was already too late to identify the man, for the door was closing behind him. "The sheep it is then," he said, turning back to the maid. "But ye dunna ken what yer missing."

Betty smiled. "I assure ya I do, Scotsman," she said, letting her gaze skim down the midline of his body, over his chest, his abdomen, the sporran that hid his jewels. "But I won't be missing it for long."

Chapter 2

An hour after his encounter with Betty, Roman walked out of the inn. Dalbert had kept his mug filled, and though Roman drank, he was not fool enough to become intoxicated. The task ahead would require all his wits; far too many unsavory characters now knew about the jewels he carried with him.

Firthport was a bordertown and a seaport, raw, unpredictable, deadly. Somewhere far off, a woman laughed. The sound carried eerily in the night air, floating to a dark figure that hurried down a distant alley.

The young man glanced quickly about. Tonight he was John Marrow, a portly, somewhat besotted businessman minding his own affairs.

The Queen's Head appeared in the dimness. It was a long building, made of gray stone and thatch. A narrow ribbon of smoke twisted from the chimney into the night sky.

Marrow stepped up to the door, tested the handle once, then rapped loudly on the stout plank. "Open up!"

Silence greeted him from inside. He knocked again. "Open up I say."

Still no response.

"Who do you think you're lockin' . . ."

The door opened. A man stood on the far side, holding a single candle and scowling. He was big and German and smelled very distinctly of caraway seeds.

"Who do you think *you* are?" he growled.

"Oh!" Marrow belched and staggered back a step. "There you are then, LaFleur. And about time, too."

"Who the hell are you?"

"I'm Marrow. John Marrow. Fine innkeeper you are, forgettin' . . ." He belched again. "Forgetting your own guests."

"You're drunk," said the landlord. "And you're no guest of mine."

Marrow reared back in offense. "I beg to differ. As I'm sure you know, LeFleur, I stay at the Queen's Arms every month when I come—"

"I am not LeFleur. I am Krahn, and this is not the Queen's Arms. 'Tis the Queen's Head."

Marrow's jaw dropped. For a moment he struggled with his hat, as if trying to raise the brim to get a better look at the landlord's face. But the hat won the battle and remained firmly in place, low over his eyes, hiding his own features. "The Queen's Head?" he said, sounding befuddled, as he staggered backward again. "The Queen's Head. Oh! Head! Well, damn me if I don't always get those bloody royal parts mixed up." He laughed uproariously at his own joke. The landlord's expression remained sour.

But Marrow was unperturbed by the other's lack of humor. He patted the innkeeper's shoulder. It was a big shoulder, he noticed, heavy with muscle and bone. "Yes, well. 'Tis a fine establishment you've got here. And close t' hand. Do you perchance let out rooms, my good man?"

Surprisingly, the landlord was able to look

even more dour. He did so, then finally spoke. "I've three I rent out. But I've only one available."

"Lovely."

"And *you'll* pay in advance," he added, not attempting to hide any particular prejudices he might foster.

Marrow nodded and almost toppled forward while doing so. "Whatever you say, my good man," he said, and after digging about in his pouch, finally brought forth a coin.

The landlord took it with a grumpy nod, motioned Marrow inside, and closed the door behind them.

The stone steps were irregular and narrow. Marrow managed to conquer them with only a few false starts. They ended on a narrow landing, facing three slatted doors.

Krahn pushed one open.

Marrow stepped inside. "Ahh. A lovely room." It had a single window, narrow, but wide enough to squeeze through in an emergency. "A handsome room, but it's not facing north."

The landlord's brows could lower to a surprising degree. "What are you babbling about?"

"I always sleep in the north room." Marrow belched again. "For luck."

"Not here you don't. The north room's taken, and if y' wake up the Scot I'll toss y' onto the street myself," he said, leaning forward aggressively.

Marrow backed away, holding up a hand. "Did I say north?" he squeaked. "I meant . . ." He let his head wobble a bit as if the room had begun to spin. "This'll be . . ." His head bobbled more violently. He staggered toward the bed. "Perfect," he said and crashed facefirst onto the mattress.

For a moment the landlord stood watching him in silence, then, "Aye. It will," he said, and closed the door behind him.

*   *   *

Roman made his way swiftly and silently through the night. Stopping in the shadow of a wattle-and-daub building, he held his breath and listened for anyone who might be following. There were no such noises, but that did not mean he wasn't being followed. A hundred eyes had seen the jewels he kept in his sporran.

Striding down the street again, Roman cursed himself for being a fool. It wasn't like him to be distracted. But there was something about the woman called Betty, something that drew him. Still, he knew better than to let a maid sway his concentration. Mayhap it was simply fatigue that had made him lose focus, for he was indeed weary. Bone weary. Firthport was not unlike other cities he knew. There was a desperation here, an undercurrent of evil that wore at him. But he would soon be returning home. He had but to stay the night, then deliver the necklace to Harrington in the morning. By the following evening he would be returning to the soothing peace of the Highlands.

But first he must survive the night.

The Queen's Head appeared through the mist. For just a moment Roman stopped to reconsider. Was there something sinister there, or was he seeing ghosts where there were none? Perhaps he should go to a different inn. But no. He made the decision quickly. The sooner he was out of sight of prying eyes the better.

Herr Krahn opened the door at Roman's second knock. The narrow stairs up which he traveled seemed unduly steep. Roman opened the door and stepped heavily into his rented room. Fatigue washed over him like a tugging tide, but this night he would not sleep, for it was far too risky. No, tonight he would stay alert and guard the jewels.

*   *   *

Midnight had long ago come and gone. Roman paced. The floor was cool beneath his bare feet. The bright red ceremonial tartan he had worn lay in a heap near the bed. Piled not far from it were his tunic and footwear. But for the amulet that hung from his neck and the sporran suspended from his shoulder, he was naked. Still, the air from the open window did little to revive him.

He paced again, singing in Gaelic and trying to think—about David who needed him, the Mac-Aulay who trusted him, Lady Fiona who believed in him.

He would not fail her. The candle sputtered out. Darkness washed in, heavy and dank with fetid memories.

He would not fail, he repeated. He was a Forbes—the son of Fiona and Leith. But he was not truly of Lady Fiona's blood. His steps slowed. The blood of Dermid flowed in his veins. Dermid! The man's face appeared like an old scar in his mind. Roman started, certain for a moment that he was there in the room with him. He heard his own childish whimper of fear. Or was the noise from some other source? He couldn't tell. For a moment he was thrown back in time to when he was young and helpless, alone in the world but for Dermid, a man who harbored evil, unspeakable secrets.

He must escape. But . . . No. Roman shook his head. Dermid was dead. There was no danger here. He was an adult with a sacred task to perform. He must not fail. The necklace must be given to Harrington. David MacAulay must be escorted back to his homeland.

But how could he do that without rest? The bed called to him. He had to rest or surely he would fail. But he would not sleep. The straw tick moaned beneath him as he lowered himself onto the edge. He would sit for a while. Just sit.

Memories crowded in again. Dark, ugly. He pushed them back. He was Roman of the great clan Forbes, trusted friend, respected diplomat. He was not evil. He would not fail. But the darkness laughed and closed about him like death.

Roman awoke with a start. He felt strangely heavy, but he managed to sit up. His head was groggy. And he was naked, and . . .

" 'E's awake!"

"Well, pop 'im, y' dolt!"

Something swung toward him.

Roman ducked instinctively. Reality washed in on him as a club hissed through his hair, but he had no time to be grateful for that near miss, for someone was lunging at him. He sprang to the side. A flash of steel arced through the night.

"Get 'im!"

Someone grabbed at him. He swung wildly. His fist connected with a skull. A man grunted and fell away.

"Brain 'im!" someone croaked.

But Roman had already launched himself at the nearest man. He hit him dead center, propelling him to the floor. Even in the darkness, he could see the blade. Roman grabbed the villain's wrist and slammed it down. Knuckles cracked against wood. A scream of pain and rage ripped the night. Roman rose and swung again. Cartilage cracked! The body below him went limp.

Something creaked behind him. Roman swung around and braced his back against the floor. A body flew toward him. Slamming his feet upward, Roman connected with his attacker's midsection and tossed the man over his head.

The wall reverberated with the impact.

"I got it! Let's get outta 'ere!" croaked a voice

from the far corner. Silence answered him. "Acre? Blacks?" he said tentatively.

No one answered.

Roman rose slowly to his feet. "Looks like you're alone, lad," he said, and took a step toward the shadowy figure.

"I uh . . ." There was a squeak in the man's voice. "I didn't mean no 'arm."

"Then give me the sporran and I'll give ye na harm."

"Yeah, sure. I—" he said and leapt.

The weight of his assault knocked Roman to the floor. A blade flashed downward. Roman jerked sideways. The knife whizzed past his head and stabbed into the wood beneath.

It was all the delay Roman needed. Sweeping his arm sideways, he crashed his fist into the villain's ear. In a moment, Roman was astride him, ready to strike again. But there was no need, for it seemed all three of his nocturnal visitors were unconscious.

Panting, Roman slipped off the flaccid body and stumbled across the room. His sporran lay where the thief had dropped it. He dipped his hand inside. No necklace. He fished wildly and swore. Still no gems.

With a quick stride he yanked the door open and flew down the stairs, sporran in hand.

The remains of a fire glowed in the hearth. He rushed across the room and stoked it into flames, then, tossing the poker aside, dumped out the contents of the ornate pouch. No necklace!

He rose with a snarl and raced up the stairs. Back in his rented room, he rifled through the thieves' clothing. Still nothing.

Retrieving his plaid, he buckled it quickly about his waist.

The nearest man groaned. Roman grabbed that

one by the shirt and leaned into his face. "Where
is it?" he asked softly.

When no answer was forthcoming, he dragged
the man down the stairs to dump him in front of
the fire.

He fell in a heap and groaned at the impact.

Settling back on his bare heels, Roman watched
his captive awaken. He had lank, greasy hair and
a scar that ran through his right eyebrow and
down his cheek. He twitched as consciousness returned.

"Where is it?" Roman asked again, just as softly,
carefully enunciating each word.

The thief jerked and cowered backward. "What?
I don't know what you're talking about."

"The necklace. Where is it?"

"I don't know nothing 'bout no necklace."

Roman reached out. The thief cowered away, but
Roman did not touch him. "How about pokers,
lad?" he asked, bringing the metal pole slowly forward. "Do ye ken aught about them?"

"I didn't take it!" squawked the thief. "I didn't
take it."

"Then where is it?"

"I don't . . . I don't know what you're talking
about."

With a jerk, Roman thrust the sharp end of the
poker past the man's face and into the fire behind
him. "Think hard," he suggested quietly.

The thief swallowed and stared sideways at the
glowing faggots. "I didn't take it," he whispered.

Roman nodded toward the pile of discarded
items that had been dumped from his sporran.
"Then why isn't it there?" he asked, reaching for
the poker. The end glowed an entrancing orange.

"Ain't there?" whispered the villain. "But we
was told 'twas in the pouch." He suddenly stiffened. "The Shadow! 'E got 'ere before us."

Roman eased back an inch. "What?"

"Not again! Jesus! Not again! I'm as good as dead. Dagger's gonna kill me."

"What are you talking about?"

"The Shadow," he moaned. "Damn his soul! He's done it again."

"Who's—" Roman began, but a gasp from behind stopped his words.

Still crouching, Roman turned on his heels. Herr Krahn stood in the doorway holding a club as thick as his arm. Behind him, a woman gaped, her uplifted candle throwing her wide eyes and cloth cap into stark relief.

"What the hell's going on here?" growled her husband.

Roman ground his teeth. What the hell, indeed? "Who or what is the Shadow?" he asked slowly.

"The Shadow?" The big man lowered the club. His wife sidled sideways a scant step, eyes still round as oranges. "What's this all about, then?"

"I've been robbed," said Roman.

"Gonna slit my throat," the thief moaned.

"The Shadow?" The big landlord advanced with a scowl. His wife came with him, staring. "Here? In my house?"

"Here and gone like a ghost," whispered the thief. "Damn 'im. 'E must a already took it when we come. Turned hisself into smoke and slipped down the chimney. Or crawled under the door like a snake."

"Have you heard of this Shadow?" asked Roman, facing the landlord.

"I have heard tales same as everyone. But whether they are true . . ." The big man shrugged.

"Oh, they're true. 'E's real," whispered the thief. "'E just ain't 'uman."

Roman turned back to the man on the floor. "Who is this Shadow?"

The thief shrugged. " 'E ain't nobody. Or 'e's everybody. 'E ain't anywhere. But 'e's everywhere. I gotta get away. Gotta get away." He shifted his eyes wildly about.

"How would he know I had the necklace?" asked Roman, trying to reel the man back to reality.

"How?" He laughed, but the sound was wild. "The Shadow knows everything 'bout everyone. 'E just knows."

Roman scowled. "Who is he? How does he look?"

" 'E looks like an old man. A babe. A puff of smoke."

Stifling an oath, Roman rose to his feet. "Who has been in this house while I was here this night?" he asked, turning to the pair by the entrance.

The landlord shook his head. "Just a young couple, them and their little one. But I know them well. Then there was the young fool what come in just fore you. He was in the room across yours. Marrow was his name. John Marrow. But he was too drunk to . . ."

Doom echoed in Roman's mind. Grabbing the woman's candle, he took the steps three at a time. The slatted door banged open, revealing an empty room.

Roman swore in quiet earnest, then turned toward the couple who had followed him up the stairs. "How did he look?"

"He . . . He . . ." Herr Krahn scowled as he scrutinized the room. The bed had not been slept in. Not a thing was out of place. "He was a stout man. Fair tall . . . I think. He woke me up. I—"

"What color was his hair? What did he wear?"

"He had a hat. It covered his face. All dark, he wore. He'd just woke me up. I couldn't see much."

Roman drew a deep breath, steadying his temper. Now was not the time to lose control. "Tell me about the Shadow," he said evenly.

Krahn pulled back his big shoulders and lowered his brows. "The Shadow," he murmured as if just connecting the incident with the name. " 'Tis said he's the ghost of an old beggar what lived on Laurel Street."

The wife eased up beside her husband. "Some say he takes from the rich and gives to them in need."

"Well, I'm in need," said Roman, low-voiced as he clenched his fists. The landlord raised his club. His wife ducked behind his back, but Roman strode past them back into his own rented room.

It took him only a few moments to wake and question the other two villains. But despite his threats and their obvious fear, they told him nothing more than he'd already learned. If the necklace was gone, the Shadow had been there before them.

Roman straightened, feeling rage spur through his system as he headed for the stairs.

"Where . . . where be you going?" asked the woman.

"Ta catch a shadow," said Roman.

Chapter 3

It had been three days since the necklace was stolen. Three days! And in that time Roman had delayed meeting with Lord Harrington. Instead, he had searched every back alley, had questioned everyone from potters to lords about a man named John Marrow, for without the gems he had no bargaining power, nothing with which to win the lad's freedom. But not a soul had heard of Marrow.

The Shadow, on the other hand, was a different matter entirely. The Shadow was a specter, a beggar, a prince, the devil incarnate. Every person had an opinion, and the opinions varied as greatly as the people's positions in life. Thieves envied him, the downtrodden revered him, and the gentry feared him. Though the stories differed greatly, one thing remained consistent. The Shadow took from the rich and gave to the poor.

But who was the Shadow? And where was he? Roman scanned the occupants of the Red Fox. The inn was busy again, loud and boisterous, as if attempting to drown out the harsh realities of the world outside its doors.

Someone had stolen the necklace. Someone was to blame. But who? Had he met the thief? Was he the sailor in the corner? The drunk on the floor?

"So, guvnor, you're back."

Roman lifted his gaze. Betty stood beside the table. She wore the same revealing gown he had seen on her before. Her breasts looked just as plump and pale, her smile just as seductive. But Roman was in no mood to appreciate her charms.

It had been three days since he'd slept. Three days of hopeless searching and scorching self-incrimination. He shouldn't have fallen asleep until the necklace was delivered. He shouldn't have failed.

"You don't look so good, luv," she said. "Mayhap you're not accustomed to our English brews."

"Mayhap," he said dryly, and took another swig of ale.

"Betty, darlin', we need another round," someone called.

"And a kiss."

"Not for you, George," she replied, glancing at the man who had spoken.

"Just a kiss," George pleaded. He was a big man, and fat.

"Seems to me you was the one what said that to Sara. She's round as a melon now and sick every morn."

Chuckles answered her rejoinder.

"That's me, Betty, luv, potent as your rum."

"And just as stale," added his companion. "But give *me* a kiss, Betty. I've spawned no babes."

The maid placed a fist to her broad hip and laughed. "That's because you *are* a babe, Arthur. Your brother would paddle your behind if he knew you was 'ere."

"I'd rather you did the paddling, Betty," said Arthur.

"Don't tempt her, boy," someone called.

" 'Twould be worth a few bruises," someone else argued.

"And your wife will bruise you, Birley, if you won't be gettin' yourself 'ome," she said.

"Ahh, Maggie's grousing all the time," complained Birley into his mug.

"As would you be, if you was carrying your fourth babe about in your belly," Betty said.

"You can't blame a man for stopping by for a pint now and again," said a balding man near the door.

"But I could blame him for losing five shillings at tables when his wife is working her fingers to the bone to keep the wolf from the door, Cleat Smith," she responded.

Cleat lowered his balding pate. "I'll win tonight. Robert owes me a game."

"Robert Redman will forever play ya men for fools if ya act the fools," Betty warned.

"He could beat you with his brain tied behind his back," Arthur said.

"He's no better man than me," Cleat argued. "He ain't got anything I ain't got."

"Only smarts and a whole lot more money," rejoined someone unseen from Roman's position. That viewpoint was met with chuckles.

Cleats rose to his feet, his face turning red. "He ain't got—"

Betty moved smoothly through the crowd. She placed her hand on his arm. "He ain't got Katherine, Cleat," she said softly. "But you do, so long as you keep your wits about you. Now go on home to her afore you make her worry again. You know how she adores ya."

He turned his gaze from the others. The anger drained from his face. "She does, don't she."

"She does indeed. Now 'urry 'ome. Oh, and . . ."
Reaching into the pocket that hung from her belt,

Betty pulled out a coiled length of scarlet ribbon. "Give this to your Rachel."

"You know how she favors red," Cleat said, bobbing his head and blushing. "You're a good one, you are, Betty. You'd make someone a fine—"

"Don't go trying to pawn your sister's boy off on her again," said George. "She ain't that desperate."

"Desperate hell! If you need a man, Betty, I'll volunteer."

"Me too!"

Cleat hurried toward the door as a dozen voices chimed agreement, but Roman was lost in thought.

He had searched the city for three full days, only to find that fate had brought him full circle.

Betty was the answer to his prayers.

Betty Mullen hurried down the dark alley. The hair on the back of her neck rose, standing on end as she glanced hastily from side to side. She'd had the feeling of being watched ever since leaving the Red Fox. Twice she'd stopped and listened.

No one followed her, she assured herself. She would know if they did. Still, she breathed a sigh of relief as she slipped the key into her front door.

"Betty."

She shrieked and spun toward the voice. The man that emerged from the darkness was even bigger than he had seemed at the inn. "Scotsman!" she said, trying to sound relieved. Her heart thundered in her chest, but wisdom and experience told her to act the bold barmaid and not the frightened mouse. "What be ya doing 'ere?"

"Me apologies." He stepped closer, but when she backed away he stopped as if sensing her fear despite her efforts to hide it. Beside her door, a single lantern illuminated the night. It did little to cast light on either his features or his intent. But she had no need to study him, for she had done so before now.

His nose had once been broken. It bowed slightly in the center, giving his face a rough appearance made more severe by his sheer size. His hair was dark and long, caught back at the nape of his neck with a single strip of leather. He had large, square hands, hands that could swing a scythe ... or a sword.

She reached for the door handle behind her.

"Forgive me." His expression was as intent as that of a hunting wolf, but he remained several feet from her and finally leaned a wide shoulder against the wall, as if forcing himself to relax and wait, lest he frighten her away. "I didna mean ta startle ye."

"Well you did. Now what do you want, Scotsman?"

"I'd like to speak ta ye." He tilted his head slightly. Half his face was illumined now, making the bump in his nose more dramatic. Had he injured it in a brawl? He would be a hell of a man to get angry, she knew. The quiet ones always were.

She shrugged, showing a bit more of her bosom. But the movement failed to distract him. She tensed a bit more. "Go ahead. Speak, then," she said, keeping her tone casual.

He remained still a moment, then nodded toward the door behind her. "Inside. In private."

She was tempted to laugh. But though he acted civil, she knew it would be foolish to offend this man. Why was he here and why hadn't she heard him follow her? He was too large for stealth, wasn't he?

" 'Tis privacy ya want?" she asked, then shrugged again and pushed the door open. "I suppose if it's that ..." she began, then slipped through the door and thrust at it with all her might.

But his arm blocked its path and prevented it from closing.

She gasped and shoved at his hand. But in a moment he was inside with his back pressed to the door.

"What do you want?" She heard fear in her voice and cringed. Only a fool would let her enemy see her fear. Unless it was feigned. And it was not.

"I willna hurt ye, lass," he said, his tone low, his eyes dark and unfathomable. "I but wish ta talk."

"And nothing else?"

She watched him watch her. Young Daniel from just down the way had faithfully lighted the candle on the flat lid of the nearby trunk. Its light chased shadows across the Scotsman's rugged face.

"Not unless yer offerin'." His voice was heavily burred with the Gaelic accent. It spurred up memories. She pushed them away. "Are ye offerin', Betty?"

She had played this game a thousand times, she reminded herself. Fear could only make her the loser. So she forced laughter. Inside her cloak was a blade as sharp as death itself. If she could make him relax his vigil, she could have it at his throat in an instant. "I don't usually conduct business here, Scotsman."

His shoulders dropped a smidgen as he tilted his head and glanced toward the bed behind her. "It seems a likely place."

His meaning was clear. He thought she was a whore. So much the better. Misconceptions had often aided her cause. "It's too dangerous to bring strangers here."

"I'm na stranger," he said. "Ye know me."

Why was he here? What did he want? If she screamed, would anyone come? No. She'd have to depend on her own defenses. Keep him talking. "I know you have a necklace worth a king's ransom.

Are you offering that to me, Scotsman?"

He straightened slightly, and though he didn't move toward her, she tensed, ready to flee. " 'Tis what I came ta speak ta ye about."

"Truly?" Her tone was casual, but the pace of her heart increased a bit more. "And all along I thought I was only jesting."

He stopped, raising his brows in question.

"I'm flattered. Not all men think my favors worth a king's ransom."

She had hoped he would laugh. She was disappointed.

A muscle in his jaw flexed. Anger flashed in his eyes as he stepped forward. "The necklace has been stolen."

She gasped. "No! That lovely bit? 'Tis sorry I am, guvnor."

"Are ye?" His hands clenched to fists, but she forced herself to remain immobile. In truth, there was nowhere to run. Not in these close quarters.

"Course I am, luv. I've been thinking 'bout 'Arrington's offer for a stone or two, and I was 'oping you'd come ta make me a deal." She smiled. "I don't mean to seem immodest, but some say a night with me is worth more than jewels."

His gaze was sharp and hard as he watched her. "So ye dunna ken anything about me loss?"

Betty opened her eyes wide. "About the theft of . . . 'Ey!" she said, placing her fists on her hips. Her fingers were only inches from her hidden blade. "You ain't accusing me of nothin' are ya?"

"I need it back." He was directly in front of her in an instant. For a big man he was very quick. " 'Tis of utmost importance."

"Then ya shouldn't be wastin' time 'ere."

She could almost feel him forcing himself to relax. "Where should I be?"

She raised a brow. "Out chasing the thief," she said.

"But I'd rather be here."

So it was lust she saw in his eyes. Relief seeped through Betty's limbs. Lust was a guest she knew how to handle. "Would ya indeed, Scottie?"

"Aye, I would." There was some sincerity in his tone, but there was more. Perplexity mayhap.

Crossing her arms, she hugged them to her torso and puckered her lips into a pout. Furtively, she closed her fingers over the handle of her blade. "And I suppose I'm supposed ta simply forgive the insults ya spewed at the Red Fox."

One corner of his lips twitched. "I think ye gave as good as ye got, lass. When it comes ta sharp tongues, yers could carve mutton."

She shrugged and slipped the knife from its hidden sheath. "A girl's got to have some way to protect her heart. Specially from men like you."

"And what kind of man am I, lass?"

"The kind ta make a girl cautious, lest she get in over her head."

He remained silent for a moment, and when he spoke his voice was quiet and beautifully burred. "Then ye dunna find me unfavorable?"

The surprise that lighted her face was real. Unfavorable? What a strange question, but she did not have the luxury to understand it, only to use it. "No," she whispered. Half-closing her eyes, she rose on her toes. Her lips were inches from his. "I find ya . . . very appealing."

He lowered his mouth. Between their bodies, Betty tipped her knife upward, prepared to strike. But suddenly her wrist was trapped in his hand.

She gasped, snapped open her eyes, and stared into his face. His gaze had not dropped, but bored into her eyes with the intensity of flame.

"If ye find me appealing, lass, I'd suggest ye

drop the dirk," he murmured. " 'Twould surely make me less becoming ta have a blade stuck between me ribs."

Before she could speak, the knife was snatched from her hand and flung away. It clattered unseen against the far wall.

"Yer surprisingly predictable, lass," he said, still holding her wrist.

Fear flooded her like the indomitable wash of tide. She wasn't predictable. Unpredictability was the only reason she had survived so long in this city. Who was this man who could read her thoughts? And what was he reading now? "What do ya want?" she rasped.

She felt his tension as if it were her own, a bowstring of singing emotion strung between them and reverberating with ... With what? He stood very near, close enough for her to smell the faint hint of caraway. But also close enough to catch the illusive scent of man.

The muscles in his lean jaw flexed again. "I want the necklace back."

She released her breath with an effort. "Then why come here?"

His grip loosened almost imperceptibly. "Because ye can help me."

"Help ya?" She forced herself to laugh, hoping it would dispel some of the tautness in her muscles. It did nothing but echo in the room like the eerie chuckle of a ghost. "And why would I do that, Scottie?"

"Because I'll pay."

So he was offering her money again. "Pay?" she asked, letting her tone bloom with interest.

"For information," he said, and loosened his grip a bit more on her wrist.

"And why me? Why come to me?"

"I watched ye at the inn."

"You and a 'undred others, Scottie. So?" She laughed again, trying to ignore the intensity of his eyes, the casual strength of his hand on her arm. She could feel the heat of his body and the hard press of his thigh even through the many layers of cloth that separated them.

"So I ken the truth."

"Truth? About what?" Her heart was racing as she waited for his response.

The silence was heavy and seemed to last forever.

"Ye are na as dense as ye seem, lass. Ye ken things."

She didn't turn away. Didn't deny his words. Didn't shift her gaze away from his. "I'm sure I'm very flattered, Scotsman. But I wonder, what things might you be speaking of?"

"The Shadow."

Her stomach pitched at the words. "The Shadow! So that's it!" she exclaimed, and, jerking her wrist free, stepped away. "Ya think the Shadow took yer precious gems!"

He neither dropped his gaze nor changed his expression. "What do ye know of him?"

"Only a thousand or so tales. He's a lord. He's a beggar. He's a saint."

"Nay!" Roman took a quick step forward, but she stepped back just as quickly, pulling her arm to her body to keep out of his grasp. "Dunna tell me fairy tales. For ye believe them na more than I."

"Nay, I do not. There is no Shadow."

He was silent for a moment, then, "Ye are wrong. And I think ye know it."

"Truly?" she asked, raising her chin slightly. "Perhaps ya think I have the Shadow here, hidden under my bed."

" 'Twould seem a terrible waste of yer bed. Who is he?'' Roman asked, advancing.

She stood her ground and raised her chin to maintain contact with his hawkish eyes. " 'E's King 'enry. Only na one knows but me, on account of we're lovers.''

"Truly? Ye and auld Henry. He doesn't seem yer type." The corner of his lips jerked in irritation, but his tone remained level.

That control worried her. Wild rage was more easily overcome than deep thought. That had been proven a thousand times. "Certainly," she said, her tone flippant. " 'E says there's not another that can match my . . ." She smiled, letting the expression steal slowly across her face and lifting one shoulder so that her left breast was pushed more fully into view.

He watched the movement, but when his gaze returned to hers, his expression remained the same, remote. "Yer what?" he asked dryly.

She snorted. "My intellect," she said, and turned away to pace across the narrow room. It contained little more than a bed and two trunks. Against the far wall, a small table boasted a cracked plate of bare bones and little else. She plopped herself onto the nearer trunk. The bent staves that bound it were unadorned, and the hasp that closed it was dark and pitted with rust. "Isn't that why ya came? Because of my intellect?" she asked, and lifted a pale shoulder again.

He watched the movement. "Mayhap ye are trying ta make me forget why I came," he said softly. "Mayhap that is why ye do that?"

She straightened her back and scowled. She had little use for thinking men, or men of any sort for that matter. "Do what?"

"Listen, lass," he said, pacing across the room to bend down and place his hands beside her hips on the trunk. "I'd like nothing more than ta stay and let ye corrupt me, but . . ."

"Corrupt ya!" She jerked to her feet, but he didn't move. Their faces were only inches apart and his gaze absolutely level. She sat back down with a jolt. "Someone corrupted ya long before ya came 'ere, I'll warrant."

He grinned. It was not an expression of happiness, but rather, it denoted something else, something deeper—a man's disillusionment with himself, perhaps. His jaw was covered with a reddish brown beard that contrasted sharply with the straight, white rows of his teeth. "Mayhap yer right, lass. I should have said, I'd love ta let ye seduce me, since ye long ta so."

Standing abruptly, she managed to push him away. "Would ya now?" she asked, anger goading her. "Well you're flat out of luck then, mate, cuz I've no wish ta do no seducin' tonight."

"Not even for a stone from the coveted necklace?"

Anger ripped free from its bonds. "Not if you gave me the entire piece, wrapped in golden cloth and delivered . . ." she began, but he was watching her very closely. Too closely, like a wolf might study a hare.

She pursed her lips, shutting off the crisp words. 'Twas her mother's voice she used when she was angry, and her mother's perfect English would do her little good here. She knew better than to lose her temper. Damn it, she knew better.

"Delivered by who, Betty, King Henry?" he asked, still watching her.

"That's right, luv," she said, making her tone heavy with accent and disdain. "Not if 'e brought the thing 'isself and promised me every rock."

He let her words fall into the silence. "Yer a strange whore, Betty," he said softly.

Anger swelled up again, but she pushed it quickly back into oblivion. "I got me pride same as you."

"What do ye ken of me own pride?" he said softly.

She scowled, but before she could formulate an answer, he straightened to his full height.

"I'm na asking ye ta lie with me," he said. "Just ta give me a wee bit of information."

"I told ya, I don't have no information. I don't know who the Shadow is."

"At the inn, ye seemed ta know everyone," he said. "Their jobs, their wives, their business."

"Them's just the regulars," she said, but she wondered if her tone was too breathless, if he saw something in her eyes. He watched her narrowly.

She forced a laugh. "Ya think maybe Cleat be the Shadow? Or Birley?"

"I dunna ken. But I think ye do."

"Well, I don't," she said, and jerked about.

His gaze followed her. "But ye can find out."

She paced across the floor to the dark fireplace. Anger threatened to well up again. She felt it in the tightness of her throat, the stiffness of her body, but she'd forgotten herself once. She wouldn't do so again. With a hand on the poker she turned and forced a smile. "What would ya give me?" she asked softly.

"I'll give ye one of the stones."

"From the necklace?" Her laughter was beautifully harsh. "Ya must think me a bloomin' idiot. Why would I believe you're goin' ta get the necklace back if the Shadow was the one what stole it?

"No! Ya want me help, ya'll pay me soon as I get ya the name."

He nodded once, his gaze not leaving hers. "I'll give ye four pounds English if ye tell me his identity."

She let her mouth go round and soft. "Four pounds?"

"Four if ye tell me his name. Six if ye know where he lives."

"If you're so well off, why do ya need the necklace back so bad?"

"I owe it to Harrington."

She laughed. "A bribe to keep someone quiet? Ya must a killed someone pretty important."

He narrowed his eyes at her, and she shrugged.

"Round Firthport, life's cheap. Ya could kill off 'alf the town and buy most folks' silence with only a shillin' or two."

"Ye think I killed someone?"

She shrugged. "If not that, then what?"

For a moment she thought he might answer, but instead, he turned and strode to the door. "Get me the name," he said, and was gone.

Betty closed her eyes and clasped her shaking hands tightly together. Sweet Mary. She had to get to James, and fast.

Chapter 4

Fatigue weighed heavily on Roman. Sleepless-
ness and frustration had taken their toll, but
he did not dare rest now. He had planned to return
to his rented room to sleep, but something held
him in the deepest shadows outside Betty's door.

Even he couldn't say why he was there for certain. After all, she had agreed to try to obtain the
true identity of the Shadow, had agreed to give that
information to Roman for a price.

But there was something...something he
couldn't quite explain that kept him from leaving.
She had promised to help him, true, but that was
after she had denied the possibility of there ever
being a Shadow. Of all the people he'd questioned,
no one had completely disregarded the notorious
thief's existence. In fact, they had seemed to thrive
on the idea of an avenging angel of sorts. A man
who would not only take from the rich, but would
give to the poor.

Betty had been the only one who had refused to
take comfort in such a concept. Why? Was it because she knew more than she was telling?

But even if she did believe, would she assist Roman in his search for the thief? For a moment, there

had been a spark of something in her eyes. Defiance perhaps?

"I got me pride same as you," she'd said. But what did she know of his pride? Mayhap she assumed he possessed the renowned pride of the Highlander, pride to match her own. But if Fiona and Leith Forbes had left him to fend for himself, if he had lived a life as lowly as a Firthport whore's, would he have pride? Or would he have sunk to the depths he knew himself capable of reaching?

Who was this maid named Betty? What had he seen in her eyes? Disdain? Hatred?

Mayhap. But there had been something more. Something that had barely tickled the nerve endings of his awareness.

He had left her room intent on reaching his own, on finding sleep, but something had stopped him. Perhaps she didn't plan on identifying the Shadow at all. Perhaps she planned on warning him.

Thus, Roman waited now in the dark, letting the minutes scrape past. Fatigue smothered him. His eyes fell closed, but he wrested himself from sweet oblivion. Just a little longer. The night dragged by, pulled along by the invisible strings of time.

Nothing stirred. The city slept.

He had been wrong. Betty was just what she seemed to be, or at least was going nowhere tonight. Relief flooded him. He could return to his own bed now and find the sleep his body . . .

What was that? A noise? Or had he simply sensed something?

Despite his fatigue, every nerve awoke with a start as he stared through the darkness toward Betty's door. It hadn't opened. And there was no other exit, so surely she was still inside. But perhaps she was preparing to leave. Or perhaps she was at the single window, peering through the scraped and tightly stretched leather that covered it, searching the darkness.

Roman remained motionless, staring at the window until his eyes watered. He saw nothing, but something had changed. Something had happened.

From behind the house, a dog growled. It was deep-throated and barely audible. But in a moment it fell silent, as though startled before recognizing a friend. Another hound perhaps.

Or maybe a nocturnal visitor of another sort. But who would be out at this hour? Was Betty expecting a visitor?

Roman waited. Nothing happened. No other sounds disturbed the night.

He was a fool. Betty was probably fast asleep.

But something had disturbed the dog. Perhaps a wild cat had wandered into the city. But wouldn't he have continued growling then, or begun barking? A familiar person might have quieted him. One of Betty's regular customers. But if such was the case, he hadn't reached the door. Why? Had he somehow sensed Roman's presence? And if so, why would he concern himself with Roman?

Unless he was the Shadow himself!

Roman erupted from his hiding place. In his present state, it seemed so logical. Darkness rushed past him. He dashed around the corner of the house and down an alley, listening, trying to determine from where the growl had issued.

A stone wall rose up in front of him. He vaulted over it, through a garden, and onto the opposite wall. Across the street, a dog barked once in deep protest. Roman found its large, pale shape in the blackness. Beside it a shadow moved and slid away.

What was it? Or who? Not taking his gaze from the spot where the shadow had been, Roman jumped from the wall and dashed toward it.

There it was, rushing away. It was a person. He was sure of that now. And who would be out in this dangerous part of town in the dark of night? If not The Shadow himself, surely it was someone who could shed a ray of light on the underbelly of Firthport.

Silent and swift, Roman sprinted down the alley, concentrating with every fiber of his body on the figure he followed.

So intent was he on catching his prey that he barely heard the deep-throated growl. The dark figure had suddenly disappeared around a corner. But if he hurried . . .

The dog struck him like a destrier at full gallop. Roman hit the ground with the hound on top. Teeth sank into the bunched wool of his plaid and grazed his chest. Twisting wildly, Roman rolled the dog beneath him. The beast growled, scratching his face with huge, horny paws as it tried to escape.

With the strength of desperation, Roman pried his heels against the ground and lurched to his feet, but the dog gained his balance and lunged again. Roman raised an arm to shield his face. The hound hit him squarely on the chest. As he fell, Roman thrust his arm hard into the beast's mouth. It gagged, trying to break free, but in that moment, Roman bent his legs, caught the hound on the balls of his feet, and thrust with all his might.

The dog flew through the air and hit a nearby stone wall with a thud. Roman leapt to his feet and spun about, crouched and ready for the next attack.

The hound rose more slowly. Staring through the darkness, he whimpered once, then shook his head and sat with a tentative wag of his tail.

The night grew silent.

Roman turned his head, searching the darkness. The Shadow was out there, not far away. His gut told him it was so. And his gut was never wrong.

* * *

A gust of laughter burst forth from the corner of the Red Fox. Roman glanced toward the source of the sound and pushed down his burning frustration.

Whoever he had seen in the darkness behind Betty's house had disappeared. Although he had searched, doubled back, and searched again, he'd found nothing.

Finally, he had returned to his rented room, and there he had slept for several hours. Still his eyes felt scratchy and his nerves raw. The noise and hubbub of the Red Fox irritated him. But not nearly so much as Betty's bright-eyed demeanor.

Dressed in a faded green gown that laced neatly up the back, she looked as fresh and sassy as ever. With that characteristic sway of her generous hips and a quip ready for all, she moved amongst the tables. Apparently, nothing had disturbed *her* sleep, not his own furtive presence, or the absence of a lover.

Who, then, was the man who had sneaked through the darkness, quieted the immense white hound, and disappeared into the night?

He could be someone of no significance, of course. Roman had told himself that a thousand times, but instinct told him otherwise. And instinct had brought him back to the Red Fox once more.

There was something about Betty that made him certain she knew more than she admitted. Perhaps it was the fact that she had denied the Shadow's very existence. Or perhaps it was the way she moved, or spoke, or laughed, or . . .

Hell fire! Perhaps it was *her* that kept bringing him back and not his quest at all.

He should be concentrating on recovering the necklace. He had promised Laird MacAulay that he would see his lad safely home. He had promised

Fiona. And yet here he was again, watching a buxom maid move about the room like a seductive dancer. Flirting, teasing, then hurrying off, a pitcher in each hand, her wide hips. . . .

Roman stopped in mid-thought. Flirting and teasing. True, she did that in abundance. But nothing else. Strange, wasn't it?

Roman had been in his share of taverns and inns, had seen a good many serving wenches. Yet never had he seen one that consistently teased and drew away. A barmaid's salary was not a large one and was often supplemented by funds she could garner on her back.

But Betty had not taken any of the men's proposals. At least not that he had seen. And Betty surely wasn't the kind of woman to spend all her nights alone. No, she was a hot-blooded one. So who was she sharing that heat with?

It was a question to which Roman planned to find an answer.

Glancing about the inn, Roman studied faces. There was no lack of variety here. The Red Fox's patrons varied from toothless gaffers to smooth-faced lads.

But what kind of man would most appeal to a barmaid? Roman wondered.

A man with wealth. That narrowed down the field considerably. A man young enough to appreciate her charms. The field narrowed still more. A man not too hideous to look at. That eliminated even more.

With these new criteria in mind, Roman scanned the crowd, noticing every man's expression. There was not a man there who didn't occasionally cast an appreciative eye at Betty, but there were only a few whose gazes rarely strayed to anything else.

Not far from the kitchen door sat just such a man. He was large and fair-haired with finely tai-

lored clothes and a slightly sloppy expression
stamped across his sharp, Scandinavian features.
More than once, Betty had stopped by his table to
exchange a few words. He was a handsome man,
young and intoxicated enough to guarantee a loosened tongue.

It didn't take long for Roman to order two more
drinks and work his way over to the man's table.

"I weary of drinkin' alone," he said, his own
voice slightly slurred as if he, too, had imbibed too
much. "Thought we might share a mug if ye have
na objections ta drinkin' with a Scotsman."

The young man raised his gaze to Roman's.
"Nay." His Norwegian accent seemed as heavy as
his lids, which were half-mast over ice-blue eyes.
"We be two fish in a foreign sea, aye?" he said,
motioning limply toward Roman's plaid. His eyes
scanned Roman's height and he smiled. "Or do
you think we are more like two bulls in the sheep's
pen, Scotsman?"

Roman pulled a stool from under the table and
sat heavily. "I wouldna mind being in *her* pen," he
said, nodding toward Betty, who laughed with a
trio of men across the room.

"Ahh," said the other with a sigh. "The softest
lamb of them all."

Roman nodded, making certain the movement
was casual. "Ye've tamed the wild ewe and found
the tender lambkin within, then, have ye?"

"Ahh." The large Norseman sighed again. "That
I have. She bleats for only me, now. Has ever since
I first come to Firthport some months past."

Could this man be the Shadow? Betty had spoken to him at some length. Roman drank again,
calming his nerves.

"Ye're a lucky man indeed, sir . . ."

"Call me Larnes."

"Yer a lucky man, Larnes, for she be a bonny lass, and na mistake."

"Aye, she is that, and soft as rose petals in my hand."

Roman forced a sigh himself, though he'd felt nothing of that rose but her thorny tongue. Still, he couldn't deny that there was softness there that begged to be touched. "I was hopin' ye could suggest a good inn at which ta stay, but . . ." He chuckled. "I'm guessin' now that ye haven't had a need ta pay for a bed. Not with Betty sleepin' just upstairs as she does."

For just a moment, Larnes looked sheepish, but then he chuckled and drank again. "It do make it convenient."

Roman drank, too, hiding his scowl behind the rim of his mug. It seemed Larnes, like most men, had few qualms about lying about his sexual exploits. Betty's room was some blocks away, and if the Norseman was indeed her lover, he would surely know as much.

"Ahh, well, ye've saved me from wasting my desire on her, then, Larnes, since she's yers and is na likely ta stray. I might as well question another about renting a room. Cheers," Roman said, and, leaving the Norwegian an extra drink, rose to question the next man.

"Tangle with the wrong woman, Scottie?"

Betty stood only a few inches from Roman's table and looked down at him with a smile. Apparently, his visit on the previous night hadn't made her bitter toward him.

Perhaps men accosting her at her door was a regular event. One that came with the job.

Or perhaps not.

"Every woman but ye is the wrong one, Betty," Roman said. He borrowed the line from his uncle

Roderic's repertoire, for he had seen Roderic the Rogue charm queens and peasants alike. And if ever Roman had needed a dose of that charm, it was now.

"She must be part cat," Betty said, nodding toward the scratches on his cheek. "Else she hasn't yet figured out where a knife will do the most good when a man won't take no for an answer."

The dog's claws had been as vicious as a wolf's. But she didn't need to know the source of his wounds. "Strange how some women react in the final throes of passion," he said, and rubbed his chest as if remembering those moments with fondness.

Betty snorted. "Aye, and it's even stranger how men lie about their escapades."

Despite everything, Roman could not help but smile. Beneath Betty's floppy white cap there was a brain as sharp as a Highlander's dirk. Had circumstances been different, he would like to learn who she truly was—Betty the woman, the real person. But fate had laid its torturous course. So for now he would play this game. "Surely ye dunna suggest that I have fabricated me bonny companion of last night."

" 'Tis either that or ye sit 'ere all night 'cause ya'd rather swill ale than spend another night in 'er arms. Though I couldn't blame ya. Looks like one more time might well do ya in."

"I'm tougher than I look." Though Betty's face looked round beneath her homely cap, it was a pretty face, thin compared to the plumpness of her body. But even if she had the face of a warthog and the form of a goat, her eyes would have fascinated him. They were large and expressive, and though their color was hidden in the poor light of the room, they seemed to speak of things hidden in her soul.

She canted her head, letting her gaze skim him. He knew what she saw—not a pretty boy, but a big man with too little charm and too much history. "I doubt a stallion in full armor would look tougher than you, Scotsman," she answered, her lids slightly lowered over mesmerizing eyes.

"Should I be flattered?" he asked.

The moment hung suspended between them. But finally, she pulled herself from his gaze with a jerk and glanced toward the kitchen. "Listen, it's time ta go so—"

"Should I be flattered?" he repeated.

But she wouldn't be drawn in again. "Go ahead if'n it makes ya feel better, Scotsman," she said. "But ya're gonna 'ave to be flattered someplace else, cause we're closing . . ."

"I been thinking," he interrupted, letting his voice slur just a little. He'd spent the past five hours in that inn, had spoken to a dozen patrons, and ordered nearly as many drinks, only two of which he had tasted himself. "It canna be safe for a bonny lass such as yerself ta walk home in the wee hours of the morning."

"So you're worried for my safety, are ya?" she asked, then leaned down to grant him a view of her splendid cleavage as she looked into his face. "Or are ya plannin' ta give me somethin' ta worry about, Scottie?"

"Me?" He motioned toward his chest with a wobbly hand. There were only two other patrons in the place. One was the young Norseman who claimed to have tamed her. He had passed out with his head on the table. The other man wasn't quite so lucky, and lay sprawled on the floor at an unlikely angle. "Ye surely mistake me for someone else."

"Aye," she said. "For a moment I thought ya was the bloke what barged into me house last night."

"Nay. I assure ye I would do na such thing ta a lady."

"But what would ya do ta *me*?" she asked.

"Ye surely misunderstand me intentions," Roman said, sounding offended.

"Do I now?"

"Aye."

" 'Twould be the first time, then, luv. Usually I understand men's intentions perfectly well."

"Is yer experience so vast, then?"

She nodded. "I've had my share."

Leaning closer, he narrowed his eyes and caught her gaze. "I dunna deny that ye draw at something in me, lass."

"And I can guess what that something is," she said, dipping her gaze to the tabletop, as though she could see through its surface and beneath his plaid.

She turned to go, but he caught her wrist and rose to his feet. "Ye belittle me affections," he said.

"Watch out, Scottie." She shifted her gaze down to where his plaid was slightly misplaced. "Your belittled affection is showing."

He grimaced. "Ye do know how ta wound a man."

"A girl's gotta protect 'erself somehow."

"Let me walk with ye ta yer home, and I'll do the protecting."

"Go away, Scot."

"As soon as we reach yer door."

She paused. He didn't miss the opportunity her silence afforded.

"I'll worry the night through if ye dunna let me accompany ye."

"Ye'll pass out and not think about me again," she argued.

"Na," he said, and found that his denial was strangely honest.

She drew a heavy breath. Her breasts rose and fell prettily with the inhalation. "Ya promise ta leave once we get there."

"Me vow is me blood," he said solemnly.

"Aye, luv, and it'll be all over the ground with various body parts if ya don't keep your word." She turned away. "I'll fetch my things."

The opportunity seemed too perfect to pass up. Taking one step forward, Roman patted her behind.

'Twas amazing how quickly she could spin back toward him. Grabbing his hand, she raised it between them. "This will be *one* of the first body parts to go," she vowed.

"Ye've a way with words, lass," he said, and, lifting her hand in his, lightly kissed her knuckles.

Something sparked between them. Stark surprise showed on her face, but in a moment, she regained her composure. Yanking her hand from his, she turned quickly away and hurried toward the kitchen.

Roman expelled air through his teeth and watched her exit. He'd felt no hint of her true figure through the gown that covered her hips. How many layers did she wear under that faded garment? he wondered. And why would she wear more than necessary in the heat of the inn? Was her figure padded? And if so, why? Some men liked plump females, he knew. But was that her reason, or was there something more?

Every time he saw her it seemed she but added to the mystery. Roman sat in silent thought until suddenly he realized how much time had elapsed since she'd left the common room. The conniving little scamp! She'd gone out the back way without him. He'd bet his life on it.

Roman hurried from the front door. Once outside, he scanned the darkness until he saw a figure flitting through the night.

With a smug smile, he trotted down a side street, turned a corner, turned again, hurried on, and finally stopped to listen. For a moment no sound met his ears. But a soft breeze blew from the south, finally carrying the sound of footsteps, light and quick as a vixen on the prowl.

He waited a moment longer, then stepped away from the building.

"Betty," he said.

"Sweet Mary!" she gasped, stumbling backward. "What the devil are you doing 'ere?"

"Walking ye home? Ye agreed ta allow me, ye ken."

"I 'ad no wish to wound your feelings with a refusal, Scotsman. But you're beginning to irritate me."

"I told ye I would worry."

"I'm a big girl, now. Ye needn't fret on my account."

"But I do."

"Then go fret somewhere else."

He watched her carefully. In the light of the inn, her cap hid her features. Or did her cleavage draw the eye to such an extent that her face was hidden? Whatever the case, here in the dark, he found that he saw her with his imagination. And he imagined her naked—slim, supple, and in his arms.

For a moment he forgot to breathe. Electricity sparked between them. "Betty." Her name was a breath on his lips.

But suddenly she backed away, her eyes wide and liquid in the darkness.

He didn't approach her, though holding back was difficult. "What be ye afraid of, lass?"

"Afraid?" She laughed, but the sound was ner-

vous. "You're thinking of someone else, surely.
There's not a man I fear."

"Then mayhap ye can protect *me*," he said.

She tilted her head and stared up into his face.
"Somehow, I think ya can 'andle yourself, Scotsman."

"Nay." He tightened one fist in sudden irritation. How was it that her presence distracted him
from his quest? "I lost the necklace," he reminded
them both.

Shrugging, she stepped around him. "The
Shadow is but a wild myth concocted to give hope
ta them that's got none. I've learned nothin' ta
make me think different, if that's why you're 'ere."

He fell in beside her. She was a good-sized
woman. How did she move with such quiet grace?

"Mayhap I'm here just ta be near ye," he said
quietly.

"Because you're attracted ta me . . . brains?"

He knew sarcasm when he heard it. "Mayhap,"
he said seriously.

She glanced quickly up at him. For a moment,
he saw something indiscernible in her eyes, but it
disappeared quickly, and she laughed.

"I know your kind, Scotsman. Have known a
thousand like ya."

"A thousand?" They'd reached her door. He
leaned against the jamb, casually hiding the key-
hole from her. " 'Tis a fair number, when in
truth . . ." He paused and lifted a hand to gently
brush her cheek. "I've known none like ye."

She drew a sharp breath between her teeth. But
her tone was still casual. "Ya should get around
more, Scotsman."

"We could go inside and discuss me lack of experience."

"Give it up, luv."

"Why would I do that now, lass?" he asked, leaning forward.

She scrunched back. "Because ya'll only be disappointed."

"I doubt that," he said, backing her against the wall, and bracing one hand on each side of her body.

" 'Tis true," she said, but her voice had dropped to little more than a whisper.

"Why?"

"Because." She licked her lips. Gone was the saucy maid with the hearty laugh and quick wit. "I'm . . . I'm spoken for."

He raised a brow. "Yer wed?"

Now she did laugh, though the sound was shaky. "My kind don't marry, Scottie. But I've got me a man. And 'e don't like competition."

"Really?" He watched her eyes carefully. He had heard this same tale from two of the men he'd questioned. But many of the others had vowed to have slept with her, only to cast suspicion on their honesty by things said later in the conversation, just as the Norseman had. "Why didna ye tell me that afore?"

"In truth, 'tis none of your affair."

Her skin looked smooth as a Highland loch.

"I'd like ta make it me affair, lass," he said, and leaned toward her lips.

"I told ya," she said, quickly pressing back against the wall. " 'E's very jealous."

Their faces were less than a handsbreadth apart.

"Me too," Roman whispered, leaning closer still.

"And powerful," she added, smacking a palm to his chest.

They stared at each other in silence for a moment, then Roman eased her hand from his chest and held it in his. Gently, he turned it up and kissed the center of her palm.

"A bonny hand," he murmured, then kissed her fingers, one at a time and slowly. "With bonny fingers. Slim. Delicate."

"And 'e's wealthy," she said, but her words were barely audible.

"Who?"

"My . . ." she began, but just then he sucked the tip of her pinky into his mouth and raised his gaze to hers. "Lover," she managed somewhat breathlessly.

Releasing her finger, he gently kissed her wrist. A pulse beat there, hot and wild. He held her arm in one hand while sliding his fingers along it with the other. She shivered at his touch, then gasped when he kissed the sensitive crease of her elbow.

"What's his name?" Roman whispered the question against her skin. It smelled of a thousand flavors, from cinnamon to sweet wine. It made him think of others places, just as soft, yet even more intoxicating.

"Lass?" he said softly.

"What?" The word was little more than a breathy gasp.

"What's his name?"

"Who?"

He had never played the rogue, but her tone flattered him, and he chuckled. "Yer lover's."

"Oh." She made a halfhearted attempt to pull her hand away, but he held it easily. "That's none of your—"

"I dunna believe there is a lover," he said, and touched his tongue gently to her arm.

"There is," she gasped, trying to pull away.

"Ye lie," he said, and trailed his kisses past her elbow.

"I do not."

"If there were a man, ye'd tell me his name. But

since there's not, ye've na reason to bar me from yer—"

"Harry!" She said the name quickly. " 'Is name is Harry."

He stared at her. She was breathing fast and deep. " 'Tis a most common name," he chided.

"Well, I assure ya, 'e's not a common man," she said, trying again to wrest her arm away. " 'E's a nobleman."

He let her take her arm back but trapped her between his own again as he placed his palms on the wall. "A nobleman's lackey, ye mean."

"A duke," she said, pursing her lips. They were fine lips, lush, full, cherry bright.

"I canna help but wonder," he said, then paused to watch her watch him. "Could yer lips be as sweet as they look."

"Don't you dare try it," she warned.

He leaned closer still. "Why not?"

She pushed her back against the wall even harder. "He'd . . . 'e'd be terrible mad."

"Who?"

"The duke."

"Does he scare ye, lass?" he whispered.

"What?" Their gazes met with a jolt.

"Does he hurt ye?"

For a moment she seemed transfixed, but then she shook her head jerkily. "Course not. 'E's sweet and considerate."

"And skilled?" he asked, slipping his hand up her arm and across her shoulder to her neck. It was as smooth and soft as rich velvet. He watched her swallow.

"Skilled?" Did her voice squeak?

"Does he make ye shiver at his touch." He slid his fingers up her slim throat. She trembled as if on command. "Does he make yer blood run hot and wild?" he asked, touching the throbbing pulse in her neck.

Her eyes were as wide as a doe's. "Ahh. Yeah."

"I think ye lie again, lass."

"I don't."

"I've met me share of dukes. They're a boring lot."

"Not . . . Harry."

"Do ye love him then?"

He watched her face, sensed her emotions, evaluated her silence.

"Has he tamed the wild vixen of the Red Fox?"

She snorted and straightened somewhat, seeming more like the fiery lass he had met less than four days ago. "Do I look a dolt?" she asked. The sauciness had returned to her tone. "I ain't foolish enough ta love 'im. But I ain't stupid enough ta turn down 'is money, either."

"He pays ye well?"

"'E pays for the 'ouse." She nodded toward the humble cottage behind her. "Ya don't think I can pay for this with my wages from the Fox, do ya?"

"It hardly seems like enough for the pleasure of yer company, lass."

She swallowed, but kept up the bold tone. "Well, I got me a bit of a nest feathered when this one don't work out no more."

"Mayhap I could feather it better."

"I know a bird in the hand when I sees one," she said. "And I ain't about ta send it flyin' whilst I chase after one on the wing."

"What if it's a bigger bird?"

Some of her nervousness seemed to fade, and when she chuckled, the tone seemed sincere. "Are ya always so concerned about size, Scotsman?"

"I'm just trying to impress ye. What with thousands of men ta compete with, I figure I'd best pull out me best weaponry."

"Please don't," she said, and to his own surprise, he laughed.

She watched him. Silence settled in, then, "Ya should laugh more, Scotsman. It becomes ya."

"Let me come in, and I'll laugh all night."

She smiled. Someone had lighted the lantern beside her door again. The light glistened on her teeth and eyes. "No," she said.

"One night," he whispered.

"No."

"Scared I'll spoil ye for the others?" he asked, and leaned closer still.

"Terrified," she said, and pushed at his chest.

"Who's ta know?'

" 'E will. 'E'll know."

"Is he coming tonight?"

"Aye. And ya'd best be gone when 'e does, or there'll be 'ell ta pay."

He sighed and placed a hand over hers where it rested on his chest. "I'm a stranger in a strange land. I suppose it would be unwise to offend a duke."

Her fingers were long and slim and felt warm beneath his.

"Aye, it would, indeed," she said.

"Ye're sure?"

"About . . ."

"Ye dunna wish for me company."

She scowled. "Ya don't take a hint easy, I'll say that for ya, Scotsman."

He drew her hand to his lips. "There are those who say we're a stubborn lot. Ye'll tell me when ye learn anything about the Shadow?"

"I tell ya 'e's naught but a myth."

"Mayhap yer right." Roman released her hand with a sigh. "But there's a good sum in it for ye if ye find out different. Perhaps ye could ask yer duke regarding him."

She nodded once. "I will," she said, and fished out a key nestled tight and snug between her breasts.

He watched her in awe, and she glanced at him and scowled.

"I couldn't think of a safer place ta keep it."

Roman exhaled slowly. "Strange, I can't think of anywhere more dangerous," he said, and, turning, walked away.

Chapter 5

Harrington House was large and ostentatious. Roman silently studied the anteroom, where he was told to wait. It was decorated in bright reds and royal blues, from the brocade on the chairs to the tapestries on the walls. The arched windows were made of stained glass, a far cry from the scraped leather that kept the weather at bay in most of the hovels in Firthport. It was not the first time Roman was made aware of the differences between the English classes. Neither was it the first time he wished to return home.

But again his night watch had been fruitless, for neither Betty nor her clandestine lover had passed the door of her cottage. Before the gray light of morning had seeped up from the east, Roman had left his hiding place in the shadows and stumbled off toward his own rented room.

Four hours of sleep later, he had asked directions and found his way here. Now he sat in silence. Without trying, he could hear two men speaking near the door. He supposed one was the viscount he had come to see.

"I thank you for coming, Lord Dasset."

" 'Twas my pleasure, I assure you," said the second man. "You have a lovely daughter."

Harrington sighed. "My apologies for her . . . reticence."

Dasset laughed. The sound was low. "Nonsense. I do not consider a silent woman undesirable."

Harrington was quiet for a moment, as if thinking. " 'Tis glad I am to hear that. And I assure you she will be more herself next time you call."

"I'll look forward to that moment."

They said their good-byes. Roman waited.

Footsteps echoed down the hall.

"So you have finally deigned to show your face, Scotsman, after being in Firthport for more than half a week."

Roman rose to his feet and turned to view Lord Marcus Harrington for the first time. He was of medium height, thin, boasting that peculiar kind of nose that some would call regal and some would simply call large.

"Lord Harrington," Roman said, nodding in deference.

"My son suggested you may have sold the necklace to the highest bidder and were now living off the proceeds." The viscount took a step into the room. Light through the vivid stained glass cast his shadow at a crooked angle. "Perhaps that would have been preferable to having you appear like this . . ." He waved his hand up and down as he appraised Roman's battered appearance. "Had Lord Dasset seen you, I would have been hard-pressed to explain your presence. There are enough people already who know of my daughter's . . . indiscretions. I've no wish for Dasset to know." His eyes were watery, his gait stiff as he crossed the room to prop himself on one of the spindly-legged chairs. "Despite his attitude, he possesses the power and the wealth to keep the gossips quiet if he takes her to wife. And with the necklace added to the dowry I think he will see the wisdom of doing so. I assume your presence here means that you have not sold the necklace but have brought it to me, albeit late. Sit down."

Roman did as commanded. "I am here," he said. For a moment he offered no more. But rarely had delay aided his cause, and he doubted it would do so now. Thus, he continued on. "But I fear I come without the necklace, for it has been stolen."

"Stolen!" Anger showed in the old man's eyes. His face grew red. "Stolen!" He rose abruptly to his feet, but suddenly his hands shook and his breath rattled in his throat. Seating himself again, he lifted a bell from a nearby table. The tone of it was sharp and loud in the close room.

A servant bearing a chalice appeared in less than a heartbeat. Harrington's face remained a vivid red, but he ignored the cupbearer and kept his gaze on Roman. "Dalbert warned me you might come here with such a tale," he said, his voice little more than a croak.

" 'Tis na a tale, me lord, 'tis the truth. 'Twas stolen from me as I slept at the Queen's Head."

"While you slept!" Harrington croaked. "Damn you . . ." His voice wheezed into a cough. The servant rushed over, but he was waved back. "Damn all you Scots!" he raved, pushing himself to his feet again. "You lie!"

Roman sat very still. "Me faults may be many and varied, me lord, but a liar I am na. The necklace was stolen from me as I have said."

The old man began to pace. "And of course you have searched long and hard for it!"

Roman drew a careful breath. Something about this man reminded him of his uncle Dermid. In his mind's eye he saw the upraised fist, heard his own whimper of fear.

"Have you searched?"

Harrington's words echoed in the room. Reality

caught Roman in a hard grip. The past was gone. Dermid was dead and rotting in his grave. But memories were strange things, for it seemed they could fly up on the wings of fatigue and frustration and consume him at any time. "Yes, me lord, I have indeed searched long and hard," he said.

The viscount's wide nostrils flared. "Huh!" he spat, then coughed spasmodically and waved frantically for the servant, who handed him the chalice. Drinking it quickly, he handed the cup back and said, "huh," again, in a voice much reduced in strength.

"Ye should have that cough attended, yer lordship," Roman said. It was the tone that made him a valued diplomat. It was also the tone he had used to soothe a drunken uncle.

"Don't try to soften me with your false concerns!" roared Harrington. "I know your thieving Scottish ways. You've sold the necklace after all and plan now to appeal to my sense of goodness. But I tell you . . ." Harrington began pacing, rapping his cane against the floor as he creaked across it. "I've got no sense of goodness. Not in this. Your bastard countryman raped my daughter." He stopped to turn and stare at Roman, his eyes bloodshot, his breath coming hard. "He raped my Christine," he rasped, but the rage was slipping now, being replaced by a sadness that even his stiffbacked pride could not hide. "MacAulay will die."

Roman drew a careful breath. "Will it help?" he asked softly.

"What's that?" Harrington turned his head to hear better.

"Will it help if the lad is killed?" Roman asked. There was no use denying MacAulay's actions. Not now. "Will it erase the stain from your daughter? Or will it only darken it?"

The old man scowled.

"If David MacAulay dies, every soul in Firthport will know the reason," Roman said. "The gossip of your daughter's disgrace will be like carrion for the crows. But if we settle this as gentlemen, who will know?"

He had struck a blow. Harrington looked as if he might actually crumble from it. But he remained erect. Roman couldn't help but admire him the slightest bit for that.

"I'm sending her to London," Harrington said.

There. The sadness again. He could see it in the old man's eyes. "Your only daughter?" Roman asked. "Far away in the sordid bowels of London?"

The viscount's face paled even more. "There is nothing else to be done," he whispered, more to himself than to Roman. "Nothing else. But I . . . What shall I do without my . . ." He faltered, but suddenly a young woman swept into the room.

"I'll not go," she said. She was dressed in a gown of black. Her hands were clasped before her and her eyes were wide and round in her pale face. "I'll not."

"Christine!" said the old man. But the single word sounded more like a prayer than a reprimand.

"I'll not go, Father," she repeated more softly.

Harrington's lips puckered and his brows lowered. "You'll go where I say. But for now you'll get yourself to your rooms."

"No! Tell me where he is. Let me go to him." Her fingers unclasped quickly and spread in frantic appeal toward her father. "Please."

"Get from my sight or I'll . . ."

"You'll what, Father? Strike me?" she asked, pulling her hands down to her sides and forming them to small, white-knuckled fists. "Do you think you can beat the love from my heart?"

"Don't speak of love!" he roared. "For you know

nothing of the meaning. You've shamed me and this house, and now you dress in black and talk of things you cannot comprehend. If your mother were here, she would choose a noble of the peer for you just as I have. She would wish for you to . . ."

"She would wish for me to find a man that I can respect and cherish. And cherish him I do, whether you wish it or not."

Harrington drew himself to his full height, pulling his cane from the floor and clasping it tightly to his chest. "Utter those words again, child, and I'll see him hanged on the morrow."

Her face turned deathly white and her lips parted in surprise. "You wouldn't!" she whispered.

"I would!" vowed Harrington.

"Father, please." She stumbled forward, but the old man held up a hand. "I'll hear no more!" The words rang in the room, followed by the silence of impending death.

Roman's mind scurried for words to mend the situation, but Harrington turned toward him with slow finality. "I've the power to see him dead," he said. "Don't you think I don't."

In that instant Roman saw everything. The old man's pain. His pride, his power, slipping from his failing hands like wine through a broken chalice. He nodded once. "Aye, my lord. Ye have the power."

Harrington nodded in return. "You've a score of days," he said rustily. "Bring me the necklace in that time, and the MacAulay will yet see his son returned home and intact."

Less than three weeks! When he had hardly a clue to the whereabouts of the necklace. Roman was about to plead for more, but the old man shook his head.

"One day past. One *minute* past, and he'll die as surely as you live and breathe."

It was fully dark when Roman reached Betty's house. He had tried to think of some way to retrieve the precious necklace. Perhaps if he had another priceless piece of jewelry, he might lure the Shadow out of hiding and catch him. But he had no access to such jewels and no hope of obtaining any. Thus he had returned to his only hope, Betty Mullen, the rough jewel of the Red Fox.

Another dull, sleepless night stretched before him. He slipped silently into the shadows and tried to get comfortable in the shallow niche of a stone wall not far from the house he watched so intently.

Time ticked away. Fatigue settled in. The huge white hound could be seen as no more than a glimmer of gray in the blackness. Would he bark if someone approached?

Roman shifted his gaze back to the house. If only he could move about to keep himself awake. But he had paced in his rented room, and still the necklace had been stolen.

He had paced, Roman thought, and realized that he had forgotten his endless strides across the room in a hopeless attempt to remain alert. In fact, he had forgotten much of that night. True, he had been tired. But wasn't it strange that memories of that time were just returning to him now? He was a light sleeper. If haunting dreams hadn't assured that, living with men called the Rogue and the Hawk, had. Even in sleep Roman had learned to sense trouble. But not that night, for the weariness had been strangely heavy.

Roman scanned the darkness again. Shadows, deep and unrevealing, smothered the house. He shifted his gaze away, across the narrow alley, then turned back to the house.

All was darkness, stillness. But . . . Something was different. The house's shadow had shifted. Roman stared, unblinking, until his eyes hurt. But nothing changed.

Roman blew out his breath, but just then he realized the shadow wasn't there at all. It was at the back gate, then beyond, without so much as a creak of hinges. It was a ghost or . . .

Roman shook his head, trying to awaken, for surely he had fallen asleep. But just then he heard a sound like the sharp intake of breath.

"Jesu!" he swore, and launched himself from his hiding spot. For just a moment the shadow froze, but then it swept away, no longer a shadow but a living being. A man. Roman was certain of it now. The white hound thumped his tail ingratiatingly. Roman rushed on. His prey was fast and knew the terrain. Suddenly, he was gone, vanished from sight in the middle of a blind alley.

Roman careened to a halt, glancing wildly about. He couldn't have disappeared. He wasn't a ghost.

There. Atop the roof, a flitting shadow, a whisper of sound. In a second Roman was climbing. Thatch scattered as he scaled the roof. The thief was in sight again.

Along the center of the building, then down, sliding on his backside and falling to the ground, for the Shadow was running again and nearly out of sight. Roman thundered after him. His chest ached from the exertion, but fury pressed him on, down another alley. Mud sucked at his shoes. The odor of urine fouled his nostrils.

A pig squealed, and from somewhere in the darkness, a man cursed. Roman paid no heed to any of this.

The Shadow was less than a rod ahead and losing ground. He disappeared around a corner. Roman bolted after him.

Hell fire! Suddenly his prey was almost out of sight. Roman put on a final burst of speed and barreled down on the flagging runner as if he were standing still.

Closer. Closer, until, without taking time to think, to draw an extra breath, Roman leapt.

He hit the man's back dead on, bowling him over with sheer impetus.

"What the 'ell?" grunted the man, but Roman was in no mood for explanation.

The man was huge. Both tall and fat. Roman rolled him over with some difficulty, puffing all the while and wondering how the hell this tub of a man had led him such a wild chase.

"Where is it?" Roman rasped.

"What the 'ell?" the man said again, his eyes showing wide rings of fear in the darkness.

"Where's the necklace?" Roman panted. But just then he heard a noise behind him. He knew he should turn, knew he should duck, but his muscles were weary, his reactions slowed.

Even as he twisted something hit him like a sledgehammer to his skull. Pain erupted in his head, crashing his brain with bright lights and clanking sounds. But the agony didn't last long. The noises drifted to silence, and darkness came for him.

"'Bout time ya wake up, Scotsman."

Roman heard Betty's voice above the clatter of pain that echoed in his cranium. He tried to sit up, but the clatter turned to an insistent clang.

She pressed him back down. "Was I you, I'd stay put lest ya bust your 'ead wide open."

"What happened?"

"Ya been 'it over the 'ead."

Memories bloomed in painful colors. "The

Shadow," he whispered. "I had just caught him when someone hit me from behind."

"The Shadow, 'ell," Betty snorted. "Ya attacked poor old George. Near scared him into 'is grave. 'E and Birley was just 'eading 'ome. Lucky for George, Birl 'eard 'im 'ollerin; otherwise, who knows what ya would 'ave done ta 'im?"

"George?" Roman tried to shake his head, but the cacophony of pain discouraged such a bold idea.

"What the 'ell were ya doing, Scottie?"

"The Shadow," Roman murmured. Reality was a slippery thing. Exhaustion and pain seemed more real, unconsciousness far more tempting. "He was there, just outside yer house."

"The Shadow?" Betty opened her eyes wide. Roman could see her face clearly, which was of some comfort to him considering the resounding clatter in his head. "Outside me own 'ouse?" she said as if dazzled, then laughed. "Mayhap 'e was coming ta see *me*. I suspect I should be fair put out that ya scared 'im off. Could be 'e wanted ta take me away from it all. Come and live with 'im in comfort, aye?"

She laughed again. Roman scowled. "How the hell did I get ta yer house?"

"George and Birley brought ya. And lucky they did, too. Cause Backrow ain't no place ta be takin' a nap."

"Backrow?" Roman fingered his aching skull, and found, to his surprise, that there were no gaping holes. "Where's that?"

"'Tis where foolish Scotsmen go when they're tired of livin'," Betty said, pushing his hand away. "What the devil were ya thinkin'?"

"I told ye . . ." Roman began, but his own frustration increased the pain in his head, and things were far too blurry to understand, much less try to explain. "Why did they bring me here?"

She shrugged. "Ol' George ain't too bright, but 'e's got a good 'eart. Seems 'e didn't want ta see ya killed in your sleep. Despite the fact that ya'd just scared the livin' soul out of 'im. Once Birley knocked ya cold, they recognized ya from the Red Fox and figured I'd see ta ya.

"Guess there's some advantage ta dressing in that little gown of yours, Scotsman. It makes ya stand out in a crowd."

"It's a plaid," Roman said. It seemed as good a thing to argue about as any. Nothing made sense anymore. Nothing was simple.

"Why do ya wear it?"

He opened one eye to peer at her. Dressed in a voluminous white nightgown, she looked different, younger, innocent. Her hair was the color of spun gold, falling in static waves about her shoulders.

"Why do ye wear *that*?" he asked.

"I was sleepin' afore I was so rudely awakened."

"Ye see," he said, turning his gaze to the ceiling. It was pitched in shadow, as was so much of this strange world he'd fallen into. "With a plaid, ye dunna need separate clothes ta sleep in and wake in. Ye simply unbelt the thing and use it for a blanket. 'Tis a practical tool, as is everything Scots."

"Truly?" He could hear the laughter in her voice. "Is that what ya are then, Scotsman? A practical tool?"

He turned toward her. In the irregular, flickering light of the candle, she no longer looked merely bonny, but breathtakingly beautiful, with a regal innocence that stunned him. "Who are ye?" he murmured.

"Who am I?" Her face became immediately somber. Taking a damp cloth from a nearby bowl, she touched it to the bump on his head. He realized now that he was in her bed while she knelt on the floor beside him. "Are there other things you've forgotten, Scotsman?"

Taking her wrist in his hand, he pulled it to his chest. Their gazes met. "I didna mean it like that, lass. In fact . . ." He paused, thinking. "I remember everything I've learned about ye. The way ye look as ye sway between the tables at the inn. How yer eyes darken when yer angry. The sound of yer laughter when yer teased. But I wonder, who are ye truly, lass?"

Their faces were mere inches apart. "I'm Betty." Her breath was a soft fan of air against his skin. "No one else."

"Then why am I here?"

She shook her head in confusion.

"Ye didn't need ta take me in, lass. Ye could have turned me away. Why would ye care if I live or die?"

"Do ya think I got no 'eart just because I'm a 'ore?" She tried to pull her hand away, but he held it firmly.

"On the contrary, lass. I think ye have the heart of an angel. And I wonder how."

"How what?"

"How ye remain untouched?"

For just a moment—for one frail, fleeting second, he could see all the way to her soul. But in an instant, it was locked carefully away, and she laughed. "Ya must a 'urt yer 'ead real bad if ya think I'm untouched, luv."

"I wonder," he murmured.

"Well don't. I could teach ya things to make your mama shudder."

He canted his head. Surprisingly, it felt better. "Consider me yer eager student then, lass."

She rose with a snort and pulled her hand from his. The vixen from the Red Fox had returned, but she seemed smaller somehow, more fragile. "Ain't I told ya about 'arry?"

"Ahh, aye," Roman said. "Yer duke."

She almost seemed to wince, but rallied speedily, and said, "Yeah. 'E won't like ya bein' 'ere."

Roman was silent for a moment. Perhaps he would be unwise to tell her what he'd learned, but it seemed he'd been unwise ever since coming to Firthport. Why change now?

"There seems to be a limited number of dukes in these parts," he said softly. "I asked around. There is na one named Harry."

For a moment she remained expressionless and motionless. But then he noticed the brightness of her eyes and the tremble of her bottom lip. "Are ya sayin' 'e lied ta me about 'is name?"

Roman scowled. She'd said she was too smart to be in love with this man, but he knew now that she'd lied. He saw it in her face. Whoever the lucky bastard was, she was not only faithful, but infatuated. "I mean he's not a duke," he said softly. "There are na dukes in Firthport."

She laughed shakily. "Not a duke? That's . . . ridiculous. 'E told me 'e was, but that I couldn't tell no one about 'im. Told me 'e loved me, that 'e wanted ta make me 'is wife, only 'e couldn't on account of 'e was already married."

"Betty . . ." Roman stood up and stepped toward her. "I'm sorry."

"You're lyin'," she said, but her tone was high-pitched, and she backed away. "You're lyin' cause ya want me ta betray 'im."

Roman stopped. "I'm not lying, Betty. I talked ta people who would know. They said there's no duke in Firthport or anywhere near."

"You're just sayin' that cuz ya think ya can toss me on me back then."

Roman shook his head. "I wouldna do that, lass. And I wouldna lie."

"Yes, ya would. I know ya would. I know 'e loves me, and . . ." Her words faltered, and her face fell into her upraised hands. "Sweet Mary, I knew this would 'appen. I knew it would," she sobbed.

Roman stepped awkwardly forward. She melted into his arms like snow in sunshine.

" 'E said 'e loved me. 'E said 'e did. But 'e 'adn't been 'ere for months. Every day . . . every night, I told myself, 'e'll come. And then last night . . ." She shook her head and sniffed against his shoulder. Her arms were tight and strong against his back. "Tonight, 'e did. It was so sweet. So fine. But then 'e ups and says, it's over. All over! 'E didn't 'ave no feelings for me at all. 'E was only usin' me," she sobbed.

"There now, lass," Roman soothed, stroking her hair. It felt as smooth and soft as kitten fur. "There now. Na man could be a man and na have feelings for ye."

"Yes 'e could. I'm just . . . nothin', nothin' at all."

"Yer a woman, Betty." He stroked her hair again. "Soft and kind and giving. And that's the best this world has ta offer a man."

She sniffed again. He stroked again.

"A beautiful woman with softness and fire and laughter. Na man could wish for more."

" 'E said someday 'e'd take me away. 'E said 'is wife would never 'ave ta know. But 'e's been lyin' all along."

"He's the Shadow, isn't he, Betty? That's why ye said there was na such man?"

"The Shadow?" She chuckled, but the sound was dull and muffled against his shoulder. "Oh, 'e'd laugh if'n 'e 'eard ya say that. 'E'd laugh, 'e would. 'E liked ta think 'imself a brave adventurer, but 'e barely 'ad enough nerve ta venture out alone in the midst of the night. The littlest thing scared 'im. In fact, if 'e 'eard a noise, 'e'd up and run."

Roman scowled over her shoulder. So the man he saw last night was not the Shadow at all, but only some frightened little weasel of a man who would use Betty's lovely body then break her tender heart.

"Is that . . ." Betty drew away slightly. Her face was filled with anguish. "Ya thought the Shadow was my lover. That's why ya walked me 'ome that night. That's why ya've been 'angin' about. Ya was 'opin' ta catch the Shadow."

"Nay. I . . ." Roman began, but she backed abruptly out of his arms.

"Ya were 'iding out there in the dark, just waitin' like a spider when 'arry left 'ere. Then ya chased 'im down. Ya weren't interested in me at all. Ya were tryin' ta use me just like 'e did."

"Nay, Betty, I . . ."

"Well!" She laughed. The sound was harsh. "Ain't ya the bloomin' idiot! All this time believin' in the Shadow when Dagger's men probably took the jewels in the first place. And 'ere 'arry fooled ya just like 'e fooled me. 'E led ya a merry chase all the way t' Backrow, and there Birley clonked ya on yer foolish 'ead."

"Betty, I didna mean ta—"

"Get out," she said. Her tone was low, but it was steady. "And don't come around again."

"Listen—"

"Out!" she shrieked, and, picking up the nearby bowl, flung it at his head.

Roman ducked, managing to escape the flying crockery. "If ye'll but listen, lass—"

"Out!" she screamed again. Searching wildly, she closed her hand over the flaming candlestick.

Roman liked to think he knew when he was beaten. Yanking the door open, he stepped outside and swung the portal closed behind him.

It had been one hell of a night. A wild chase. A concussion. A raving woman. And the realization that every clue he had about the Shadow was false. But she had said something . . .

Dagger probably took it anyway, she'd said. But Dagger who? That's what he had to find out.

Inside the house, Betty held her breath and listened to Roman's retreating footsteps.

Sweet Mary, it had been one hell of a night, and the best performance of her life.

Chapter 6

The building where Roman sat might loosely be called an inn. It was dark and dank, with a low, sooty ceiling and a peculiar stench.

Customers were scattered about the place, men with furtive, evil eyes. Hard, half-dressed women groped their current companions with poorly concealed boredom.

Disgust rose in Roman, but there were other emotions—darker, more sinister ones. Ones he dare not admit to lest he find himself pulled below that black undertow.

He thought he had dredged the bottom of the human pool before now, but Firthport's hideous underbelly had proven far more fetid than he could have imagined.

It had taken him three days to find this place, three days of searching, questions, threats.

But here he was, sitting in a dark corner, watching a man he had met only once before. The man who had tried, but failed, to steal the necklace.

Perhaps he had once been given a name. Perhaps by a mother who had loved him. But now he was known only as Scar, a name initiated by the line that ran diagonally through his right eyebrow and across his cheek.

Endless investigating had told Roman that Scar was one of Dagger's men. Had the scum lied to him on that night at the inn, then? Had he somehow stolen the necklace and pretended he had not? Could he have been that good an actor?

It was possible, but was it not more likely that another of the ring of thieves had taken it before-hand?

It didn't truly matter. For tonight Roman's search would come to an end. He quieted his impatience and waited. Scar looked nervous, edgy, and loud. Some hours ago he had teetered over the brink of intoxication. Now he was cantankerous and garrulous.

At frequent intervals, Roman could hear fragments of the boasts he threw toward his companions, a motley group of unimpressed, vapid-faced villains.

"Called me in personal," Scar said now. "Ta thank me for all my 'ard work, I'm thinkin'. I done 'im a good turn in Eddenberry that—"

"I 'eard ya botched up a job last week. Let the goods slip right through your fingers." A sallow-faced man took a deep swig from his mug and stared into his companion's eyes. "Maybe 'e's meanin' ta . . . *thank* ye for that."

Leaning across the table, Scar grabbed the other's shirtfront and rose with a jerk. "That weren't my fault. Ya 'ear me. It weren't."

The man hung limply from Scar's fist and smiled with dark teeth. "Ya gonna tell '*im* that?"

Even from a distance, Roman could see Scar's hand tremble. It fell away from the other's shirt. He glanced wildly about as if he saw wolves circling for the kill. "It weren't my fault."

"Then ya'd best go tell 'is Lordship that."

Scar licked his thin lips. "I'm tellin' ya, that ain't why 'e called me in."

"Sure of that, are ya?"

Scar nodded, but the movement was jerky and erratic.

"Then ya'd best 'urry on yer way so as ta collect that big reward 'e's waitin' ta give ya."

"I'll do that." Scar straightened. "I'll do that right now." He stumbled over his chair as he backed away, righted himself, and glanced back at his peers. "Don't be plannin' on seein' me round 'ere no more," he said, and disappeared through the door.

The sallow-faced man chuckled and drank again. "Oh, I won't," he said into his mug.

Rising noiselessly to his feet, Roman, too, exited.

The air outside was ripe with rotting fish and fetid urine. Windblown, tattered clouds skittered past a pale, half-moon. In a moment, Roman saw a dark figure hurrying away.

He followed at a distance until the light of the moon was completely quelled and darkness lay like a blanket about him. Then he hastened his step.

Ahead, Scar was muttering to himself as he stumbled along.

"Always done right by 'im. Always."

The alley down which they passed gave Roman little cover, still he had no choice but to follow. Tonight, he would meet Lord Dagger. Tonight he would learn the whereabouts of the necklace, no matter what it took.

"Snuffed that lad in Eddenberry with 'is own knife." His pace slowed and he chuckled. "Pretty thing. Even cleaned the blade 'fore givin' it over. But did 'e give me so much as a farthing for my trouble? No. 'E owes me, 'e does." He slowed even more.

The smell of the sea was sharp here. From a nearby building, light spilled from a window and a woman laughed, the sound high-pitched and eerie.

Scar turned toward the noise with a start, but kept stumbling along.

When he finally stopped, Roman pressed his back against a nearby wall and watched as Scar rapped his knuckles against the door of a long, low building made of stone. A warehouse of sorts, he would guess.

In the darkness, Scar shuffled his feet and knocked again, a bit louder. Finally, the door opened. No light seeped from the interior of the place.

"What do ya want?" The voice from inside the building was as deep as the night.

"I'm ... I'm 'ere," said Scar, his own tone high-pitched.

There was a moment's delay, then Scar disappeared inside.

Roman remained still for a moment, then, when nothing moved, he crept around the far side of the building. There he found another door. It was boarded up, but there was a chink in the crooked wooden boards. Squatting near the building, he peered inside.

A single candle had been placed upon a crate. But its light seemed to cower in the darkness.

"So ..." The person who spoke was unseen, but his voice was clear, and strange in some indefinable way. "Ya've come."

"Yeah, I ... I came. Like you asked." Scar's voice seemed loud. Standing near the candle, he'd removed his cap, which he twisted in his hands. The light, pale and feeble, illuminated little more than his face, setting off his scar in harsh relief.

Roman could see little by the exclusive light of the single candle. But he thought he could make out five other people, four standing, one seated on something high.

The silence was as dark as the room, heavy with tension.

"Ahh, Pete, Pete didn't say what ya wanted me for," Scar said, squirming slightly.

Silence again. Oppressive, long.

In the blackness, the seated man shifted slightly. Roman squinted, trying to discern a face.

"What do I want?" the seated man asked. "I wanted to thank ya, o' course."

"Yeah?" The relief in Scar's tone was nearly a tangible thing. "That's what I told 'em at the wharf. That's what I told 'em."

"Ya mentioned my name?"

"No! No!" Scar said. "I just said I'd done a good job, and I was in for a reward, is all."

"A reward. Aye. Ya'll get your reward. And do you know why?"

Scar licked his lips again and smiled, a ghoulish expression. "Cuz of the jeweled knife I got from the lad in Eddenberry?"

The shadowed man rose to his feet. Roman held his breath, waiting. It must be Dagger himself, but since he didn't enter the light, illumination was not shed on his identity.

"The jewels were paste," he said. "No, Scar, it's not the knife. 'Tis the fact that ya taught me somethin'."

"Me?" Scar was still smiling. "What could I have taught *you*?"

Dagger chuckled, pacing now, back and forth, just out of the circle of light. "Remember the necklace ya were to get for me?"

Scar's Adam's apple bobbed. The smile dropped from his face. "That weren't my fault." He shuffled his feet and gripped his cap tighter. "It weren't my fault. The necklace . . . it was gone when I found the Scotsman."

" 'Tis my point exactly. 'Tis what ya taught me. That no matter what . . ." He stopped and seemed to wave one arm in a semicircle. "Some . . . nobody can still ruin my plans."

"It was the Shadow!"

"Ya know, I think you're right. And what do ya think we should do about the . . . Shadow?"

"Kill 'em?"

Dagger chuckled. "I like the way ya think, Scar. Always have."

"I can do that for ya. I can kill 'im."

"Do you know who he is then?"

Scar grimaced a smile. "I can find out. I got me ways."

"Sure ya do. And ya've proven yourself useful to me in the past," he said, stepping forward.

"Yeah." Scar bobbed his head. "I've been useful."

Dagger stepped into the light. His back was to Roman, his face visible to Scar. Roman saw the villain's eyes widen as he looked at Dagger's face.

"But ya've failed," Dagger said, and lifted his hand in a casual signal.

Four men approached the circle of light. Candlelight glimmered off uplifted blades.

"No! Pete! God, Blacks, call 'em off!" Scar screamed, stumbling into the darkness. The men closed in. Shrieks and blows echoed against the stone walls. But in minutes the sounds of death subsided.

"Now . . ." Dagger's voice was husky, like a man just sated. "What should we do?"

"We'll find the Shadow," someone said, stepping toward the light.

"And how will ya do that? Even Angel can't convince the fence ta talk."

"Maybe Angel's gettin' soft. Maybe 'e'll 'ave ta step down and let a new man take 'is spot."

"And what do you mean by that, Blacks?"

"I mean, I been workin' 'ard for ya. And I got me own people on the job."

"Your own people?"

"Yer . . . yer people, I mean. And I 'eard of a 'ore. They say she knows the Shadow—intimate like."

"A whore?"

"Yeah, rumor 'as it."

"I'd hate to think my empire runs on rumor."

"We'll find 'im."

Dagger was silent for a moment, then, "Aye, ya will. Where does this whore live?"

"Don't know exactly, but she works a place called the Red Fox. I got Wads there now."

Chapter 7

Roman sprinted down the dark streets and back alleys of Firthport.

Betty!

Dear Jesu! They were after Betty! Somehow, they had associated her with the Shadow. How, he didn't know. Perhaps it was his own fault. Perhaps he would be to blame if she were harmed.

If! Hardly was there a question. Not after what he had just witnessed.

Roman's lungs burned. He'd seen a good many cold-blooded deeds. But never had he witnessed anything like tonight.

If they would do that to one of their own, what more would they do to get information from Betty? She knew nothing of the Shadow. Could tell them nothing at all.

Down one more alley, across a street. A dog barked. Roman careened around a drunken man who stumbled in his wake. And then there it was. The Red Fox.

He crashed through the doors. Only three people remained in the common room.

"Betty!" he gasped. "Where's Betty?'

A man squinted at him through blurry eyes a moment before his head drooped to the table.

Another watched him. "Ya got it bad for her," he said.

"Where is she?"

A large man with a spattered cloth tied about his waist entered. "What's all this racket about then?"

"Betty!" Roman rasped. "I need ta know where she is."

The big man scowled, stepping closer. "Why—"

But Roman had no time for delays. He charged across the room and into the kitchen. One glance around made him fear the worst. "Where is she?"

"Here now—" the cook began, but Roman grabbed the man by the shirtfront and growled, " 'Tis life or death."

"She's . . . she's just left."

"To her home?"

"Where else?"

Faces blurred as he ran past the tables. Outside, the air seemed tense, waiting. On he ran. Irregular cobblestones tilted him off-balance. Exhaustion threatened to overcome him. A scream split the night. It ripped through the darkness, then halted in mid-shriek.

Dear God, don't let me be too late!

There! Up ahead, a cluster of people jostled about. A dark form jolted away.

"Grab 'er!" someone croaked.

A man gave chase. He caught her about the waist. Betty screamed again.

Roman was close now. He slowed to a walk, trying to control his breathing enough to speak.

" 'Ello mates!" Roman's Firthport accent was poor, but mayhap they would chalk it up to intoxication. In the darkness it would be difficult to tell that he wore a plaid and was not one of them.

The nearest man jerked about to squint at him in the darkness. Something gleamed in his hand. " 'Oo the 'ell are you?"

"Me?" Praise God! She was alive, still standing. That much Roman knew. But her face was deathly pale in the blackness, and she stood absolutely immobile, as if she were in shock. If he gave her an opportunity, would she be capable of running? "Dagger sent me."

"The 'ell 'e did!" said the man with the knife. He seemed to speak for them all. Was he the man Blacks had sent? What was his name? Wads? 'Twas Roman's best guess.

"Blacks may trust ya, Wads, but there is others that thought I should come."

The nearest man tried to peer through the darkness, but made no objection to the name. "Who thought that?"

"I'm sure you'll understand if'n I don't care ta say."

The moon had found a hole in the tattered clouds. It shone against his back. By its light, Roman could see the man's scowl.

"Why'd ya come?"

"Maybe thems higher up wanted ta make certain ya didn't botch things up," Roman said smoothly. His breath was returning, and with it, a strategy.

"What's your name?" asked the second man.

Betty was held with her arms behind her back. Roman could make out the pale fabric of her gown stretched tight across her chest.

"Name's Angel," Roman said, remembering the man mentioned in the warehouse. The man that was trying to get information from the fence.

There was a sharp gasp from the nearest villain.

Roman forced a chuckle. He needed a weapon, something bigger than the dagger in his garter. "Ya 'eard of me then?"

"I . . . I 'eard of ya. But I thought ya was busy—with other things."

"Other things haven't worked out. I'll need the girl."

"She ain't no girl," said the man holding Betty. He twisted her arm and she screamed in pain. "She's a 'ore."

The other two chuckled. Roman tried to follow suit, but his own humor sounded rather rusty, like a hinge too long unused.

"Hand over the girl," he said, but he'd lost his accent and with it, his credibility.

"You ain't Angel," said the nearest man, bringing up his knife. "'Oo are you?'"

Roman took a step closer, smoothly, slowly. "Maybe I'm the Shadow."

A man gasped and then tried to stab him.

In that instant, Roman pulled the dagger from his garter. It flashed from hiding, sank into flesh and sliced upward, ripping from hip to ribs.

Roman launched himself at the second man with a snarl. The villain swung a club, but Roman danced back, then sank his blade deep into the man's throat. He went down gurgling on his own blood.

Roman straightened. His body vibrated with bloodlust, sang with it, revelled in it!

"Come any closer, and I'll kill the 'ore. I swear I will," warned the third man, but the knife he held at her throat shook.

Roman laughed. The sound was deep and unearthly. He was Satan incarnate. Nothing could stop him. "Kill her then," he said, his voice barely audible in its deep timbre.

"What?" croaked the villain.

"As you said, she's just a whore. It doesn't matter to me if she lives or dies. But the Shadow can't let his competition go unchecked. *You*, I'll have ta kill."

For a moment the villain was paralyzed. But suddenly he thrust Betty away from him.

She shrieked as she fell.

Roman bounded after the villain with a snarl. Death! Blood!

Then reality took hold. Sanity settled in.

Roman turned like one in a haze of confusing emotions. "Betty." She lay very still. He hurried toward her. "Betty?" He squatted near her, but she didn't answer.

Ever so gently, he turned her over. Her face was lax in the moonlight, devoid of pain, for she was unconscious. He felt her throat for a pulse. It was there, strong but erratic.

Scooping her into his arms, he glanced at the men on the ground. They lay sprawled like broken marionettes, black pools of blood spreading from their bodies.

Bloodlust boiled up again, demanding, screaming. Betty moaned in Roman's arms, drawing him back to sanity. He pulled her to his chest and rose. She was light, limp, silent. The night slipped past him. In minutes he was at her house.

It wasn't easy getting the key from her hiding spot, but he managed, unlocked the door, and stepped inside. A candle burned, illuminating her face, the pale stretch of her neck.

He crossed the room and laid her on the bed. She moaned again but failed to open her eyes. A blackish bruise had formed on her brow. A trickle of blood was smeared down her throat.

She was wearing the same pale green gown as the day before. He loosened the laces and slipped open the bodice, revealing more of her curves and tempting him with hidden treasures.

Bloodlust had given way to lust of another sort. He clenched his hands to fists. There was evil in his blood—evil called forth by this sinister place!

But no. Though his uncle had been depraved, he was not of that ilk. He was the son of Fiona's heart. She had said it was so. He drew another deep breath. His hands shook.

The wickedness of Firthport's underbelly called to the dark side of him. But he had to fight it. He had to leave this helltown before it was too late, before he found out what he truly was, what he truly could be.

But circumstances or the devil himself held him there. And Roman had a mission to accomplish first.

Thus, he slipped Betty's bodice downward to examine her more thoroughly. She gasped and moaned.

Carefully, he tugged her sleeves free. Her right arm lay at a peculiar angle. Hell fire! He knew little of mending fractures. Still, there was nothing he could do but slide his hand up her arms and feel for breakage. Nothing felt peculiar in her arm.

But her shoulder was strangely twisted. It was dislocated. Roman was suddenly certain, for he had seen an old soldier sustain just such an injury. He had been holding the lead of a stallion that had been distracted by a passing mare; the stud had tossed his head in the air. The sound of the man's shoulder popping could be heard from a distance of ten rods. He had stood in shocked disbelief for a second, then fainted dead away.

Betty had withstood the pain better than the old soldier had. But there was no time to waste now, for though Roman had watched Fiona grind Bernard's arm back into its socket, he had been a lad of no more than twelve years. The memory was dim. Still . . .

Reluctantly rolling her onto her side, Roman grasped her upper arm in one hand and placed his other palm upon the joint.

Setting his teeth against the pain of his patient, he twisted the arm forward. Betty jerked beneath his hands and wailed. The sound was high-pitched and agonized. God help him! Sweat dampened his brow, but he pulled back on the limb, pushing as he went and praying with a fervor that all would be well.

The bone slipped into the socket with a muffled pop. Roman stood for a moment, his hands remaining where they were, his breath coming hard. So God had not yet abandoned him to the evils of Firthport. Roman set Betty's arm back across her body.

His gaze touched her breasts. The tops of them were just visible above her loosened bodice. They looked pale and smooth and delicately female. Ever so gently, he reached out to touch her. The Norseman at the Red Fox had been right, it seemed, she was as soft as a rose petal.

Lust struck him again but with a softer stroke now, and almost tenderly. The poor lass. Surely she had not deserved such abuse. His fingers skimmed upward, across her collarbone, along the smooth length of her neck. Certainly such a lass could find better employment than what she had. Especially now that her lover had left her. Perhaps after all this was behind him, he could help find her a better occupation, or at least a decent man. Surely there was someone in Firthport who would want her. True, she was plump, but . . .

His gaze skimmed over her arms. In his rush to mend her, he had failed to notice that they were slim and delicate. He pulled the bodice farther aside and saw now that beneath her gown, she wore a strange, white garment. It was constructed of a lumpy fabric that lay in ungainly rolls against her skin.

Pulling the bodice away, he saw that padding

stretched from her shoulders on down. He peeled it quickly away, removing the skirt as he went, until she lay naked and pale beneath his hands.

Roman stared. Why would a whore shield such a body as this with layers of padding? Why would a whore want to appear fat and misshapen? And tall. Her shoes had heels as tall as his hand was wide.

Betty awoke with a shriek, clutching her shoulder and trying to sit up.

"Lass," Roman said, bending over to hold her still. "Yer safe now."

She glanced wildly about, her eyes wide with shock and pain.

"Yer home," he said, smoothing his hand down her hale arm. "Safe."

But she shook her head. "They know," she whispered. "They know."

"Know what?"

Her gaze clasped onto his, held. "How did I get here? Did they follow us?"

"They didna follow us, and I carried ye, lass. Yer . . ." Their bodies were very close. Hers seemed small and soft against his. "Yer lighter than I would have guessed. A fact for which the padding may be accountable."

"They'll find me. They'll come."

He scowled, holding her still. "They dunna know where ye live, lass. That much I know for certain. Ye are safe from them, at least for a time."

She drew a deep breath, relaxed a little, then gasped as she viewed her own nakedness.

"Yer ahh . . ." He cleared his throat as he dragged a blanket over her legs and higher. "I fear yer arm was twisted from its socket. I ahh . . ." He shrugged, trying to explain her lack of clothing, "I had to press it back in."

She hugged her hurt arm closer to her body

while tugging the woolen to her chin. "And what was wrong with my legs?" she asked.

Roman cleared his throat again. "Na a thing, lass. Ye can take me own word on that."

She blushed. He saw the color, pink and soft, staining her cheeks like the first light of dawn.

"Why do you pad your clothing?" he asked softly.

She licked her lips and darted her gaze about the room. "I think that is hardly your affair."

He shrugged. Her cheeks were still colored, and he could not help but smooth a finger down to her chin. "It could be said that ye owe me a favor, lass."

The blush drained from her cheeks. "What . . . did you have in mind?"

Was there fear in her eyes? And if so, why? What kind of whore would be afraid of the intimacy between a man and a woman?

"In truth, lass," he said softly. "Seeing ye thus gave me enough pleasure. I ask for no more than a bit of honesty."

She pulled a deep breath through her mouth. Her shoulders relaxed marginally. "Did you . . . Did you kill them?"

Roman drew his hand reluctantly away and rose to his feet. Memories flooded back, and with them, self-incrimination. He could have merely wounded them. He could have frightened them away. "Aye," he said, turning as he crunched his hands into fists. "They are dead."

"Thank you."

Roman turned back. "Dunna thank me."

"Why?"

"Because ye dunna ken what I am."

"Then what are you, Scotsman?"

"I . . ." His throat felt tight. "I didna kill them for ye."

"You knew them?"

"Nay," he said. "I knew them na. I but knew their kind."

She seemed to have relaxed a bit. "Tell me, Scotsman, are ya always so confusing?"

"I am usually neither confused nor confusing," he said, turning away. "I fear Firthport brings out the worst in me." They were difficult words to say, but hearing them gave him some relief, allowed some feeling of normalcy.

"So tell me, Scotsman," she said softly. "This is yer worst?"

He turned slowly back, finding her eyes. "I killed them, lass, for na reason."

"I like to think my life is worth something."

Self-doubt galled him, but her beauty soothed the raw, emotional wounds. Still, he did not deserve to be soothed. "Ye misunderstand, lass. I did not kill them for ye."

"They had no quarrel with you, Scotsman."

"I ken that but—"

"Why were you there if not to protect me?"

"I . . ." In the beginning he had come to protect her. But in the inferno of the battle, he had lost control. 'Twas an unforgivable sin. "I didna have ta kill them," he said.

She watched him very closely. "Ahh. So ya think ya could have just asked them nicely to leave me be, I suppose."

Roman said nothing.

"They would have killed me, Scotsman," she said softly. "Without regret, without feeling, they would have killed me, had it not been for you."

Her words gave something back to him—something that had been lost in the alley.

"Why, lass?" he asked softly. "Why would they kill ye?"

She laughed, but the sound was hollow. "Because they were Dagger's men."

Roman shook his head. "Who is this Dagger?"

She remained silent for a moment. "I thought ya knew. Ya told them as much."

"Tonight I saw . . ." He paused. The memory seemed little more than a black dream. "The night the necklace was stolen, three men broke into my room." He turned away, confusion crowding in. "But the necklace was already gone. I remembered one of the men's faces and followed him to Dagger."

"No!" She gasped the word.

Roman turned toward her in surprise. "What's wrong, lass? Is it yer arm?"

"My arm?" She laughed aloud, but her face was pale. "You don't know who you're dealing with, Scotsman."

He relaxed a smidgen. "I've some idea."

"He'll kill you," she whispered. "Or worse."

Taking a few steps, he approached her bed. "Would ye care, lass?"

"Stay away from him. Leave Firthport." Her eyes were bright with emotion.

What did those eyes show? Fear? For him? "I canna."

"Why?"

"Because I made a vow."

"Is it worth your life?"

He paused a moment, then, "Aye, lass. It is."

"Then you're a fool."

He watched her face, alive with a passion he could not understand. "Is there nothing for which ye'd risk yer life, lass?" he asked softly.

"No."

"Ye lie."

Their gazes held a moment longer, but then she turned away. "And you're wrong, Scotsman.

There's nothing more valuable than my own skin."

Her profile looked cameo perfect in the light of the flame. He could not help but reach out and touch her cheek. "Mayhap yer right, lass," he murmured. "'Tis naught more valuable than your skin."

She turned slowly back to him. "I meant to me."

"'Twas my meaning also. Mayhap I would feel that there's nothing more valuable to me than yer skin."

She swallowed. He watched a blush stain her cheeks. "I 'adn't 'eard that Scots were charming."

He paused, as surprised as he was flattered. "And I haven't seen a whore blush."

She turned away.

The room fell sharply quiet.

"I suppose ye'd like ta retract yer last opinion of me," he said softly.

She turned back with a shrug. Her lips, full and bright, were lifted in a small self-deprecating smile, but he wondered if he saw a hint of sadness in her eyes, not quite hidden away. "I think most would agree that saving my life was a rather charming thing to do, Scotsman, whether ya call me 'ore or not."

"Lass . . ." She seemed very small suddenly. Small and helpless and in need of someone more clever than himself. "'Tis sorry I be."

"That ya saved me life."

Roman made a noise of self-disgust and closed his eyes. "Forgive me, lass, I'm na good at this sort of thing."

"And what sort of thing might that be?"

"Wooing women."

Her mouth fell open, and she blinked.

Roman frowned. "'Tis a bad sign that ye couldna even guess what I was attempting ta do."

She laughed. "Scottie, no one woos a 'ore."

He found her gaze with his own. "Then yer na a whore, lass. Because that be exactly what I'm trying ta do."

"Well..." She sounded breathless and looked the same. "Don't."

"Why?"

"Because I..." She shook her head. "I'm..."

"Yer a wee, bonny lass," he said. "Soft." He ran a finger gently over her bare shoulder. "And kind, I think, though ye wouldna admit it."

"I am not kind," she said angrily.

"I said ye wouldna admit it. How well I know ye already."

"Ya don't know me at all, Scotsman."

"Then tell me about yerself, lass."

She shook her head sharply.

"And why not?"

"Because I will not waste my time on a dead man."

He raised his brows in surprise. "Do I smell that bad then?"

She snorted. "Make jokes if ya like. But if'n ya dare tangle with Dagger, yer as good as dead."

He watched her eyes. They were beautiful beyond description. "Ye dunna give me much credit, lass, considering the circumstances."

"Which are?"

He shrugged. "Two of his men are dead. Do ye forget the battle so quickly?"

"I haven't forgotten," she whispered. "But there are more. Scores of them. Ya can't win. Not if ya challenge 'im straight on."

"Then how can I win?"

She opened her mouth, then shook her head as if to retract the words. "I didn't say ya could."

"But what were ye thinking?"

"Nothing."

"What do ye know of this Dagger?"

"I know he kills for pleasure. And he has a ring of thieves that do the same. That's enough."

"Who is he?"

"No one knows that," she said. "No one dares even speak his name."

"Mysteries," Roman said. "Firthport seems full of them. No one knows the Shadow. No one knows Dagger."

"The Shadow's not real," Betty said, her tone harsh, her brow bruised and furrowed. "But Dagger is. He's as real as he is deadly. Stay away from him. Even if ya got the necklace, even if ya found it, it'd do ya no good, cause 'e wants it, and 'e won't stop till 'e finds it. It'd only get ya killed the sooner. Go home," she whispered. Her words fell into silence. The candle hissed beside her. "Please," she added softly.

"Ye see," he said, reaching out again to trace his fingers gently down her cheek. "Ye are kind."

"And you're stupid," she said, angrily swiping his hand away. "Why won't ya leave?"

"Me duty lies here. I made a vow."

"To who?"

"Me mother."

She stared at him for a moment, then laughed aloud. "And would your mother not rather ya keep yourself alive than fulfill your stupid vow?"

Roman remained silent for a moment. The Highlands were there in his mind suddenly, easing his soul. "'Tis hard to say what me mother would think. She is a . . . unique woman."

"Go home, Scotsman, before it's too late."

"It's too late, now, lass."

"No!" she said, grasping his shirt with her left hand. "I will not be responsible for your death. I will not."

He stared into her eyes. "How could ye take that responsibility?"

"Don't ya see?" she asked, shaking with feeling, but just then she realized his gaze had fallen away.

Her blanket had deserted her, it seemed, and his gaze, green and intense, had been snared by her breasts.

She swallowed hard, but she did not draw the blanket up, for perhaps this was her only chance. "What'll it take, Scotsman?" she asked softly. "What'll it take ta convince ya ta leave?"

His gaze lifted to hers. Fire burned in his eyes. She watched him tighten his jaw, watched him clench his fists and hold himself back.

"Dunna tempt me, lass," he murmured hoarsely. "Ye dunna ken what I'm capable of."

Dear God, forgive her! "Then show me," she said, and slipped the blanket from her body.

Chapter 8

As a child, Roman had seen a brooch made of ivory found in a distant land and brought to the Highlands by a thousand twisted trails. He had thought it the most beautiful thing on earth, smooth, precious, lovely.

Her skin was like that. By the light of the single candle, it glowed as if with a fire of its own. She'd lost her coif and half her pins in the melee with Dagger's men. Her golden hair hung in loops, half-upswept, half-down.

It was the hair that he could not resist. Perhaps it was the incongruity of its wild disarray against the neat slimness of her body. Perhaps it was the sheer femininity that drew him. Sitting on the saggy mattress, he dipped his fingers into the wild mass, releasing the surviving pins. The golden strands sighed across his hands, soft as a kitten's fur against his fingers and seeming to caress his very soul. He drew a careful breath, breathing her scent, feeling the very essence of her as he burrowed deeper, sliding his splayed fingers against her scalp.

Her breathing was raspy. Her eyes fell closed. Her head dropped back a bit as she leaned upon one palm.

"Lass." He could not help but lean closer and whisper something to her, for her beauty touched his soul. He slipped his hand onto her neck, caressing, soothing. Her flesh was soft and warm. Her throat was slim, long, elegant. He traced its sharp tendon with one finger, then slid lower, over her collarbone and softly, ever so softly along the outside curve of her right breast.

She shivered violently against his touch and breathed hard, fast exhalations that rasped softly against his face.

Roman slid his fingers around her sides until he felt the sharp ridge of her backbone. He skimmed his fingers lower, slowly lower, until she arched away from his hand, pressing her breasts upward.

They were beautiful, firm, capped by taut, rosy-hued nipples. He leaned closer, holding hard to the reins of self-control, making each movement carefully until his lips touched the crest of one breast.

She shrieked softly and jerked beneath him.

"Lass." Roman raised his head, scrutinizing her face. It was taut with intensity and rapt concentration, beautiful beyond words in the glow of the tallow candle. "Lass," he repeated, tightening his arm where it lay about her back. She felt no more substantial than a flower, no more corrupt than a sanctuary. "Who are ye?"

Her eyes snapped open like one who's been slapped. "Betty," she said, her tone raspy.

He could not help but smile, for there was passion as bright as a rose in her face. "Yer more than a simple name, lass. More than . . ." He shrugged, finding no words. "Who are ye?"

She shook her head, looking disoriented. "I'm . . ." She exhaled again, sharply, and tentatively lifted her injured arm to touch the leather lace that secured his simple shirt.

"Ye tremble," he said softly. "Why?"

She shifted her eyes to his chest, clumsily loosening his laces as she did so.

"Why?" he whispered again, leaning closer still so that only a breath of distance remained between their faces. "Do ye tremble with fear, or do ye tremble with passion?"

She pursed her lips and finally met his gaze. Her eyes were wide and wild. "I'm not . . ." She shook her head and paused. "I've not done this . . . with any but . . . Harry for quite some time."

He watched her face, the pain, the honesty, and in that moment he wanted nothing more than to protect her from the harsh realities of the world, to hold her in his arms and keep her forever safe. But she was not some virgin to be coddled, and he must keep his head.

"Why do ye do it with me, lass?" he asked, sliding his hand languidly down her back.

She shivered again and closed her eyes. Roman cupped her buttock and she moaned, letting her lips part soundlessly as he caressed her.

He slid his hand lower, feeling the smooth length of her thigh. He lifted her leg, bending it toward him, feeling the velvet strength of it. Her knee was sharp, her calf smooth, her instep high, and her toes, as he slid his fingers down them, were tiny delicate pods.

Her hands gripped his shirt, bunching it in her fists and pulling it up. Its great length scraped upward until it lay in folds about his waist. She slipped her hand underneath to press her palm against his abdomen.

Roman sucked air between his teeth. His muscles were taut with tension and anticipation. Her hand slipped higher, over the rippled tension below his ribs to the trembling breadth of his chest. She brushed his nipple. He trembled more violently, then exhaled carefully, trying to remain sane, to think.

"Why me?" he asked again, but her hands were soft and warm, eager and skilled.

"Could I just . . ." Her breath was a soft fan of air against his cheek. Her eyes were closed. "Could I just . . . feel you against me?" she whispered.

He had to think, keep his head. But her lips were slightly parted and her breasts pale and hard-tipped.

He all but tore his brooch from his shirt and his shirt from his chest, before sitting silent to watch her.

Betty bit her lip, then slowly, tentatively, set her palm to his left pectoral. The flesh was marked with three long scars. The muscle leapt beneath her hand. She swallowed hard and almost drew away. But she must do this. She must. It wasn't that she wanted to. It wasn't that he drew at some part of her that she had long tried to disavow. It wasn't that his kindness wooed her or that his strength weakened her. But . . .

His shoulder was capped in muscle. His arm, heavy and taut, rippled beneath her fingers, and his chest, when she wandered back in that direction, was as tight as polished stone and adorned in the center with a strange amulet of sorts.

"Teeth," she murmured, lifting it from his chest. "I wondered what it was."

He opened his eyes. "Wondered? When did you see it?"

Sweet Mary! Had she lost her mind? She must be careful—and smart. Now was surely not the time to let down her guard. "At the inn," she said, trying to keep her tone even. "It lay outside your tunic for a time." She dared not look into his eyes. "'Tis a strange charm to wear about your neck."

He drew a deep breath and watched her. "It but

reminds me who I am, lass, and where I come from."

She forced herself to relax and finally lifted her gaze to his. His eyes were intense, mesmerizing.

Taking her hand in his, he turned the amulet so that they both viewed it clearly.

"A wolf," he said softly. "I was but a lad when it attacked me best of friends."

She could imagine him as a boy, laughing, carefree, before the world had caused the pain she sometimes saw in his eyes. "I'm sorry," she said softly.

"Ye dunna need ta be sorry, lass. I carried me Dora ta a healer. She recovered well and bravely."

Betty ran her fingers gently over the stripes on his chest. "Dora was a lucky girl ta have ya for a friend."

His eyes smiled, but his lips only tilted the slightest bit. "Dora was a hound."

She remained silent for a moment, thinking, examining him. "You risked your life to avenge a *dog*?"

"Aye." He nodded once. "But she was a good dog."

What kind of man was this? "You jest," she said softly.

"Rarely," he countered.

"Why would ya do such a thing, Scotsman?"

"She was me friend, was Dora, and a gift from me da."

She touched the trio of scars again. "And was the revenge worth the pain?" she asked.

He shrugged. Muscles danced in his arms and torso. "Killing the beast did great deeds for me reputation. Laird Leith dubbed me 'Wolf.'"

"They called ya Wolf?"

He nodded.

"And would that be a good thing where ya come from, Scotsman?"

The smile was back in his eyes. "When one grows up with a fighting Hawk and a charming Rogue, 'tis best ta have a wee bit of the beastie in ye, lass."

Beast? Is that what he was? A wolf? Cunning, ruthless, deadly? Memories of the night flooded back. "Ya didn't owe me anything, Scotsman," she whispered. "Why did ya help me?"

He drew a deep breath. His beard was dark and cropped close. Beneath the hair, his face was lean and sculpted, as if a fine artist had lovingly molded it in his hands. But more likely, the sculptor would have been a woman, creating the image of manhood.

"Maybe I did it simply to kill!" His tone was as deep as night, his expression suddenly harsh, but she shook her head and gently replaced the amulet against his chest.

" 'Tis not true," she said softly.

"And how do ye know that, lass?"

"I know men."

His hand touched her arm and smoothed downward, sparking sharp sensation along that limb and outward. "And what do ye know of me?"

He would be her bane! The end to all she had strived for for so long. The thought struck her suddenly, and she jerked.

"Lass?" he asked, looking puzzled.

"Go home, Scotsman," she said, tamping down her fear, pushing away the sudden premonition. "Before it's too late."

"Too late for what?"

"For you."

"But I've found something here that interests me," he whispered, gently cupping her breast. "A phenomenon. A mystery."

"A whore," she whispered, trying not to shiver. "I wonder."

Panic was beginning to rise, but she held his gaze with her own. "I'm offering myself ta ya, Scotsman. Isn't that enough proof?"

He touched her cheek again, softly, gently. "But ye've na said why, lass."

His eyes were deep and earnest, but he was dangerous. She had to remember that. And yet . . . "Ya don't know Dagger," she whispered. " 'E'll see ya dead. 'E will, if'n ya don't leave."

His hand stopped on her cheek. "So yer offering yerself," he said softly. "If I agree to go."

She forced a laugh. It didn't sound too unreal, considering the circumstances. "It seems real noble the way you say it, Scottie. But the truth is . . ." She lowered her gaze. He was built like a fine stallion, hard and lean and powerful. "Like I says, it's been a good long time for me, but for 'arry."

Despite her attempt to dismiss it, she could feel the heat of his gaze on her face. "Then there be na strings attached ta yer offer?" he asked.

Her heart was beating hard and fast. "Ya may think a 'ore ain't got no soul, Scotsman. But it ain't true."

She stared at him, smiting him with her gaze and hoping he'd turn away. But he did not. Instead, he watched her with eyes as steady and hard as a hunting wolf's.

She felt the blush of her emotions heat her cheeks. "I've done me own share of sinnin'," she said. "I won't 'ave yer death on me soul, too."

"So ye think I saved ye so that I could incur yer gratitude and collect yer debt. Ye think I calculated the risks and decided the possibility of death was worth a fuck with the Red Fox whore!"

Anger flamed within her like a windswept blaze. She raised her hand to strike him, but he had already caught her wrist in a casual grip.

Think! She had to think. Betty smiled, forcing her muscles to relax and raising her brows as if in concession. "And ya were right, Scottie," she purred. "I'm well worth the risk."

Their gazes burned. His grip tightened, and she felt it shake. Passion rode him hard, and she knew it. But in a moment, he dropped her wrist and pulled the blanket over her body.

Jerking to his feet, he turned away.

Confusing emotions battled within her. Something deep inside made her want to cry out to him, to pull him back to her, to feel the warmth of his body touch her soul. But good sense knew better. Still, despite the width of his bared back, the strength of his taut arms, he looked so alone. Like a boy in a man's body.

"Scottie," she said softly, against her will.

"Go to sleep," he said, without turning back. His tone was gruff, taut, hard-edged.

"With you here?" She almost laughed at the ridiculousness of the idea.

"What?" He turned abruptly toward her, his fists clenched, his eyes bright with anger and uneased passion. "Do ye think ye canna trust me?" he asked, stepping closer. "Do ye think mayhap I'll be unable ta keep meself from ye during the night?" His chest was bunched with muscle. "Is that what ye think? That a barbaric Scot like meself canna be trusted with a . . . with a body like yers?"

Betty swallowed and managed to force her gaze from the scarred width of his chest to the sparking intensity of his eyes. "Mayhap . . . mayhap I can't trust meself, Scotsman," she whispered.

Chapter 9

Roman stood gaping at Betty like a fish tossed abruptly into thin air. He blinked, feeling breathless and disoriented.

He was a Highlander, a diplomat, a barrister. He had skills. But not women skills. Whores were one thing. He'd had his share of bonny women, eager for his coin. There had been guilt, but somewhere in his soul, he had believed it right that he was there with them.

And perhaps somehow he thought it right that he was here with Betty. But only if he was with Betty the whore. Betty, the woman, was another matter. And her desire confused him. Other women had desired his coin and perhaps his position. But even Sharlyn, whom he had planned to marry, had not attempted to hide the fact that he did not interest her as a man. It would have been a marriage of the most convenience, useful for diplomatic and political reasons. But her father had found someone more diplomatically and politically desirable.

"Well . . ." he said, his tone sounding raspy to his own ears. "Well, I . . ." He tightened his fists, loosened them, tightened them again. He was acting like a child, and he knew it. "I'll be here." He nodded to the floor. "If ye need me." He swallowed, cleared his throat. "I mean . . . if yer in need of me ministrations . . ." He drew a deep breath and for a moment, considered knocking his head against the nearby wall. "Yer arm," he said. "Or . . . any other part of . . ."

Hell fire! He was an idiot when it came to women. "I'll just . . . I'll be going ta sleep now, lass." Before he made an even bigger ass of himself.

"Not 'ere, Scotsman," she said softly.

He canted his head. "What?"

"I said, ya can't stay 'ere."

He straightened slightly. She was wounded. Dagger's men might return. He was staying. And he was ever so grateful to find a firm disagreement to settle his mind on. "And why would that be, lass?"

She shrugged. Her shoulders were bare, distracting as she tugged the blanket slightly higher. "I won't 'ave ya interfering with business."

He lowered his brows. "Business. Ye said ye were closed for business. Because of Harry."

"Well, 'arry is gone, and a girl's got to make a living. I won't 'ave ya scaring away me . . . customers."

"Customers! Damn right I'll scare away yer customers," he growled, leaning into her face.

"Ya've no right ta interfere with my business," she hissed.

"Business!" He clenched his teeth, gripped his fists tight, then drew a deep breath as if calming himself. "What'll it take then?"

His change of pace, confused her. She scowled. "Take?"

He leaned closer, cupping her chin in his palm. "How much?"

"I offered myself once." She raised her chin and tried to look haughty. "Ya refused."

"I couldn't afford the conditions," he murmured. "But if we're talking coin, that's different. How much?"

"Go away, Scotsman. Ye've no right to me."

"I saved yer life." It seemed the argument had changed somehow, had shifted sides, but he couldn't seem to stop the words. True, he had saved her life, and, therefore, he owed her protection. It didn't make sense, not even to himself. Yet, somehow it seemed true.

"Ya saved me life," she spat. "But ya'll not own me soul."

"What the hell does that mean?"

"If'n we ... do it ... we do it on me own terms. Ya'll leave Firthport before the dawn."

He ground his teeth. "I made a vow ta finish what I started."

"Then ya'd best be about fulfilling it," she said. "Get out. I won't 'ave ya dying in me own place. Daggermen 'ave a tendency to make a terrible mess of a man."

Roman snorted. "And what do they do ta women?" She paled at his words, but it gave him little satisfaction, only an itching desire to take her in his arms. Instead, he steeled himself. "I'm staying, lass," he said, and bent to douse the flame.

"Don't snuff the light." She looked even paler now and smaller, like a child afraid of the dark. He opened his mouth, wanting to ask why, but she shook her head. " 'Tis a foolish habit to leave a light burning, I know. But 'tis mine."

"I have na wish ta be burned ta death in me sleep."

"So long as you're in Firthport, that'll be the least of your worries, Scotsman," she said softly.

He turned away with a snort and pulled his shirt back over his head. Loosening his belt, he removed his plaid, wrapped it about his shoulders, and settled onto the floor.

She watched him for a moment, then turned away, carefully pulling her nightgown over her head and wounded shoulder before lying down.

The night stretched into silence. Fatigue numbed Roman's thoughts. Dreams stole in. Soft and beckoning at first, they slipped into darkness, pulling him down with them, threatening, throttling.

Roman awoke to a scream. Reality flooded back. He yanked his blade from his garter and jerked to his feet.

The room was dark, but even so he could see the girl sitting upright on her bed. The villains were . . . He turned, crouched, ready. There was no sound but her ragged breathing.

Roman turned again, straightening slightly. "Betty?"

"No!" she screamed again. "Mam! Nooo!"

He rushed to her and grabbed her flailing arms to crush them between their bodies. "Betty! Betty! Wake up. 'Tis a dream."

She awoke with a jolt, her body stiff in his arms.

"All is well." He released her arms and gently stroked her cheek. " 'Twas a bruadair," he said, slipping into his native Gaelic. "A dream, lass, nothin' more."

"Da." She breathed the word like a prayer, softly burred into the darkness. "Ye came back for me, Da?"

Her eyes were as wide as a child's, her fingers tight with desperate strength as they tangled in his shirt.

"Shhh, lass," he soothed. "Shh. I'm here. Na harm will befall ye."

"Cork said . . . Cork said ye were dead, Da." Releasing one hand from his shirt, she raised it to his face, feeling the rough stubble of his short beard.

"But I say na. Ye wouldna leave yer little lass, for I be yer sunshine. Ye always say 'tis so."

"Shh, lass, ye've had a scare is all," he said.

With a moan, she clasped her arms about his neck, squeezing him close. "Ye'll na go again, will ye, Da? England be so cold and frightful. We'll go home, now. We'll go home."

Roman held her tightly to him and stroked her hair. "I'm here, lass," he crooned.

She snuffled once. Through her nightgown, he could feel the warmth of her breasts pressed against his chest.

"Da?" Her tone was uncertain now, small as an infant's. "Where is Mam?"

Roman closed his eyes. Who was this woman and what had she endured? "Betty." He said her name softly, but she stiffened instantly. He felt her throat constrict, her muscles tighten.

She pulled away slowly, as if afraid to look into his face. "Scotsman."

Her composure returned with shocking speed. But he didn't release her, couldn't quite force himself to relinquish his hold. "Lass," he breathed, watching her face in the darkness, " 'tis sorry I be."

She laughed abruptly. "Nay." She cleared her throat and tried again to pull from the shelter of his arms. " 'Tis I who should apologize. I . . . um . . ." She turned toward the guttered candle. "The light went out."

He touched her face again, wanting to draw back the child that needed him, that trusted him as he had so often wished he could trust. " 'Tis me own fault," he said. "I should have lighted another candle. But I didna know."

She laughed. The sound was no less haunted than the last. " 'Tis of no concern, of course," she said, finally succeeding in pulling from his grip and slipping her bare feet to the floor. He shifted his weight, allowing her to pull the blanket from beneath him. She drew it about her shoulders like a shield and walked to the trunk where the candle had once glowed. From a nearby shelf, she took a new taper and a flint and steel, but her hands shook. He saw it, and taking two steps toward her, settled his fingers over hers.

"Speak ta me, lass," he pleaded.

She kept her face averted. " 'Tis late, Scotsman. I am fatigued, 'tis all."

"Nay." Her hands felt cold beneath his. " 'Tis na all. Ye knew the dreams would find ye if the candle failed. They have haunted ye afore."

She moved away toward the dark fireplace. "They are dreams. Nothing more," she said, striking a spark from the flint and steel. It landed on a heap of fuzzy tinder, placed just so as if carefully tended for just such an occasion. The spark caught fire, blazed quickly.

"Nightmares be the dark beasts of memories come back ta haunt our sleep," Roman said softly.

She turned, her face a porcelain cameo against the backdrop of the small fire. "And how do ya know that, Scotsman?"

He crossed the floor to squat in front of her. Her blanket lay in folds about her, and her hair, soft as thistledown streamed about her shoulders in molten waves of gold. "The beasts come for me also," he said.

The tiny blaze crackled and grew. Her small face was somber.

"I'm sorry."

He took her hands. They felt clammy in his own. "As am I."

She drew a shaky breath, and he could not resist pulling her closer, so that she was cradled against his body. Although she felt stiff and uncertain, she did not draw away. "What are your beasts, Scotsman?"

He gazed over her head at the fire. "They were spawned long ago, lass, and best left ta sleep if they will."

"Long ago." She nodded. "But still they snarl and snap, waiting to devour me."

He tightened his arms about her. She felt small and fragile. "Yer da would na wish for his memory to haunt ye so." He settled onto his buttocks, shifting her between his legs and wrapping his plaid about both of them. "How did they die, lass?"

For a time, Roman thought she would refuse to answer, but finally she spoke. "He was an Irishman." She said the words softly, with the singsong burr that her father must have had. "A farmer."

The fire crackled again. She was cradled, warm and soft between his thighs.

"And yer mother?"

"She was as bonny as the spring flowers." She laughed, then sobered and swallowed. "He always said so. He had a small, gilt-framed portrait of her. I always thought it so lovely. They must have taken it. I never found it. Not after . . ." She swallowed. "Da always said Mam was the flower and I was the . . ." She paused.

"The sunshine," Roman murmured, remembering her words.

She turned toward him. There were no tears, just dry, hopeless sadness.

"They killed him," she whispered and closed her eyes. "Perhaps Grandfather hoped she would return home with them. Perhaps . . ." She shrugged, shaking her head. "But he did not know."

Roman stroked her hair, soothing her and himself. "Didna know what?"

"That she would choose to die rather than be left without him."

"No, lass," he crooned and closed his eyes to pull her closer still. "She didna take her own life."

"Nay." The word was small. "She went to save him from the fire. But . . ." She shook her head like one lost in another time. "The flames were so big—unearthly bright I thought. She would certainly die there. Certainly. And I could not force myself to go in."

"Oh, lass. Ye surely canna blame yerself. Ye were wise ta stay out."

"Wise," she whispered. "Aye. That I am. Wise enough to leave them to their deaths. Wise enough to survive by whatever means I might."

He exhaled softly, feeling her pain tighten his chest. Guilt was an old companion, but a poor friend that had given him no joy. "Ye canna let their deaths haunt ye."

She shook her head. " 'Tis not their deaths that haunt me," she murmured. " 'Tis their love."

"How so?"

She didn't answer, but sat very still. "Are ya married, Scotsman?"

"I was nearly so once."

"Did ya feel some love for her?"

"Love? Nay. But I would have given her a good life."

"Then why didn't ya?"

He watched the fire for a moment. "Her father found someone more desirable." Roman had never quite admitted the relief he'd felt, but he admitted it to himself now, in the silence that followed.

"And your parents, did they not share a love?"

The dark beasts of memories were hunting again. He beat them back. "Why do ye ask?"

" 'Tis said what a child learns at birth cannot be untaught. I fear it may be true, for I could not marry unless 'twas for true love," she whispered.

"And thus ye are alone?"

She nodded. "So ye see, what we learn as children we must forever bear."

"'Tis na true," he countered, "for me own parents were gentle folk, while I . . ."

"What?" she asked, touching his face. "Are ya saying ya are not gentle, Scotsman?" she asked. There was humor in her voice, as if her short acquaintance with him had shown her his true self. But she did not know him.

"Ye would be well advised na ta be so trusting, lass," he said dourly.

Now she laughed aloud. "Trusting? I think ya mistake me for someone else, Scot. There are many things said about me, but none would say I am too trusting."

The irony of her words was not lost on him, for she was cuddled in the intimate fork of his legs. "What do ye do with a man ye trust?"

"Ya'll never know," she said.

He smiled, though he didn't know why, and tugged her closer against his chest.

"Scotsman?" She touched the wolf teeth that hung from his neck.

"Aye?"

"The necklace ya 'ad at the inn—why did ya 'ave it?"

He scowled. For just a moment, he had forgotten his mission, reality, the world outside her door. If just touching her could do that, how much more would her kiss do? "Because women make fools of men," he intoned, glancing down at her, and finding to his surprise that his amulet had been loosed from his neck and lay in her small palm.

"How—"

"It must have come untied," she explained and casually handed it back to him. "It seems to me, men do a fair job of making fools of themselves, Scottie."

Her mind was like summer lightning, quick and bright and fascinating. He eased an arm about her back again. "My foster mother's family are called the MacAulays. David is her . . . cousin of sorts. A likable lad." He glanced down into her face as she watched him. Never had he been in such a position with a woman. And yet, never had he felt more free to talk. "I suppose ye dunna need ta hear the lad's lineage."

She smiled a little, the expression as soft as an angel's. "I listen with bated breath, Scotsman."

He smoothed her hair behind her ear. Why did such a simple touch make his heart sing? "The short of it is, young David became enamored with a woman of some substance."

"Enamored with?" Her smile lifted a bit more. "Might that be a Scottish term for something a bit more base?"

Roman grimaced. "David be a good lad, ye understand."

" 'E bedded the girl?"

"Aye."

She stared into space for an instant, then shook her head. "I fear I see no connection between a bit of fornication and a necklace worth a king's crown."

"It seems the lass's father has long coveted the necklace, and—"

"Sweet Mary," Betty sighed. " 'Tis a bribe to keep the scandal quiet."

" 'Tis more than that at risk," Roman assured her. " 'Tis David's very life."

Betty paled, letting her gaze drop from his face. "His life?" she murmured.

"Aye."

"Where is this David MacAulay being kept?"

"I know na."

"In a gaol? Black Hull, mayhap?"

"I dunna know."

"Pray 'tis not Devil's Port."

"Wherever David be, the lass's sire holds the key. I've but to give him the necklace and he will release my kinsman."

"But can't ya exchange the necklace for other pretty stones? Won't—"

Roman shook his head. "The lass's sire is in na humor to compromise. 'Tis the necklace or nothing."

Betty drew away from him, taking her warmth, his comfort, and rising abruptly to her feet. "He's fooling. Making ya sweat, is all."

"I dunna think so. Mayhap afore he would have been flexible, but it seems his daughter has raised his ire by insisting that she loves the lad." He raised his brows, watching her closer. " 'Tis said once ye've had a Highlander, ye'll na settle for less." He said the words to lighten her mood, but her face remained tense and solemn in the fire's dancing light.

" 'Tis a tight spot," Roman said, watching her pace. "But His Lordship has given me a score of days ta see the necklace returned."

"A score!" She stopped pacing to stare at him. "Ya'll not live that long, Scotsman. Not 'ere in Firthport. Not if Dagger wants ya dead."

"I'm flattered by yer faith in me, lass."

"Ya jest!" she said. "Because ya don't know 'im."

Roman remembered the warehouse, the terror, the smell of death. "I think I've some idea."

"Then leave. Now. Please."

"After I retrieve the necklace from Dagger and—"

"Ya don't even know Dagger has it!"

"If na him, then who?" Roman asked, frustration rising. "Surely na the Shadow, for ye say there is na such man."

She was silent, pale.

He watched her closely. "Is that na what ye said, lass?"

She shook her head slowly. "Nay."

"What's that?"

"Nay," she whispered. "There is no such man."

Roman rose slowly to his feet. "A man's life hangs in the balance as we speak, lass," he said softly. "A lie might tip the scale."

"There is no such man," she said again. Her face looked strained and ghostly white, her eyes wide and bright. "But—"

Footsteps suddenly sounded outside.

Roman glanced at her, then drew his blade and placed himself between her and the door.

"Let me in!" someone called from the far side of the door. "For God's sake, let me in!"

"Liam," she said, turning.

Roman grabbed her wrist. "I thought ye trusted no one."

"'Tis Liam," she said, pulling from his grasp. But he caught her wrist before she reached the door.

"Think, lass. What could he be wanting?"

"They're comin'! They know!"

"Sweet Mary!" She threw open the lock. "Liam! How do you . . ." she began, and screamed.

Chapter 10

Something lunged from the darkness. Candle-light gleamed on metal. Liam shrieked in pain and fell. Roman dragged him inside, then slammed his weight against the door. But someone was on the opposite side, holding it open.

Blood stained Liam's sleeve. A man cursed on the far side of the door. Another added his weight to the heavy timbers. Roman's body jerked as the door bumped open a scant inch farther. Fingers appeared in the crack.

Panic rose in Betty's throat. They had come for her! She had to escape! But how? She scanned the room, thinking. The fireplace was near. A log burned there. She reached for it and swung.

Sparks lit a fiery arc through the night air, then spattered outward as the wood thundered against the exposed fingers.

There was an agonized shriek. The fingers disappeared. Roman heaved at the door until it thudded closed. Betty reached for the lock, but already the door was being shoved open again.

Liam added his weight to the portal, but his arm was bloody and his face pale. "I tried ta warn ya," he gasped. "I come as soon as I 'eard."

Roman braced his feet against the floor. "Who

the hell's out there?" he asked through gritted teeth.

"Daggermen. They're Daggermen. They know!" Betty stumbled backward, her face white.

The door inched open. A blade slashed through the crack.

Betty shrieked and crashed her weight against the portal again. It moved only a bit.

"How?" she gasped.

"James. They got old James."

"Dear God."

"What?" Roman said, shoving at the door.

"Ya gotta go, Tara," Liam whispered "Ya gotta get out. Now! I'll hold 'em as long as I can."

"I can't leave you here."

The door bumped again. Roman grunted. Liam groaned.

"We can hold them," she said.

Men cursed and shouted on the far side of the door. Roman shook his head. "You got a plan?" he asked Liam.

The boy nodded to the far side of the house. "Another way out."

"Go!" Roman whispered.

"Nay!" Betty shook her head.

A man yelled. Suddenly, a blade slipped between the planks of the portal, just missing Betty's midsection. She screamed. Roman swore, and leaning his shoulder against the door, raised his fist and thumped her on the head.

She dropped like a rock into oblivion. Liam's jaw fell.

"Take her," Roman ordered.

"But . . ."

"Now!" Roman yelled, and, letting the door swing wide, whipped his short blade from his garter.

The first man died instantly. He dropped his

sword. Roman scooped it up with his left hand and swung.

The second man screamed and fell. The four behind him stumbled back. Roman could only hope now that Liam could handle Betty. He could only pray there was indeed a second exit as he parried and thrust, slashed and ducked.

Behind him, the door swung closed. He stood with his back to it. A villain lunged at him. Roman blocked the stroke, sweeping the blade downward, but not soon enough. It slashed across his thigh. He hissed in agony. The man swung again, but Roman whipped his dagger upward. It lodged in the villain's gut. He staggered backward.

But three others remained. They came as a group, charging him in a semicircle of death. The first swung. Roman dodged, then dodged again. But he'd miscalculated. His back slammed against the door. It sprang open. He stumbled into the room, trying to right his balance.

The villains rushed in after him.

Roman swiped with his sword. A long, curved blade spun from one man's hand. Roman slashed again. Blood spurted from his opponent's arm. He fell against the wall.

"Damn it!" he screamed. "Get 'im!"

The other two pressed forward. "Where is she?"

Roman crouched, waiting, holding his sword in his right hand. His left was empty, stretched out to the side for balance. "She doesn't know anything about the Shadow," he hissed.

The nearest thief laughed. "Is that what she told ya, Scotsman?" He advanced slowly, licking his lips. "Did she tell ya she didn't know nothin'? She musta been a good fuck ta convince ya ta stay and die for 'er. And now she's gone, probably humpin' the Shadow while I kill ya."

Where was the exit? Was she safely gone? Roman dared not shift his attention from the advancing men. "She doesn't know the Shadow," he repeated, stalling for time.

"Of course she don't. The fence was just jestin' when he said she did. Course he was about to die at the time. Just like you are," said the thief. Then he sprang forward.

Roman parried and retreated. There was no time to think, only to thrust and swing. Behind the two that attacked him, the third man tore open one of the wooden trunks. Clothing flew into the air.

A sword sliced Roman's biceps. His feet faltered. He stumbled back against the bed. Death screamed his name.

"Here!" the third man yelled.

A thief jerked, distracted. Roman stabbed. His sword slid between ribs and deep into flesh.

The thief's jaw dropped. Blood oozed from the corner of his mouth.

Roman yanked his blade free and scrambled onto the mattress.

"Here ya are!" crooned the third man, not noticing his fallen comrade or his own injured arm. A necklace spilled between his fingers, alight with white and blue gems. "And what a beauty ya be, stolen back from that bastard Shadow."

Roman's world spun. The necklace! How had it gotten into Betty's trunk?

The nearest villain grinned at him. "The Shadow stole it and gave it to his whore. How does it feel to be fucked by them both, Scotsman?" he asked and swung.

Rage erupted in Roman. With a war cry, he whipped his sword upward, sending the other's blade sideways. The villain was knocked off-balance. Roman stabbed.

The thief fell backward, his knees buckling, a snarl on his lips as blood gushed from his chest.

Roman raised his sword and balanced unsteadily as he searched for the last man. But he had already gone, rushing into the darkness with the necklace. The room was empty except for death and himself. Roman staggered toward the door, but his legs refused to carry him farther. He fell to his knees. The world tilted crazily, and then he crashed to the floor, where blackness descended like the angels of hell.

Roman didn't know what woke him. Neither did he care. Once he thought he heard the skitter of nervous feet. But darkness took him again. Time marched on unmarked.

Pain gnawed at his thigh. Smoky light seeped in through the open door. He realized fuzzily that he was lying on his back. From far away, a woman cackled, or was it in his mind only?

She'd betrayed him, lied to him. Nay! She'd fucked him as the bastard had said. Fucked him and left him to die.

He turned his head. Death! It was all around him, filled his nostrils and his mind. But it did not disgust him. Instead, he reveled in it. He would find her. And when he did, death would be his ally!

Pushing himself to his feet, Roman realized that his brooch was gone, as were his sporran and plaid. The scavengers of Firthport had little shame and no mercy, it seemed. But he did not care.

He found his sgian dubh—his black dagger. It was covered with dried blood. Gripping it in one hand, he staggered through the door dressed in nothing but his knee-length tunic. The sun seemed ungodly bright. The earth moved beneath his feet, pushing him onward. His head spun. People stared and scurried out of his way. He approached the Queen's Head. Its door opened. Mistress Krahn gasped when she saw him.

"I need boiling water. Food." His voice sounded strangely distant to his own ears. The stairs tilted at odd angles beneath his feet.

Seating himself on the bed, Roman removed his shirt. Time was irregular. The mistress of the inn appeared with food and water, then backed away, her hands clasped before her.

"I could—" she began.

Roman raised his face to hers. She froze, quailed beneath his gaze, and rushed from the room.

He sat alone, tore strips from his shirt, cleaned his wounds. It seemed almost as if the pain belonged to someone else now. Binding his thigh, he reached for the food and ate, though he was unaware what he consumed. In his mind, he formed plan after plan.

He wrapped himself in the ceremonial tartan he'd set aside and limped to the door.

Mistress Krahn was just scurrying away when he opened it.

"I have little enough money," he said.

She stopped, staring at him with eyes round as bantam eggs. "I beg yer—"

"I have na money ta speak of, but if ye'll find me clothes I'll give ye me plaid."

"Yer—" She blinked, staring at his face, then skimming her shocked gaze down his body. He stood in nothing more than a hastily donned tartan. His chest was bare and bleeding.

"It's Highland made and bright red." He canted his head and lifted the thick fabric from his thigh, staring at her. "Like me blood."

Her jaw dropped. "I'll . . . I'll find clothes," she gasped, and rushed away.

Three days passed. Roman wandered through the back alleys of hell, questioning, searching, sewing together clues like small pieces of a patched blanket.

The sun was setting. He sat in a small inn, dressed in black trunk hose. They gripped his thigh wound with aching pressure. The doublet he wore was equally tight. On his head was a hat brimmed in the front. Between his shoulder blades, rested his sgian dubh in a makeshift sheath.

"I had a cousin named Shamus," he said, tasting his brew again. It burned his stomach, as his anger burned his soul. He hadn't eaten since the previous night, for he saved his few coins for spirits. People gathered at inns, people drank at inns, people would tell him where to find a young man named Liam. And Liam would lead him to the woman.

Roman almost smiled. He wouldn't inquire about the wench. Nay, that would only be another exercise in frustration, for he did not know who she was.

She had called herself Betty. Dagger's men had called her a whore. Liam had called her Tara, and Roman had called her much, much worse.

"He's dead now," Roman said, continuing his staccato conversation with hardly a thought to what he said. He would find the girl, and when he did, she would pay. "Poor auld Shamus. Was a good lad. He was of the O'Malley clan."

"O'Malley?" The bartender paused with his rag to lean on the bar. "Of Shannon lawn?"

"Aye," Roman agreed, nodding once. "Don't ye be tellin' me ye know them."

"I come from Coirce Glen, just over the rise from there."

"Ye dunna say." But of course he did say, for Roman had already learned what he could of the innkeeper. He knew that this man catered to an Irish clientele. But he was only a means to an end.

"So who was this Shamus O'Malley?"

"Ahh." Roman drank again. "He was a friend,

he was. A fine friend. But he died after a battle with an Englishman."

The innkeeper's face flushed red. "Damn their hides."

"Aye, damn 'em all," Roman agreed. "They forever kill the flower of our bonny lads."

"Aye, they do that."

"But I come nonetheless, cuz I promised Shamus I would deliver a token to his love."

"In Firthport?"

"Aye, she's an Englishman's daughter. And so the duel that cost his life," Roman said.

"And who is this woman?"

Roman shook his head. "Shamus wouldna say. He but said that enough blood had been spilled. He wouldna let me die in his defense." Suddenly, he slammed his mug upon the table and squeezed his eyes tightly closed. "But what I would give if I could."

The innkeeper jumped at his abrupt movement, then leaned closer. "Then how will ye deliver the token?"

Roman exhaled softly and looked at the soot-darkened beams of the ceiling. "I am ta deliver it to a man named Liam. 'Tis said he knows everyone, even Englishmen's daughters."

"Liam?" the innkeeper said, but his voice was quiet now, and he glanced right and left. "Liam of Backrow?"

Roman said nothing, but nodded once and drank again. He kept his movements casual, but every fiber in his body was taut.

Backrow. Liam lived in a section of town called Backrow. And Betty, whom he now called Tara, would not be far away.

Roman remained perfectly still. Hidden in the shadows of a gray stone house, he watched Liam's door. The black-haired lad had been in and out of the place a number of times. While he was gone, Roman had slipped into the room.

It had been dark, small, and devoid of the one person he hungered to find.

The door opened. The lad stepped out again. It was near evening. Shadows lay long and spidery across the street. Roman didn't look up, but remained as he was until Liam disappeared around a corner. Then, quiet and solemn, he straightened and followed.

The sun slipped toward the west. The noise of Market Street was winding down as the vendors' cries stilled. A boy of nine or ten wheeled a rickety barrow past. From it wafted the heady scent of the remains of his loaves.

Roman's stomach churned a complaint, but he ignored it and walked on. Liam stopped. Roman turned, examining a few items still displayed by a vendor.

But soon he was moving again. From up ahead came the sound of laughter. Light shone through the smoky glass of an inn. Scents issued out, confusing in a jumble of haunting aromas.

Liam bought a bit of smoked fish from the last stall and slowed his pace. Nibbling on the piece, he finally leaned against a wall near the inn and waited.

Roman slipped into the black shadow of a building and pressed himself up against the stone to watch.

Time slid uneasily by. Two men exited the inn. They were loud, raucous, inebriated.

A boy rounded a corner. Dressed in tattered hose and a drooping hat, he looked to be no more than thirteen. He carried a mended net over one shoulder. The dull end of a fishhook was laced through the loose weave of his rough shirt. He whistled as he strolled along with a fluid motion to his step. But in a moment, he stopped, seated himself on a step, and pulled something from his pocket. Was it an apple? Something edible? In the falling darkness, Roman couldn't be quite certain. Still, his taste buds ached at the thought.

Roman cleared his mind and hurried his gaze back to Liam. He must not lose his concentration. Eventually, the Irishman would lead him to the lass. He had to be patient.

A richly garbed man exited the inn. A leather pocket dangled from his belt. His face was flushed, and on his arm was a brightly dressed doxy. She laughed hardily up into his face.

A hound, drawn by the smell of Liam's fish, rounded the corner. "Ay," yelled the Irishman. "Get the 'ell away from me."

The gentleman turned his head. His companion scowled. The fisherboy stretched and sauntered past the pair.

The dog disappeared down the alley. Liam turned nonchalantly on his heel and walked back in the direction from which he had come.

No. Not another fruitless night. Not another false lead, Roman thought. But then the fisherboy turned his head. For just a moment, the gentleman's pouch was visible in the lad's delicate hand before it disappeared from sight. The boy was a thief—with hands like . . .

Something clicked in Roman's brain. Something . . . But . . .

Hell fire! That was no lad. It was Tara.

Chapter 11

Exhilaration bloomed in Roman's chest. He had found her! She would pay!

But already she was slipping back into the crowd. Jerking from his trance, he followed the ragged figure. She seemed in no hurry, but stopped now and then. With one hand in her pocket, she chatted with a vendor, then moved on. Laughter wafted on the evening air.

Roman barely noticed. Revenge was near. But he would not rush it. Would not let his emotions take over. He would follow her, stay calm and quiet, and finally he would have his hands on her. He stopped at a fruit seller's booth, glanced over the produce, then walked on. He was closer now, closing the space. Tara was busy talking to a buxom young woman who sold flowers behind a small stand.

Closer. Closer still.

"They match yer eyes," Tara was saying. "But they ain't nearly so pretty as you."

"Go on," said the girl. "I know yer kind. All flattery and no substance."

Roman moved closer still. He was nearly touching her now. But her back was to him and her words burned his mind. Tara? Flirting with the maid? He must be wrong. Led on a merry chase yet again. His hunger and impatience must have deceived him. But in that moment, she turned.

Eyes as blue as heaven smote him. His hand shot out without thought, circling her arm.

Her eyes went round, her jaw dropped. She stumbled back a step, but he held her in a firm grip.

" 'Tis good ta see ye again . . . lad," he said, his voice barely audible to his own ears.

She'd gone pale and stiff. "How?" she whispered.

He smiled. Never had the sight of terror pleased him, but now it satisfied his soul and soothed his aching wounds. "Surprised ta see me?"

"How did you escape them?"

A thousand memories crashed back on him. The clash of sword. The pain. But worst of all, the knowledge that he had been betrayed by the very woman he had fought to save.

"Let us walk a ways. I'll tell ye the tale."

She shook her head and tried to pull away, but he tightened his grip and gritted a smile.

" 'Tis a story of honor and lies, of valor and defeat. The kind of tale any lad would love," he said, and turned, towing her along beside him.

They moved easily through the crowd, though her movements were stiff. An alley gaped off to their left. He turned into it and stopped.

She stared up into his face, her eyes still round with disbelief. "How did you get away?" she breathed.

"I kilt them," he admitted flatly. "I kilt them!" he whispered, leaning closer. "All but the one that found the necklace." He tightened his grip. Anger rode him with a fury. " 'Twas a wondrous chain of sparkling gems. And I wondered, where did ye get it, Tara?"

She stared at him as if she had not an inkling of what he spoke.

"The necklace!" he said, shaking her. "In yer trunk."

He waited for an explanation. It would be a lie, and he would laugh in her face. Revel in his revenge.

"You weren't hurt?" she asked breathlessly. Beneath his hand, her arm felt slim and frail. And her eyes! Even in the shadows of this godforsaken alley, they reminded him of a Highland loch, as deep and unfathomable as eternity.

He shook himself. "Nay!" he said through his teeth. "Of course I was na hurt. 'Twas an even fight, after all. Only six ta one. Only six bloodthirsty bastards with nothing ta live for. But I had a reason to survive." He moved an inch closer. "I had revenge."

The alley was silent. His face must have reflected his shaky emotional state, for there was true fear in her eyes now.

"What are you going to do with me?"

He laughed. His thigh throbbed with pain. His belly coiled with hunger. "I could kill ye with me bare hands," he said.

She stood perfectly still, watching him.

Even in this ragged boy's garb, there was something about her that drew him.

"But I willna," he whispered, staring into her eyes and knowing betrayal, feeling it in his soul. "I willna kill ye. Nay. For ye will lead me to the Shadow. And Dagger will pay me well for him."

"Ya think I would betray the Shadow?" Tara rasped, low-voiced.

Roman leaned closer, glaring into her face. " 'Tis yer choice, lass. Either I take the Shadow to Dagger—or I take ye. And I dunna think ye would like how he treats young women who be trying to horn in on his territory."

She gasped. Her eyes grew larger still . . . then rolled upward, and suddenly she went limp and slipped to the ground in a heap.

His hand dropped from her arm in surprise. "Tara?" he said, reaching for her again.

But suddenly she was rolling away. Roman grabbed for her. But she was on her feet in an instant. He snatched her coat, drawing her back. She turned like a cornered cat, claws extended. He caught her arms, but in that instant, her knee came up. He twisted instinctively. White-hot pain slammed into his thigh.

Lights exploded in his head. His hands fell uselessly away. Darkness threatened. But one thought rolled back oblivion. She was getting away!

Somehow he forced his legs to move. He stumbled forward. Rage, blood red and hot, filled his head. She was there, just in front of him. He jumped, catching her by the shoulders and pulling her to the ground.

She shrieked and kicked, but he held on, dragging himself up her body until he lay across her. His breath came in great gasps. His heart hammered against her back. Pain skittered through him. He lay immobile, waiting for the agony to ease.

Finally it did. He propped himself up and rolled her over.

"Ye'll na get away this time, lass. Nay. This time 'twill be ye who pays."

"I did not wish for ye ta die." She was still breathing hard. Her face was pale and finely shaped.

"Ye are the mistress of lies," he said, reminding himself of the pain that came with believing her.

"But 'twill avail ye little. For I will turn ye over ta Dagger."

He watched her draw a breath and knew that he must indeed be evil, for even now, when he planned his revenge, he still desired her. "I will give ye ta Dagger na matter what ye say," he whispered, but against his will, he leaned closer, as if his lips were pulled to her mouth by an invisible force.

"Ho!" chuckled someone. "What have we here?"

Roman jerked his head upward. Twisting off the girl, he turned to find two men standing not a rod from him.

"Looks ta be some interesting entertainment," said the second man. He wheezed out a chuckle and shifted his eyes nervously sideways. "Don't ya think, Sam?"

"Interesting indeed."

Roman rose warily to his feet. Pain clattered down his thigh, but there was no time to consider that now, for more Firthport inhabitants had slithered out from under their slimy rocks. "I caught the boy stealing," he said, pulling Tara to her feet. "I'll be taking him before the magistrate."

"Sure. After yer done buggerin' 'im," said Sam, chuckling. "I 'ate ta ruin yer fun, but we got us our orders. Said ta bring in any thieves we come across."

"Bring them in where?" Roman asked.

"That ain't for ya to know," said Sam. "Now ya just be on yer way."

Roman shifted slightly, positioning himself casually between Tara and the newcomers. "The boy owes me," he said simply.

The second man wheezed out a sound rather like a laugh. "I wouldn't mind watchin' 'im do 'im, Sam."

Sam licked his lips. They were pale and pulled

into a thin line like a grimace. "You forgettin' orders, Gourd?"

"Dagger didn't say—"

"Shut up!" rasped Sam. "And you," he said, addressing Roman and slowly drawing a blade from a sheath. "Get outta the way."

Roman glanced at the knife, shrugged. "Listen. I'm willing to share."

Gourd nodded and wheezed. "There's enough there for the three of us."

Sam licked his lips again. Lust was in his eyes, ugly, dark, terrifying.

Tara shuddered. She felt Roman's grip tighten on her wrist.

"I'm not selfish," Roman said, and chuckled. "In fact there's something you should know about him."

Gourd narrowed his eyes. "What's that?"

"Come here," Roman invited.

Tara pulled harder. Panic was welling up, drowning thought. She yanked at her arm.

"I like 'em fresh and sassy," said Gourd.

"I'll tell you a secret 'bout this one."

Gourd moved closer, pulling out a dirk. "If this is a trick, I'll carve out yer gizzard."

"Oh, it's a trick," Roman said, "but you'll like it."

Gourd was standing only inches away now, shifting his knife nervously. Sam was close behind.

"What is it then?"

Roman chuckled. "He's really a . . ." he began, then shook his head and rubbed his neck as if in disbelief.

The knife appeared from the back of Roman's tunic like a flash of lightning. It swept through the air and lodged in Gourd's throat.

Tara shrieked.

Gourd gurgled on his blood and stumbled backward, groping at the handle.

"Run!" Roman ordered, but Tara was frozen to the spot.

Sam swore and made a wild swipe with his knife. Roman dodged. He swiped again. Roman jumped to the side, but he stumbled over Gourd's lifeless body. In the next instant, Sam's blade ripped across Roman's arm, splattering blood into the air. Sam laughed.

"I'd like ta kill ya slow, only the boy's waiting fer me," rasped Sam and lunged. But Roman had found his balance. He leapt to the side. Sam stumbled past and turned with a snarl. But in that instant, Roman had wrenched the blade from Gourd's neck. Sweeping it upward, he planted it deep in Sam's stomach.

The villain rose on his toes and stumbled to a halt. His fingers curled into talons. The knife dropped to the ground. A moment later it was covered by Sam's twitching body.

Roman stood staring down at the carnage he had wrought.

"Come on." Tara tugged at his sleeve.

Roman remained immobile, starring at the men at his feet.

"Come," she said again.

He turned on her with the suddenness of a wolf. "Leave me."

She started back. Rage glowed in his eyes. But his arm trembled and dripped with blood. "Someone will be coming soon," she whispered.

"Get the hell out of here!" he yelled, and swung to push her away.

She ducked, then caught him when he nearly fell. "You're hurt."

He laughed; the sound was low and dark. "Not as bad as them."

"Come. I'll see to your wounds," she said.

He grabbed her by the shirtfront, dragging her up to his nose. "Don't ye ken what I can do to ye?"

She swallowed, nodded once, dangling like a felled hare from his fist. "Aye, you could have let them have me."

For a moment, an unreadable expression overtook his face. Terror, pain, sorrow. But then he pushed her back. "Get away from me."

Voices rose behind her. Tara glanced nervously in that direction, but no one was in sight as of yet. "You're giving up then? Decided to sacrifice MacAulay's life, have ya?"

Roman straightened slightly. Some semblance of sanity returned to his eyes.

"If that's more of Dagger's men, you'll not survive the night, Scotsman," she said. "And with you will die the lad's only chance of returning to his homeland. But if that's what you want . . ." She turned and ran away.

Behind her, Roman swore, but in a moment, she heard his following footsteps. Voices bloomed behind her. She turned to see men pointing after them. It took only a moment for Roman to catch up to her. Grasping his arm, she pulled him along. They would be followed, but she knew each alley like an old friend, every loose rock, every unlocked window.

"Here." She eased open a door and tugged on Roman's sleeve. He stumbled inside, then leaned against the wall. His gaze was sharp and steady as he watched her, but he held his wounded arm almost casually against his chest.

"How bad is it?"

He said nothing, but remained as he was, still watching her.

She scowled. Blood had soaked the sleeve. By the

light of the fire, she could see the stain.

"Sit down," she said, nodding toward the bed. It was a narrow tick that lay on the floor and covered a good deal of the room's space.

He didn't move.

Anger slowly brewed in her. She hadn't asked him to find her. If he had never interfered in her life, she would have had no need of his heroics. "I wonder how a one-armed beggar would fare in Firthport," she mused.

He leaned his head back against the wall, still watching her. "Mayhap I'll become a thief."

She snorted. "You're not made of the right stuff, Scotsman."

"Ye've na way of knowing what I'm made of, lass."

She watched him. Never had she met another like him—a man who would avenge a dog, protect a whore. Oh, she knew him. "Sit down, Scotsman, before you fall down."

He slid down the wall until he landed with his buttocks on the floor and his legs bent and parted. She knelt beside him. His sleeve had been slashed, but it was impossible to ascertain the extent of the damage without removing his shirt.

She scowled, knowing she was a fool. But regardless of his unwanted interference in her life, he had still kept her safe. "We'll have to take it off."

His head remained tilted back against the wall behind him, exposing the breadth of his dark-skinned throat. The chuckle seemed to rise from there. "And what is it ye wish for me ta take off, sweet Tara? Is that yer name, or shall I call ye something else?"

She'd seen delirium in the wounded before and wondered now if such was the case here.

"Ya need to take off your shirt," she said.

"Ahh." He chuckled again. "Me hopes be

crushed. But, aye, yer free ta remove whatever ye wish from me person.''

She hesitated a moment. He was in a fey mood, and she did not trust it. But neither could she allow him to bleed to death. She reached for his shirt, but soon realized the difficulty involved in removing it.

"I'll need to cut it off.''

He chuckled again, but did not explain the reason. Instead, he merely nodded.

Taking a knife from a shelf by the hearth, Tara sliced his shirt open down the front. It parted like the Red Sea before Moses' staff, bearing an expanse of rippling muscle and . . .

"Sweet Mary,'' she breathed, staring at the scattered wounds that marred his chest and belly. She raised her eyes to his face. "How . . .''

His gaze was dagger sharp and icy cold.

She swallowed and ever so gently touched a finger to a wound that marred his chest just below the toothed amulet. "You were wounded for me,'' she whispered.

He said nothing. Silence stretched between them.

"Why?'' she asked into the gathering darkness.

She watched him draw a breath. His nostrils flared. Ever so slightly his muscles relaxed beneath her hand.

"Once there was a lad,'' he said, looking past her toward her humble pallet. "Small he was, and alone but for his uncle . . . and his hound.''

Tara waited in silence, for it seemed as if he had forgotten her presence.

" 'Twas . . .'' He paused, and for an instant, she thought she felt him tremble, though it was a hard thing to believe, for he was built like an indomitable stallion, hard and lean and invincible. " 'Twas a mean existence,'' he murmured. "Na goodness was there. Na so much as a kind word. Nay, na from Dermid. Evil. Deep as eternity. I felt it in him. I knew it was there. And sometimes . . . Sometimes I felt meself drowning in it, felt it cover me head and pull me under like a dark tide."

Tara remained unmoving, transfixed by his sing-song tone, his distant gaze.

"But there will forever be dreamers." He chuckled softly to himself, but the sound was tortured. "It seems there were those who believed there was good in me. They taught me ta search for good in others. But even as I search—I kill."

"They would have killed me."

"I told myself a thousand times that you deserve to die," he murmured.

"But you could not do it, Scotsman," she said softly. "Because you are good."

Their gazes seemed to hold for an eternity. But finally Tara moved away. Going to the small hearth, she reached for a ladle and stirred the contents of a pot that steamed over the fire. She then swung a kettle of water nearby. Pulling a cloth bag from her pocket, she dumped the contents into a second pot and moved it near the blaze. Rising to her feet, she went to a small trunk. From it, she brought forth an old shirt that she ripped into strips.

She could feel him watching her, his gaze sharp and feral. Rage and pain emanated from him. He hated her. And why shouldn't he? She had left him to die in her own house. True, she had been given no choice, for Liam had dragged her unconscious from the place. Still, she should have gone back, should have looked for him. Terror had kept her away. Terror of finding him dead, of being killed herself. Thus, she had once again immersed herself into the life of a petty thief. But in the night when there was nothing to occupy her mind, she had thought of him and prayed for his survival even though she knew there was no hope.

Yet here he was, alive and hale. Tara turned to stare at him. Relief flooded through her. Their gazes clashed. She quickly lowered hers. To him, she was a calculating wench who looked out for herself and none other. She must make certain it stayed that way. But it was tempting, just this once, to let down her guard.

She turned slowly, feeling the tension caused by his presence. There was a lean, hungry look about him. A look she had seen a thousand times before, a feeling she had felt in her own gut.

"How long has it been since you've eaten?"

He remained silent, as if reading something in her face. She turned nervously away, paced to the fireplace, and ladled a portion of broth into a wooden bowl. Upon a stone ledge near the fire sat a squat jug of deep green glass and a dark loaf of bread wrapped in a white cloth. Taking the loaf, she carried it and the bowl to him where he sat near the door, and, squatting, extended the meal toward him. She saw the hunger in his eyes, felt the slight tremble of his muscles as if it shook her own.

"There is not," he said finally, his tone deep and low.

"Not what?"

"Not good in me," he whispered. " 'Tis but a hoax."

He sat on her floor like a small boy wounded in her defense. He did not demand to know how she had come by the necklace. He did not now seek revenge. Instead, he mourned the lives of two villains with souls as black as hell. "So you've been pretending to be good, have ya, Scotsman?" she asked.

He gazed past her into the flame. "Aye. Roman

the Wolf, so serious, so steady, so staid. Na reiving was tolerated when I was at Glen Creag. Na even the meanest theft. The Hawk would play tricks, and the Rogue would . . ." He seemed to relax a smidgen more. "Roderic the Rogue would do anything. But Roman was forever the guardsman of the weak and the frail. The protector of justice."

For some reason beyond her ken, she longed to touch him. "But 'twas all an act," she whispered. "To keep the evil in you at bay."

Surprise showed stark and wild in his eyes, and for a moment, she thought he would question how she knew, but instead, he set his jaw in a hard line. " 'Tis na longer at bay. The evil is freed." His fist tightened.

Against her will and better judgment, she moved closer. His skin was warm beneath her fingertips, and gently, ever so gently, she smoothed his shirt over his shoulder and down his arm. It fell away from the oozing gash across his biceps. "Then why this?" she asked. "Why did you not let them have me?"

Silence held the place. The mouth-watering steam from the hot soup wafted between them.

" 'Tis ye that will lead me to the Shadow," he intoned, his eyes flat and steady. "And I will have me revenge."

She watched him closely. Revenge had made him save her? Revenge and nothing more? 'Tis what he said, and she must believe him. She must, to save her own life. She drew that knowledge about her like a protective veil and rose jerkily to her feet.

"So you think to turn the Shadow over to Dagger? Is that it?" Her voice was shrill, her hands tightly clasped against the tattered fabric of her boys' garments. "You think to cause his death?"

"Aye." His voice was deep and menacing.

"Well, you won't!" She spun toward him. "You won't because he is already dead."

Roman's eyes widened, then narrowed into a scowl. "Ye lie."

"Sweet Mary!" she sobbed, conjuring up every bit of sorrow she could. This must be her finest performance if she were to survive. "If only 'twas true. If only . . ." She collapsed to the floor, feeling the misery sweep through her like a blaze gone wild, making herself believe she was what she said she was—the Shadow's woman. She was alone, so alone with no hope without the Shadow.

She never heard Roman move, but suddenly he was beside her, gripping her arm in a hard clasp and pulling her upward. "Ye lie. The bastard stole the necklace, and—"

"Aye!" Tears wet her face and blurred her vision. She swiped them aside. "Aye, he stole it," she whispered. She had played a thousand roles since coming to Firthport. She could play this one. "As he stole many things. But never for himself. He believed in sharing."

Roman's scowl deepened. He loosened his hold on her arm. "What's this new lie?"

She clasped her arm where he had held it and settled back on her heels. "Ya do not know the evil that is Firthport," she whispered. "The hunger. The fear. 'Arry fed the hungry, abolished the fear."

"Harry?"

She closed her eyes, willing up the necessary emotions. "Some of what I said before was true. 'Arry was my lover. My love. And now he is gone. But he was not a duke. He was a simple man. Simple and perfect," she whispered. "But now I am alone."

"If he is dead, why do Dagger's men still search for him?"

She laughed. The sound was eerie. Her expression would look wild in the shifting light, she knew, and her hands shook. "Are you so naive as to think Dagger is the only evil force in all of England?" She shook her head. "The Shadow went where he wished, took what he fancied. No lock could hold him out. Every door was open to him. He was a jester, a knight, a peasant. An angel," she whispered. "But angels cannot long survive in hell."

"If he is dead, who kilt him?"

She shook her head. "He took from the rich, and the rich have power." Turning, she paced away, embracing thoughts of her father, her mother, her loss. Tears stung her eyes. "For all I know it could have been the girl's father who first wanted the necklace. Mayhap he craved revenge just as you do." She stopped and let her eyes fall closed. "It matters naught who killed him, only that he is gone forever. Only that my life . . ." She paused, feeling overwhelmed by the sadness that rushed up at her. She felt the floor tilt, felt herself tip sideways.

"Here." Roman gripped her arm and eased her to the mattress. "Sit." Retrieving the meal she had left by the door, he brought it to her.

She shook her head, keeping her eyes closed. "It's for you," she whispered. "I, too, believe in sharing."

"Eat," he ordered, but she shook her head.

"There is no reason," she whispered. "Why should I wish to prolong my life with him gone?"

"Mayhap ye dunna," Roman said. "But I do. For 'tis ye who will help me get the necklace back."

Chapter 12

S he lied. That much he knew. But what parts of her tale were untrue exactly? He did not know, and so there seemed little reason not to play along. But he would be cautious now. Question every word, doubt every nuance.

Who was this woman? A barmaid, a whore, a thief? He watched her closely, focusing all his concentration on her.

In a moment she nodded. " 'Tis right that I help you. 'Tis right." She laughed, the sound hollow. "We cannot win against the Dagger's army. I know that this venture will cause my death. Yet, even though I know death is the vehicle that will take me to my 'arry, I am afraid. I am a coward," she whispered.

Whatever she was, she was not a coward, Roman thought. She had removed the floppy hat, and her hair, blond and full and soft, fell down her narrow back in long cascades. "Drink," he repeated, pushing the cup toward her.

"No." Her voice was stronger now. She forced a smile. "Ya saved my life. 'Tis the least I can do to give you food and drink, Scotsman."

"Roman."

She tilted her head in question.

"Me name," he said. " 'Tis Roman of the clan Forbes."

Lifting the bread and bowl from the floor, she raised it toward him. "Eat, Roman of the Forbes."

It was a kind of discipline that had kept him from the food, but hunger was overpowering now, filling his senses, weakening him both physically and mentally. He tried to swallow the painful fill of his salivary glands, but he had waited too long, and the food was too close. Not since childhood had he known such hunger.

He took the bowl with shaking hands and tipped it to his mouth. It smelled of sweet onions and fine fowl. It tasted so rich and heavenly that the sharp necessity of it hurt his mouth.

She studied him over the edge of the bowl before handing him the bread. He tore off a piece, remembering control, holding on to discipline as if it were a lifeline tied to the last vestige of sanity.

Slowly, carefully, he dipped the bread into the broth. The taste filled his mouth and his soul.

Tearing a bit of crust from the loaf, Tara nibbled on it and watched him. But he barely noticed her now. When she handed him the cup, he drank, and when she refilled the bowl, he ate again.

Finally, he was sated. Seated on her mattress, he leaned his head against the wall and studied her.

"So 'twas ye that told the Shadow of the necklace?" Roman asked.

She turned away, and on her cheeks was a flush. Of shame? Or was the expression a hoax like everything else?

" 'Twas I," she whispered, wringing her hands and seeming to draw herself into her own memories. " 'Tis true. There is a . . . a babe in Middlecastle. Wee Sineag. No bigger than a gosling is she." Her voice was singsong, haunting, reminding him somehow of the wild winds of his homeland.

"With hair as bright as an evening blaze. She coughed so, ya'd think 'twould split her in two." Tara paused and seemed to shake herself mentally. "'Arry he . . ." She clasped and unclasped her hands, looking almost surprised to find herself in her own hovel with no babe in sight. "He could not bear to see another suffer. Some of the money from the necklace would have gone to buy an elixir."

Roman watched her face, searched for lies. There was pain in her expression. Pain and sorrow, and nothing else he could discern.

"How did ye know where I stayed? How did ye find me?" he asked.

"Caraway seeds."

Roman narrowed his eyes.

"Mistress Krahn of the Queen's Head uses it heavily in her cooking. I could smell it on ya."

"Ye lie," he said, but her words seemed too outlandish to be anything but the truth.

"Nay. 'Tis true," she said. "'Arry taught me much before . . ." She drew a deep breath and lifted her chin slightly, as if fighting back tears. "Oft he said that we use but half our senses. He taught me to use all I have. He gave me worth, gave me . . ." Her bottom lip trembled. "He gave me much."

"So ye told him of the jewels, and he went to the Queen's Head disguised as John Marrow. After that 'twas an easy enough task ta slip beneath me rented bed and wait until I fell asleep."

Tara shrugged. "I do not know his exact methods. All I know is that he had the necklace before morning."

"Why did he give it to ye? Why did he na sell the jewels and give money to the babe's mother?"

Something fleeted across her eyes. She rose abruptly to her feet. "James is . . . James was missing."

Roman waited for an explanation.

"He was a fence for stolen goods. The only fence 'arry trusted. 'Twas I who usually delivered the goods. In fact . . ." She turned, twisting her hands. "The night you watched my house, 'twas I you chased, for I was trying to take the necklace to James. I escaped down the hatch beneath the trunk in my old house."

"Thus I never saw ye leave."

She nodded. "I thought I was safe, then I heard ya and started running. Ya nearly caught me, for my legs were failing. But I saw an open window and scrambled through."

"I ran on and attacked George, who happened to be returning from the inn."

"Poor George." The tiniest spark of humor flashed in her eyes. And though Roman knew he should hate her, he could not help but want to see her smile.

"Poor George?" he said. "'Twas me that was beat upon the head. And 'twas me that barely escaped the white hound."

One corner of her bonny lips tilted upward. "You neglected to take him a gift to calm him."

For a moment Roman puzzled over her words, but then the truth dawned. "Ahh, so that was the purpose for the plate of bones I saw in yer house the first time."

"He was a wonderful watchdog," she said. "He would growl at anyone not bearing gifts and warn me of goings and comings. But since that day he only wags his tail and whimpers when someone passes by. I cannot help but wonder why."

"We had a disagreement."

She watched him. "Mayhap you have a chance against the Daggermen after all, Scotsman. But I . . ." She paused. "Not I. For they know I was in-

volved with the Shadow. Dagger will not rest until
I am dead."

"How does he know?"

"They killed James. I feared he was in trouble
when I went to deliver the necklace and he wasn't
'ome. I feared the worst, that he would tell the
Shadow's identity. But even the Dagger couldn't
break that loyalty."

"But the fence told Dagger about ye?"

"Aye, and I cannot blame him. Dagger has . . ."
She shuddered. "Dagger has ways of making men
talk. But James is dead now. Out of their reach."

Her face was mobile and alive, expressing her
sorrow, her resignation. Was she lying now? Damn
him! He could not tell. "We live for the living," she
said softly. "I'll see to your wounds."

Moving to the fire, she wrapped a rag about the
handle of the water kettle and lifted it from its
swinging metal arm. After pouring some of the water into a bowl, she replaced the kettle and slipped
his sliced shirt past his wrists.

Bare but for his amulet, his chest looked like the
massive torso of some ancient warlord.

Tara swallowed, then dunked a cloth into the
steaming water and wrung it out.

For a moment, their gazes met.

"This will hurt," she warned.

He nodded, then flinched as she settled the
warm cloth against his biceps. His muscles
twitched, but he remained as he was.

The wound was long but not deep. She washed
it carefully. Beneath her hands, his skin was warm,
his muscles rigid and mounded. She lifted a strip
of cloth and wrapped it carefully about his arm.

Every moment he watched her. The room was
silent but for an occasional crackle from the fire.

"You've . . ." She swallowed again. He had
saved her life, true, but she could not allow herself

to trust him. Not now, not ever. "You've neglected your wounds," she said softly.

"In truth I barely noticed them. What of wee Sineag?" he asked.

She lifted her gaze to his. Who was this man who would concern himself with a wee lass he had never met? She forced herself to shrug, trying to act unconcerned. "Mayhap God will see fit to see her healed without intervention," she said, and turned the conversation aside. "Your limp is new. Surely you took note of your leg wound?"

" 'Tis something to be said of rage," he said. "It blinds one ta pain. In truth, I've been living to find ye."

She swallowed. Even though she vividly remembered their time alone together in her room, she knew it was not infatuation that caused him to follow her. Nay. Hardly that. It was hate. And yet, even knowing how he felt about her, she could not seem to keep her hands from him.

"I'll tend to these," she said, touching a healing laceration.

A muscle jumped beneath her hand, but before she could draw away he caught her wrist. "Why?"

His gaze was like the arc of a hot, green flame. She battled to continue to breath.

"Once there was a girl," she whispered. "She was a small lass, alone but for an old man called Cork, a man who thought she did not deserve to die in a filthy Firthport alley. There will always be dreamers," she said, mimicking his words from not long before.

"Who are ye?" he whispered.

"Betty," she forced herself to say, but he shook his head.

"Nay, ye are na. I dunna ken who ye are, but Tara feels right. Thus I will call ye that until I learn the truth." His hand slipped from her wrist.

Her fingers trembled, but she forced herself to rinse the rag and wring it out again. Shakily, she cleansed his chest. It was hard, crafted of fine hills and valleys. Her breath came faster.

His left wrist was bloody. She washed it, too, marvelling at the thickness of the bone, the denseness of the muscle.

Her gaze slipped downward. There was a scratch across his abdomen. She slipped the cloth over that slight wound. The muscles coiled like magic beneath her hand.

"Did I hurt you?" she whispered.

His eyes were sharp and clear, the muscles in his jaw, tight. "Nay."

"I . . ." For just a moment, for just one singular instant, she wanted to tell him the truth, to cleanse her soul, to share more than that which she could hold in her hand. But if the truth be known, her will to survive was stronger than all else. "I noticed your limp."

He merely watched her, saying nothing.

"You did not limp when first I met you."

"I did not kill people on a daily basis either, lass."

Guilt was a new emotion for her. It had no place in her life. Tara shoved it to the back of her mind for later examination, but kept the expression on her face.

"Do ye regret their deaths?" he asked, watching her.

She shook her head. "But I regret your involvement."

He reached out very slowly and touched her face, his fingers gentle against her skin. She closed her eyes.

" 'Tis strange," he whispered. "It seems ye could do anything, and I would still desire ye."

She hid her surprise, though he had voiced the

feeling she'd refused to allow herself to recognize. "I . . ." She knew she'd lost the expression of guilt, and wondered now with some fear what her face revealed. She would be a fool to drop her guard with him. And fools died young. "I'll see to your leg."

For a moment, she thought he would refuse. For a moment, the coward in her hoped he would, but finally he settled back. " 'Tis na the first time I've been at yer mercy, lass."

The points had been unlaced from his doublet. Tara licked her lips and eyed them, the fabric below, the bulge.

"I can see ta the wound meself."

"Nay," she said, forcing her gaze to his face. "Nay," she repeated, calming her voice. "Ya saved my life. And I would do what I can for ya."

"Am I allowed to make suggestions?"

She tried to control her blush, but through all her deceitful years that was the one thing she had not conquered. "Decidedly not."

He shrugged. She bit her lip, said a silent prayer to a God who listened to sinners and saints alike, and reached for the top of his hose.

"Tara?"

"Aye?" She whipped her hands back to look into his face.

"Have ye ever wondered what a Scotsman wears beneath his plaid?"

She shook her head, feeling suddenly foolish and far out of her depth.

"They wear nothing," he said. "And they wear the same under their English garments. I can tend the wound meself."

She managed to shake her head again.

"Ye could at least give me a blanket and turn away for a moment."

She retrieved the woolen with shaky hands, gave it to him, and showed him her back.

When next she looked at him, his tattered shirt had been shoved beneath his knee and he was naked but for the blanket that covered his body at a crooked angle. His chest was exposed, as were his shoulders, and the wounded width of one powerful leg. It made an erotic picture, the mighty male, awaiting her touch.

She took a deep breath as she forced her gaze to his thigh. "It has turned septic," she said, forcing the words out. He had suffered on her account. He had suffered, and she would tend his wounds. But nothing more. She was not interested in him as a person. The width of his shoulders did not impress her. The bulky curve of his chest held no appeal. And his eyes, green as a summer meadow, did not make her heart race and her soul long for intimacy.

"Lass, are ye well?" he asked.

She all but slapped herself, for she realized suddenly that she was staring at him like a dazed lambkin. "Aye," she said, and, hurrying to the fire, retrieved the kettle of hot water. The wound was puckered and oozing. She grimaced. "I fear it should be lanced."

"How do ye ken that?"

She shrugged, distracted by the duty ahead of her. "When I was a child, there was an old woman who taught me a bit about the art of healing. But not enough."

"Fiona could teach ye more," Roman said softly.

"Fiona?"

"The lady of the Forbes. There is none, as of yet, who can match her skill. Roderic's wife is . . . well, the Flame, and wee Elizabeth is still a bairn." His gaze was far off and his expression rueful. "At least ta me own eyes she is still a babe."

"Your family?" Tara asked softly.

"Aye, they be mine, if na by blood, then by kindness."

"They are not your kin?"

"My parents died when I was but a lad. Me uncle took me in." He was silent for a moment, his face taut. "Fiona . . . seemed ta think I needed a mother."

"And Dermid?" she asked.

"How do ye know his name?"

"Ya've mentioned your uncle before," she said.

"Ye've a good memory."

"It's served me well. What happened to Dermid?"

A muscle jumped in his lean jaw. "He died on me laird's blade."

"Your laird?"

"Fiona's husband." He looked away. "Laird Leith."

"Your foster father?" she asked softly.

"He calls me son."

His emotions were so clear, it seemed she could read every thought. "But ya do not deserve that name?"

He turned slowly back to her, his eyes flat. "I dunna."

Tara skimmed her gaze down his massive body. "For a man fully grown, you know little of yourself, Scotsman."

Something shone in his eyes. Was it gratitude for the words she spoke?

"Mayhap ye can teach me of meself then, lass," he said softly.

Mayhap, she thought. And mayhap she could tell him of herself, share that which she had never shared before.

But no! She was being foolish, and foolish she could not afford to be. Turning quickly away, she hurried back to the fire to retrieve a knife that lay upon the stone ledge. Picking up a small rock, she absently sharpened the blade against it as she returned more slowly to him.

Long ago, there had been a woman named Mary in the village of Killcairn, a kind woman with a doting family and a gift for healing. Long ago, Tara had imagined herself assuming that role. But fate had not opened that path to a small Irish girl with flaxen hair.

"I can lance the wound meself."

Roman's words startled her. She drew herself from the past. "What?"

"Ye look pale, lass. There's no need for ye ta do this."

"Nay, I can . . ." She glanced at the wound again. It was an ugly thing, far worse than his others. And if it did not mend 'twould be her fault. "I can see to it."

" 'Tis yer choice. But we'd best have bandages close ta hand. And Fiona would pack dry bread into the wound to draw out the poison, methinks."

"Bread." She nodded. The floor seemed to have tilted slightly, and her stomach felt strange. "I'll fetch some."

"Mayhap ye should sit for a bit, lass."

"Nay." She shook her head. The movement did nothing to set the room to rights. "I am fine."

"At least give me the blade," he said. "I'll sharpen it whilst ye retrieve what ye must."

She nodded, handing him the knife and rock, but she could not turn away, for she could not help staring at his wound.

"Lass."

She drew a deep breath and found his gaze.

"The linens."

"Oh." The word sounded strangely breathy. "Aye," she said, and turned away.

To her relief, she found that the jug of ale was

not empty. She took a swig straight from the bottle, gathered up bread and linens, and turned back.

Roman's hiss of pain made her stop in her tracks. But his hand didn't delay a moment. Instead, it moved again, slicing a cross into his oozing leg wound. Blood flowed in earnest now, soaking the tattered shirt he'd shoved beneath his knee.

"I . . ." the world tilted more dramatically. "I could have done that," Tara said.

"Ye'd best sit down, lass."

"Nay, I . . ." She paused. Her stomach lurched. "I'd best sit," she said, stumbling toward the mattress.

He reached for her. Encircling her arm in his large hand, he guided her onto the pallet, took the items from her hands, and set them on the floor.

"Lie down."

"Nay, I'm . . ."

"Lie down," he ordered, and she did so.

He quickly cleaned and wrapped his own wound while she felt foolish and dizzy beside him.

Finally, he lay down beside her.

"Are ye well, lass?"

"Aye," she said, then added facetiously, "the lancing barely hurt atall."

He smiled. Her world tilted again, but she feared it was no longer from nausea but from the beauty of his smile.

He stroked her hair back from her face, skimming it behind her ear before running his hand down her arm and finally resting it on her waist.

Touch. How long had it been since she'd been touched with tenderness? Memories of her childhood welled up again. Her father's laughter, her mother's song. There had been love there, as deep as forever. But it was nearly forgotten, nearly out of reach, drowned by a thousand dark incidents since.

The realization frightened her. There had been a time when she had vowed never to forget. Needing to feel, she reached out and touched Roman's chest. There was power there, but there was more—tenderness, caring. No matter what he said, he had been raised to love, and he had not forgotten, not like she.

But perhaps self-preservation had made her forget. Perhaps it was necessary to put tenderness behind her if she were to remain alive. She closed her eyes and steadied her mind.

Aye, she did not need this tenderness.

"I'm . . ." She tried to push away, but his arm was heavy across her waist. "I'm fine now. I'll see to your other wounds."

"Rest for a bit, lass. Dunna fret; I willna bite."

Bite? It was hardly his teeth that worried her. "I'm not . . . fretting."

"Nay?" Raising his hand, he skimmed his fingers through her hair again, touching her ear, her throat. "Ye nearly fainted."

"Well, I . . ." She shivered. His touch felt shivery warm, like an errant sunbeam breaking through a winter sky. "I um . . . should have eaten, I suppose."

He smiled, just a glimpse of humor that she thought too seldom found his face. "And here I hoped ye were overwhelmed by the sight of me masculinity."

Betty the barmaid would have come up with a saucy rejoinder. Tara the lass blushed. She lowered her eyes and turned her face away. But Roman gently caught her chin and urged it upward.

"Who are ye?" he whispered.

For a moment she couldn't speak, but finally she forced the single word from between her lips. "Bet—" she began, but at that moment, he kissed her.

Sunshine flooded Tara's life in a torrent of light, warming her system, heating her blood. His hand cupped her neck. His heart raced against hers. His mouth slipped away, kissing her jaw, her throat.

Rays of hot pleasure seared her skin, threatening her with its heat. The woman named Betty would be lost in the inferno. The Shadow would be no more. All that remained was Tara, alone and terrified.

She pushed against him, panicked, trying to break free.

He eased back. "I have frightened ye?"

She was Betty—the barmaid, the whore. She did not frighten. "Nay. I simply . . . Too much activity 'tis bad for your leg."

"Too much activity?" He grinned again, just the corner of a smile. "How much activity were ye planning?"

Her chest hurt, for her heart was racing along like a runaway cart horse. "None at all," she breathed, but seeing him thus, smiling, seductive, alluring, made her mouth go dry and her wits drown.

"Take yer clothes off."

"What?" she gasped.

Their faces were inches apart, but their bodies were much closer, pressed against each other. "Take yer clothes off," he whispered.

She tried to form some sort of denial, but Betty the barmaid had abandoned her completely, leaving her to mouth incoherent mutterings.

"I saved yer life, lass," he whispered, and suddenly his lips were against her ear, kissing it with butterfly tenderness.

She shivered. Her eyes fell closed.

"I thought . . ." She battled with her own weaknesses, trying to remember her reasons for celibacy. "I thought you were a gentleman."

"I told ye I was na ta be trusted, lass. I warned ye. 'Twas ye that denied me words," he said, and kissed the tender dell behind her lobe.

"But I . . ." She couldn't think, couldn't talk. "But I . . ." His fingers skimmed down the shallow furrow in the center of her back. Her breathing became erratic. "I . . ."

"Shh," he murmured again, and suddenly his hands were beneath her simple, boy's tunic. They were warm and strong against her skin. He was kissing her with such sweet, aching tenderness that there was little she could do but let the shirt skim upward. She lifted her arms, allowing it to ease over her head.

But now there was a new impediment, for she had bound her breasts with long strips of white cloth.

" 'Twould seem I forget that ye are a lad today," he whispered. His hands skimmed down her back, smoothing away her hose, caressing every inch of her as he scooped her closer still. Her legs seemed to open of their own accord, and suddenly his hips were clasped between them. She could feel the hard length of him, hot and eager against her sensitized softness.

Somehow, he had rolled to his back. She rode him astride, pressing her desire against his. His hands kneaded her buttocks. Letting her head drop back and allowing nothing but the hot, wild feelings to permeate her senses, she moaned.

Her skin tingled at his touch, and her head spun. She had lived in the underbelly of Firthport long enough to know the consequences of her actions, but she had been starved for human touch for too many years. The floodgates of desire burst open. There seemed nothing she could do but press against the rising tide and hope to stay afloat.

His hands eased up her back. She arched toward

him, feeling his fingers pause on the bindings that covered her chest. Not for an instant did the rhythm of their bodies slow. They rocked against each other like enchanted beings, not finding copulation, but not able to draw apart, sipping at the forbidden nectar of desire. Her bindings loosened. The clothes eased from her torso, dropping away.

She heard Roman catch his breath as one nipple peeked from its confinement. The rocking pace of his movements slowed. One hand slipped forward to scoop the fabric away and cup her breast.

Her gasp sounded much like his, but higher-pitched and breathy.

"Lass . . ." His tone was husky, deep as midnight, quiet as gentle waters. "Ye are beautiful."

Her hair had tumbled over her shoulders. It caressed his scared chest, brushed against his amulet.

"Ye are bonny beyond words," he whispered, and, urging her toward him, gently kissed her lips.

Desire erupted anew, but now the position had changed. Instead of having him trapped beneath her, his penis pressed hot and turgid against the entrance of her being.

She was so close to heaven, just inches away. He pressed gently inward. Her breathing stopped. Her heart raced on.

He eased into her tender portal a fraction of an inch. But with that invasion, good sense flooded in.

The consequences of such an act were enormous, too lethal to ignore any longer. She ended the kiss, placed a shaky hand to his chest, and pushed away, breathing hard.

"Lass . . ." He opened his eyes and ceased the seesaw rhythm of his hips. His jaw was clenched as if it pained him to stop, and for a moment, the rock hard strength of his arms shivered.

" 'Arry!" She said the name suddenly. She'd wholly forgotten that she was supposed to be mourning Harry's passing. Sweet Mary! Tara pressed in earnest now against his chest, trying to retreat, but he moved with her. "I . . . I cannot. I am in mourning!" In mourning! The words sounded foolish even to her own ears, for she was naked and trembling with desire. Still, she clung to her story.

He tried to draw her nearer. She scrambled off the bed, but he held her wrist. Scraps of cloth hung from her shoulders like a mummy's ghoulish garb.

"I didna mean ta frighten ye," he said, wincing as his feet touched the floor. But despite the pain, he stood and moved closer, entrapping her with his arm about her bare waist.

"Forgive me for me haste, lass. It seemed ye have possessed me senses. But I will move more slowly now."

It didn't matter how slowly he moved. The results would still be the same. She must escape.

But she had been captured again. It was time to think. Betty! She was Betty, she told herself. With a supreme effort, she steadied her breathing and relaxed in his arms.

He hugged her more tightly.

"There is little enough joy ta be found in this life," he said. "Let us take it where we can." He smoothed her hair against her back.

She closed her eyes. What kind of magic did he weave that he had but to touch her and she would lose her senses, forget her plight?

"But 'arry. 'E . . . 'e just . . ."

He placed a finger gently to her lips. "Na more lies, lass. Na tonight," he said, then slouched against her for a moment, as if shaken by weakness.

"Lies!" She tried to sound indignant, to hold to her role. "Ya think I lie?" She was Betty. Quick of wit, indomitable. She only needed to hold out a bit longer, for he was weakening. "'Arry *is* dead," she said.

His eyes spoke of his doubt as his hand glided up her back, under her hair, cradling her neck. "Then let him go, and let us live," he whispered as he kissed her.

She wrapped her arms about his back. "Aye," she rasped. She was the lonely woman, yearning to be consoled. "Yer right. He would want me to live." 'Twas all an act, part of her role, but he felt wonderfully hard against her, and she trembled. "Touch me. Help me forget all, if just for a small piece of time."

Their gazes met, but in a moment his head dropped back slightly, and he scowled as if puzzled.

Guilt gnawed at her. But she could not afford that emotion. "Roman?" she said, putting just the proper bit of worry in her tone. "Are you well?"

"Aye." He straightened and met her eyes. "'Tis merely yer presence that makes me weak."

"Here. Lie down," she said, urging him back onto the pallet.

He sat, but his arms remained about her, pulling her to her knees between his powerful thighs.

The intimacy of this new position nearly overwhelmed her. She willed herself not to blush, but the great length of him throbbed against her abdomen, promising pleasures she had never scaled. Pleasures she suddenly wished to. But she would have to leave, and very soon. She would not see him again—ever. The thought burned her mind. Her hand skimmed his chest. It was brawny and broad and breathtakingly alluring, adorned with that strange amulet that would forever remind her of him. She smoothed her hand upward along the leather strip. "L-lie down," she urged again, drawing her fingers away.

"Only if ye do, lass."

She managed a nod.

He pulled her gently onto the pallet. They stretched out, facing each other. Every inch of him was hot and hard and eager. He shifted his wounded thigh, and she bent her leg, resting it over his to avoid direct contact.

But this new position was more stimulating yet, for she was nestled against him warm and safe, held in his arms like a precious gift. And she was wet, achingly wet, like nothing she had experienced before.

He kissed her then, and suddenly, as simply as breathing, his manhood was between her thighs and gliding inward.

Ecstasy called. She curled her fingers around his amulet as she closed her eyes and ever so carefully rocked against him.

But suddenly his hands fell away and his head lolled back against the pillow, seeming to weigh him down.

"Roman?" she breathed, wanting more, wanting satiation.

"Lass, I feel almost as if . . ." He opened his eyes, and suddenly his gaze was not warm and gentle, but sharp and accusatory.

Reality snapped back into place. Sweet Mary, she must think, she must escape. "What . . . what is it?" she asked, managing to sound bewildered.

"Ye've drugged me," he rasped.

"What?" She opened her eyes wide. Where were her clothes? Could she make it to the door? "What are ya talking about?" she asked. She slipped from the pallet. Her feet touched the floor.

"Hell fire!" he growled, grabbing her wrist and rising with her. "Ye drugged me!"

"Nay!" she shrieked, and, twisting with all her might, broke free.

He charged after her.

She screamed, but he stumbled, and in that moment, she grabbed her tunic and fled.

Chapter 13

Roman sat in silent darkness, watching.
He was a wiser man now, colder, leaner, but wiser.

He had examined the situation from every angle, considered every word she had spoken.

He would find her, and when he did, she would pay dearly.

Unconsciousness had grabbed him like a dark troll on the previous night. He had tried to follow her, had grappled with the black demon, trying to break free. But her drug was strong.

He curled his hand into a fist. She had betrayed him, tricked him, stolen from him. First the precious necklace, and now ... He curled his fingers over his chest. Damn her hide, she had taken his amulet.

She was the mistress of lies, and he had played her fool. But no more. Henceforth neither scruples nor her compelling charm would forestall his revenge. She owed him. She would pay. 'Twas as simple as that.

Thus he waited in absolute immobile silence, watching the door of a gray hovel from the anonymity of a black shadow.

She would come, he told himself. For though she

had spewed a thousand lies, she had not lied about the sickly babe. That one bit of her dialogue had stayed with him like a tick, refusing to be forgotten, for when she'd spoken of the lass named Sineag, she had been another person, an innocent herself, it had seemed, lost in memories. Sineag! 'Twas a Scottish name. Or so Roman had first thought. But nay. 'Twas a *Gaelic* name. And Gaelic meant Irish as well as Scottish. Once he had realized that, doors had opened to him. It had been simple enough to ask about a newborn child with a cough. All it took were a few well-placed lies—lies that came easier now.

Now he would wait and watch, for she would come. Something in his gut told him that much.

The night dragged toward morning. But the door of the hovel remained closed. Even from this distance, Roman could hear a child's labored coughing. The sound wore on his nerves.

Where was Tara? Why hadn't she arrived? Had he misjudged her yet again? Had she fabricated the whole story, after all?

He could wait no longer, for the shadows were fading. He would need to find better hiding for daylight watch.

Across the street was a broken cart. It had only one wheel, and the wood was rotting through in many places, but 'twas big enough for Roman to hide in. Glancing carefully about him, he hurried to it and placed himself uncomfortably inside.

In order to remain out of sight, he had to bend his legs. They cramped. He swore silently and tried to rub the ache from them.

Dawn arrived. A chaffinch perched on the edge of the cart and cocked his head at Roman, as if sizing him up. Then, seeming to decide the human was harmless, the small finch burst into song.

Roman scowled, thinking the bird correct in his

assessment of the damage he might cause. If Tara appeared at the end of the cart, he doubted his ability to unfold, much less give chase. Nevertheless, he stayed, entertained by the little songster's music and marveling at the fact that despite it all, life continued, the dawn rose, birds sang.

The cart had a small hole from where a knot of wood had fallen. If Roman craned his neck just so, he was able to watch the door.

The neighborhood began waking. He smelled the aroma of cook fires, heard the slam of a door, and a farewell as someone left a cottage. A child carrying a basket passed the door he watched. Roman's attention perked up. A child! Tara had pretended to be a child before. She could surely do so again.

But this one was less than ten years old, and no more than four feet tall. 'Twould be a difficult disguise even for a black-hearted conniver like her.

He settled back onto the floor of the cart again. The wood had long ago been eroded by wind and weather. The softer lumber had worn away, causing sharp ridges to rise, seemingly for the express purpose of tormenting his back.

Hoofbeats clopped down the street, softly muffled by the muddy road. A flea-bitten cob trotted up, slowed to a walk, and finally stopped. From his hellish position, Roman watched the aged animal mouth its bit, then hang his head and rest, cocking one bony hip.

The driver was an old man, grizzled, bearded. He wore a slouch hat, a long, gray doublet that may have fit him years ago when he had yet borne the muscle of youth. Now it hung on his thin frame, reaching well past his thighs. When he eased himself from the cart, Roman saw that the freedom of youth had indeed left him. He was dressed in baggy hose that matched the doublet, but one leg ended at the knee.

Leaning against the cart, the old man reached inside and drew out a pottery jar. He cradled it against his chest, then turned with agonizing slowness and took a gnarled crutch from its resting place beneath the seat. Placing it under his right arm, he limped toward the hovel.

It seemed to take forever for the old man to reach his destination. Mayhap in another time and another place Roman might have seen fit to help the old gaffer. But not today. He shifted his gaze from the stooped back to the street, waiting, impatience gnawing him. But finally the old fellow reached his destination and knocked at the portal.

It opened in a moment. A woman stood in the doorway. She was young, but there were lines of worry on her face and shadows of terror in her eyes. Words were spoken. Roman knew that much, though he couldn't make out exactly what was said.

The old man nodded and handed the jug over to the woman. There were tears in her eyes and when she spoke Roman could just make out her shaky words of thanks and blessings.

The mother reached out for a moment and touched the old man's cheek. Though Roman had no way of knowing what was in the jug, it was obviously something of utmost importance. This, he knew, was a singular moment. A sterling act of kindness.

He watched the mother draw back, watched the door close.

So Tara had been right. God saw fit to help wee Sineag without the Shadow's intervention. Even in the bowels of Firthport, kindness lived.

Memories of the Highlands flooded Roman. All was not dark. All was not evil.

The old man turned. His face was hidden be-

neath the limp brim of his hat. His gnarled hands
clutched . . .

But wait . . .

The hands weren't gnarled. They were slim and
delicate and . . .

Roman launched from his hiding place with a
snarl. He sprang over the side of the cart, and, even
as he catapulted from cover, he saw the old man
jerk to a halt, eyes wide.

Less than ten rods separated them. The old man
stood paralyzed for a moment. Then, with the suddenness of a doe, he erupted into action. But instead of running, he began clawing at his clothes.
The baggy hose fell away. The wooden crutch clattered to the ground. And suddenly he was bare-
legged and running like the devil was behind him.

Tara! It was Tara. Roman knew it. He was gaining on her. She was near. So near. He reached for
her. Her doublet skimmed past his fingers. He
swore. She spurted ahead. Roman's thigh throbbed
and threatened to spill him to the ground, but he
would not lose her this time. Not if the hounds of
hell rose up and devoured him.

Sheer rage drove him on. He reached again,
snagged her coat, and reeled her back. She shrieked
as cloth ripped from her body. But suddenly the
doublet hung limply in his hand, and she was
sprinting away.

Roman tossed the garment aside with a curse
and leapt after her. But she had already turned a
corner. He careened around it and skidded to a
halt. She was nowhere in sight. A stone fence
stretched off to the right and left. Surely she was
behind it. Back in motion, he leapt over it and
stopped again. His breath came in hard gasps, and
his thigh pulsed with weakening pain.

Hell fire! Where . . .

It was then that he saw the holly bush move. It

was small, no higher than his knees, and surely not big enough to hide her and yet . . . Neither could she be a lad or an old man.

Heart still thumping, he turned in a circle as if searching for her, then, with a curse, he ran along the fence to the left.

Once past the house, he leapt over the stone and hedge, circled the hovel at a gallop, and slid to a halt at the corner.

She was there, crouched like a frightened hare half-inside the bush and glancing furtively about as she rose cautiously to her feet.

He saw it all as if in a dream. She rose. He neared. She turned, but it was far too late. His fingers curled into her shirtfront. He dragged her against him. Her gasp was loud and satisfying to his ears.

She fought like a wildcat, twisting and thrashing. His leg burned with her pummeling. His chest ached from her claws, but nothing could diminish the glory of crushing her against him.

It was not an easy task to drag her to the cart in the street. But Roman did so, barely noticing that his arm throttled her throat while his opposite hand gripped the back of her tunic near her bottom.

He tossed her into the cart, then jumped in after to weigh her down and click the horse into motion. The old flea-bitten cob could move with surprising speed when turned toward home. It sped through the mud and over the cobbles until Roman pulled it to a halt in front of Tara's door.

There was no one about. Roman dragged the bearded girl from the cart, sent the horse on his way, and pushed Tara into her own house. He closed the door and leaned against it.

They stared at each other. She was breathing hard. Her flattened chest rose and fell beneath the simple shirt. Her hose were gone, showing her slim, bare legs below the lengthy tunic. But her hat was miraculously still in place, as was the stringy gray hair that hung beneath it. Her thinning beard was several inches long and snowy white.

The sight of her thus sent a fresh wave of rage through Roman, for she was the embodiment of his own foolishness. He took a step forward. She retreated.

"What do ya want from me?" Her tone was pitched high with fear. He wanted revenge, and he was not above obtaining it at the expense of her little siren's body. Roman smiled. "Last time we were here together, we were interrupted a bit prematurely. I thought ye might wish to make up for that." He advanced again.

She retreated. "Stay away from me."

Roman canted his head. "Ye've changed, lass, for I remember ye moaning in me arms in this very room."

He had her backed nearly to the wall. They were mere inches apart.

"Indeed," he murmured. "Ye've changed."

"What do you want from me?" she asked again.

"I but want to give ye what ye wished from me. The pleasure of our bodies united," he said, leaning closer, lifting a hand to slide it around her waist. He would have his revenge. She shivered at his touch. " 'Tis what ye wanted, isn't it? Could I but feel ye against me," he mimicked. "Ye wanted me. Surely 'twas na a lie." He smoothed his hand sideways, down her hip, over her buttock. She shivered again, and her breath came faster.

"I . . ." She placed a hand to his chest and pushed, but with little strength. "I'm sorry about the drug," she whispered.

"Drug?" Roman gritted his teeth, but continued to stroke her backside. "Ye mean ta say ye drugged me? And here I thought 'twas but yer charm that made me lose me senses." He slipped his hand lower, down her thigh, letting his fingers run along the inside of her leg until they skimmed past her tunic and onto bare skin.

She jerked against him, breathing hard and fast.

"I thought 'twas surely me attraction ta ye that made the world seem ta tilt," he said. "And I thought surely 'twas the same for ye."

"I'm sorry!" She rasped the words. Her bound chest rose and fell. "I'm sorry for everything. Please . . ."

They stared at each other, both breathing hard.

"What do you want from me?"

He wanted *her*. Body and soul, writhing with ecstasy beneath his hands. He stared at her, enraged at himself, at his weaknesses, and lost in the horrible knowledge that no matter what, beard and all, he still wanted her and could not hurt her.

"Damn ye!" he swore through his teeth.

"I'm sorry, Scotsman," she whispered. "Sorry for everything. But the necklace is gone now. Out of our reach."

"Nay." He shook his head. Revenge. 'Twas revenge he wanted, he reminded himself. But she was soft and alluring, and though he vowed vengeance, one glimpse of her made him forget what he had suffered because of her, made him forget everything but how she felt in his arms, how her eyes danced when she laughed. He crossed his arms against his chest, hoping his gaze was as hard as his desire and praying she couldn't read the need in his eyes. "'Tis na out of *yer* reach, lass. I begin to think that nothing be past yer grasp."

She said nothing.

"Where's me amulet?"

"I didn't—"

"Me patience has been stretched ta the limit, lass.

If the truth be told, I have vowed to kill ye."

He watched her throat convulse as she swallowed, and felt a bit better, despite his own inability to make her pay.

"I didn't—"

He raised a hand. "Dunna lie."

She paused, blinked, then dipped her hand into her baggy tunic and pulled the amulet over her head.

He took it in his fist before slipping the leather strip about his neck. "Why?"

She pursed her lips and raised her chin. Now that he was close and cognizant, her lips seemed strangely smooth nestled between the frizzled white facial hair. "I believe in sharing."

"Strange how 'tis always *my* possessions that are shared," he said.

She clasped her hands like a shield between them, then turned to pace the floor stiffly. "Some of us have less to share than others." Betty the barmaid was back, or at least she was making a valiant effort to return. He could almost see the mask fall into place. " 'Arry is gone," she whispered. "I am but trying to survive, doin' me best to make it alone in the evil of this city." She rasped out a single sob and lifted a hand to cover her face. "You've no idea what I've been through, what with 'arry's death and Dagger's men, and . . ."

Roman couldn't stop the laughter that welled up in him. It began as a rumble of disbelief, then spewed forth in a roar of tension-relieving mirth. Before him paced an old man with curvaceous legs, a seductress's sexy voice, and the delicate hands of a musician—or a thief. A thief who could no more tell the truth than he could make her pay for her crimes. What a pathetic pair they made.

He continued to laugh, letting the noise fill the room until he was sated and the sound turned to small rumblings of humor. When his eyes cleared of tears, he found her glaring at him.

"You don't know what I've endured," she repeated as if trying to draw back the proper mood. But her cheeks were red and her eyes narrowed. "You don't know—"

"And neither do I care!" he said, sweeping forward to yank the hat from her head. Tough, white horsehairs snapped in two. The hat came free, scraggly bits of gray hair clinging to it. The beard, to which it had been attached, drooped away from her ears like tattered cobwebs.

He glared into her eyes. "I dunna wish ta hear yer sad lies, for ye have abused me sympathy far too long.

"Hell fire! Get rid of that thing," he said, yanking the beard free.

It came away in his hand. She squawked, grabbing her jaw in pain and stumbling back.

"How the hell did ye keep that on?"

"It's none of your affair," she said. "And neither is anything I do. I've done you no harm. So get out of my house."

"No harm?" he growled, circling her, feeling a need to move, to pace off his frustration. She turned with him, watching his face. "If such is how ye think, let us review the past. I had but met ye once when ye drugged me the first time."

She opened her mouth as if to deny his words, but he shook his head and went on.

"I have been the fool," he said, "But I see the truth plain enough now. Ye drugged me that first night, and I had done ye na harm."

She licked her lips. Was that honey stuck to her chin?

"Ye insulted me," she said.

"Insulted . . . Ahh," he said, nodding. "By offering ta bed ye."

She returned the nod. Her face looked haughty, or as haughty as a face could with wisps of frizzled white hair stuck to it with honey and God knew what. Her own hair, once pinned securely to her scalp, was coming loose and dangled down at strange angles.

"Ya treated me like a whore," she said.

" 'Twas me understanding that ye were a whore. Now I am na even sure yer a woman. But I know you're a thief. And ye stole me necklace."

She seemed almost to pale. But she shook her head. "I did not."

"But 'twas ye that made it possible to be stolen by drugging me."

It was her turn to laugh. "Do you think the Shadow needed *my* help?" She shook her head. "Hardly that. 'Twould have made no difference if you had been wide-awake and clutching the gems in your fist. He would have taken them anyway."

Roman didn't argue, but cocked his head slightly and circled her again. "Ye lied to me. Lied to me from the first."

"Lies leave no scars."

"Scars!" he snarled, jerking to a halt and yanking his doublet open. There was no shirt beneath it, for he had taken no time to obtain a new one. "Ye want to see scars?"

Her gaze shifted to his chest. She grimaced, but refused to turn her face away. "I did not cause them."

"I saved yer life." Anger was roiling up again, anger at himself, his weaknesses, her ungodly appeal.

"I did not ask you to. I told you to leave me be, to get gone."

He let his hands fall away from his doublet. It closed partway. "But I didna," he said. "And I willna. Na until the necklace is returned into me own hands."

"The necklace!" she shouted. "Damn the necklace. It is beyond your reach. Are you so daft that you cannot see that? Dagger has it. There is no way to get it back."

He stepped closer. "Aye. There is a way. And ye will find it."

She shook her head and stumbled back a step. "Nay. Never, for I have no wish to die."

"And neither does David MacAulay."

"I know no David MacAulay," she said. "And I do not wish to know him."

"That is good," Roman said, "for ye'll have precious little opportunity. He'll soon be dead—unless ye help me."

She pursed her lips, keeping her chin high and her hands clasped.

"Aye, he will die. And do ye ken why?"

She didn't answer.

"Na because he stole, lass," he said, circling her again. "Na because he lied. Or even because he left someone to die in his stead. He will die because he dared love."

She clasped her hands more tightly together. Beneath the glue and errant strands of beard, her face looked pale. "I care not for love."

He grabbed her arms and shook her. "But I care for vows made by me own lips. And I vowed to see him safely ta his father."

"Then you have a problem, don't you, Scotsman?"

"Nay, lass. Ye have a problem. For if ye dunna help me find the necklace, I swear before God I will send ye to the magistrate for yer crimes. David will na be the only one ta suffer. For surely loving a noblewoman is na so grievous a crime as theft."

"A noblewoman?"

He watched her. Her back was straight, her slim fingers clasped. "Aye. It seems he had the bad sense to become infatuated with Harrington's daughter."

The room seemed deathly quiet suddenly, and when she spoke her voice was weak. "*Lord* Harrington—of Harrington House?"

"Aye. She is a bonny lass. Fair-haired and fiery-spirited. Christine she is called. She reminds me a wee bit of ye, but lacks the beard."

"Ye said love. What makes ye think he loves her?"

"What difference is it ta ye?" Roman asked.

"No difference. I but wonder. What makes ya think he cherishes her and has not but used her for his own depraved desires?"

"I know the lad; he is young and full of himself. But he would not bed a woman against her will. And if I judge the lady rightly, she wouldna bed atall unless she had planned ta marry."

Her face looked strained. "They bedded?"

"Aye." He nodded in some confusion. "They bedded. And thus Harrington's rage. He says he willna lose another daughter to a . . . How did he say it? A barbarian, I believe was the term used."

"A barbarian." For a moment pain crossed her face. It was stark and clear and strangely honest. If honesty was an expression known to her. "So there might be . . . There might be a child?" she asked.

Roman scowled. "I suppose there is that possibility, though I am na privy to the lass's private state."

"And if MacAulay dies, what will happen to the babe?"

"Harrington says his daughter will wed a peer of the realm. I suspect the bairn would be raised as his own."

"Nay. A nobleman would not take the child as

his own. At least not in his heart. And what of Harrington's daughter?" Her voice was very soft again, far away.

"What?" Roman asked.

"This MacAulay that she loves—tell me of him."

Roman scowled and shook his head. "I dunna see what difference—"

"Please," she said softly. "Tell me of him."

"He has seen but two and twenty years. No more. But he has been raised to be honorable."

"And he is of . . . peasant stock?"

"Peasant? We in the Highlands dunna divide our peoples into peasants and noblemen. We be but one family. Though if the truth be known, David is the son of the laird of the MacAulays. The middle son," he added.

"And far beneath the Harrington name," Tara said softly.

Roman drew a deep breath. "The lad will soon die," he said, "unless the necklace is delivered."

She turned stiffly away. "It shall be delivered—for Christine Harrington and her love," she murmured.

"What say ye?"

She faced him. "You said you would turn me over to the magistrate if I did not cooperate, did you not?"

He nodded, feeling strangely disoriented. But he should be becoming accustomed to those feelings, for she forever tilted him off-balance. "Aye. I did that."

"And I would surely dance on the wind for my crimes."

It was an ugly term for an ugly thing. Death by hanging. He said nothing.

"I have no wish to die," she said. "And therefore . . ." She drew a deep breath, watching him. "I will see the necklace returned to you, but only if you do exactly as I say."

Chapter 14

"Exactly as ye say?" Roman asked.

Tara nodded. The decision had been made and she felt better for it. Dagger was a formidable adversary, but mayhap this Scotsman was just as deadly. In fact . . . She watched his eyes. There was something there that spoke of her own demise. Mayhap his allure was more dangerous than Dagger's evil, for he tempted her—tempted her to tell the truth, to share herself. But she must not, for if her true identity was revealed her life would surely be forfeit. Still, she could not let MacAulay die—not if Christine Harrington loved him. There was naught she could do but assist Roman in his mission and hope to send him on his way.

She rubbed her chin. It itched, as did her scalp where the brass pins dug into her flesh. She yanked them free.

Tendrils of hair slipped from confinement. She sighed, searched out the last pin, and rubbed her scalp. He watched, seeming strangely distracted for a moment.

"Mayhap ye have hopes of ordering me ta me own death," he suggested, but his tone was casual, as if the idea held little interest for him.

She paused from her chore of rubbing adhesive from her chin to look at him. It was a mistake, for her stomach pitched when she did so. Mayhap it was his eyes, deep and mysterious as the forest beyond Firthport. Or mayhap it was his form, broad and hard, marred by scars taken to protect her. Or maybe it was far more than that, something inexplicable. But whatever his allure, she had to resist it. "If ye fear the risk, Scotsman, ye'd best head for your homeland now," she said, willing her tone to be casual. "For there is little chance either of us will live through the task."

"Then why do ye do it?"

She fidgeted under his gaze. Not since her childhood had she allowed anyone this close to her person. It made her jittery. And nervousness could kill as easily as overconfidence. "I told ye. 'Twas your threat. If you turn me over to the magistrate, I will die for certain."

"So yer scairt of me threat?"

"Aye. And why shouldn't I be?"

"Ye should be, lass," he said softly. "But yer na. And so I wonder why ye agree to help me?"

Their gazes fused. She jerked hers away. "I told ya. I have no wish to die. Thus I am but taking the course that offers the best chance of survival."

"Ye lie, lass," he said quietly. "Ye have other reasons, but I ken na what they be. Hence I will play by yer rules since ye know the opponents far better. I but ask, what course we follow?"

Tara remained motionless for a moment. A plan had trickled into her mind minutes before. Perhaps she could do this thing. Perhaps she could free MacAulay and exact some revenge on Dagger at the same time. Excitement tingled in her system. Details, sharp and titillating, begged to be honed. Clothing, costumes, contacts, schedules, information.

"What course?" he repeated.

She shrugged. "I have but the seed of an idea," she said, and turned away.

"Show me the seed."

She stopped and turned toward him. "We will offer Dagger something he can't refuse."

Roman's brows were low over his eyes. He looked formidable and powerful. Perhaps he was right. Maybe she should be afraid of him. But she was not, at least not in the usual sense. "I thought ye didna ken who Dagger was."

"I do not," she admitted.

"Then how?"

"Greed," she said simply. "James is dead." He was a friend, and the only fence she could trust. She would be a fool to steal again, but the scheme called. "So how will Dagger get rid of his goods?" she mused. Filling a basin with water, she washed her face as ideas flooded her mind. "He must have his own system. A foreigner, perhaps. The necklace is very recognizable, and Harrington is powerful. Dagger will not sell it close to home. Not in Firth-port for certain and possibly not in all of England. So chances are good he still has the jewels. And if he has them, 'tis logical to assume he has others, for his thieves are everywhere. All we need is to offer him something that he can sell to the same market. Something comparable. But what?" She scrubbed absently at her face. " 'Twas a fine piece. What would compare? Jewels? Fine crockery? Royal—"

"We'll na steal."

Tara looked at Roman standing in silent disapproval, large and firm and forbidding. And she threw back her head and laughed.

"What do ye find so amusing?"

"You." She stabbed a finger at him. "A simple mention of theft and ya blanch. I have to say, it makes your threats toward me a bit less worrisome."

"So if I dunna worry ye, why do ye agree to assist in me search for the necklace?" he asked, taking a step closer.

She refused to back away. "Mayhap I feel somewhat responsible for your plight."

He was very near now, close enough so that she had to raise her chin to look into his eyes. "So . . ." He raised one hand to her cheek. She managed not to shiver beneath his touch, even when it slipped down to her throat. "Ye pity me, lass?"

He could crush the life from her with one hand. But 'twas not her throat she worried for, but her heart.

"Mayhap," she whispered.

His fingers tightened against her throat as he leaned closer. "And mayhap ye forget the men I have kilt."

She held her breath. "I do not forget." Silence echoed in the tiny room. "But neither do I forget that they were evil."

He leaned closer still. His breathing was harsh, his expression strained as his fingers tightened even more around her throat. "There is na difference between them and me," he rasped. "Na difference atall."

Fear flickered through her, but it lasted for only a moment, for through his eyes, she could see into his soul. "You are wrong, Scotsman. There is the difference of night and day."

For a moment she thought perhaps it was she who was wrong. She felt his fingers tremble against her neck, felt the war that waged within him. But soon he pulled his hand away and drew a deep breath. "What do we steal?" he asked.

She forced out a laugh. It sounded shaky and weak. "*We?*" She laughed again. The sound was a bit steadier. "We don't steal anything, Scotsman."

He scowled and watched her from beneath lowered brows.

"Tempers get people killed," she said. "Tempers and . . . passion. You'll steal nothing," she said. "But I . . ." She paused, thinking. The necklace flashed through her mind, and then, clear as morning, she saw Lord Harrington's jeweled crucifix. It was made of silver and rubies. She had been no more than ten when she had first seen it from her hiding place in the holly bushes. She remembered the scratches they had caused her, but she hadn't noticed at the time, for she'd been enthralled with her first glance of her grandfather. He had worn a richly embroidered doublet with velvet hose and the crucifix. For a moment, hungry envy had consumed her, but then she had glanced at his eyes.

The sight of them had made her cringe back into the prickly bushes, for never before had she seen such emptiness.

She had remained in the holly until dark, but finally she had returned to the tiny shack she called home. Even now, she remembered opening the door, remembered Cork looking up from the kettle above the orange glow of the fire. "Ah, lass, so ye finally arrive. I thought mayhap the fairies 'ad taken ye. Thought perhaps I'd 'ave all the stew ta meself for a change. But I see I'll 'ave ta share again." He sighed. The worry he'd tried to hide faded from his eyes, replaced by its usual twinkle for the wonders of life. "Well, are ye going ta eat. Or did ye eat at the palace, mayhap?" he asked. She had not answered, but had darted across the dirt floor to throw herself into his welcoming arms.

Tears collected somewhere in her soul, but long ago they ceased to visit her eyes.

"What are ye thinking, lass?" Roman asked.

The sound of his brogue startled her from her reverie.

"The crucifix," she said. "'Tis destined to be mine."

"Explain."

A trickle of excitement coursed through her veins. It had been long indeed since she'd challenged a house such as Harrington's, and far too long to wait to seek her revenge from him. "Surely the symbol of a lowly shepherd belongs with me rather than with a lord of the realm."

"What are ye talking about?"

She smiled. "Lord Harrington is about to make a contribution to charity."

He watched her in silence for a moment, then, "Explain from the beginning."

Clasping her hands in front of her body, she paced past him. The trickle of excitement had turned to a steady flow. "'Tis a simple scheme really. I've but to steal the crucifix, let the right people know what I've done, tell them I'm looking to become a Daggerman, deliver the crucifix to Dagger, then follow him to where he keeps his other goods." She shrugged. "And steal the necklace, of course."

"What could be simpler?" he asked.

She paced again, thinking hard. "There might be a few tight spots—making Dagger trust me, making him believe he needs me. He's got a hundred men in his ring of thieves if he has one. Why would he want me? What would set me apart from them? And then, of course, there is the matter of not letting the Daggermen kill me." She scowled, deep in thought, pacing in a circle and talking to herself. "They're a suspicious lot, and likely to—"

She stopped abruptly when she felt Roman's hands on her arms and nearly bumped into his chest. "What is it?" she asked.

His scowl was dark. "'Tis too dangerous."

She blinked once. The scheme had taken over as it always did. Focus was her forte. "Dangerous?"

"Yer a conniving little urchin," he said. "But I'll na have yer death on me conscience."

She looked him straight in the eye. "I thought that was the purpose, Scotsman. To see me pay for my crimes."

His grip relaxed a bit. "I but want the necklace returned and MacAulay freed. I've na wish ta see ye dead—na at this moment leastways."

"Then go away and leave me in peace."

He dropped his hands and turned away. "Peace! That is all I desire. But there is na peace for me until I finish what I have begun. I made me vow. And I must stand by it."

"Then let me go about my business. The sooner I get the crucifix, the sooner MacAulay goes free."

He shook his head and snorted a laugh. "Ye must think me daft indeed if ye think I'll let ye out of me sight."

"In fact, I do think ye daft, Scotsman. But I tell you now, if you don't leave me alone, I'll not get the crucifix. And if I don't get the crucifix, I'll not get the necklace. And if I don't get the necklace, your friend dies."

Roman shook his head again. "Aye, ye'll get the necklace," he said. "But I'll be there with ye the whole while."

She laughed out loud. "You?" She let her gaze skim him from head to toe, and laughed again. "You couldn't steal a kiss from a whore."

"Indeed?" he said and suddenly he was up against her with his body pressed hard and close as his arms encircled her. "Then who did I steal a kiss from when I kissed ye, lass?" His lips were very close, his arms broad and strong.

Fear mingled with excitement within her. She

pushed at his chest, afraid of the feelings.

"Ye tell me ye are Betty and nothing more," he murmured. "But how did a simple barmaid learn to mastermind a theft of this caliber?"

She swallowed. The thrill of the scheme had caused her to forget herself. "'Arry . . ." She remembered to make her voice catch as if on tears. "I knew the Shadow for a long while."

For a moment she thought he would call her a liar. Indeed, he raised a brow as if doubting every word, but finally he asked, "And the Shadow shared his plans with ye?"

She shrugged, trying to look casual. "He trusted me."

"Yer generally a fine liar, lass, but now ye go ta far." The slightest suggestion of a smile tilted his lips.

"Are ya callin' me a liar?" Indignance was hard to come by, but she did her best.

He laughed. "Na, lass, of course na. Go on. Tell me more. The Shadow—he planned the thefts?"

She nodded.

"And executed them?"

"Of course."

"And ye?"

He pressed closer still, and suddenly she remembered her strange state of undress. Her legs were bare below the knee, and her heart hammered a strange warning.

"What was *yer* job, lass?"

"I would wait," she said. "And pray for his safe return."

"So he valued ye for yer loyalty?" he asked, his breath warm against her face. "And for the beauty I've seen revealed beneath this lowly garment?" He slipped a hand down her back.

She swallowed hard. Her pulse was racing. His hand skimmed upward, sliding beneath her hair until it finally caressed the bare skin at the back of her neck. She shivered against his touch. "I . . ." She had to keep her head . . . or lose it. "I have other skills."

"Oh?"

She could sense his amusement, though she could no longer see his face. His breath fanned her ear. His kiss there was butterfly soft against its upper curve.

Her breath caught in her throat and she tried to pull away, but her effort was weak, and his grasp strong.

"Dare I ask what he taught ye, lass?" he inquired, and kissed the corner of her mouth.

Excitement sizzled through her, followed by panic. She thrust away and managed to stumble back. He followed, but she held up a hand. "Your amulet."

"What?"

"Where is your amulet?"

He lifted a hand to his chest. It came away empty—again. Shakily, she pulled the thing from beneath her own tunic where it hung from her neck.

"How the devil—"

"He taught me much," she repeated.

He nodded, suddenly thoughtful. "And we'll need every bit of that knowledge to execute yer wild scheme."

She shook her head. "Not we, Scotsman. I work alone."

"Na this time."

"I give you my word to retrieve the necklace and deliver it into your hands."

"And I'll believe ye," he said, "when I see ye declared a living saint by the bishop of Bradberry."

"So my word is not good enough for you?"

He laughed aloud. "Nay, lass, it is na. Now ye waste me time, and I've little ta spare, for David's days dwindle. But why steal from Harrington?"

"There is a beautiful simplicity in this," Tara said. "To steal from the very person that will gain from the act in the end."

"And how do ye plan to break into Harrington House in the midst of the night without anyone seeing?"

"I'll not break in," she said. "Nay. I'll use the light of day to have a look about."

He shook his head. "Then ye'll have ta choose another victim, for I canna go to Harrington House without being recognized."

" 'Tis fine, for I'll not take ya with me," she repeated.

"Aye, lass, ye will, for I willna leave yer side until the necklace is once again in me own possession. That I promise ye."

His expression brooked no argument. His eyes were steady, and his chest, where his doublet parted, showed the scars he had already gained because of her.

She had no wish to see him dead. Neither did she wish to be killed because of him. But stealth and cunning were not always the only skills needed. She could not forget his strength in battle. Neither could she forget that he had guarded the door while she had escaped from Dagger's men.

" 'Twould be safer without you," she said.

"Safer for whom?"

She wasn't certain if it was an accusation or not. But it was clear that he had no intention of changing his mind. "You canna go like that."

He scowled a question.

"The beard," she said, motioning to his face.

"What about me beard."

"It'll be shaved if you're to accompany me."

"Nay."

"Do you forget that you killed several of Dagger's men? He's a black-hearted devil and kills for no reason, but he's likely to frown on the death of his own men. Would you rather be bearded and dead or live and smooth-faced?"

"Let me think," Roman said, stroking his beard as if it were his beloved.

She laughed, letting her tension dissipate. "You made a jest, Scotsman. I did not believe ya knew how. Sit down, I'll sharpen a blade. Unless you'd rather I use pumice to remove your beard."

"Now ye jest, if ye think I would trust ye ta do either," he said, glaring at her as she moved toward the fire.

She turned, knife in hand. "You think I will cut your throat?"

"The thought had occurred to me."

She smiled. "And to me. Sit."

He eyed the trunk she'd indicated. "I've worn this beard since I left childhood behind."

She approached, sharpening the knife as she did so. "Do I threaten your manhood, Scotsman?"

He eyed the blade. " 'Tis possible," he said.

"Do I frighten you?"

"Aye, lass, ye do."

She laughed, then sobered, watching his face. She did not scare him, and it was possible, she thought, that nothing would. "Think what you will about my lies and deceptions, Scotsman, but I'll tell you this, I am alive today because of them. If you hope to return to your homeland the same, you'll heed my advice and welcome the blade."

"I doubt if merely shaving me will fool our adversaries."

"I said nothing of *merely* shaving you," she said, urging him onto the trunk. Testing the blade with her thumb, she moved behind him, but before she touched his beard, he caught her wrist.

"What do ye mean by that?"

"I see ye as . . ." She shrugged and narrowed her eyes in thought. "A jester, I think."

Chapter 15

❦❦

"**W**hat are ye jabbering about?" Roman asked, still holding her wrist.

She lifted the blade in a casual motion. "If you insist on accompanying me, you'll need a disguise. I think you'd make a fine jester."

He snorted and released her wrist. "Not in this lifetime, lass."

She glanced at the freshly sharpened blade. "That may not be too long."

"As I said, we canna go to Harrington's, so there is na need for me ta disguise meself," Roman reminded her.

"Lord Crighton!" she said, abruptly stopping her knife a quarter of an inch from his throat.

"What?" He apparently didn't dare turn his head, but tilted his eyes up in an attempt to see her face.

" 'Tis time for Lord Crighton to pay."

"For what?"

"His crimes."

"Which are?"

"Too numerous to mention, I'm sure," she said, touching the blade to his neck.

"Can I ask ye to elaborate without having me throat cut?"

She paused again, staring at the wall and remembering. "There was once a small boy. His mother was Crighton's maid. But the mother died, and the boy stayed on, doing what work he could. 'Twas down at the dock I first saw him. A narrow lad he was with black hair and sparkling eyes. He was carrying Crighton's trunk when I spied him. But the trunk was larger than he, and he dropped it."

Her stomach pitched slightly. "I remember seeing Crighton turn. On his face was the expression of a ghoul. No corpse could have looked colder. He carried a walking stick topped by a mermaid of gold. When he swung the stick across the boy's back, I thought surely the lad would die."

"We steal the mermaid," said Roman quietly.

Their gazes met. She nodded slowly.

"Tell me, Mistress Tara, did ye save the wee lad?"

There was something in his eyes. Understanding. Empathy that bordered on pain. She opened her mouth to speak, to ease his mind. But good sense rushed back. "'Arry did," she said quickly. The moment was broken.

"There are times, whole moments sometimes, when ye almost tell the truth," Roman said.

She snorted. "Don't hold your breath, Scotsman."

"How can I do aught when ye have a knife poised at me throat?"

"Ya still don't trust me? Even after that touching tale?"

He scowled, looking tense. "What makes ye think ye know how ta shave a man?"

"I've done it many times."

"Any survivors?"

She laughed quietly and scraped the blade one quick, seemingly careless stroke up his throat. "One."

He winced but didn't move his head. "Scarred?"

"Aye. Quite badly."

" 'Tis probably why the Shadow never showed his face in the light of day."

"Nay. I never shaved 'Arry."

"A wise man, I see."

"The Shadow had a very light beard," she said, scraping again. Dark, coarse hair tripped over the blade and fell unheeded to the floor. "Yours resembles Cork's." She had already finished his neck and moved to his right cheek.

"Cork?" he asked.

Memories flared. An old man's gnarled fingers on hers, guiding, teaching. Repetition. Unorthodox lessons held by a fire's orange glow. Cork's knotty sense of humor. Laughter.

"Who is Cork?" he asked again.

"He was a good man," she said. "But he is gone."

" 'Tis sorry I be."

It had been long indeed since she had performed this task. It felt right somehow and soothing. "As am I," she said. "But I was lucky to know him as long as I did."

"He was an old man?"

" 'Tis good you are at guessing."

"Your grandfather?"

For a moment, her hand shook. The blade wobbled.

"Careful, lass. I've grown fond of me nose."

She seemed stiff suddenly. Roman remained silent for a moment, letting her relax and enjoying the warmth of her free hand on his opposite cheek.

"Cork was na yer grandfather?"

For a moment, he thought she would refuse to answer. "Nay. My grandfather outlives my sire."

"Again I am sorry."

" 'Tis said the good oft die afore the evil."

He watched her carefully, searching for clues to who she was. Though he knew it shouldn't matter, thoughts of her consumed him. "Yer grandfather is evil?"

"*Voilà*," she said, drawing back as she examined his face. " 'Tis finished. Ya look quite charming."

Roman put his hand to his jaw. It felt oddly smooth. "And barely a scar to show for it," he said.

"Ya wound me," she said mockingly, but in her eyes, Roman thought he saw pain.

He rose to his feet. "Tell me yer tale, lass."

"Which one?" she asked, her tone flippant.

"The true one."

" 'Twould bore you unto death. Fiction is much more intriguing," she said, turning away.

He caught her hand. "What could it hurt to dabble in the truth?"

Her gaze lifted to his face. There was emotion there, deep and dark, but soft somehow. "How did you break your nose?" she asked quietly.

"Were we na talking about ye?"

" 'Tis a boring subject. While you . . ." She raised her hand. It was soft and warm against his cheek. "You have a good face, Roman of the Forbes. I admit it intrigues me. How did ya break your nose?"

" 'Twas a lad at Glen Creag," he said. "Two years older than I, he was. He delighted in calling me Dermid."

"Your uncle's name," she said quietly.

Roman nodded. "I didna care ta be reminded that he was me kinsman."

"Who initiated the battle?"

"I have a fierce temper," he said.

She smiled. "Do ya?"

"Aye."

"And was your hair as red as your temper?"

"How did ye guess?"

"There are streaks of auburn amidst the dark."

She smoothed her fingers into his hairline. "I bet ya were a bonny lad."

Intimacy hung between them, begging to be acknowledged.

"Who are ye?" Roman whispered.

The room was silent, but suddenly, Tara drew away. "I am the one who will steal back your necklace, but only if we plan well and carefully."

Roman scowled at her secrecy. "I was told once that women enjoy speaking of themselves. There will be some satisfaction in telling Roderic that for once he was wrong about the fairer sex."

She smiled. Dressed in ratty clothes and forgotten pieces of beard, the sun seemed to shine with that expression. "Where were you educated, Scotsman?"

"Will this shed any light on yer past?"

"Nay. But it may well help assure your future."

"I schooled in Naples."

"Truly?" She looked as if he had just enlightened her with the secret of the universe. "Might you speak Italian?"

He said something in quick Italian.

"That's beautiful. What does it mean?"

Roman watched her. Her eyes shone as blue as a Highland lochan. Her smile sparkled like a thousand moonlit waves. "Had I known Italian would cause such excitement, I might have tried it long ago."

She laughed. "What does it mean?"

"It means, ye speak Italian like a pig. I heard that a good deal while I was there."

She laughed again, then repeated his Italian phrase word for word.

Roman drew back slightly and scowled, for her diction was slightly better than his. "Ye've lived in Italy, lass."

"Nay," she laughed again, looking flushed and

flattered. "I but have . . . an interest in language."

"A *gift* for language," he corrected.

She shrugged, then quickly bent over the truck he'd recently abandoned. In a moment, she had raised the lid and was rummaging inside. "How would I say, yes, my lord."

He stared at her backside. Her tunic was pulled taut over her derriere. It was a sweet, soft curve. And her legs, bare now to midthigh, made it surprisingly difficult to breath.

"*Sì, Sua Eccelenza*," he said in Italian.

She repeated it perfectly, then tried it faster. Nearly folded in half, she rummaged about in fabric of every color and texture.

"How would I say, your wish is my command?"

He told her.

There was a hiss of impatience from the interior of the trunk. He caught a glimpse of rich velvet, sheer silk, and for a moment, he thought he saw the poor sailor's shirt with the fishhook that she'd worn not long before. But soon she straightened, pulling up several garments with her.

He pulled his gaze from her legs with an effort. "What's that?"

"Hose, jerkin, shirt, hat, shoes." She held up each piece in turn. "An Italian's costume. Is it not a thing of beauty?"

He grimaced. "It is not."

She scowled, first at him, then at the slandered clothing. "What's wrong with them?"

Roman glanced at the hose first. They were particolored, mustard yellow and white set in a diagonal design. The shirt was lavishly embroidered in black thread, and the hat was embellished with a white ostrich plume that thrust away from the huge headgear at an arrogant angle. But it was the codpiece that held his attention. It was black, padded to outlandish proportions, and studded with seed pearls that did nothing but emphasize its size.

"Where . . ." he asked, "did ye get such a thing?"

"I stole it from an Italian lord. It will be the perfect costume for you to wear."

"I preferred the jester idea."

She deepened her scowl, then shrugged. " 'Tis the best of fashion and good taste. Put them on," she said, handing him the clothes.

He shook his head.

She laughed. "You are being childish."

"Better than being . . ." He eyed the garments distastefully. "A swaggering exhibitionist."

She propped her fists on her hips to glare at him. "Mayhap you think *I* wish to be your servant, following you about like a hound on a leash. 'Yes, my lord. Your wish is my command, my lord.' "

Her propped fists showed the steep curve of her waist despite the ridiculous tunic she wore.

"Ye'll be saying that to me?" he asked, pulling his gaze from her waist to her face.

"If ya wear the costume."

For just a moment he let his gaze slip back down the trim beauty of her form. "Time is fleeting. Let us dress," he said.

Tara knew the way to Crighton Hall, just as she seemed to know everything about Firthport. While they walked, she told him bits about the baron they would visit. His tastes, his habits, his friends, his enemies.

She spoke rapidly, pausing now and then to make suggestions on Roman's costume or ask how to say a word in Italian. She would repeat each one, roll it around on her tongue, use it in a sentence with other spare words he had given her, and finally spew out a phrase that sounded more Italian than an Italian's.

"We are nearly there," she said. Slowing her

walk and slouching her shoulders, she looked for all the world like a young serving boy. Her hose were baggy, gray, and slightly worn, her tunic long, nondescript. It was an ugly outfit, but Roman thought it a thing of rare beauty next to his own ensemble.

"There is Crighton Hall just ahead. You know what you are to say, my lord?"

He looked at her askance, for her voice matched her appearance perfectly, that of a young, clumsy lad. She ducked her head shyly, and he saw now that she walked in a strange, duck-footed manner, the scuffed toes of her shoes pointed out. In her left hand, she carried a cloth bag, supposedly filled with their belongings. On her head was a droopy brown hat.

"Aye," he said. "I ken what ta say."

" 'Tis good. You are clever, my lord," she said, scratching at her hip, "for 'twill be mere moments until the baron arrives from Lord Bledham's."

"How do ye ken all this?" he asked.

"My lord?" she said, stopping suddenly and blinking up at him. Her mouth was round with bewilderment, her brow furrowed. Roman realized suddenly that she was not pretending to be Fletcher, his lowly servant. She *was* Fletcher.

"How is it that you know all this?" he asked, finding his poor Italian accent with an effort.

"Why, my lord . . ." She grinned at him in a lopsided manner. The wig beneath her homely cap was the color of dirty straw. " 'Tis me job ta know these things. Someday ya'll be as famous as Michelangelo, and I'll be your assistant."

She was fascinating to watch, spritely, genuine.

"Look, my lord," she said, turning her gamine face away and pointing a grubby finger at an approaching horseman. "A gentleman. P'raps he can help us on our way."

Roman pulled himself from his thoughts. David MacAulay's life and his own honor depended on how well he played this role. "Sir," he called out as the horseman drew near. "Might you be able to give us assist?"

The rider stopped his mount a short distance from them. The bay gelding he rode fidgeted, pulling at the reins and snorting his discontent as he shook his hirsute head. The horse's nasal discharge sprayed onto Roman's tunic. He grimaced, pulled a lacy handkerchief from his pocket, and wiped at the slime.

When he looked up, he wondered if he saw humor on the old baron's face. He was a homely man, bulbous-nosed, portly, with skinny legs that gripped the proud gelding's sides like pincers.

"And what kind of assistance might you be needing of me?" he asked, staring at Roman.

"I fear we've gone astray." Roman wrinkled his brow and cocked a knee and a wrist in unison, letting the handkerchief droop from his fingertips. He'd seen the Italian dandies do it a thousand times—and had wanted to punch them on each occasion. "My boy here assured me he knew the way to Lord Bledham's holdings." He sneered at the lad. "But curse him, he's gotten us waylaid yet again."

Fletcher kicked at a clump of dirt with the toe of his shoe and barely dared peek up through his bangs at his master. "The signorina at the inn assured me 'twas this way," he mumbled.

"Well the signorina at the inn was a twit. Anyone could see that from—"

"Why did you wish to find Bledham's?" interrupted Crighton.

"What?" asked Roman, pulling his attention from his impromptu servant.

The gelding pranced. "Why did you wish to reach Lord Bledham's estate?"

Roman lifted one corner of his mouth in unison with a limp wrist. "I'm Giorgio Merici."

The baron scowled. "And I'm Lord Crighton. What do you want with Bledham?"

"You don't know?" Roman glanced irritably at Fletcher, then elapsed into a round of sound, Italian cursing. Somehow, though Roman would never know how, Tara knew enough to blush. "I have been commissioned to paint the ceilings at Holyhead," he said finally, making certain he retained a peeved expression. "I assumed my name would proceed me."

"Edgar commissioned you?" Crighton asked.

"Lord Bledham," Roman corrected.

"The bastard," Crighton murmured under his breath. "Looking to outdo me again. What has he agreed to pay you?"

Roman assumed an expression of surprise. "I should think that should stay between the baron and me."

"I'll double it," Crighton said.

"I couldn't possibly—"

"Triple!" Crighton said, "and I'll let the entire country know of your work."

"Well . . ." Roman gasped, glancing at Fletcher, whose jaw had dropped open in surprise. "I . . . Still, I couldn't—"

"Come along. I'll show you Crighton Hall. 'Tis twice the size of Holyhead and much more masterfully planned."

"Well I—"

"Do it!" Fletcher whispered, nearly jumping up and down. "Do it, my lord. And we'll show these English some culture."

"Well I suppose it wouldn't hurt to see my canvas," said Roman. "Lead on."

*   *   *

Crighton Hall was big and square, built of gray stone and towering over the smaller homes beyond its gates.

Roman walked leisurely up the road to the door. Beside him, Fletcher was taut with excitement. His head turned with every step as he absorbed each detail around him.

In a moment, Crighton dismounted. Handing the reins to a boy who appeared from nowhere, he led the way up stone steps.

The door was wide and arched. It opened with a squeal of protest. Beside it was a settle of sorts. The back was formed from the antlers of deer and the seat was red brocade. Roman promptly seated himself upon it with a sigh.

Crighton frowned down at him. "Don't you wish to see the rooms?"

"It has been a dreadfully wearying journey." Roman sniffed into his handkerchief.

"Come along. You can rest later."

Roman rose languidly to his feet. "Mayhap I could quench my thirst at the least. Fletcher could fetch something from your kitchen."

Crighton scowled, apparently impatient to steal this painter from his friend and rival. "Very well. Follow the steps down and around then, boy. Tell Frances to send up spirits for two," he ordered, and turned away. But in a moment, he turned back. "And mind you don't pinch anything on the way, or it'll be your ears."

Fletcher puffed out her tightly bound chest. Affront was written across his face. "I've never stole nothing."

"And make certain you don't start now," Crighton said.

Roman allowed himself one glance at Tara. She was there, somewhere, under the thick facade of the serving boy. Her eyes were just as bright and alive as ever and if he looked hard he could see the merest suggestion of a smile touch her lips. But now was not the time to let her allure distract him. He followed the baron upstairs.

Tara watched them go. Life was good.

Setting the bag by the door, she hurried down the hall. Stairways led off in every direction. She ignored them all, focusing on her mission.

Where would she be if she were a golden mermaid forever captured on the end of a walking stick, Tara wondered, silently passing rooms on her right and left. Up ahead, she saw a door set with a simple, square window. Through that smoky glass, she vaguely made out the bright colors of the garden beyond.

The answer was so simple.

If she were a golden mermaid, she would reside in the anteroom that adjoined the garden. Tara set her hand to the latch.

The *locked* anteroom, she corrected, and nearly laughed out loud.

Less than ten minutes later, Tara was hurrying up the stairs, carrying two chalices of ale. Whistling, she stopped long enough to sip from one cup and continue on.

On the landing, a gilt-framed picture shone down at her. It was a lascivious piece, showing a man with five women in various stages of undress.

Tara stopped, stared. Then, lifting the chalice in her right hand, she spat into the brew and hurried on, whistling again.

"What took you so long?" asked Crighton, scowling from a doorway.

" 'Tis sorry I am, your lordship. I fear I was delayed—admiring your artwork."

Crighton grunted, took the chalice from Tara's

right hand, and turned his back to pace across the room toward Roman.

"So what do you think, Merici?"

"'Tis a lovely room." Roman sighed dramatically and waved vaguely at the endless white ceiling. "The grand sweep of the arches. The gentle curve of the plaster. The bold strength of the pillars."

Crighton smiled and took a sip from his chalice.

Tara smiled, too, first at Crighton, and then at Roman, with a tiny, significant nod.

"And there are other rooms just as grand," said Crighton, smirking at Roman. "If you're not too busy with Bledham's little house, that is."

"I'll do it," said Roman breathlessly.

Crighton chuckled and drank again. "I thought you would."

"Come along, Fletcher. We'll hurry back to the inn and fetch our supplies."

"So soon?" Crighton said. "Before you so much as finish your ale." He examined his own brew bemusedly. "It's particularly good today."

Chapter 16

Roman closed the door of Tara's small dwelling and barred it behind him. "I think I've waited long enough, lass."

She stared up into his face, her eyes alive, her dirty cheeks aglow. "You did wonderfully well... my lord."

"I look the fool."

"You look..." She paused as if there was much she would say, but dared not. Was that admiration in her eyes? "I doubt you could ever look the fool, Scotsman."

He could not help but smile. Theft was wrong. He knew theft was wrong. But theft with her...

"Are you certain you are not truly an Italian painter by profession?" she asked.

She had removed her homely hat. The straw-colored wig followed.

"Quite certain," he said.

"An actor?" she asked, turning away to carefully pack the wig in the trunk.

"A lawyer," he said, sitting down on the straw pallet to watch her. "And quite a boring one."

She turned to him. "I doubt it."

How had he survived before this moment—before he had seen her eyes aglow, had heard her laughter? What had happened to his thoughts of revenge? What kind of magic did she work on him?

"I'm assuming I didn't risk me life for nothing," he said, hoping she didn't realize how she affected him. "Ye did get it, didn't ye?"

"Oh, aye." She said it with a laugh. Pulling her tunic loose from her belt, she fished out a leather bag that hung nearly to her waist.

She tipped it onto the mattress beside Roman. Five items rolled onto the bed: the gold mermaid, a silver spoon, a spool of gold thread, and a stylish ornamental belt.

Roman glanced at each item, then raised his gaze to hers.

She cleared her throat. "I believe—"

"In sharing," he said. "But yer sharing could get us both kilt."

Her grin broadened. "That's half the fun of it, Scotsman," she said, and reaching beneath her tunic, pulled away the belt that had held the pouch securely to her body.

"And what's the other half?" he asked.

She sobered, gently fingering the mermaid's wild gilt hair. "Revenge."

"Revenge for the lad that felt the weight of the mermaid across his back, or revenge for yerself?" he asked quietly.

"Mayhap a wee bit of both," she answered just as softly.

"Who are ye, lass?" he whispered.

She pulled her gaze away, but not without effort. "I'm the one who will retrieve your necklace, Scotsman. Nothing more."

He snared her hand. " 'Tis a lie, lass," he said, tugging her back. "Ye are a woman of depth and compassion. But ye dunna let people see that side of ye."

She laughed. "That is because it is not there," she argued. "I but take care of myself as best I can."

"Nay." He shook his head. "There is much ye dunna say. But there are things I ken."

She tugged at her fingers, and he set her free. "Such as?"

"Ye could steal the night without disturbing the dawn. This piece . . ." He hefted the mermaid. The figure showed only her head and bared torso, but still it exceeded the length of his hand and weighed more than half a stone. "'Tis worth a fair bit," he said, not taking his gaze from hers. "Enough ta keep ye well for a year in this humble abode I would think."

"'Arry was the thief," she corrected, but her slim hands were clasped. "True, he was generous and would share, but—"

"There was no Harry."

Her jaw dropped. She mouthed something, then drew a breath, and said, "I'll not have ya slandering his name." Her voice shook when she said it, but Roman was far past believing her.

"He's na more real than Fletcher, or Betty, or the old man with the severed leg. In fact, he is far less real."

"How dare you?" she gasped, going pale.

He was on his feet in an instant, gripping her arms in a hard clasp. "I dare because me own life depends on it. You are the Shadow!"

"You're daft!" she hissed.

"Admit it."

"Nay! I will not. You're insane!"

"Mayhap," he said, leaning closer. "But I am also right."

"'Arry was the Shadow. 'Tis horribly cruel of ya to deny his existence," she said. There were tears in her eyes.

Roman tightened his grip on her arms. "Dunna

waste yer false tears, lass, for I doubt ye ken how ta cry in earnest. There was na Harry and ye are the Shadow."

"Nay," she said again, but her voice was weaker, her tears gone. "He was my love, my life."

"He was a figment of yer imagination. He was ye. Admit it!"

"Nay!"

"Admit it!" he growled, shaking her.

Tense silence hung between them.

"How long have you known?" she whispered.

He *had* known the truth. Truly he had. But still, hearing her admit it made his soul sing. There was no Harry, no lover who still owned her affections. "In me heart I have known for some while, I think," he said softly. "But me mind has taken far too long ta see the light."

"And what will you do with this knowledge?"

He held her gaze, reminding himself that though she held no affection for a man he could not compete with, neither did she hold any affection for him. "We've made an agreement, lass," he said, keeping his tone flat, and refusing to admit why he could not harm her. "I'll stand by it ta the end. Help me retrieve the necklace, and I'll guard yer secret with me verra life."

She nodded once, then pulled away, her narrow hands tightly clasped.

"Ye can trust me, lass," he said. He read her tension, understood her doubts. Yet he could not help the happiness that suffused him. She was the Shadow. Therefore, she was free to love another.

She turned, a scowl marring her brow. "I don't know how to trust, Scotsman."

"Trust is a slippery thing, 'tis true," he said softly. "But 'tis na unmanagable once ye get a grip on it."

She shook her head, but her fine lips lifted

slightly into a smile. "I don't think so. Not for me."

"Who are ye?" It seemed he had asked that question a hundred times. But it had never intrigued him more than now.

"Who would you like me to be?"

"Yerself."

"There is no myself, Scotsman," she whispered, and in her eyes he saw sorrow, deep and earnest.

He crossed the distance between them and took her into his arms. And from there, there was nothing he could do but kiss her.

She was warm and soft and kissing him in return. He felt her desperate need like a tangible thing, and hugged her more tightly against him.

"If there is no ye, lass, then who am I kissing?"

"Someone truly terrified," she whispered.

"Nay." He shook his head. "Nothing frightens a shadow."

"But things frighten me," she said, and shivered.

"Hence the disguises?"

"When I am Betty I can match any man quip for quip. When I'm a lad I have a youth's speed and daring. And when I am the Shadow, I fear nothing."

"What do you fear now, lass?"

"You."

"I will na harm ye," he said, gently touching her face.

She closed her eyes. " 'Tis not true. You look to find the person who I once was."

"Is that an evil thing, lass?"

"Find her, and what happens to the others, Scotsman?"

"What others?"

She motioned to her chest. "The others that I have become. They have kept me alive. When I am no longer them, I will die."

Roman tightened his arms about her, understanding. "When I was but a lad, me parents were taken from me. I lived then with me uncle. But me uncle could na be trusted, nor could the parents who had abandoned me, I reasoned. Thus I thought that none could be trusted. I must fend for meself, stay apart from the world, lest someone steal me verra life."

"But you were wrong?"

"In later years, after I had been touched by kindness, I thought mayhap it would be better to die than to live without that."

"And now? What do you think now?"

"That I must take the risk. If I dare."

She watched him breathlessly for a moment, and then she kissed him, softly, tentatively. The sensations were sweet beyond measure, yet searing, stunning. He let her lead the way, let her fingers slip beneath his jerkin. Even through the linen of the embroidered shirt, he could feel the warmth of her hands. They slid sensuously around his body, pulling him closer. She deepened the kiss. He calmed his breathing, touched her lips with his tongue, felt her shiver with desire against him.

The knowledge of her arousal heated his already warmed system. His manhood rose, nearly matching the outlandish size of the codpiece that stood like a stiff guard between them. No longer could he be content to allow her to lead the way. He slid his hands under her baggy tunic and about her back. Her skin was warm and soft. He pressed his palms up her spine, and she arched against him with a shudder of pleasure.

It was that simple movement that made her irresistible. Beneath the tunic, he could feel the strips of cloth that bound her breasts. He found the knots against her back and loosened them until they fell away. He slid his hands downward to find the laces that kept her ill-fitting hose upon her body.

He untied them without stopping the kiss, and then smoothed the coarse fabric down her buttocks. She pressed her hips forward, and he gripped her bottom and pulled her upward.

She straddled his waist.

Roman splayed his fingers, running his hands up her torso, bunching her tunic and binding clothes above them. The clothes slipped away. She drew her arms out of the sleeves eagerly, and he tugged the tunic over her head.

Her breasts were free, bare, high and firm and so lovely that he caught his breath. Ever so gently, he cupped one in his hand, weighing it in his palm before he closed his eyes and slipped it over the fullness of the curve. She gasped and arched toward him, breathing hard.

Roman opened his eyes to find her watching him. There was longing there, but there was also fear.

Desire, hard as flint and just as sharp, spurred him. His gaze slipped down her body. She gripped him with her slim, endless legs, her torso leaning away from him. Her nipples were hard and erect, pink blossoms that called for his kiss. Below that, her ribs slanted down to a belly that was flat and firm. Her waist was tiny and tight, her hips flared.

He shivered with excitement, but held himself still. "Lass . . ." His voice was husky. "Do I go ta fast for ye?"

She exhaled sharply, and he realized suddenly that she had been holding her breath. "This trust is . . ." She paused. Her eyes were wide and blue. " 'Tis indeed a slippery thing. It comes and goes, and there are times when I do not care if I trust at all."

"Trust can indeed make fools of us," he whispered. "But 'tis said that caring can make us whole."

"Caring kills," she whispered hoarsely.

"Mayhap 'tis worth the price," he whispered, and, bearing her to the bed, eased her down upon it.

He settled slowly down beside her and touched her face with careful fingertips. She closed her eyes and tilted her head into his touch. Roman skimmed his hand along the fine bone of her jaw, down her delicate throat and into the silky mass of her hair. It remained confined on the top of her head. His fingers slipped into the soft nest and found a pin. He tugged it free, then trailed it gently down her throat, her shoulder, over her breast, and down to the hollow of her abdomen. Back up, his fingers went, retrieving another pin before slipping downward. But now he followed its path with kisses, light, careful, mere whispered caresses to her shoulder, her arm, the sweet, firm curve of her breast. Until finally all the pins were placed in a pile on her flat belly.

Roman spread his fingers in her hair now. It was as soft as a dream, gold as a morning ray of light. He spread it forward until it spilled over her, covering her shoulders, brushing her breasts, spreading gossamer sheer over her rose-petal nipples.

"Tara." He breathed her name softly. "But ye are bonny, lass, beautiful beyond all I imagined." He touched her breast again, but did not allow his hand to stay. Instead, he smoothed it lower, over her curves, down her leg.

Her legs were long and pale as a lily. They were bent at the knee and pressed together, covering most of the golden triangle of hair that adorned the apex between them. Roman ran his fingers slowly down one thigh, stroking, caressing. Her lips parted and her eyes fell closed as she absorbed his touch. He could feel her muscles relax beneath his hands and soon her knees had fallen open, exposing the core of her womanhood. He slipped his hand along her inner thigh. The skin there was as smooth as finest silk, and when he reached her center, she was moist, warm, soft.

She moaned and pressed against his fingers.

Fiery bright desire raced through Roman, but he would not hurry. Instead, he slipped his hand downward to cup her warmth in his palm before sliding lower to press his wrist against her heat and caress her bottom. The frilly white of his cuff looked strangely right against her dark, golden curls.

She arched her taut body and shivered violently against his touch. Her hands came up to grasp his jerkin and hold tightly. "Scotsman," she said, breathing hard.

There was desire in her eyes, hot and eager. But there was also fear. If she called a halt, Roman thought, he was honor-bound to agree.

"Aye, lass?" His voice was husky.

"I would see you naked."

Thank you, God! He exhaled carefully, swallowed, said another silent prayer. "If . . . if ye call me Roman," he whispered.

"Roman," she breathed, and, shivering, kissed him.

Fire. Hot and wild and consuming!

It was all Roman could do to untie his jerkin without breaking off the kiss. But she was impatient now and pushed him away far enough to assist his efforts. She pulled the garment off. The shirt beneath was fastened with a row of small bone buttons. They opened with magical quickness beneath her skillful hands.

His chest was bare but for the amulet of teeth. Lying beside one nipple, it made him look all the more fierce and untamable, Tara thought. She skimmed her hands over his chest, unable to resist.

"When I first saw you at the inn you wore this," she whispered, touching the wolf teeth. "You were naked, and I was the Shadow, there on a mission." Tentatively, ever so tentatively, she touched the nub of his nipple and felt the muscles underneath coil beneath her hand. "Never have I been so tempted to pull out of a role, to touch..." She swept her palm over his nipple again, and again the muscles beneath her hand jumped. It was a marvelous feeling, full of life and heat. An experience like none other.

"Do you..." She paused, breathing hard and seeming to feel each drop of blood that coursed wildly through her veins. Slowly, she pushed his shirt off one shoulder. It was broad with bone and muscle, powerful and exhilarating. "Do you perhaps feel what I feel?" She searched his eyes, wondering.

His lips were near hers, and his hair, dark as midnight, fell across his bare skin in highlights of black and cinnamon.

"There be lightning in me blood," he whispered.

She could not help but smile. "Burning," she said.

"Aye," he murmured, and kissed her. But she was no longer content to allow things to remain as they were. It was a simple thing to free the laces of his hose. The shirt slid away from his chest. The hose slipped away from his hips, and the codpiece paled beside the power of his erection.

She let her gaze settle on it for a moment, before shifting her eyes away.

Roman pressed the hose lower, but they clung to him as if loath to leave his powerful thighs. He wrestled with them for a moment, pushing them down and finally sitting on the edge of the bed to peel them away.

Tara stared at the broad strength of his back.

"Scars." She whispered the word, and reaching out, touched a jagged strip that marked his back.

He didn't flinch, but turned slowly toward her.

"You have scars," she whispered, meeting his gaze.

"From long ago and best forgotten," he murmured, wrapping her again in his arms.

But she shook her head. "Scars are not forgotten. They are hidden or they are healed."

"Then heal me, lass," he whispered, and kissed her.

She leaned back into the mattress. There was excitement, yes. But there was more here. There was depth and feeling, and a man with hands so slow and strong that she felt she could die beneath his caress and not care. What was this wild longing?

His hands roamed her body, smoothing over her breasts, her thighs. His kisses followed, slow and hot and lingering.

He settled between her legs and she welcomed him there, bending her knees, feeling the warmth of his nakedness with gladness. His manhood was rigid and hot between her thighs.

His kisses slipped from her lips, down her throat, and lower until he found the crest of her breast.

She arched against the sizzling sensations. And somehow, like silver magic, he was inside. Both stopped their movement. He seemed as hard as an oaken bough. Every muscle was bunched and controlled, every fiber taut and ready.

She felt his shiver of anticipation and could wait no longer. Tightening, she bucked against him. The hounds of desire were set free. With a groan, he thrust forward.

The portal to Tara's core ripped free. She felt it give and welcomed the opening, for now he was sunk deep within her and she could wrap herself around him and glory in the wild ride.

There was no time for thought. No time for delay. They rode together at a desperate pace, gasping for air and satisfaction.

She filled her fists with his hair and drove against him, reaching for something that demanded attention.

Harder, faster. Muscles writhing, breath rasping.

She felt him grow inside her, felt the bulge of hard need, and then he was pulsing, pushing her over the edge of desire. She heard his groan, saw him arch back his head, and felt the release of her satiety. Her head felt light and her muscles useless. Her hands fell to the mattress.

Roman eased away, then rose to his feet.

So this was sex, what she had waited so long to experience. She smiled ever so softly to herself.

"How dare ye!" Roman said, looming, dark and angry over the bed. "How dare ye be a virgin!"

Chapter 17

"What?" Tara blinked up at him, naked, sated, confused.

Roman stood with his fists clenched and every fine muscle tight with anger. "How dare ye be a virgin?"

She was tempted to laugh, tempted, but not so foolish.

"You're . . ." She pushed the hair out of her face. The amulet swung lazily against his glorious chest. It fascinated her, but she managed to keep from touching it or him. "You're upset because I was an innocent?"

"Innocent!" He all but snarled the word, then threw up his hands to circle the tiny room and come back to glare at her once more. "Ye are na, nor probably ever were, an innocent."

"But, I thought you said—"

"Ye lied!" he exclaimed, jabbing a finger at her. "Ye lied again, even about . . ." He waved his hand toward her, as if encompassing her entire being. "Even about that!"

She could not help but smile now, just a mite. "You're angry."

He made a sound that reminded her very much of the beast whose teeth he had stolen.

"From the start ye have lied, connived, schemed! But I thought, foolishly, I see, that in this one thing . . ." He raised a stern forefinger to shake it at her. "In this one thing I thought ye would be honest."

"How exactly did I lie to you, Scotsman?" she asked. Sitting up, she wrapped her arms about her bent legs to stare at him from a better vantage point. She was naked and cooling, but somehow her nudity failed to bother her. 'Twas a fact she would have to consider later.

"How?" he rasped. "Ye said ye were a whore."

"Oh."

Bending his forefinger into his fist, he paced again. "Usually when a woman says she is a whore, ye can believe her. 'Tis a fairly certain thing. For if they are apt ta lie, 'tis usually the opposite they say. But na with thee. Nay! Na with thee. Jesu, I should have known better."

She watched him pace. Not until this very moment had she noticed how truly beautiful he was. She'd admired his strength, his fitness, his nobility. But now even the slight bend to his nose fascinated her. The way his eyes flashed, how the muscles in his massive thighs flexed when he walked.

He shook his head. Dark hair brushed his shoulders. Scars marred his back. And suddenly she wanted to kiss those aged wounds.

"I should have known ye were na capable of honesty. What a fool I was ta think otherwise. 'Twas obvious from the start that I could na trust ye. 'Twas—"

" 'Twas wonderful," she murmured.

He stopped in his tracks. His breathing ceased. "Lass," he murmured, but then he shook his head and glared at her again. "Ye'll na soften me with sweet words. 'Twas na as if we but shared a fine meal or a . . ." He tossed up his hand again, as if mere words were not enough to express his anger. "Or a stolen kiss in the wine cellar. I stole . . ." He closed his eyes and rubbed them. "Hell fire, I stole far more than that!"

"I may know little about the ways of men and women," she said, still watching him, "but theft is a subject I know a fair bit about. And I would say, what you took 'twas freely given."

He lowered his hand to stare at her. "Could it be that ye are so naive that ye dunna realize the significance of this?"

"Significance?"

"I took yer maidenhead!"

"Somehow, I never imagined a man would be upset by such a situation."

"Well then ye have never imagined me!" he said. The amulet danced as he thumped his bare chest. "Ye think I can simply turn me back on me responsibility?"

Tara drew a steadying breath and reeled herself in from the soft void of contentment. For a moment she had forgotten who he was—the beloved foster son of a laird, a nobleman, wealthy, privileged. But she would not forget again. "So that's it, is it, Scotsman? You think I am binding you to me?"

His dark brows lowered a bit more over his eyes.

"You think I have tricked you and now plan to force you to pledge your troth?" She forced a laugh, but the effort hurt her chest. To cover the pain, she slipped her feet to the floor and bent to retrieve her garments. "Well, you needn't worry, for I have no such plans."

Clothing was strewn everywhere. She rummaged angrily through it. "And I'll retrieve the necklace as I vowed. You needn't worry on that account either. This changes nothing. I'll—" she began, but suddenly, his hand encircled her arm and he jerked her upright.

She gasped, peering at him through a veil of golden, misplaced hair.

"Ye'll not," he said, glaring into her face.

"What?"

"Ye'll na go ta Dagger."

She tried to pull her arm from his grasp, but he held her still, so she glared at him from where she was. "'Tis what I vowed to do, and I will do it. This changes nothing."

"This changes . . ." he gritted, then filled his nostrils with air and flexed his jaw, "everything."

"Was this not your idea from the first? 'Twas it not you who insisted that I retrieve the necklace?" she asked. "Or am I going mad?"

He smiled. It was a wolfish sort of grin, beguiling, bewitching. "Yer going mad," he said.

"Nay!" Forcing her gaze from his face, she finally managed to yank her arm from his grasp. "But ye are *making* me mad. I vowed to retrieve the necklace, and retrieve it I will." She tightened her lips and her fists. "Harrington will not create another orphan. Not while it is in my power to change his course."

"What say ye?" Roman asked.

She swallowed, realizing abruptly what she had said. He was making her lose her focus, reveal her secrets. 'Twas a thing she could not afford to do. "I said I will fulfill my vow," she said simply.

"Ye said Harrington would not create another orphan. What did ye mean?"

She shrugged, finally giving up on her search for clothing and tossing the garments angrily to the floor. "He is a noble. Nobles have a knack for making orphans of children. I but guess that he's no different."

Roman shook his head. "'Tis na what ye meant," he said, taking a step toward her.

"Tis." She backed away and scowled up at him.

" 'Tisn't," he said, and wrapping his arm about her bare waist pulled her close for a kiss.

The heat of it seared all thought from her mind. Her muscles loosened, and she forgot to breath.

" 'Tisn't," he said, drawing the kiss to an end. "What did ye mean?"

"Huh?" She tried to think, but his body was hard against hers. His abdomen rippled with strength and against her breasts, his chest was packed with tightly sculpted muscles.

Somehow, her arms had found their way about his waist. She bit her lip and tried to reprimand her hands for their downward exploration. But his buttocks were hard and seductive. She cupped her palms over them, skimming lower.

His nostrils flared. Between their bodies, she felt his desire stir to life.

"Scotsman?" she whispered, holding his gaze. "Could you do it again?"

Passion flared in his eyes. He leaned forward. Their lips met, but suddenly, he jerked away.

"Nay!" he said, glaring at her. "Ye are but trying ta distract me again."

She blinked at him, feeling bereft. "I but asked," she whispered.

He took a step forward, then shook his head emphatically and stepped back. "Hell fire, woman, ye are driving me ta distraction! Scotsman!" He turned rapidly away to rave at the unoffending wall. "Scotsman! she calls me. She doesna even use me given name. Roman! Me name is Roman!"

"Roman," she whispered, and, quite suddenly, she pressed up against his back, with her arms round his waist and her breasts hot and firm against him.

He swallowed.

"Roman," she repeated softly into his ear. "Can you do it again?"

"Nay," he said, but when her small hand closed around his erection, he shuddered. "Nay, lass, I'll na do it again. A virgin ye were, and I'll not be responsible for yer ruination."

He was sure he felt her smile against his back. "A bit late to worry about that, Scots . . . Roman," she whispered.

"Lass . . ." he rasped. She was doing wicked, wonderful things with her hand, sliding it slowly along the length of his shaft. "Lass, I . . ."

"I'm no lass," she said. " 'Tis two and twenty, I am."

"Ye lie," he managed.

"Aye." She chuckled. Her breath was soft and warm against his shoulder. "I do that. But not about my age. I have seen better than a score of years and never have I felt the magic that ballads are written about. Not until tonight."

She tightened her grip slightly. He groaned and let his head fall back a fraction of an inch.

"I would feel the magic again. Now."

Roman shook his head. It was, without a doubt, one of the hardest things he had ever done. Pride should have spurred through him. But pride was not one of the myriad feelings that coursed through his system. Desire pretty much overrode everything else.

"I'll na do it again," he said, eyes still closed, head still inclined back.

"Why?"

Her other hand had joined in the assault. It stroked his thigh, brushing his gonads, burning his system.

"Why?" He rasped the word. If he had the least bit of discipline, even a wee bit, he would move away. Instead, he stood like one in a trance. "Have ye given na thought ta this deed? Do ye na ken what the results might be? What if a babe should be planted within ye? What if one already has?"

"There is no babe," she whispered.

He forced himself not to turn. He could not make himself move away, but he could manage to remain as he was, and as long as he did that, she was safe from him.

"How do ye know that?" he said, forcing himself to return to the subject.

"You should not assume that I am naive just because I was a virgin," she said, stroking again. Her other hand had moved up to skim his abdomen. " 'Tis not my time to conceive."

"How do ye ken that?"

"I learn what I can where I can. Some of my best teachers have been of less than sterling repute."

There was a steady rhythm to her stroking. He swelled and throbbed beneath her hand.

"If I were a lesser man, I'd thank God for the low moral status of yer teachers," he rasped.

She laughed softly against his shoulder. "If you were a lesser man, I would not be begging for your favors."

Her right hand slipped lower to clasp his gonads in a gentle grip.

"Sweet . . . Mary!" he gasped, going rigid, before forcing himself to relax a smidgen. "Is it . . . Is it begging ye be, lass?"

"Aye. I am begging."

"It would be . . ." The rhythmn of her hands seem to have set the pace of his heart. "It would be unseemly to refuse a lady's begging," he said, and, against his better judgment, turned in her arms.

"Aye, it would, Scotsman," she murmured.

"And yet . . ." he said, wrapping his arms tightly about her and kissing her with all the passion that roared through his system. "I *will* refuse."

"What?" Her lips were red and swollen, her eyes filled with wild desire.

"I will na do it again, lass, unless ye tell me yer true name." Liam had called her Tara, and it seemed right. He called her the same, but suddenly it seemed of utmost importance that she trust him with her full name.

"Tis . . ." she began, but he cupped her buttocks in his hands and pulled her from her feet. She wrapped her arms about his neck and her legs about his waist, letting these new sensations sear her to the bone. "Betty," she whispered.

She was wet and open and ready, but he shook his head. "Nay, lass," he said. "Betty is the barmaid."

"Fletcher?" she ventured, breathing hard.

"It would be difficult ta convince me that ye are a boy just now," Roman said, smoothing his hand along the back of her thigh, letting his fingers brush the soft moistness of her. She shivered in his arms.

She opened her mouth again, but he kissed away the lies until they were both breathless and aching.

"Who are ye, lass?" he whispered.

They had formed a steady rhythm, bumping gently against each other, reaching.

"Who I once was is of no import," she said, breathlessly searching for fullfillment.

Roman scooped her higher, a hand on each buttock as he gritted his teeth and held her off the aching rod of his desire. " 'Tis important ta me, and I will know," he said.

"Roman," she whispered, pulling herself closer until her nipples touched his chest, "please do it again."

His skin burned where her bright, erect nipples touched him, but he held himself rigid and waited for the hardest edge of his desire to pass. Then ever so slowly, he lowered her onto his waiting rod.

He watched her eyes fall closed, heard her gasp breath through her teeth, felt her shiver of pleasure, and nearly lost control.

But he managed to stop himself when she was barely impaled on his staff.

"Yer name!" he rasped.

Her fingers wrapped in his hair, tugging. Her back arched, her legs squeezed harder as she pushed against him. But he would not give in.

"Roman!" she pleaded, pushing harder.

"Ye know me name," he said through gritted teeth. "But I dunna know yers, and until I do—"

"Tara," she said, meeting his gaze from mere inches away. "'Tis Tara O'Flynn."

"Tara." He breathed her name, and with a shiver of relief, lowered her fully onto him.

She inhaled sharply, and pressed into him, her back arched, her eyes closed.

It was a fast ride, wild, exhilarating. This time there was no time to consider the other's pleasure, only the pulsing climb toward heaven, and the rapid tumble down into satiety.

Every muscle in Roman's body quivered with weakness, but he managed to lower them both to the nearby bed.

She was soft as butter in his arms now. Sweet and warm and impossible to let go.

"Tara," he murmured against her ear.

She opened her eyes, and for a moment he saw fear there. But he smoothed a few strands of gossamer hair behind her ear and kissed the corner of her mouth.

"Trust me, Tara," he whispered.

"I think mayhap I already have."

He stroked her hair again, watching her eyes fall closed and feeling a strange emotion fill him. It was deeper than contentment. In fact, it was deeper than euphoria.

"Tara?"

"Aye?" Her tone was very soft now, like the voice of an angelic child.

She was neither an angel or a child, he reminded himself. But it did no good.

"How is it that ye saved yerself all these years? Surely ye had a good many offers."

"Offers?" She chuckled softly and opened her eyes to stare at him for a moment. "Aye, I had offers. Some kindly, and some not so." She reached out to gently stroke his face. "I learned much as a barmaid. Noblemen and peasants—it seems they are much alike where lust is concerned."

Her fingers were feather soft against his cheek. Too soft, for it brought to mind other parts of her anatomy that were softer still, other parts that might have been mauled by some drunken swine.

Roman pulled her fingers into his hand and wrapped them tight in his own. They were slim and fragile. He closed his eyes, trying not to think of the men that had lusted for her, had tried to take her, willing or no. "Did they . . ."He tried to stop the question but he could not. "Did they hurt ye, lass."

She smiled again. The expression looked sleepy, ethereal, and yet strangely earthy. "Have you not learned that I am tougher than I appear?"

He tightened his grip. "Aye, but—"

Bringing his hand to her lips, she kissed his knuckles lightly. "I managed to resist them all, Scotsman," she said softly. "Until you. But had I known what I was missing . . ." She shrugged one shoulder. It was pale and bare, half-hidden by her spun-gold hair and so strangely sensual that he could not help but scoop his hand over the smooth curve of it. His fingers looked dark and hard between the silky sheath of her hair and the ivory hillock of her shoulder that she pulled close to her cheek. "If I had known what I was missing, mayhap I would not have resisted so long." Turning her head, she kissed the back of his hand, then shifted her sapphire eyes to his. "Tell me, Scotsman," she whispered, "had I chosen another, would I still have felt the earth move?"

The imp had been set free and shone wild and seductive in her eyes. He knew she was intentionally teasing him, and yet something coiled in his gut. It felt strangely like jealousy. Like an animal instinct so deep he could hear its snarl of rage.

"Nay," he said, quite proud of the steady assurance in his tone. "With the rest ye would have been lucky ta remain awake. Only with me will ye feel the earth move."

Chapter 18

$\sim$ $\circlearrowright$ $\curvearrowright$ $\sim$

Roman awoke slowly. Half-remembered dreams filled his senses with suffusing warmth.

Tara. Memories of her name, her face, her form, filled him with rejuvenated desire. Still half-asleep, he reached for her, but found nothing. He opened his eyes, scowled, rolled over and—

"Hello, handsome," said a husky voice.

Roman jolted to a sitting position, scrambling for blankets to cover his nudity.

The woman laughed and took a step closer. Her black hair fell nearly to her waist. In the mirror behind her, he could see it fall in midnight waves down her back. Her hips were broad and swayed as she moved.

Roman found a blanket, dragged it over his lower body and skimmed the room with his gaze. "Where's Tara?"

"Tara?" Her accent was a thick Yiddish, her face nearly hidden with the fire at her back. "Och. She left, looking . . . satisfied." She purred the word. "And now I see why." Her gaze traveled leisurely over him, seeming to sear the blanket as it went.

But Roman had no time to consider the woman's

blatant sensuality. He was on his feet in an instant. "What the hell did ye do with her?"

"Her?" The woman tossed back her hair, revealing more bared skin above a jewel-bright drawstring blouse. "Why would you want that skinny wench when you could have . . . me." She skimmed her hand down her throat. The movement was slow, sensuous, seductive. The hand was slim, fine-boned . . . and strangely familiar.

Roman checked himself and settled back onto the mattress. He had managed to draw the blanket about his waist, but it gapped open now, revealing his leg past midthigh.

"That depends," he said, making his own tone husky and suggestive. "Who ye are?"

Her gaze flitted to his thigh, and for a moment he thought he saw her falter. But then she tossed back her head and smiled. Her teeth were tremendously white against the dark skin of her face. "My name is Salina, princess of the Roms."

Roman raised his brows. "Ye've na need ta lie about yer heritage ta impress me, lass, for yer figure has already done that quite well."

"I *am* a princess," she said. Her eyes flashed in the uncertain light.

Roman merely canted his head and grinned, as if the truth was of little importance. "How long will the skinny one be gone?"

She glanced at the door with a scowl. Beneath the scarlet scarf bound about her head, he saw her brow wrinkle slightly. "She did not say."

"Well then," Roman began, and rising, let the blanket fall to the floor.

Her gaze snapped to his lower regions, but already Roman had reached her. In an instant she was in his arms and he was crushing her lips with a fierce kiss.

For a moment she was still, but soon she was

struggling wildly against him. He tightened his arms about her, quieting her thrashing until he finally drew away and looked into her eyes. They were as blue and angry as intense flame. She opened her mouth to speak, but he raised a finger and placed it over her lips.

"Did I forget ta tell ye *my* part, lass? I be Theaelo, the greatest lover in all Romania."

He watched Tara's expression change from anger to bewilderment to doubt and finally removed his finger from her lips.

For a moment she did nothing but glare at him, but finally she spoke. "You didn't know who I was."

"Did I na?"

"Nay." Her anger was evident in her tone, but there was something else that sounded soothingly like jealousy.

He smiled and kissed her again. "You underestimate me, lass. I knew ye from the first."

"You lie."

He smiled again. "Usually I dunna, lass. But I'm trying to learn. And 'tis said 'tis good ta learn from the best."

She scowled as if uncertain of his meaning, then backed away. He let her go. "You didn't know who I was."

"Had ye grown an extra nose and dyed yer skin black as sin with yonder walnut stain, I would have known ye still."

"How?"

" 'Tis plainly ye." He shrugged. In truth, he had been fooled for a moment. Even now it was difficult to believe she was the same woman he had made love to just hours before. But the walnut shells on the table and the steaming pot nearby had told him she'd been brewing a dye to color her skin. "Ye couldna fool a simpleton in that costume."

She watched him closely for a moment, then shrugged and turned toward the fire. "It better fool simpletons and otherwise, because your friend's life depends on it."

Roman sat very still as he considered her words. So his guess had been right; she planned to use this disguise to regain the necklace. "How so?" he asked.

She stirred something in the pot, then pushed the metal arm back over the fire. "I need to convince Dagger that I am a thief. But I cannot be merely one of the throng. I will have to stand out. Be different."

Roman clenched his fists and stayed as he was. Had he not been so sated, he would have heard her preparing the dye. He would have to be more aware. But it seemed her charms were as effective a drug as her herbs. "Ye will certainly na look like one of the lads in that garb," he agreed.

She turned back toward him. Her eyes looked haunted with doubt, but she did not voice it. Instead, she said, "That is exactly the plan. Dressed like this and bearing the golden mermaid, he'll gladly accept me into the fold."

"Why?" Roman asked, keeping his tone steady.

"Consider your own reaction to my disguise," she said coolly. "As I told you earlier, noblemen and peasants are much the same where lust is concerned."

"And what if they should become . . . lusty?" he asked, rising slowly to his feet. "How far will ye play this part?"

She shrugged flippantly, but her mouth was pursed and her eyes very bright. " 'Tis hard to say," she told him, turning away.

But in an instant, he had grabbed her arm and

turned her back toward him. "Ye'd best say, lass. 'Twould be a foolish thing ta visit Dagger dressed like that."

She raised her chin and glared at him, but her eyes were suspiciously bright. "Because you think he might find me desirable?"

Roman clenched his jaw and tried to control his temper, but it was flaring, threatening. "Exactly," he said.

"Ahh." He felt her relax beneath his hand. "So you can philander where you like. Do as you please. Hell!" she swore, but softly as if she were merely passing the time of day. "Why not bed Salina so long as the skinny wench is gone. Mayhap you've never had a gypsy girl in your vast experience."

His anger slipped a notch. He relaxed his grip a little. "Ye think me experience vast?"

"You're a skillful lover, as you well know, Scotsman. And I do not deny my own . . ." She turned her face away. "My own ineptitude."

He swore softly. He had wounded her, and that knowledge tore at him. "Me own experience consists of three women," he admitted softly. "Not . . . Not all at the same time," he hurried to add. "And none of them . . ." He shook his head and putting his hand on her chin, turned her face gently back toward him. "None of them mentioned me skill."

Her eyes were morning bright against her dyed skin.

"Ineptitude." He breathed the word, nearly overcome by the sight of her sadness, the soft feel of her so close to him. " 'Tis ye that makes the earth move, lass. Na me."

"You did not know me," she said, but there was doubt now, and he smiled.

"I cannot tell ye how yer jealousy moves me, lass. But I will tell ye true. I knew 'twas ye as soon

as ye called Tara a skinny wench, for no one..."
He paused and slipped his hand down her body.
"Na one could call ye skinny, for ye are bonny be-
yond words."

"Truly?" She whispered the word.

"For just a moment I thought that Salina was
indeed a gypsy. I thought she had mayhap harmed
ye in some way, and I thought I would kill her if
it was necessary ta hold ye safely in me arms
again."

Sheer relief shown in her eyes, but in an instant
she hid it and turned her face away. "Well, you'd
best tell me how you discovered it was me, so that
I might improve my disguise."

He shook his head. "Ye've na been listening ta
me, lass," he said softly. "Ye'll na be risking yer
life by visiting the Dagger."

She watched him for a second, then slowly
reached out to lift the wolf teeth from his chest.
"How did you get this, Scotsman?"

He scowled, but finally answered. "Have I na
told ye that tale?"

"Aye, you have. And I wonder now, were you
not in danger when you challenged the beast?" she
asked, running her fingers up the leather.

He nodded. "Aye. There was some danger."

"Then why did you do it?"

" 'Twas something I had ta do."

She nodded. "And this is something I have to
do."

He shook his head. "I'll find another way ta free
David."

"Nay. You won't. Time is running short, Scotsman, and you'll not be able to see him safely back
to your homeland without my help. He'll die, and
'twill be your fault ... and mine."

Something in her expression intrigued him.
"Why do ye care, lass?" he asked.

For a moment he thought she would answer. But finally she shrugged. "Even a thief can have feelings. Call it a whim. Mayhap now that I have felt a lover's flame, I can feel for the lovers, and cannot bear to see one die."

"And mayhap ye are a chronic liar that willna let herself trust me."

"Mayhap." She smiled gently.

The expression stopped his breath. "Lass," he murmured. "Please dunna risk—"

"Shh." She covered his lips with her forefinger. "Think who I am, Scotsman," she said softly. "I am the Shadow. You said so yourself. Once there was an old man. I called him Cork, for I did not know his true name. His fingers were gnarled and bent, but he taught me sleight of hand, and I like to think he taught me something besides." She watched him very closely, her bright eyes so blue and intense it was as though he looked straight into heaven. "There is little good I can do in this world, Scotsman. Let me do this."

"But what if . . ." Terror gripped him. "What if I lose ye?"

For a moment she remained motionless, but then she kissed him, very gently. "Then I have tried to do what you would do. What is right."

Roman shook his head and drew away. " 'Twas na long ago that I knew right from wrong," he said. "Murder, theft, lying. They were all wrong. But now . . ." He shrugged.

"I wager you are a fine lawyer," she said softly.

He would wager that he could not live without her. "Dunna do this," he said.

She smiled. "But I *am* a liar, and I *am* a thief."

"Ye wouldna have ta be. Come back ta the Highlands with me, lass. Be my—"

She pressed her fingers firmly to his lips. "Things said in passion are oft regretted," she said.

Reaching up, Roman pulled her hand away, but she shook her head and smiled.

"Your friend's time is fleeting, Scotsman. Will you let me help him?"

"There have been times I have acted the fool," he said softly. "And mayhap at times I have even thought meself ta have some power. But I am na longer vain enough or fool enough ta think I can stop ye."

"Good."

"But this I say, lass. Ye will na go alone. Na so long as the heavens shine above and Hell calls me name."

"I will not risk your life by taking you with me, Scotsman," she said.

For a fleeting instant, warmth spurred through him. She must be concerned for his well-being, he thought. But perhaps not. Perhaps yet, despite everything that had passed between them, she was fooling him again and but planned to escape. "I'll be with ye, lass."

She scowled. "I have planned well and carefully," she said, sweeping a hand sideways to indicate her hair, her costume, the nearby needle and thread that waited to be plied again. "I managed to fool even you in my own house with my disguise only half-complete. I will fool them. But you . . ."

"What about me?"

She shrugged, looking slightly apologetic. "I will go as a Rom," she said, her accent impeccable, her disguise the same.

"So shall I be also."

She laughed. "Let me hear your speech."

He scowled at her. 'Twas her life they were discussing. 'Twas her continued survival, and it angered him that she could treat it so casually.

"Say, I am Theaelo of the proud wild Roms."

"I am Theaelo of the proud, wild Roms," he said, sounding, even to his own ears, like a drunken Swede. He nearly grimaced, but managed to deepen his scowl and add, "and I go with ye if I must tie ye ta me wrist."

She shook her head. "You'd never be believed. Rom men are wild, fiery, unpredictable, not noble and loyal ..." Her voice trailed off as her gaze skimmed his naked form, then she shrugged. "They wear bands of gold through holes in their ears," she said and turned abruptly away as if that one fact explained everything. Bending, she began to rummage in her trunk.

Not far away, her sewing needle winked in the candle's light. Roman plucked it out of its fabric, then, seeing one Italian shoe on the floor, lifted it up. It was a stupid-looking thing, but it had a solid heel. Putting it behind his left ear, Roman glanced into the mirror, and stabbed his lobe.

At precisely that moment, Tara straightened and saw him in the mirror. He watched her mouth fall open, then smiled as he pulled the thread through his ear.

"Have ye a ring ta put through the hole?"

She turned, slowly lifting a hand toward his ear. A single drop of blood welled up and slid languidly down the black thread. "You stabbed yourself."

Roman grasped the bottle of ale from her shelf, pulled out the cork, and took a swig. "I am Theaelo of the proud, wild Roms," he said. The statement was heavily burred.

"Oh." She looked bewildered, and somehow that baffled expression improved Roman's mood immeasurably.

"No ring?"

She shook her head, still looking dazed..

" 'Tis na a problem," he said, and digging inside the trunk, found what he searched for.

In a moment he had pulled the fishhook from her sailor's shirt, doused it with ale and pushed the dull end through his ear.

Tara's jaw dropped a fraction of an inch lower. Roman glanced at himself in the mirror. The straight end of the hook extended behind his lobe a good two inches and was smeared with blood. The hook lay sharp and shiny against his flesh. He nodded and turned his gaze to her.

"We go together, lass," he said, placing his fists on his bare hips, "even though ye look a bit tame for the part."

Chapter 19

Tara pulled her gaze from Roman's mutilated ear. Every time she thought she knew him, he surprised her. 'Twould be a far better thing if she could predict his actions, for then surely she could set the thought of him on the shelf beside all the other details that jostled for her attention.

"I've no suitable garments for you to wear," she said. "Therefore—"

"I will go," he said simply.

She turned away with a frown and began rummaging in the trunk. She had been collecting for more than a decade. Garments and fabrics crowded wigs and paste beads. But nothing seemed appropriate until, toward the bottom of the trunk, she found a pair of brown leather hose.

She held them up to the wavering light of the candle, then shifted her gaze to Roman. He'd wrapped himself in the blanket, but even so, she could see the garment would be too small.

She shrugged. " 'Tis the best I can find."

She handed over the hose, then began rummaging in the trunk again.

Although she tried to ignore him, she could not help but know he turned his back, nor could she fail to hear the blanket slip from his body.

A tunic. She must find him a tunic, she told herself. But she had mirrors, and they were her downfall, for they made it all too easy to watch him. All she had to do was raise her eyes the slightest bit and she could see him. His back was very broad. It was darker than she would have expected a lawyer's back to be, and that made her wonder what kind of activities exposed his torso to the sunlight. Or was he that dark-skinned all over and she had simply failed to notice? Her gaze slipped lower, granting her an answer when she saw the dramatic rise of his pale buttocks.

She drew a steadying breath and watched as he stepped into the hose. They were too small, and he bounced slightly, trying to force himself into them.

The bouncing intrigued Tara even more. She craned her neck, trying to see into the second mirror and ascertain the effects his movements were having on his frontal body parts.

But the looking glass was too small. He bounced, and she craned until finally he had persuaded the hose to encompass his hips and thighs.

She saw the muscles in his back flex, saw his bulging triceps strain and knew he was trying to close the codpiece that covered his crotch.

Tara bit her lip. Though she was unhappy about his insistence on accompanying her, she had no wish for him to injure himself in his attempt to fit into the leather hose. Mayhap she should offer to assist him, she thought devilishly, but in that moment he turned.

She ducked her head rapidly back, hands clawing at the fabrics in the trunk.

"Here," she said, turning quickly, ruffled blouse in hand. "I found . . ." But she could not quite finish the thought. Her gaze skimmed over his mounded chest, his narrow waist, his tightly confined hips and thighs.

"Tight," he said simply.

"Nay!" she said, but the word was squeaky. She cleared her throat and tried again. "Nay. I think it looks . . ." She shrugged, wondering if her face was as red as it felt. "The style is bending toward snug."

"Snug," he said, "has been exceeded by about half a cow's worth of leather. Should I feel the urge ta breathe, I'll have ta leave the room."

"Aye," she murmured. Sweet Mary, he was a sight to see. Raw male, untamed hair, hardened muscles, and not an ounce of fat to lap above the narrow waistband.

" 'Twill na be a problem, of course," he added. "I have always felt that breathing is overvalued."

"Aye," she murmured again. Maybe it was the wolf's teeth hanging dead center between his nipples that intrigued her so. Or maybe it was the fishhook in his ear. Surely it wasn't merely his blatant masculinity, for she had spent the entirety of her life in the presence of men, and half of that she had been a man herself. But she had never managed to look like *that*.

"Unless ye wish ta do me bodily harm, lass," he murmured huskily, "ye'd best na look at me like that whilst I'm trussed into this garment."

Tara snapped her gaze to his face. "I didn't . . . I wasn't . . ."

He watched her, his green eyes steady, his nostrils slightly flared.

"I . . ." she began, but finally she merely handed over the shirt. "Found this for you," she finished in a rush.

"Lass," he said, catching her hand, "should I be flattered?"

Her lips moved. Her mind refused to. But finally she snapped herself from her trance and left the shirt in his fingers as she jerked her hand free. "Put it on. Put it on,'' she said, turning away.

She could feel him watching her, but refused to turn back. Hers was not a life of leisure. Far from that. She could not afford to act like a brainless ninny every time he showed a bit of skin. She could not afford to dwell on the night just past. In fact, she could not afford to think of him at all. She had to plan and plan carefully or forfeit her own life for her carelessness. She turned, ready to tell him so.

He lifted his gaze to hers and raised his brows. ''I dunna mean ta find fault, lass, but the fit seems a bit suspect.'' The ruffled sleeves barely reached past his elbows, and the bottom hem did not meet his hose. She could see a narrow strip of dark hair visible between the shirt and waistband. For just an instant she considered sliding her fingers through that hair.

She cleared her throat and tried to do the same with her mind. ''It seems the lad that wore that was a bit smaller than you.''

He canted his head at her understatement. She cleared her throat again and turned back to the trunk, but her mind was running wild and her fingers fumbled. In a moment she was looking at him again.

''I can find none other.''

Roman shrugged. Gripping the bottom of the shirt, he pulled it over his head. A hundred tempting muscles flexed. ''I'll go without,'' he said.

Tara licked her lips then snapped her gaze to his. ''What?''

''I've seen me share of gypsies,'' he said, '' 'Tis na uncommon for them ta go without a shirt.''

She felt her mind grow limp. ''Nay.''

He crumpled the shirt in his hands. They were big hands, powerful, but she could well remember the gentleness they possessed.

"What say ye?" he asked.

"I said nay!" She was angry suddenly. She was not some mealy-mouthed milkmaid, boggled by the merest sight of flesh. She was the Shadow, Betty, Fletcher, and a hundred other people who did not blanch at anything, so why was she acting like some silk merchant's fat daughter? "I'll not deny that last night was . . ." She paused and tried not to sigh. " 'Twas quite pleasurable," she said. "But we've work to do now."

His brows raised higher. "Do I argue the point?"

"No. Your . . . your chest . . ." She placed her hand beside his amulet. "Your chest argues," she said breathlessly.

"Yer pardon?"

She stared at him. Surely he knew the effect he had on her. Surely he knew that the sight of him thus turned her mind to mush, that the deep burr of his voice sent quivers through her being. He was not stupid. "Fine," she said and drew her hand quickly away. "Go without a tunic. See if I care. And here . . ." She handed him a crimson sash. "To tie about your waist. 'Twill accent your . . ." She waved her hand a bit wildly. "Everything."

"Yer angry at me," he said.

"No, I'm not."

"Aye, ye—" He paused and scowled. "Where's me amulet."

"You cannot wear it this night."

His scowl deepened. " 'Tis a lucky token of sorts. I will wear it."

"Dagger's men may recognize it."

"How could that be?"

"I noticed it the first night at the Queen's Head. Dagger's men may have, too."

"Ye noticed it?"

"You were naked." Tara felt herself blush. "I could not help but see . . ." She nodded in the general direction of his chest and cleared her throat. "I could not help but notice . . . I was intrigued by . . ." She paused, feeling panicked. "I noticed it," she finished in a rush.

The room went quiet.

The corners of Roman's lips twitched. "Dare I hope the sight of me . . . amulet sparked some lascivious thoughts in yer mind."

"I . . ." She opened her mouth, closed it, opened it again, then, like magic, produced the amulet, seemingly from thin air. "There it is, then. Put it somewhere safe," she said quickly. "Now we've very little time and much to do if you wish to save your friend."

He didn't shift his gaze from her face, but spread his legs and crossed his arms against the muscular expanse of his chest. It was a strangely erotic stance, she thought, and the roguish smile that tilted his lips did nothing to detract from his appeal.

Think, she must think, and not about his chest— or any other body parts.

She turned stiffly away. "I am Rom. I am Rom," she said, rubbing her brow. "Salina they call me. And you are Theaelo, my . . . protector." She paced again, not allowing herself to look in his direction. He would make a fine protector, dark, large, dangerous . . .

"Lass, I—"

"Silent!" she said, abruptly turning toward him.

He raised his brows in question.

"You'll be mute," she said with a relieved sigh.

Roman settled his palm on the dirk at his waist as he entered the dark interior of the nameless tavern. He would have been happier with a sword, but he had none. He would have been happier still if the Hawk were here with him, lending his immense strength and his steely nerve. But the Hawk was in France and not expected to return for some weeks. Roman was Tara's sole protection, and that thought wore at him. She had masterminded the scheme, and she insisted on assuming the risk. But not she alone. Liam had been notified, thereby involving one more innocent.

Well, *innocent* was stretching the term, he thought as he followed Tara into the dimly lit inn.

Or rather, he followed her hips. Draped in black-and-purple fabric, they swayed as she walked. A cloth bag hung from her girdle. Her feet were bare, and strapped to her right ankle was a string of tiny bells that tinkled with each step.

The tavern settled into silence as all eyes turned to watch her entrance.

Roman stared straight ahead. He knew the kind of species that inhabited this place, could feel their hot, hungry gazes burn at Tara. Hell fire, he must be the king of fools to allow her to do this.

"I wish to see the Dagger," she said in a loud staccato.

It had been quiet before. Now, not a soul breathed.

"Did you not hear me?" She slapped the palm of her hand on the nearest table.

Two men jumped. One swore. A man scurried from the kitchen. He was missing a front tooth, and a sprig of greasy hair drooped over one eye.

"I wish to see the Dagger," she repeated, louder still.

The toothless proprietor looked nervous. "We don't know no Dagger here."

She turned her head and spat.

Roman watched her spittle bead up in the dust at the innkeeper's feet. There were more than twenty men here. Each one of them watched her with barely concealed bloodlust.

"Coward!" She said the word very succinctly, even with the Romanian accent.

"What did—"

"I said you are a coward!" Tara repeated, tossing her head. "You are, every one of you, cowards or you would not be afraid to tell the Dagger of my presence."

A man rose from the nearby table with a grin. At his side was a short, curved sword.

The hair at the back of Roman's neck rose. He took a single step toward Tara and remained still with his gaze on the man's face.

"And who might you be?" the man asked.

Tara turned slowly toward him. The ankle bells jangled. She snorted, tossing her head back slightly. "Not one to talk to the likes of you, worm."

There was very little warning. "Whore," the man snarled, grabbing for his sword.

Sheer, desperate instinct made Roman react. He lunged, and immediately wrapped an arm about the villain's throat and dragged him up against his bare chest.

The room was silent again but for the man's gasping breath.

Salina laughed, the noise quicksilver light. "Meet Theaelo," she said, stepping up to the man Roman held captive. "He does not talk, but he hears, aye? And he does not like to hear me called a whore." Drawing nearer still, she lightly slapped the captive's cheek before trailing her fingers down Roman's bare arm.

Their gazes met. Fire sizzled in hers. Rage boiled in Roman's veins. Damn her for taking such risks!

"I am Salina," she said, turning quickly toward the patrons, as if the question had been tangible and coming from that front. "Princess of the Rom. And I wish to speak to the Dagger."

A man rose slowly from a stool. His hair was

snowy white and his voice soft when he spoke. "And why do you wish to speak to him . . . Princess?"

She turned her gaze very slowly toward him, as if wondering if it compromised her supreme position to do so. "Because I have this." In one fluid motion she lifted the golden mermaid from the bag and held it aloft. There were a few murmurs, but most men remained quiet, all attention riveted on the golden object.

" 'Tis a pretty piece. Can I see it?" asked the white-haired man.

Salina laughed, and, without lowering her gaze, dropped the mermaid back into the bag.

"What is your name, White Head?" she asked, stepping forward.

Panic welled up like a cold tide in Roman. Thrusting his captive back toward his table, he paced after her, dirk drawn.

"They call me Angel," said the man with his ethereal voice.

"Angel!" She laughed, closing in on him so that they were nearly touching. Sensuality steamed off her. "Do not underestimate me just because I have tits, Angel. I have come to see the Dagger, and see him I will."

The inn was quiet, and then Angel laughed.

"I've a feeling he would be quite disappointed if he did not meet you. Albert will take you to Cape Hood."

"Cape Hood?" she asked.

Angel smiled. The expression was nothing if not ethereal. " 'Tis where he conducts his . . . business."

Tara turned slowly, absorbing her surroundings. Cape Hood. She knew Roman had been here before, had watched a man being killed. For a moment pure panic seized her. She should not have brought him here. Should not have dragged him into her thievery. He was a barrister, a nobleman. But no. He was much more than that.

Though she tried, she could not forget how he had held her during their lovemaking, during her nightmares. He had stroked her and cuddled her, and with his touch, light seemed to return to her world.

She should not have allowed him to come along. But . . . She turned her gaze to Roman. In the night, the huge warehouse was lighted with only one candle. The building seemed to echo thoughts as clearly as it did words. Roman stood only inches from her side. Even without touching him, she could feel his warmth, his strength.

He was not a lad to be allowed or disallowed to do anything, she reminded herself. He was here because he had insisted on coming along. She had to remember that, had to focus. She was Salina, Romanian, proud, fearless.

"I have waited already too long," she said, rising to pace the dirt floor. Roman rose with her, saying nothing.

"They'll come soon enough," Albert said.

"Soon enough has come and gone!" she said, turning to pace again. "When—"

The sound of approaching footsteps interrupted her. She stopped, drew a deep breath. She *was* Salina. Nodding once, she took a seat on a crate some yards from the candle.

A door creaked open. For just a moment she could see a man silhouetted against the relative light of the outdoors, a lean man of average height.

Silence settled over the building.

Salina sat very still, very straight, staring at the dark figure that stood well outside the pale circle of candlelight. The quiet stretched out before her, but she remained silent, waiting, her expression unchanged. Roman stood beside her, immobile, watchful.

"You wanted to see me," said Lord Dagger. His voice was low and bland, but with a strange inflection that did not quite match the dialect of his peers.

Tara canted her head slightly and tilted her lips into the semblance of a cool smile. "I still don't *see* you."

The hidden form chuckled, and although he did not move from the shrouding shadows, she could feel his gaze sweep over her. "Angel tells me you have something of value . . . on your person."

She inclined her head like a princess and raised her brows at the obvious double entendre. " 'Tis a pretty enough piece I've brought."

"Move into the light," Lord Dagger said.

She remained as she was. " 'Tis you that's in the shadows, Daggerman, and I have a yearning to see what valuables you might have . . . on your person."

"On your feet, whore," said Albert. She sensed him moving closer, heard a scuffle, a gasp of breath, and then a yelp of pain as he thudded against something solid.

She turned with casual slowness toward the disruption. Roman stood with his legs braced far apart and his bare chest rising and falling with his steady breaths. In one fist he held a dirk.

"Who is the watchdog?" Dagger asked.

"He is called Theaelo," she said, turning her attention slowly back to Dagger.

"Does he talk or just attack on command?"

"Theaelo considers it a privilege to guard me in silence."

Dagger chuckled. "I might feel the same if there are . . . rewards."

She nodded curtly at the compliment. The dust

felt cool and soft against her bare feet. "I think we can come to a mutually . . . rewarding arrangement."

"I've been known to satisfy."

She offered him a pouting smile. "There is satisfaction and there is satisfaction, Lord Dagger."

"Indeed," he said.

She drew out the golden mermaid.

For a moment he was absolutely quiet, then, "Lord Crighton will be quite upset."

Tara felt as if her heart were about to beat its way free of her chest. She raised her brows slowly. "You know the piece?"

"I've admired it."

"And I stole it."

Silence again.

"How?"

She dropped the mermaid unceremoniously back into her bag and paced a few feet. "Every woman must be allowed her secrets."

"But yours are so interesting, Princess. I wonder why you come here."

She stopped with the light to her back. It would show her silhouette and little else. "Let us just say that I have no wish to marry a man as doddering as my grandfather."

"So they planned to marry ya to an old man?"

Turning with a jerk, she paced again, angrily now. "I am young!" she said, drawing a fist toward her bosom. It was dyed, pushed high, and well exposed above the drawstring décolleté of her simple blouse. "I have needs."

"Indeed."

She stopped again, giving him a glimpse of her profile in the candlelight before she turned toward him. "And I have talents."

Though she wasn't certain, she thought he held his breath.

"I am offering you the mermaid as goodwill,"

she said simply. " 'Tis yours with the agreement that what I bring to you henceforth will be shared half and half."

"You steal it, I sell it," he said simply.

She lifted her chin a smidgen. "You'll not find another as good as I."

"Have ye, perhaps, heard of a man called the Shadow?"

Her heart thundered on. "I admit that I only just arrived in this place you call Firthport. I've made few acquaintances."

"He's been a thorn in my side."

She smiled. "Then let me be a soothing potion."

"A tempting potion you make, too. But I've found that fools act in haste. Hence, I propose a new proposition. You keep the mermaid for now. I have a mission for you, and if you are successful in that theft, we will be partners. Three parts for me, one part for you."

She smiled and shook her head. "No. I will steal what you like, but you will get half and I will get half."

He laughed. "As you wish then, and later, we will make more personal terms."

She stared into the impenetrable darkness at him, then walked back to Roman and settled a hand on his bare chest. "I enjoy personal," she purred, and walked toward the door.

Chapter 20

"**Y**e'll na even think upon it," Roman said. The journey home had been long and slow, for they had taken a circuitous course and stopped often to listen. But no one followed them. Still, they'd barely spoken until the door was closed and barred behind them.

" 'Tis the only way," Tara said, lighting a candle. "I've but to steal the bracelet Dagger covets, and the necklace will be ours."

Roman gritted his teeth and stormed across the floor to swing her around, but when she lifted her face he saw the aching fatigue clear as sunrise in her eyes.

"Lass," he said, worry etched in his voice, "are ye well?"

"Tired," she said, her knees buckling.

Catching her gently, Roman lifted her into his arms and carried her to the bed. She did not object, but lay quietly with her eyes closed and her head pillowed against his bare chest. It was a feeling of such exquisite agony, that for a moment he could not speak.

"Thank you." Her breath was feather soft against his skin.

Roman settled onto the low pallet, still holding

her. Letting his own eyes fall closed, he absorbed the feeling that tantalized him. "For what?"

"For saving my life."

He tightened his grip. Terror had been the course of the evening, terror and more terror as he remembered the murder he had seen committed in that same warehouse not many nights before. But Tara was safe now, at least for a while.

He drew a deep breath, still trying to relax.

The risks she had undertaken were immense. It seemed there were a thousand things he should reprimand her for. But she felt so soft and light in his arms, so fine and delicate. Still, those characteristics only made his worry deeper.

"Ye did na need ta be so bold, lass," he said, remembering her sharp staccato voice, her flirting, her hand, warm, but softly trembling as she had stroked his chest for all to see.

It had been a strange sensation, mixed with equal amounts of eroticism and terror.

She opened her eyes and met his gaze. "My apologies," she said softly. "I fear Salina is not a subtle character."

Roman frowned into her eyes. "But ye are na Salina."

"Aye, I am," she said. "There is a part of me that is her and a part of her that is me."

"I fear tonight ye were all her. And bold enough to age me fifty years."

She smiled, a soft tender smile that Salina would never wear, and reached out to run a single finger gently along the raised vein in his right hand. "Boldness covers fear. 'Tis a tiresome thing holding back the drowning terror." She shivered a little. "The evil in that place was too thick to let me breathe. But you . . ." Her gaze met his. "I think you have no fear, Scotsman."

Images of Albert lunging toward Tara stabbed

through Roman's mind. Terror welled up again, but he pushed it back and touched her face. Her skin was velvety soft, but her dark, false hair felt coarse against his fingers. He pushed it aside, then eased the kerchief and wig from her head.

Her golden hair was confined with pins. He released them one by one, massaged her scalp, and watched her eyes fall closed again. He knew the moment sleep took her. Her lips parted slightly and her breath was kitten-soft against his skin. His chest ached with that light contact.

"I do fear," he whispered into the quiet. "I fear losing ye."

Roman awoke with a start. Daylight shone through the wooden shutters. What had he heard? Tara stirred in his arms. He glanced at her, set his hand on his dirk, and rose quickly to his feet.

" 'Tis me. Liam," came a voice from outside.

Roman unbarred the door and the boy slipped in.

He was no more than thirteen years of age. Lean and gangly, he grinned at Tara, then flitted his gaze to Roman. His dark eyes hurried up and down before settling on Roman's pierced and hooked ear. "I knew when ya decided to go fishing you'd hook a big one," he said to Tara, and laughed.

Roman noticed Tara's blush, but she covered it quickly.

"You followed Dagger?" she asked.

"Aye, I followed him," said Liam, "but I lost him. 'E 'ad a 'orse, a fine dark steed. Fleet as I am, I fear the 'orse was the faster."

"What direction did he go?"

"North, up Cartway."

"Cartway," Tara mused. She had begun to pace, her fair brows pulled low over her eyes. "Who is he?"

Liam shrugged his shoulders. " 'E is a murderin' thief with a ring of murderin' thieves that surround 'im. Do ya need ta know more?''

She paced again, then shook her head. "No. You're right. All I need to do is steal the bracelet as Dagger requested."

Liam paced to the hearth. There was a small loaf of bread there, which he took and consumed with astounding speed.

"How far did ye follow Dagger?" Roman asked.

"Till me lungs gave out," said the boy.

"Did he turn, slow down?"

"Nay." Liam scowled. " 'Tis sorry I am ta disappoint ya, Tara."

" 'Tis no matter," she said. " 'Twould have made little difference if I knew his family tree and entire history. We know what we know and will have to be especially careful because of it."

Roman considered saying again that she would not go through with this theft, but there seemed little point, so he stood in silent thought.

" 'Twas a thrill to watch ya work," Liam said. "Wouldn't a never knowed ya weren't Rom. Me . . ." He shook his head. The bread had already been consumed. He reached into his pocket now to draw out a coin and roll it with silvery quickness between his fingers. "I can do the light-hands work. But won't never be anyone ta compare ta your acting."

Pure admiration shone in Liam's eyes. Or did it? Was there, perhaps, a touch of envy? Roman wondered. Why did Tara trust this boy so when she trusted none other.

"Where were ye that ye could see so well?" asked Roman quietly.

Liam rolled the coin again. It flashed between his fingers only to suddenly appear in the other hand seemingly by magic and without conscious thought. "I was on the roof. By the by, ya done a fair job of acting yourself, Scotch. The silent Rom, all muscle and balls." He laughed. "What ya gonna do now, Tara?"

She paced and bit her lip. "I've little choice but to steal Harrington's bracelet as he asked."

"Nay. 'Tis too dangerous," Roman said. "We'll find some other way."

"What other way?" asked Tara.

Roman turned toward her, fear for her making his stomach churn. "Any other way."

"There is little time remaining," she said. "And we are so close. We've but to steal Harrington's bracelet, take it to Dagger, and find out where he stashed the necklace."

"So simple," Roman said, "if ye dunna mind dying."

The room fell quiet.

"And do ye, lass?"

"I've no wish to die."

"And I've na wish ta let ye," Roman said.

"You do not hold my life in your hands, Scotsman," she said. "You may look the part of the bare-chested protector, but I've been surviving alone for a good many years. And I'll not have you telling me how to live my life now."

Anger slowly flooded over Roman. "Ye'll na go," he said.

She lifted her chin at him. "Oh, I'll go. I'll have the bracelet. And if you're too stubborn to take it, 'tis fine with me. I'm certain I can think of something else to do with it."

"Ye'll na—" Roman began, but Liam's words intersected his own.

"Mayhap Scotch is right, Tara. 'Tis dangerous, even for you."

Tara turned her gaze to Liam's. Roman narrowed his eyes and wondered what passed between them. Something unsaid. Something merely understood.

Tara sighed. "Let us consider it then. Mayhap we will think up a better plan. What do we know of Dagger thus far?"

" 'Tis said 'e killed James" Liam said softly.

"I've heard as much," she said.

"Old Bertram the Hand was there when they pulled James from the firth."

"First Cork and now James," Tara murmured. "Must Bertram watch all the old masters die?"

" 'E says you're the master now," Liam said.

Roman watched her turn her face toward the lad. They were immersed in their own world. A world of crime and intrigue. He had no part in that world. He was a barrister, a diplomat. And yet, somehow their worlds had become enmeshed. Her life had entwined with his own, and suddenly he did not wish to live without her, no matter what world she lived in.

"If James was a master at redistributing stolen goods, why would Dagger have him killed instead of employing his expertise?" Roman asked.

"James was more than a fence," Tara said. "He was a legend. Thieves would come from as far away as Rome to sell their goods. But he got a good deal of business from here in Firthport."

"A bloke could enter in his back door one day and James would sell it out the front of 'is shop the next."

"And the magistrate did nothing to interfere with his dealings?" Roman asked.

Liam shrugged. " 'E didn't steal it, 'e only bought it, and there was plenty a times when the former owners was just 'appy ta get their goods back. They didn't care 'ow it was done."

Roman scowled. The entire situation went against everything he stood for, but he was out of his element now. "So why did Dagger kill James?"

"Dagger must have his own system for distributing stolen goods," Tara said.

"Or mayhap finding out 'oo the Shadow was was more important than fencing goods," Liam said.

"What do ye mean by that?" Roman asked, dread seeping over him.

"That's why 'e took auld James. Cause 'e knew the old fence was one of the few that knowed about the Shadow."

Roman felt his stomach pitch. "So he might know—"

"If he knew I was the Shadow, I'd be dead now," Tara said. Her tone was flippant, but her eyes . . . "They learned that I was associated with the Shadow, but James must have . . ." Her voice broke. She turned away. "He must have died before they could force him to identify me."

Roman gritted his teeth. "Are ye saying Dagger tortured James ta find out who ye were? And now ye're playing about with—"

"Playing about!" She snapped the words at him. The worry in her eyes was no longer hidden, but was mingled with anger and frustration. "Mayhap this is a game to you, Scotsman. But 'tis not to me. 'Tis deadly serious. I am not a barrister who can fall back on the law to save me. In fact, 'tis the law that would do me most harm. I am not the son of a lord. There is nothing holding you here. At any time you can hie yourself back to your homeland and forget Firthport ever existed. But this is my own place in the world."

"There may have been a time when I was above begging, lass. But 'tis na longer true. Please," he said softly, "dunna follow this course. We will find another way to free David MacAulay."

"I can scale the walls of Harrington House," she said quietly. "I can get the bracelet."

"'Tis said old man 'arrington is guarding 'is daughter well," Liam said. "'Tis said 'e 'as 'ired men to make certain she stays put."

Tara was silent for a moment, but then she shrugged. "I've fooled guards before."

"And what if 'e recognizes you?" Liam asked.

Tara turned quickly toward the lad.

"What do ye mean, recognizes her?" Roman asked.

For a moment, she only stared at Liam, but finally she spoke. "Liam has long feared that someone would recognize me as the Shadow. But the Shadow is dead."

Roman watched her carefully, considering every word. But if there was more to this situation than what she admitted, he could not tell. "Then let the Shadow lie in peace," he said softly. "As ye said, I am a diplomat, a barrister—there is another way for me ta achieve me ends."

Tara caught his gaze and smiled gently. "I suppose I should be happy to forgo this job." She shrugged. "All right, Scotsman, 'tis for you to think up a better plan."

"You'll not try for the bracelet?" Liam asked, his tone dubious.

Tara laughed. "Despite what you may think, I have no wish to stand in line beside MacAulay for the hangman's noose."

Liam exhaled noisily, then flipped the coin between his fingers again. "'Tis glad I am to hear that, Tara, for you've still to tell me 'ow you stole the mermaid."

"You're far too young to know," Tara said.

"Then I'll take my leave," Liam said, "and try to grow up faster."

"Grow up any faster, lad, and you'll be a gaffer

before you've grown your first whisker," Tara replied. Again, her tone was flippant, but she reached out and touched the boy's hand, and for a moment, it tarried there. "Take care, Liam."

"I shall, but I will also learn what I can about the Dagger," he said.

The door closed noiselessly behind him.

The room fell into silence.

"Then ye'll na steal the bracelet?" Roman asked, watching her back.

She turned with the elegant grace of a flower in the wind. Her golden hair flowed like silken waves about her shoulders and her teeth looked snowy white against her darkened skin. "If I did not know better, I would say that you do not trust me, Scotsman."

He scowled at her. "I dunna. And for good reason."

She approached him with swaying hips, her colorful skirt sweeping her ankles. "Then I vow, I will not steal the bracelet until we have considered all options."

Her arms slipped about his waist. They were slim arms, but strong and resilient, like the woman he loved.

Terror coiled in Roman's gut. "Who are ye now, lass, Salina or Tara O'Flynn."

She laughed. "Mayhap I am both."

He watched her eyes. They were the crystalline blue of angels'. But he must not be misled. "And mayhap ye are all Salina this day," he said.

She shook her head and lifted her skirts.

Her ankles were narrow and fine, her calves slim and shapely. But just below the knee he could see the delineation where the walnut stain stopped and the pale skin began.

"You see, I am part of each," she said. "But I had best return to myself before it is too late and the dye will not be undone. Then who knows, mayhap I will be Salina forever and every man I see will be scurrying for cover."

"I did not see Dagger running for cover," Roman said, scowling as she turned away.

She fanned up the fire with quick efficiency, swung the water kettle over the blaze, then glanced over her shoulder at him.

"In fact, methinks he was more than interested," Roman added.

Straightening, Tara lifted three lemons from a wooden bowl on her small table, and glanced at him again. " 'Twas my hope to ... distract him, Scotsman."

"Distract him!" Emotion welled up in Roman's chest. It was hot and angry, and he did not like it, for emotion got people killed. "Ye could have found a thousand ways ta distract him. Ye did na have ta flaunt yer—"

"You're jealous." She looked up at him from where she leaned over the table. Her breasts were pressed high and full against her meager blouse. Her tone was soft, and yet her words cut through his bluster like hot steel through snow.

"Nay." He meant to say the word with force, but only managed to push it out on a husky breath.

"Why?"

So absurd was his denial that it was as if he had never spoken. "There are men of the world, lass," he said, clenching his fists once. "But I am na one of them. I canna hold ye in me arms, feel yer passion beneath me, then watch ye flaunt yerself to another."

She squeezed a lemon. Her fingers looked as smooth as lily stems against the yellow rind, but her gaze did not leave his. "So you are not a man of the world?" Her tone was husky, sensual, awakening some primitive need in him.

He clenched his fists. "Nay, I am na."

"Are you certain?" She stood slowly.

He watched her. There was a sensuality that robed her. "I am a man of the earth, solid . . ." She rounded the table, approaching him. Her blouse had slipped off one shoulder and threatened to reveal more. He cleared his throat. "Boring," he said.

"I don't find you boring," she whispered. Her hair was like golden, gossamer wings, her eyes as deep as eternity. "In truth, I have never dreamt I could feel what you make me feel. When you touched me . . ." She paused. Roman could see the steady thrum of a pulse in her fine throat. She let her eyes fall closed for a moment. "I felt like I was truly alive for the first time. When I felt your flesh against mine . . ."

Desire roared to wakefulness in him.

"Your heart against my heart," she said, reaching out for a moment before drawing her hand back to curl her fingers against her breast.

It was full and dark-skinned, and he knew if he touched it, he would be lost to all thought. And he must think.

"Roman," she murmured, breathing hard, "touch me."

The hell with thinking! With a growl, Roman drew her into his arms. Their lips clashed.

Raw, hungry desire consumed him. Her hands were like quicksilver, everywhere, hot, enticing. He was not sure whether he freed her breasts or whether she had, but suddenly her blouse slipped below her nipples. Soft and intoxicating she was.

He drew one pink nipple into his mouth, suckling, licking, feverish with excitement.

She gasped and bucked against him. In a moment her legs encircled his waist and his erection was straining out between the unlaced plackets of his hose.

He tried to slow down, to take her gently, but she was not gentle. Indeed she was as hot as flame in his hands, moaning, begging, demanding. When she entrapped him hot and throbbing in her hand, he could wait no longer. With a groan of aching impatience, he yanked her skirt up and drove into her.

Desire met desire on even ground, each striving for fulfillment. She arched against him, her head thrown back, her breasts bare and pushed toward his mouth.

He reached out, flicking his tongue over her nipple. She caught his hair in her hands and a primal cry of lust rose from her. With that, Roman erupted in a volcanic explosion.

He pumped hard and fast. She matched his pace, pressing against him with all her strength until their movements finally slowed to a shuddering halt.

He felt her grow lax against him, felt her legs unclasp as her feet slipped to the floor.

But he could not bear to let her go. Though he felt limp with weakness, he lifted her into his arms and carried her to the bed.

The pallet rustled as he joined her there. When he leaned over to kiss her, her lips felt feathery soft, though they looked bruised by the passion he had expended on her.

He lifted his gaze to hers, searching for resentment, anger. "Did I hurt ye, lass?" he asked.

"Nay, Scotsman. Did I hurt you?"

He could not help but smile and kiss her again. When he drew back her expression had gone sober.

"Why are you not married?" she asked.

He watched her eyes. "I waited for an advantageous match."

"Advantageous," she said. "What does that mean?"

Never, not if he lived to see a thousand years would he know anyone as desirable as she. He knew that suddenly, beyond the shadow of a doubt.

"I have known hunger, lass," he said.

He had not meant to be cryptic. The words had simply come, but somehow she understood.

"And so ye would marry for wealth," she said. There was no condemnation in her voice, but perhaps there was sadness. " 'Tis what is expected, I'm certain."

"Expected?" He looked into her eyes. There were riches there. "Amongst the Forbes, there is naught to be expected but the unexpected."

While one of her hands toyed with his hair, the other remained softly curled against her breast, which was dark-skinned nearly to the nipple, where it faded to delicate ivory. The image fascinated him, drew him. He kissed the hand, the fingers, the breast.

"In truth, lass, I believe I have been expected to marry . . . conservatively, to a prominent family. A diplomatic union."

"It is your family's custom to choose your wives such?"

He pondered that. "The women of the Forbes are . . ." He shook his head, trying to find the proper words, but it seemed all diplomacy had fled. "Well, they are dangerous. But I think me family expects me ta find someone more . . . staid." She would fit in admirably among the Forbes women, he thought, but he did not say it, for emotions and sensation were coming at him too fast to sort them out one from another.

"Staid?" she asked softly.

"Ta suit me own disposition."

"Staid." She nodded. Four pink welts marked the path where her nails had raked his chest. She followed that course with a gentle finger. "Mayhap they misjudged you."

"And mayhap ye bring the animal from me own soul. But in truth, lass," he said softly, "I dunna think the Forbeses choose their wives atall." He let his fingers slip down her back, and his mind slipped away to the far distant hills of the Highlands. "Sometimes when I was a lad, in the midst of the night I would believe I was yet with Dermid. I would forget Fiona's tender touch, or mayhap I would dream that I couldna quite reach her." Even now he felt that aching terror coil within him. He clenched his fist and drew a deep breath. "I would creep down the hall and sit at Fiona's door. Sometimes there was na sound, but sometimes I would hear her voice, or her laughter. Then there would be Leith's tone, deep and contented, filled with laughter and thought. 'Twas Leith that told me the truth," he said softly. "Fiona was na chosen, he said, she was sent from heaven above."

Tara lay very still, her eyes wide, her expression tense. "And your brothers' wives, were they heaven-sent also?"

"I have na brothers auld enough to wed, but me foster uncles, Roderic and Colin, have married."

"And were their wives gifts from heaven?"

He smiled at his own thoughts. "Mayhap the Flame was sent from somewhere else," he murmured. "Somewhere that would foster a good hot fire. But aye, lass, she has been a gift ta the Rogue."

Her fingers had slipped from his hair and now stroked his neck. The feather-soft feeling was tantalizingly sweet. "But you did not think you deserved such a gift," she whispered. "And thus you sat alone by the door in the dark, listening for Fiona's voice?"

Memories crowded in. "They wouldna allow me to sit there for long, lass."

"I am sorry."

Roman shook his head and drew himself back to the present. " 'Twas na like that. 'Twas me own decision ta be alone. She always knew when I was there. Somehow . . ." He shrugged. "She always knew, and she would come. Finally, there seemed na point in running away. Her touch didna seem so terrible. Her kindness did not seem so frightening, though mayhap . . ."

"What?"

"Mayhap ye are right; I never believed I deserved it."

"You deserve every gift there is," she said softly.

"Why do ye say this?"

"Because I know you, Scotsman. You have seen the depths of depravity, yet you have remained unstained."

He opened his mouth to argue, but she placed her fingers on his lips and smiled. "I am a fair judge of people, Scottie, and I am a skeptic. If I say you are good, you are good.

He was lost in her eyes, in the kindness of her words. "Love is a frightening thing," he whispered.

He had not meant to say those words and wished now to reel them back, but the damage was done.

He could see the terror in her eyes, and though she did not move, it seemed he could feel her draw away. "I know little of love," she said.

She was wrong, but mayhap she did not know it. He held her tightly. "Don't ye?"

Her gaze lifted again, haunted, ethereally blue. She shook her head, but the motion was stiff and jerky. "Love kills, Scotsman. That's what I know. And no matter what you think, I do not wish to die."

"Love can heal," he said quietly.

She shook her head again, but the movement was no more certain than before. "I have no proof of that."

"I am proof," he said. "For I surely wouldna have lived had na Fiona saved me. And ye, lass . . . I have heard ye speak of Cork. There is something in yer voice when ye speak of him."

Her eyes fell closed. "He died because of me." Her words were hushed. Roman remained very still. "I was young and I was full of myself. I had stolen a buckle from a passing lord. Cork . . ." She shook her head. "He had taught me to study my victims before I stole. He said that if I got caught, I would hang and I would hang alone. He would not risk his life for me."

Roman stroked her hair back, wanting to take her pain.

"They suspected me of the theft. I was naught but the little urchin that lived with Cork. They came to his room, accusing me. But he laughed and said I was not clever enough to make such a theft. 'Twas he that had taken it, he said."

"They hung him?" Roman asked.

She would not look at him. "Cork had always said he would not dance that dance. He was killed trying to escape. Bertram saw it all."

The fire crackled behind her.

Her lips trembled. He kissed them. Her mouth was sweet and eager. She held him tightly to her, as though she clung to life with that embrace. Their kiss lingered, but finally it ended.

" 'Tis sorry I am, lass."

" 'Tis how he said he wished to go. I mourned his death. I mourned him," she whispered. "But now I wonder if even in that I was selfish. 'Twas myself I felt pity for."

" 'Tis what we do, lass. We dunna fret for those

gone ahead, but those left behind. Still, dunna ye see how Cork's love healed ye, lass?"

"I see how it killed," she said, "and yet . . ." She touched his cheek so gently that he felt a need to press into her caress and close his eyes to the sharp need it caused. "What we've done. It feels . . ." She smoothed her palm along his cheek and he took her hand and kissed it gently.

"Like love?" he whispered.

"I do not know," she murmured. "But I long for it again."

What kind of magic did she possess that all she need do was touch his face or speak his name and he quivered to have her again?

Their lovemaking was slow this time. Ever so slowly, he eased the blouse from her body, and ever so slowly, his kisses fell where they would, her arms, her breasts, the delicate hollow below her sternum.

Her abdomen was trim and flat, her hips softly flared, and her legs endless and shapely. He kissed every inch of them, smoothing his hands along them, lifting her knees, and finally, when she trembled for him, he slid easily into the warm, tight sheath of her body.

Where before a tempest had blown, now soft waves rocked them. They were slowly lapped closer and closer to the shore of contentment, until finally, sated and languid, they drifted onto the warm sand of fulfillment.

Sleep was a cozy blanket wrapped about them. Roman pulled it around him and fell into the darkness.

Warm dreams caressed him. He was basking in the aftermath of their lovemaking. Her name was Tara O'Flynn, and whether she knew it or not, she was his, and his alone. He had been a fool to think he could settle for less than this. A fool to believe he could be satisfied with a diplomatic union. He had been reared in an atmosphere of fierce love and fiery passion. 'Twas not a legacy to be forgotten. True, he was not worthy, but suddenly he knew that Tara had been sent for him, just as Fiona had been sent for Leith, and Flame had been sent for the Rogue.

Roman reached across the bed now, needing to feel her against him. His hand touched her empty pillow.

So, she had left the bed. He smiled to himself. Who would she be this time? A fine lady? A bawdy barmaid? Or perhaps, herself, a golden-haired nymph with hands that could take him to heaven. He opened his eyes, searched the room, then sat up . . . and swore.

Hell fire! She was gone!

Chapter 21

❧ ⌒⌒⌒ ❧

Tara hurried down the dark streets toward Harrington House.

Roman would sleep. Of course he would sleep. Jewel, the old whore of Backrow, had told Tara more than once that sex was the strongest sleep tonic a man could consume. And they had had sex. Quick and hard, and long and slow. She had planned the first time, and it had been shamefully simple, for Salina had taken over, had seduced him, had seduced *her*. But the second time . . .

Tara's breath came faster at the memory of his hands, strong and gentle against her skin. His chest was as hard as . . .

A dark shape bounded into view. She started back with a gasp, but it was nothing more terrifying than a dog chasing a rat.

Sweet Mary! What was wrong with her? This was no time to daydream. She was the Shadow, resurrected from the dead. But she would be dead in earnest if she didn't concentrate. Her ability to focus had kept her alive all these many years. She must focus now.

She was the Shadow. Wrapping her thoughts about her, she hurried along until finally, dark and looming, Harrington House appeared.

She sat in the darkness, watching, becoming one with the night. Instead of washing the dye from her face, she had darkened it further with the aid of molasses and a fine layer of silt. Her hair was hidden beneath a flat, brown cap, and her hands were covered with dark, kid gloves. She would be nearly impossible to see, she knew. Thus, she sat, studying the situation until she could make out every detail.

There, just next to the chestnut tree that drooped heavily over the lane, stood a man. So old Harrington *had* hired guards, or at least one. But no, at the corner of the house was another man.

A thrill of anticipation snaked along Tara's spine. There was little point in being a thief if the job was too easy. And this job would not be easy.

Smiling to herself, she slipped from her hiding place and went to inspect the back of the house.

One guard watched that side of the huge manse, but he was bored and restless. Only minutes after Tara arrived there, he rounded the house to talk to his companions.

After that it was a simple enough task to slip to the back door. It was almost a disappointment when it opened so easily under her hand. In a moment, she was inside and skimming up the stairs, the soft soles of her shoes silent against the stones, the wood, the carpet.

The house was quiet, but for the sharp hiss of a cat from the kitchen. Apparently there was a feline argument about who patrolled the larders while the cook slept. But Tara need not worry about the kitchen. Even if someone awoke to reprimand the cats, they would not find her.

For more than a decade she had been a thief, planning, scheming, surviving on her wits. Mayhap it could have been different. Mayhap long ago she could have gone to Lord Harrington and told him the truth. Told him she was his granddaughter—the child of the daughter whose death he had caused. But she had not. She would like to think pride had prevented her from doing so, but the truth was far less noble. Fear was a hard thing to admit.

But she would not think of that now. She had to concentrate. Where would he keep the bracelet for which she searched?

He was an old man, old and bitter and greedy. He would keep it close to himself, she reasoned, and so she crept, silent as the night, down the hall to where she knew his room to be.

There was no servant at his door, and he had left the portal partially open.

Heaven smiled on her. She smiled back.

Inside the room, some light managed to find its way through the thick, smoky glass of his window.

Tara stepped beside the door and waited, scanning the room, her nerves stretched taut. No servants near the bed. Harrington slept alone. And there he was, in the middle of his large, curtained mattress. His back faced her.

The trunk at the end of his bed opened with only a quiet creak. Tara leaned the cover back and sat still, waiting in silence in case the sound had alerted the old man. Patience was a necessity. Harrington slept on.

Tara removed her gloves, closed her eyes, and thought with her fingers. She felt fabric, wood, metal. But the metal was heavy and coarse. She moved her fingers swiftly on. At the very bottom of the trunk she found a small leather pouch and drew it out. The contents tumbled silently out. A ring of gold and diamonds winked in the faint light at her. A pair of buckles lay side by side. But there was no bracelet.

Silently, she slipped the items back into the pouch and shoved them carefully beneath the clothes. The trunk closed with a nearly inaudible moan.

Without standing up, Tara skimmed the room again, but nothing obvious caught her gaze. And wouldn't the old man be obvious? After all, he had hired guards. Why hire guards, if you could not trust them? Which meant that the bracelet was not here.

But where?

Where else but his daughter's room.

For a moment Tara remained motionless.

Something akin to dread seeped through her, for long ago, when the girl had been no more than eight years of age, Tara had seen her. Christine Harrington, blonde, beautiful, pampered in frills of pink and white—the daughter of Harrington's second wife.

Grubby, hungry, and hidden in the holly bushes, Tara had sneered at the girl. For Tara had been all of thirteen years of age, old and wise and cynical. But on her way home that night her heart had ached with regret.

She did not want that ache again. But at that moment, Roman's image invaded her mind. His solemn face was tilted down toward her, and in his hands there was a quiet magic.

The bracelet would be in Christine's room. Thus, she would go there.

The hall was silent and very dark.

Whereas Harrington had not had a single servant at his door, his daughter had two. From her spot around the corner, Tara could hear them breathe in quiet symphony. Ever so carefully, she peaked around the corner. The one by the door was a woman. She knew it by the way she slept, curled up like a child. But the other was a man, who did not lie down but slept sitting in a half-erect position.

Tara eased back behind the corner of the wall. Sweet Mary! She had not asked for an easy task, but she had hoped it would be possible. As she listened, the guard's breathing changed. Tara knew he awoke. She waited in silence, hoping fervently that he would fall back asleep.

It did not take long for him to do so, but what now? If he slept so lightly, surely he would awaken long before she managed to sneak into Christine's bedchamber. Unless . . .

Within minutes, Tara was back down the steps to the kitchen.

Easing the door open, she stepped inside. On the long, plank table, a cat rose and stretched. Tara hurried to the larder, spied a bit of cheese, and after stealing a small piece, nabbed the cat and hurried up the stairs toward the bedchambers.

The tabby had a bad temper and a good deal of heft. He nosed at Tara's fingers, trying to trace the intoxicating scent of cheese. But it had not far to travel before Tara reached her destination.

Near Christine's room, there was another chamber, a weaving room. The door opened quietly beneath Tara's hand. Placing the cat inside, she closed the door and set the cheese a scant inch away.

Quiet as dusk, Tara hurried down the hall and into a doorway to wait.

It didn't take long for the cat to be tempted by the cheese. Having explored the dry interior of the room, he had returned to the door, sniffed the cheese, and thrust a paw beneath the portal. He almost reached the delectably stinky thing and dragged his claws back across the wooden floor to reconnoiter and try again.

A series of strange scrapings and scratchings followed. Tara waited, poised for action.

Despite the noise from the cat, Tara knew the moment the guard was awake. She held her breath, waiting, tense. She heard him rise to his feet and sensed more than heard his knife slide from its sheath.

A shiver ran up her spine.

For a big man, the guard moved quietly. She saw him stop where the hallway branched. She held her breath, knowing he was searching, but in a moment he had ascertained the source of the noise. Still, he was cautious when he moved toward the door. It opened beneath his hand.

"What the devil ya doing in here, cat?" he asked, but before he could say another word, Tara had slipped from her hiding place and down the next hall.

There was no time to waste now. Not an instant. Stepping past the maidservant, Tara pushed the door latch with firm conviction, stepped into the bedchamber, and drew in observations with lightning speed.

No one awake. No servants. Big room. Bed. Tapestries. A trunk. Tara exhaled silently and leaned her back against the wall for a moment, still drawing in perceptions and waiting for her pulse to slow.

A fire still glowed in the hearth. By that light Tara could see the small form that graced the bed. Christine, beloved daughter of Lord Harrington. Her hair had perhaps darkened a mite since Tara had first seen her, but it was still golden, plaited now in two long rows that rested atop the blanket.

She slept soundly, peacefully. What would it be like to rest so well, knowing no one would break down your door and accuse you of theft. Surely, no gallows haunted her dreams, and hunger had never gnawed at her belly.

Tara drew herself from her reverie. There was no time for such thoughts now. A large trunk sat at the foot of the bed, but Tara ignored that, for a studded leather chest sat on the window's sill. She was across the floor in a moment. The chest opened silently beneath her hand. Again her fingers trailed through the items within. Three tiny gold buttons, a gilded frame facing down, a silver chain, but nothing else. Tara frowned and absently fiddled with the frame.

It felt strangely familiar to her fingers, strangely . . .

She turned the portrait over and caught her breath.

"Who are you?"

Tara snapped her gaze to the girl in the bed. She was sitting up, and though her face looked pale with fear, she clasped a knife in her fist and her voice did not quaver.

Tara glanced toward the door.

"Stay where you are," Christine said. "Stay where you are, or I'll scream."

Turning her head just a little, Tara looked toward the window, but the girl read her thoughts again.

" 'Tis locked," she said, "from the outside. You can believe me; I've tried it." She was lovely, with wide blue eyes, and when she stepped from the bed her feet looked very white and ultimately dainty.

Tara remained transfixed, for it was as though she had seen this woman a thousand times in her mother's face.

"Who are you?" asked Christine, placing her back to the wall and lifting her knife a bit higher. "What are you doing here?"

It was time to leave. Past time, and Tara knew it, but she could not move.

"Who are you?" Christine took a step closer. "Are you . . . the Shadow?"

It was as though Tara was caught in a dark dream tangled in reality. She tried to deny Christine's question, but she could not move. She had to leave, but she still held the tiny, gilt-framed portrait in her hand, and the blue eyes mesmerized her.

"Please." The girl's whispered voice shook suddenly with earnest appeal. "I will not tell a soul you were here. You can take what you like. I will tell Father 'twas lost. But I beg a favor of you."

The room was pitched into silence. Tara said nothing.

"There is a man, a Scotsman. David MacAulay. He has been unjustly accused and sits now in a gaol somewhere. Please, if you could but find out where he's kept. You must have some knowledge of that world, and there is . . ." She took a step closer. "There is no one else I can send."

Tara backed away.

Christine stopped. "Please," she whispered again. "Take what you like."

Tara lifted the tiny portrait. "I would take this."

The girl frowned. " 'Tis a picture of my half sister. I cherish it, but the frame . . ."

Tara tightened her grip on the portrait. In her mind a small shack burned and her mother screamed.

"I'm sorry," said Christine, shaking her head. "Take it. The whole thing. 'Tis of little import in comparison to what might be lost." She hurried across the distance now, gathering the items that had fallen from the leather chest. "Take the buttons and the—"

Reality jolted Tara. "Where is the bracelet?" she asked, jerking her mind back in focus.

"Bracelet?"

"Of diamonds and sapphires."

"Ohh." She said the word on a soft exhalation. "It isn't here."

Damn it. Tara backed toward the door. But

Christine followed her, still holding the knife loosely in one hand.

"Wait. I can get it for you. I can get it."

Tara stopped. She had been here too long. She must leave, but Roman needed the bracelet. "How?" she asked, turning her attention back to the girl.

"Father is hosting a Lady Day festival. He says it is in honor of the virgin, but he only hopes to lure men here to marry off his disgraced daughter. Lord Dasset is vying for my hand, you know." For a moment, Tara thought she would cry. "He is powerful and immensely wealthy. And so Father thought . . ." She shook her head and lifted her chin slightly, as if drawing herself back to the present. "I refused to go. But if I change my mind . . . if I promise to attend, he'll get the bracelet." She was speaking quickly but quietly, little above a whisper. "Come here on the first day of May, and I'll give it to you if you promise to do as I ask."

Tara glanced about. Had she heard a noise below her?

"Please," begged Christine.

Tara focused her attention on the girl. "All ya want me ta do is—"

The door suddenly crashed open and the guard leapt inside.

Tara spun about. She didn't want to die, not here in Harrington House.

"Nay!" Christine leapt suddenly between the guard and Tara. "Nay. You'll not hurt him."

"Out of my way!" growled the guard, but instead of obeying, Christine threw herself at the man.

Tara darted for the door. The guard caught Christine by the hair and tossed her aside. Tara skidded to a halt, only inches from the man's outstretched knife. He lunged, but she jumped backward in time. The blade hissed past her, barely missing her midsection. In her panic, she tripped, falling to the floor. The guard smiled and advanced, but in that moment, darkness filled the doorway. There was a movement, a growl. Suddenly, the guard fell, crumbling like a dry scone to the floor.

Tara gasped.

Roman stood like a giant, half-naked barbarian, chest heaving and eyes shooting sparks.

"Get the hell out of here!" he ordered.

"I need to—"

"Outta here!" he snarled, and lifting her by her shirtfront, tossed her toward the door.

"But wait!" Christine found her feet and stumbled toward Tara. "Please!"

"If you look amongst your guests, you'll find me. Remember the name Fontaine," said Tara, but already Roman was dragging her from the room.

"Mistress, I—" The maidservant stumbled sleepy-eyed into the room.

Roman stopped, bare chest heaving, the guard's knife gripped in one huge fist. The woman stumbled back a step and shrieked. Roman growled and the maid's eyes widened, then they rolled back in her head and she fainted dead away.

"What was that?" croaked an old man's voice. "Samuel? Edgar!"

Roman bolted down the hall, dragging Tara with him. They flew down the steps toward the front door looming ahead.

"Not that way!" Tara hissed. "The guards!"

But Roman yanked the door open and stormed through. Beside the steps, a man lay bound and gagged in something that looked suspiciously like a small, ruffled shirt. But Tara had no time to consider it, for footsteps were thundering toward them from all directions.

Shouts filled the air. Roman was running, and she was running with him, hanging on to his hand, gasping for breath and life.

Something hissed above their heads, materializing into an arrow that twanged into a nearby tree.

There were shouts and curses, threats, and near misses. Finally, the night grew silent but for the sound of their footfalls and their gasping breath.

Tara slowed to a walk. "We are safe now," she said, but Roman wouldn't let her stop.

Pulling her along, he dragged her down the silent streets until finally they reached her home.

Roman pushed her inside and barred the entrance himself, then leaned back against the portal and stared at her.

The house was eerily silent. Tara cleared her throat and avoided his gaze. "'Tis good we reached home, for dawn is breaking."

No comment.

She glanced at him. He looked huge and forbidding against the door. She tried to ignore his expression as she poured water into a basin and washed the molasses and silt from her face. "I . . . I suppose I owe you my thanks." She dried her face with her sleeve and chanced a smile. "What you lack in finesse you make up for in . . ." She cocked an arm. "Brute strength." His expression didn't change. "Though I fear you owe me a good, ruffled shirt," she said, rambling on. "Of course—"

"Were ye planning the theft the whole time?" His tone was grave.

Tara studied him in the darkness of the room. Her fingers fidgeted. "What?"

"While we were making love, did ye feel anything, or were ye but distracting me whilst ye planned another theft?"

She had felt a thousand things, things so gloriously thrilling that she had found no words for them. But she must not dwell on that. She survived by her wits, by her cool-headed logic. And when he was near, cool-headed logic failed her.

Tara pulled her dark cap from her head and shrugged her shoulders. "I like to think I'm more than a thief, Scotsman. I am an artist in my own way." And he was a barrister, a noble. She would be a fool to believe there could be anything lasting between them. "I cannot afford to be distracted by a bulging muscle or a manly chest. I cannot afford to feel."

She never heard him approach, but suddenly she was swung around and his eyes glared into hers.

"Damn ye! Ye are na Salina, so dunna pretend ye are."

For a moment she could not breathe, for he was there—so close, so large and solid and alluring, that all she wanted to do was collapse in his arms. "You are wrong," she said instead. "I am Salina, just as I said I was. I am Salina and a thousand other women you haven't met. And none of them can you trust."

A muscle flexed in his jaw. "But all of them I desire," he said, and pulling her into his arms, he kissed her.

He was not for her. He was not, she reminded herself frantically. But she wanted him. With all her heart and soul, she wanted him, and she could not help but kiss him back.

Her arms wrapped about him of their own accord. Her heart pounded madly against his.

"Tell me ye feel nothing, lass," he dared, his tone coarse as whiskey.

She could not speak, for he seemed to fill her senses, leaving her numb and aching.

"Tell me!" he said, shaking her.

"I . . ." She gathered her wits like wayward bits of straw. She could not let herself love him. She

could not. It would only cause pain, for she was
naught but a thief. She did not belong in his life.
No more than she belonged in Harrington House.
She had seen what happened when nobles and
peasants combined. People died. "I feel nothing."

"Ye lie!" he growled, and kissed her again.

When had she become so weak? When had she
realized that life was not life without him? It was
merely existence.

He drew back, his eyes an intense green flame
and so damned alluring that she felt as if her soul
were being sucked from her body.

"Tell me ye feel nothing, lass."

"I—" she began, but he kissed her again and as
their lips joined, he lifted her into his arms.

The bed creaked with a sigh beneath them. His
kisses were flaming velvet against her throat. A
button fell beneath the magic of his hands. The
cloth that bound her breasts was pushed aside. She
felt air touch her nipple, but in a moment it was
replaced by his mouth. She gasped and arched
against him.

"Tell me, lass," he murmured.

"I . . ." she moaned, but he suckled again and she
lost her thought to the searing sensations.

The binding cloth eased lower, baring her other
breast. His tongue flicked over it. Life sparked
there, hard and hot and tantalizing.

Tara gasped air through her teeth and gripped
the bed sheets in clawed fingers.

"So ye feel . . ." He circled her nipple with his
tongue while his fingers trickled soft and enticing
down her abdomen. "Nothing?"

Her dark trunk hose opened to his fingers. She
trembled beneath his touch.

"Say it, lass," he urged.

She opened her eyes. Damn him for making her
feel. "You could make a linen robe tremble with

desire," she hissed. "But that means nothing. Salina feels. Desires! Craves!"

"But ye are na Salina." His fingers slipped beneath her codpiece. She tingled against his touch. "And this goes much deeper than the cravings of a lusty woman."

"Nay!" she denied, suddenly frantic. But he kissed her lips again with desperate passion.

"I thought I had lost ye." His statement fell with flat finality into the silence. "And I thought, 'twas time for me ta die were ye lost ta me."

His arms tightened about her. Her soul leapt within her, but she could find no words to speak.

"I knew where ye had gone, and I called meself a thousand fools. If ye had been lost . . ."

Tara tangled her fingers in his hair, trying to think, to ward off the emotions that bombarded her. "Tis . . . tis what I do, Scotsman," she said. "I steal."

Very slowly, ever so slowly, he pushed himself up on his elbow to stare into her eyes. "No more," he said.

"What say you?"

"Ye'll steal na more," he said, his tone absolutely steady. "Ye'll return to the Highlands with me."

For one wild moment hope and joy flared through her. They would leave Firthport together. They would be wed. Life would be wonderful. But no! Reality settled in like a heavy rock in her stomach. She was a thief. He was noble and a man of honesty. Even if he could forget their differences, society could not. Fairy tales were not for her. Far better to bask in their moments together, then send him away, whole and hale.

"I'll not go with you, Scotsman."

His expression didn't change in the least. "Aye, ye will," he said. "As soon as I free MacAulay from the gaol."

"Free MacAulay!" Panic surged through her. He was not the kind of man to do nothing. If he knew where MacAulay was kept, he would surely do anything necessary—take any risk—to get him free. "You said you did not know where he was being kept." *She* knew, for Liam had friends in the lowliest of places.

"But I have found out." Roman smiled, breaking her heart. "He's kept at Black Hull. I'll go there this night and get him out. We'll leave for the Highlands at—"

"Black Hull!" She gripped his shirt in desperation. "You cannot go there. 'Tis a hellish place."

"I can go, and I must," he said, trying to pull her hands away.

"Nay!" She gripped tighter. "You cannot go there. They'll kill you."

" 'Tis the risk I must take," he said, freeing himself of her hands and moving away.

"But he's not there!" she gasped, grabbing his sleeve. "He's in Devil's Port!"

"Devil's Port?" Roman turned slowly back.

Tara read the truth in his eyes. "Damn you, Scotsman!" she said. "How did you know I'd learned his location?"

"Mayhap I've learned a wee bit of yer trickery, lass. And mayhap I thought ta distract ye just as ye distracted me."

She held her breath. "You cannot get him out of Devil's Port. No one can. Not even I."

He narrowed his eyes at her. "Ye'll na try, lass. Ye'll stay safely here until the lad is free and we are on our way to the Highlands."

Terror as cold as hell burned in her. She tightened her grip in his shirt. "You'll not go there, Scotsman. Tell me you'll not."

Roman placed his hand gently on her fist and watched her eyes. "I've na choice, lass. I gave me vow, and me vow is me blood. There's na other way."

"But there is," she breathed. "I've but to go to Harrington House and—"

"Nay!" His voice resounded in the room, and his hand tightened like a claw about her. "Nay," he repeated. "Ye'll na risk yer life again, lass. 'Tis me own task that needs doing, and ye must stay here until it is complete. Please!" He whispered the word. "Swear to me on your mother's soul."

Tara stared into his eyes. They were honest eyes, steady, bold. She could not disappoint those eyes. "I swear to you, Roman," she said softly. "I will *not* stay here while you go to your death."

Roman gritted his teeth and swore between them as he hefted himself from the bed. "Then I'll bind ye up and leave ye here whilst I go."

She was off the pallet in an instant, facing him with an open shirt and binding clothes that hung from her shoulders like tattered clouds. "You think some paltry rope can hold me?" She laughed, feeling frantic with fear. "Nothing can hold me. Nothing! And when I get free, I will challenge the gates of Devil's Port."

"Ye willna."

"I will go there," she vowed, deep-voiced. "And I will tell them I am the Shadow."

He grabbed her arms. "Ye willna!"

Their gazes clashed, hot and fast.

"Aye." She spoke slowly, softly. "I will. That is *my* vow. Unless you abandon this foolish idea of breaking MacAulay free, unless you do things my way."

Closing his eyes, Roman gritted his teeth and exhaled sharply through them. "Yer way?" he said, his tone weary.

Excitement surged through her. "'Tis simple.

Harrington will be entertaining only three nights hence. Christine will be there and—"

"How do ye know this?"

"I spoke to her."

"Spoke to her! Hell fire! She knows who ye are."

"Don't be absurd, Scotsman. She has no way of knowing. Look at the way I am dressed. She offered to give me her bracelet, offered me anything if I—"

"Of course she offered ye anything," Roman interrupted again. "She was terrified and but wanted ta pacify ye until she could have ye captured."

"Terrified?" Without trying, Tara remembered the girl's expression. In that moment by the bed, she was reminded of her mother. So proud, so regal. "Nay. She was not frightened, but she was concerned for MacAulay."

"What about MacAulay?"

"She said that if I would but find where he is kept, she would give me the bracelet."

"And ye would believe her?" Roman stormed. "More likely she would have ye thrown into the gaol beside MacAulay."

Tara shook her head. "Nay. She would not."

"And how, pray, do ye know that?"

"Because I have seen women in love afore."

Roman opened his mouth, but no words came out. He narrowed his eyes and exhaled. "Indeed?"

She watched him carefully. He was a big man, steady, intelligent, cautious. "Indeed," she said.

Tara felt she could almost see the thoughts that ripped through his mind, but he did not voice them.

Instead, he said, "I willna see ye die, lass. I willna have it."

She could not quite stop the smile that lighted her heart and lifted her lips. "Long have I been in this business, Scotsman. They've yet to kill me."

He shook his head, his face a mask of worry. "Harrington will treble his guards. Ye willna be able to sneak into his house again."

"I will not try."

Roman all but winced. "Not another costume."

"Nay, not a costume, Scotsman. A new identity. A French lady, I think."

"Nay," he said, but the word was little more than a moan.

"I've still three days to make my gown," she said, beginning to pace.

"God save us."

"My skin." She touched her face, considering. " 'Twill take some time to get the color out."

"Dunna even think upon it."

"Lemon juice, salt, hot water. A long bath."

"I said nay!"

She turned toward him with her shirt still open and her binding clothes about her waist. "I'll need help bathing."

"I said . . ." He paused. She watched him fill his nostrils with air. "Help ye bathe?"

"Aye." Salina was back if only for a brief appearance. "Help me bathe, Scotsman," she said, looking up at him through lowered lashes. "We'll talk as we soak, and if you do not agree with my plans, we will think of a better scheme."

He exhaled gently. A muscle flexed in his jaw. His gaze skimmed lower, over her breasts, her waist, her hips. "We'll talk," he said, and she smiled.

Chapter 22

"'Tis almost without risk," Tara said. She sat before the fire, her nimble fingers stitching gold thread into the fine, black fabric that had once been the Shadow's tunic.

Now it was to be part of a French lady's gown.

Hell fire! Roman closed his eyes for a moment. Mayhap he should have gone to Devil's Port as he had planned, but if he knew anything about Tara O'Flynn, it was that she would do as she said. She would follow him there and heaven have mercy on them after that.

"We'll wear black," she said. "The colors are bright this season. 'Twill make us more noticeable."

Roman quit his pacing for a moment. "Noticeable?"

"Aye."

"And pray, wee lass, why would we wish ta be noticed."

"Well 'tis simple." She smiled up from her stitching. "We do not want to seem as if we wish to be inconspicuous. Surely that would make us conspicuous. For who of the gentry does not go to great lengths to stand out in the crowd?" Picking up a narrow band of silver fur, she began to sew it above the cuff of the wide, slashed sleeves.

Roman scowled, pacing again, feeling irritable and cagey. "And where did ye steal the fur?"

"I did not steal it." She was a thief. How she managed to sound offended, Roman would never know. "Liam gave it to me some months ago."

"Liam?" Roman said. "Where did he get fox?"

"It's not fox. It's cat. 'Twas giving chase to a mouse and did not see the cart." She shrugged, tilted her head, and raised the fur for closer inspection. "Dead immediately."

" 'Tis like Liam ta give a dead cat as a gift." Roman said. "And 'tis like ye ta march into Harrington House wearing the damn thing on yer sleeve."

"I thought I might sew a bit of it onto your cap, also."

"Heaven save us."

" 'Twas your idea to accompany me. But—"

"We'll na discuss it again."

She shrugged. "As you wish. We'll appear as brother and sister, of course."

"Brother and sister? Why?"

"Harrington is looking for a husband for the girl. 'Twould make little impression to bring a married man. Don your hose."

"What?"

"The black hose you were wearing when you first found me."

"Why?"

"I may need to do a bit of altering to fit the new codpiece onto it."

Roman stared at her. He was getting accustomed to the idea of her being a thief. It was the fact that she enjoyed it so much that worried him. "What codpiece?"

"The one you wore with the Italian costume," she said, stitching again.

"I've na wish ta wear that awful piece of hardware again."

She glanced up as if surprised, but he wondered if there was a smile in her eyes. "Why ever not?"

He scowled. He was her senior by several years. He was a scholar, a diplomat, a Highlander, rugged, ready, raw. How was it that she made him feel like a green lad? It made him irritable. "Some men may feel a need to pad their . . . endowments," he said, placing his fists on his hips. "But I dunna."

There was definitely a sparkle of glee in her eye. It made him more irritable still. She was taking a grave risk going to Harrington House. Damn it all, at least she could be somber about it.

" 'Tis merely part of the costume," she assured him. Setting her stitching aside, she rose to her feet. "I did not mean to insult you. In fact . . ." She approached him. Her hair was as gold as sunlight, shiny clean and wispy soft from the bath they had shared the day before. It was surprising, really, that two people of their size could fit into that small vat. But there were good things to be said about a tight squeeze. Just the memory of it warmed Roman's blood. He deepened his scowl, trying to cool it. "I am very . . ." She paused again and stopped a few inches in front of him. Was she blushing? But surely after what they had done together in the vat, it was too late to blush. "I'm more than pleased with your . . . endowments," she said softly.

Be that as it may, he was *not* wearing that ungodly codpiece, he promised himself.

"Far more than pleased," she whispered, and reaching up, placed a slim hand on his chest.

Her touch burned straight through to his heart. He cleared his throat. "Truly?"

He could see a pulse beat in her delicate throat, and her eyes were intensely blue, focused on his own. It seemed that whatever Tara did, she did with all her soul.

"Aye." She whispered the word. "I had no way of knowing what your touch would do to me."

He knew he was a weak-kneed fool. But he could not help but kiss her lips. They were too red, too full, too sensual to resist. He did not even try. "Your touch does the same to me and more," he murmured.

"I could not bear it if you were hurt," she whispered. "I could not bear it if I failed you, if your costume was less than perfect." Her voice broke. "If you were found out because of me."

"Dunna fear, lass, all will be well."

"But what if I fail? What if I am not clever enough to do this?"

"There is none, nor has there ever been, a woman half so clever as ye. If there is a way ta do this task, 'twill be done because of ye."

She leaned her cheek against his fingers. "You trust me?" she whispered. "Even knowing what I am, you still trust me?"

"In most things I am na such a fool as ta trust ye, for ye are a liar and a scamp," he said philosophically. "Yet, in this, I can do naught else."

"But MacAulay's life . . . and your life, depend on me. What if—"

"Nay lass," he said. "Ye are right. Na one will recognize ye." He touched her cheek. "Yer skin is as soft and pale as a princess's. Surely ye are na wandering gypsy. Yer bosom. . . ." Gently, ever so gently, he cupped his hand over her breast. "'Tis so full and fetching. No one would dream of thinking ye might have played at being a boy. "Ye are clever beyond words, lass, and ye well know it."

"But—"

"Shhh. Ye will plan, and I will protect. We will be an invincible pair."

She smiled; the expression was tremulous. "If the codpiece offends your sensibilities, Roman—"

"Nay." He kissed her softly again. "Ye were right and I was but foolish. 'Twill be the perfect piece for a foppish Frenchman's costume."

"So." There was a chuckle from the far side of the room.

Roman yanked his dirk from his sheath and spun about, but it was only Liam, grinning at them from near the door.

"Ya convinced him to wear the codpiece."

"How the devil did ye get in here?" Roman rasped.

"Sweet Mary, Liam," Tara sighed with her hand still on Roman's arm. "I should have never taught you to lift a bar. You scared me half unto death."

Liam chuckled, his angular face alight with pleasure. "Do not let me stop you from doing what you were. 'Tis forever an education."

Roman knew Tara had manipulated him again. She had wooed him into agreeing to wear the damnable codpiece, but it had been worth it to hold her in his arms and soothe her. Still, mayhap 'twould be best not to let her know he knew her ways so well. "What does the lad mean by that?" he asked.

"It most likely means he has much to learn," Tara said, "a fact I am inclined to agree with."

"I meant—" Liam began, but Tara interrupted him.

"Did you get the invitation?"

Liam chuckled again and pulled a piece of parchment from somewhere inside his shabby doublet. "Duly stolen, copied, and delivered, m' lady, to one Mistress and Monsieur Fontaine."

Tara drew her hand from Roman's arm and took the invitation from the lad. "The carriage and team?"

"What carriage and team?" Roman asked.

"You can hardly expect us to walk to Harrington House in all our finery," Tara explained.

"What carriage?" Roman repeated.

"Victor is currying the horses even now," Liam said.

"What horses?"

Liam cleared his throat, looking quizzically from one to the other.

Tara smiled and gave her hand a casual toss, as if the subject was of no importance. " 'Tis the team of an elderly dowager," Tara said. "She'll not miss the horses."

"In truth, 'tis a shame how little exercise the steeds get," Liam added. He had the grin of a mischievous satyr, Roman thought. "Near to a crime to leave such fine horseflesh rotting away in their stalls."

"And ye approached the dowager and convinced her of this, I suspect," Roman said. "I imagine she was quite grateful for your offer ta exercise the beasts."

"Truth be told, I beat the groom at a game of tables. It seems Victor was quite sure he had won and wagered a bit over his head. A bad sport, these games of chance, as my mum used to say." Liam smiled. His charm reminded Roman dangerously of Roderic the Rogue.

"Ye cheated," Roman deduced.

"I did that," Liam said proudly. "And Victor was more than 'appy ta offer the team to see 'is losses returned."

"We'll all be hanged," Roman intoned, beginning to pace again.

"Come, Liam," Tara said, glancing worriedly at Roman. "Your costume is all but finished."

Roman scowled and watched them chatter over the groom's garments she dragged from a trunk.

He didn't want to know where that costume had come from.

Less than ten minutes had passed when Tara walked Liam to the door. "Just after dark then," Tara said, "and have a care not to lather the team."

"I wouldn't think of it, m' lady," Liam vowed, and, bowing from the waist, left them.

"If ye stuff me codpiece with any more padding, I'll think ye've got ulterior motives," Roman said, looking down at Tara.

"I . . ." She jerked to her feet and stumbled back, blushing. Roman watched her in fascination. He could never guess how she would respond. Like a child, a vixen, a lady? They were all part of the woman that was Tara O'Flynn. "You're supposed to be my brother."

Roman shrugged. "'Twas a bad choice, methinks, for I may have some trouble pretending such a platonic relationship."

His doublet, which had been created from a number of garments, had been stylishly slashed, enlarged, and padded in the popular peasecod style, making him look older and stouter. He wore plain, black hose but for the ostentatious codpiece, which was adorned with gold thread and seed pearls. Tara had trimmed his hair to just above his shoulders and combed it straight down so that it covered his pierced ear. A black velvet cap was perched on his head.

It was doubtful he would be recognized as the bearded Scotsman who had first come to this city.

Tara fretted with the frilly, white cuff of his tunic, then scowled into his face. "What's your name?"

He cocked his head at her. "Are ye feeling quite well, lass? Me name is Roman and ye well know it."

"Mon dieu!" she said. "Try to remember your part or we will . . ."

Roman could not help smiling at her, for she was so bonny and sober, immersed in her role as a fine French lady.

With her fists on her hips, she pursed her lips. "You're teasing me," she said. "You'll pay for that."

Roman lifted her hand, kissing it. "I will take that as a vow and anticipate the punishment."

She did nothing in half measures. Even when she blushed it seemed to go clear to the bone. He stared at the beautiful display above her daring décolleté. "Yer identity is surely safe, lass. I doubt there will be a man there who will raise his eyes above yer neck."

The blush deepened.

"Tell me, *ma petite,*" he said, pulling her closer, "how far does the blush reach?"

Yanking her hand from his grip, Tara jerked about and hurried to the far side of the room.

Roman followed her. Mayhap he was beginning to understand her a bit. For even he felt different when he was dressed differently. Right now, for instance, he felt as randy and carefree as any French nobleman. Mayhap 'twas a bit of what she felt when she "became another." Or perhaps it was simply the joy of her company that made his heart feel so light. "Tell me, lass," he began thoughtfully, then made a wild grab for her. She shrieked and managed to slip out of his grasp. He crossed his arms over his chest and let her go, but even from behind he could see that her ears were red. "Are ye truly so easily embarrassed, or is it all but a well-refined act?"

She waited a moment before she turned. But when she did her persona was firmly in place.

"A lady does not act, *mon frère*," she said. "A lady *is*."

She had braided her hair and coiled it about the crown of her head. A cap of black and gold adorned the neat plait, and below that, everything was bosom. Or at least that was as far as Roman could coax his attention. When she glided up to him, however, he managed to realize she was several inches taller than usual.

"Ye grew," he commented.

"A bit of height only makes it easier to look down my nose at the common English," she said, and lifting her skirt slightly, displayed the platform shoes hidden beneath.

"M' lady," said Liam, stepping inside, "your carriage waits just round the corner so as not to attract . . . God's nuts, ya grew!"

"Joseph!" she admonished, looking shocked even as she used the lad's newly invented name. "I'll not have you using such language in my presence."

Liam grinned. "Don't she do that good though, Scotch. She'll be the mistress of thievery until the day she dies."

Sobriety returned to Roman with a start. Until the day she died! 'Twas his task to make certain that day would not come for many years.

Shrubs trimmed in the shape of animals lined the cobbled walk of Harrington House. Even in the dark, Roman could make out their shapes strewn with white hawthorn blossoms.

The carriage glided to a halt. Liam opened the door with a flourish. "We have arrived," he said. His bow was elegant, his grin was not.

Roman scowled, first at him and then at the looming shrubbery. Confidence was a strange thing. It came and it went. His had gone. But when he glanced at Tara, he saw that hers was intact. Or at least, if it was not, he would never know it by her expression.

"Are you ready, *mon frère*?" she asked.

"*Oui*," Roman managed, though he failed to dredge up the frivolous tone he thought more appropriate.

Tara puckered her lips. She had stained them bright red and very tempting. "Are you feeling quite well?"

"One question only," he said quietly. "Why do you look young and vivacious and I look . . . fat?"

Her laughter was silvery sweet in the cool spring air. She had procured a feathered fan from somewhere and covered the lower half of her face now. "Is it the truth you wish for?"

He nodded, trying to follow her moods and her leads. But she was like quicksilver, changing with the speed of light.

She leaned closer, her bosom full and seductive above the low neckline. "If you looked your usual self, I would never be able to keep you for myself. Even as it is, every woman here will wonder what lies within your codpiece. 'Tis my task"—she looked up at him through silky lashes—"to make certain they do not find out."

For a moment Roman was tempted almost beyond restraint to take her back to her room and make slow, hot love to her. But she was already disembarking.

Two footmen approached their carriage. Lanterns had been set out on long poles, and laughter could be heard from the house.

Tara offered her hand to the nearest servant. She was all elegance and smooth sensuality. Roman clamped a firm hand over his possessiveness and his nerves and followed her down the cobbled lane.

The door was opened by a servant who requested their names.

Roman's stomach coiled as he scanned the crowd before him. He was far out of his depth. This was not his method. He was accustomed to stating the truth and accepting the circumstances whatever they may be. But that was before he had met Tara O'Flynn, for while he might be willing to accept whatever circumstances came his way, he was not willing to let her do the same. Thus there was little he could do now but play the game by her rules.

Keeping his expression bland, he glanced about the entrance through which they passed. It was huge and arched. Hung with tapestries and painted in deep, rich colors, it seemed somehow far different than both other times he had been there. But those times he had come as someone else. Once as Roman Forbes, begging a favor. The other as some half-civilized barbarian who did nothing but bang guards into oblivion and drag Tara to safety.

Hell fire! If they were recognized . . .

"I am Elise Fontaine," Tara said, "and *mon frère*, Lord Fontaine." Her accent was impeccable, her elegance all but tangible.

From the top of the carpeted stairs, Lord Harrington hurried down toward them. His spindly legs were encased in forest green hose, his upper body swathed in a short, voluminous gown of the same bright hue. 'Twas a gay costume, but there was, perhaps, a certain desperation as he took Tara's hand.

"My apologies, my dear, do I . . ." He paused as their gazes met, and his tone quieted. "It almost seems as if I knew you . . . long ago. But . . ." He shook his head, looking bemused. "Do I know—"

"I invited them, Father," said Christine. She hurried down the arched hall from the left. She wore a light blue gown of patterned velvet. Her cheeks were pale, her blue eyes very bright, and on her wrist, she wore a band of sapphires and diamonds. "Elise?"

For a moment, Roman held his breath, for uncertainty was obvious in Christine's tone.

"Christine," crooned Tara, sweeping her arms wide to pull the girl into her embrace. "I would know you anywhere, *mon amie*. I heard so much about you."

There was just a moment's delay before Christine caught the inference and played along. 'Twas quite apparent she had expected Tara to arrive and had spent no small amount of time considering what she might say. "And Elizabeth talks of little else but the summer you and she spent together."

For just an instant, Roman saw a congratulatory gleam in Tara's eye. In fact, she nodded once as she smiled and gently pressed the girl to arms' length. The bracelet, Roman noticed, was still on Christine's arm.

"You are fully as beautiful as I supposed you would be," Tara said, beaming. Not in a thousand years would Roman have guessed she was acting. "Lizzy did not exaggerate a bit, did she, Seymore?"

Hell fire! He didn't know any Lizzy, and he was beginning to sweat. "*Non*," he managed, and Tara laughed with that tinkling, silvery sound that was all her own.

"*Mon frère* of many words," she said. "I think, could it be, you have smitten him dumb with your beauty, Christine?"

"Lady Christine," called a young nobleman dressed in scarlet hose and waistcoat, "your guests are begging to hear you sing. Come." The young man walked, or rather, Roman thought, he *tinkled* toward them. "The world grows dull without your beauty to lighten it."

Roman managed to contain his scowl, but there

was little wonder the girl had been smitten by David MacAulay, he thought. Highlanders may have their faults, but at least they were men and not . . . fairymen.

"But . . ." There was a certain degree of desperation in Christine's tone as she was guided away. "Elise has just arrived. And I—"

"I shall entertain Lady Fontaine and her brother," interrupted her father. "Go with Lord Beaumont now. 'Twill give me a moment to learn something about Lord Fontaine."

Christine pursed her lips slightly, but she nodded and, taking Beaumont's arm, disappeared through the archway.

Tara studied Harrington as he watched Christine depart. He was but an old man, she realized, and though that thought was no new revelation, it still surprised her somehow. He was old and frail, and mayhap long past hating.

"She is indeed a lovely child," Tara said, still watching him.

"My only daughter, now that Maude is gone." Harrington's voice was quiet and scratchy. "I suppose I have spoiled her shamelessly. Yet, she reminds me of mistakes long past. Mistakes I must redeem." His expression was somber, as though he had forgotten the presence of his guests. "I will find her a good match." His gaze strayed to a man dressed in russet brown. "Yonder is Lord Dasset." Tara turned her gaze to the one indicated. He was not a particularly handsome man. His height and build were average, but he had a decided air of self-confidence. Silver streaked his hair. He turned to Harrington, nodded, then slowly shifted his eyes to look at Tara. She felt the impact of his gaze and could understand why Harrington might consider him a desirable match for his daughter. If he was looking for someone who could protect her, there was little doubt that this man could. Tara sensed power here. But she sensed something else as well. "A good match," Harrington repeated thoughtfully, "mayhap 'tis the best a father can offer his child."

Tara pulled her gaze from Dasset and managed a smile. "Lord Beaumont looked to be a likely candidate."

"Likely to be an idiot and waste his father's fortune. She needs a solid man," Harrington said, but then he caught himself. "Forgive me," he said, extending his arm to her. "We have only just met, and I am rambling on as if we've known each other a lifetime. 'Tis the trouble with becoming old. But I will bend your ear with my problems no more. So you are a friend of Lady Elizabeth?"

Tara took his arm, but for just an instant she trembled. "Is there a person in all of England that is not Lizzy's friend? Even Seymour adores her," she said, extending her other arm to Roman. "And he is so staid, he hardly likes anyone."

Harrington glanced at Roman through shrewd old eyes. "There is something vaguely familiar about you, Lord Fontaine. Have we, mayhap, met before?"

Roman did not so much as glance at Tara, and his expression remained perfectly steady. Regardless of his disclaimers, he made a fine actor, and could make a better thief if his scruples would not ruin it for him.

"I have business in England with some frequency," he said. " 'Tis a possibility we've met before. Do you know the duke of Perth, perchance?"

"Nay. I cannot say that I do. Is it business with the duke that brings you here?"

"In actuality, I have some business to discuss with the MacGowans of Dun Ard."

"Business? With the Scots?"

Roman nodded solemnly, and Tara almost smiled. So he was not afraid to tread on familiar ground in the fear that he would be recognized. In fact, it seemed he almost challenged Harrington to do so. And what better way to disguise oneself than with confidence?

"In fact I have business with the lady of the MacGowans," he said.

"A lady?"

"Have you not heard of the Flame and her steeds?"

"Nay."

"You shall," said Roman.

"To be quite frank, I am surprised to hear you would deal with the Scots," Harrington said, stopping near a large banquet table.

Tara could feel Roman's arm tighten beneath her hand. "And why would that surprise you, Lord Harrington?"

"They are a . . ." For a moment pain and anger showed in the old man's eyes. "An immoral lot."

"Immoral?" Roman questioned. Tara stared at him. Confidence was to be desired. But defending his countrymen, was not. "Nay. They may be, at times, too fervent, but they are not immoral."

The anger was gone from the old man's eyes. Pain and disillusionment remained. "I speak from some experience," he said.

"I, too," Roman said, ignoring the slight squeeze Tara gave his arm. "And never have I dealt with a more honest people."

"Honest?"

"If a Scotsman says 'tis so, 'tis so."

"There are those that would agree with you," Harrington said, gazing after his daughter. "And there are those who would argue."

"Those who would argue do not know the Scots

as I know them," Roman said. Tara squeezed his arm again. Again he ignored her.

"And would you . . ." The old man stopped but finally continued. "Would you happen to have some acquaintance with the MacAulays?"

"The MacAulays . . ." Roman began. Tara gripped his arm harder. "*Non*," he said finally. "I do not believe I know them."

"I have known them some time," said the old man. "In the past they have been honorable. But . . ." Again his gaze swept to the door where Christine had disappeared. "She is my only daughter."

This man was her enemy, Tara reminded herself, but there was pain in his eyes, pain she almost wished she could ease.

"Honorable," Roman said with a nod. "The Scots are that, and brave and loyal, and generous and—"

Tara snapped her attention back to the matter at hand and squeezed his arm with all her might. Their lives hung in the balance here, and he was waxing philosophical about his countrymen.

"Of course they can also be barbaric," Roman finished lamely.

"Barbaric," Harrington agreed, though his tone lacked conviction. "But mayhap we have all acted the barbarian at some time.

"Lord Crighton, 'tis glad I am you could come," he said, drawing himself from his reverie as a gentleman approached. "You should speak to Fontaine here. 'Twould seem you share an interest in horses."

Sweet Mary! Tara thought, 'twas Lord Crighton without his mermaid staff. She longed to look at Roman, but he was already bowing toward the man who had once commissioned him to paint ceilings.

"And you, my dear," Harrington said, taking Tara's hand in his. "Ye remind me of someone I knew long ago before I was a fool. Would you honor me with a dance?"

For a moment, Tara quelled, but she could not fail now, for their lives hung in the balance.

Roman tried to relax as he walked through the open door near the banquet table. They had been at Harrington House for several hours, but he had not seen Tara for some time. As for himself, he had fooled Crighton, thus he could fool everyone else there. The worst was over.

"Lord Fontaine," said a man who stood near a shrub shaped like a boar's head, "I'm Dalbert Harrington. 'Tis a pleasure to meet you."

Roman almost swore aloud. He hadn't seen Harrington's son since their first meeting at the Red Fox, and he had no wish to see him now. "The pleasure is mine," he said, stifling an oath.

Dalbert nodded as if he were prone to agree. Light from a high, nearby lantern showed that his lids were strangely lowered over his eyes. It took no scholar to realize he was drunk. "So you're Lady Fontaine's brother."

Roman waited a moment for him to continue, but when he did not, Roman nodded. "*Oui*. She is mine." He had not meant to make that statement sound quite so possessive, but now that the words were out, he felt no desire to reel them back. "'Tis growing late," he added. "Have you perchance seen her?"

It seemed to take a moment for the question to seep into Dalbert's whiskey-soaked brain. "Aye, I've seen her. In fact . . ." He turned rather clumsily just as Tara rounded the corner of the house. Her hand was placed on a gentleman's arm. She was alluring beyond words. Her laughter was gay, her smile dazzling, her figure hourglass perfect, with her breasts pressed high and her waist cinched to an impossible width. "There she is now."

Just then she looked at Roman. Their gazes met. Roman felt his pulse race with that brief contact. Jealously flared up. She could flirt so easily, entice without effort. She nodded, then walked on past.

"Good God," Dalbert murmured, drinking again, "she's got a great pair of . . ." He glanced at Roman, chuckled, drank again. "Eyes."

Animal rage spurred through Roman. He had almost forgotten that Dalbert had put his hands on Tara. She had been Betty then, but it mattered naught what she called herself. She was his, and he would not tolerate any man dishonoring her.

"*Oui*." Roman forced a smile. "*Oui*, she has our mother's eyes. Very blue. Much like the water in your fountain just yonder. And by the by," Roman said, taking Dalbert's arm. "I had a question about that fountain. Would you be so kind as to accompany me there?"

"Well, I really must relieve myself," said Dalbert, but Roman towed him gently along.

" 'Twill only take a moment."

Roman reentered Harrington House feeling considerably better. It seemed Dalbert couldn't swim even in three feet of water, and had decided to take a wee nap beside the fountain after the exertion he'd expended on splashing about.

Roman skimmed the crowd. It was not difficult finding Tara, for she was the center of attention. Not a small percentage of her audience was male. Roman moved closer.

"I do love your gown," said a woman with an outrageous hat and a nose far too long for her face. "What kind of fur is that?"

Roman held his breath.

Tara laughed. "My tailor assures me 'tis a rare kind of golden ermine only found in the northern regions of Finland," she said, drawing her attention back to her audience. "But if the truth be told, I think 'tis naught more than a dead cat."

Her listeners dissolved into laughter.

Only Tara O'Flynn could speak the truth like a lie and a lie like the truth. And only Tara O'Flynn could steal his heart with the dexterity of a magician. That knowledge gave him no peace.

"Cat or golden ermine . . ." said the man Harrington had referred to as Lord Dasset. He emerged gracefully from the crowd. There was something strangely familiar about that voice. Something strange. But what was it? "You would look royal in either." Roman watched him lift Tara's hand to his lips. "Rather like a gypsy princess I once met."

Realization ripped through Roman like a summer storm. Lord Dasset—Lord Dagger! They were one and the same.

Chapter 23

Every instinct vibrated within Tara. This was Lord Dagger. A noble, a gentleman—a murderer. She knew it. She sensed it. But did he recognize her? And if he did, what would he do about it?

She tilted her head and smiled as he kissed her hand. "A gypsy princess?" she said with her heart hammering wildly. "I know not whether to think that an insult or a compliment."

"Most assuredly a compliment," he said. His gaze was sharp, though there was the suggestion of a smile on his lips. "The princess was quite intriguing."

"Sister mine," said Roman from her right. "Have you recovered from the ache in your head?"

Sweet Mary! For just a moment Tara was tempted almost beyond control to reach for Roman's hand. But now was not the time to show fear, for surely Lord Dagger could smell that emotion the way a hound could smell blood.

"I feel much better," she said, turning her smile on Roman.

Just a glimpse of him calmed her. For he was, as always, strong and stolid, stalwart and steady. But he was also in grave danger, for if Dagger recognized her, he would also recognize Roman.

Dagger turned. Tara's heart beat faster yet, but she held on to her smile with terrible tenacity.

"Lord Dasset, may I introduce *mon frère*, the baron de la Fontaine."

Dagger's gaze locked onto Roman's. But Roman didn't flinch. Instead, his eyes remained absolutely steady until the other finally nodded.

"Lord Fontaine. 'Tis my pleasure to meet you," said Dagger. "I was hoping to ask your permission to dance with your lovely sister."

No emotion showed on Roman's face. Neither did his gaze turn to hers. "I fear this day has been a long and wearing one. I was just about to take Elise home."

Not now. They couldn't go now, Tara thought. She had not yet captured the bracelet, and even if she had, it would surely seem odd if they scurried away just after their first introduction to Dasset. If he was not suspicious of them yet, that surely would make him so.

"*Non.* So soon? The night is yet young," said Tara.

Roman's eyes were exquisitely green and deadly flat. "I hate to risk you to another headache, *ma soeur*," he said, but in that moment, she knew he worried about a far greater risk. So he, too, had recognized Dasset.

Still, the greatest risk lay in being too hasty. Turning her gaze back to Dasset, she said, "My brother coddles me. I would be delighted to share a dance."

Dasset nodded and turned his gaze to Roman. "If you wish to return to your room, I would be honored to accompany your sister home."

For one panicked moment, Tara feared Roman's stoic expression might crumble. She saw a muscle flex in his jaw, but finally he spoke, his tone as well controlled as before.

"She is my only sister," he said. "And though she is a bit headstrong . . ." He turned toward her. Though his brow was comically arched, she could feel his anger and worry as clearly as Dasset's hand beneath hers. "I would be loath to leave without her." He nodded shallowly. "I will wait."

Dasset led her away. Fear was like a cold blade against her back, but she would not let it show. Surely, even if he recognized her, he would not turn them over to the magistrates. 'Twould make no sense. But then, nothing she had ever heard about the Dagger made sense. He killed without reason, it was said—without reason, and without remorse.

Roman watched Tara walk away, her hand held high on Dasset's. A thousand emotions crashed within him. But fear won out. Fear for her. Dear Jesu, he should never have let her convince him to come here. He had to save her, take her away, before it was too late.

He took a step forward, but suddenly a hand caught his arm.

"Lord Fontaine."

He turned with a scowl.

Christine stood there. She smiled, but it failed to reach her eyes. "Are you enjoying yourself?"

His attention flickered away. He had to get Tara from Dagger's grasp. "I was just about to leave. If you don't mind I—"

"I know who you are." Her voice was a tiny whisper, but certainly loud enough to draw his attention back to her. "When I first met you, I thought you were not the kind to give up on my David. I prayed you were not. It took me some time to piece together the puzzle, but I know you now. Where is he?" Her voice was softer yet.

Turning back toward Tara, he convinced himself that she was well before looking at Christine again.

"Please tell me," she whispered. "Please."

"He's in Devil's Port."

For just a moment, Roman thought she might faint. He reached out, catching her wrist.

"Are you well?"

She straightened slightly, but still looked weak. "I need a bit of air is all. Will you assist me?"

He glanced again toward Tara. She was laughing up into Dagger's face. She was a consummate actress, he reminded himself. Or could it be she enjoyed the flirtation. And what if Dagger was only playing a part, too? What if he were only pretending not to recognize her?

"Please," Christine said, drawing his attention away.

He could hardly walk away while she collapsed onto the floor. They made their way through the crowd. The arched entrance welcomed them with the silence of a tomb. But soon they were outside. The air felt cool against his face.

Two men passed, deep in discussion.

"I thought you had left." Christine said when they were past. "I thought . . ." Christine took a deep breath, steadying herself.

"You should not be out here with me," Roman said.

" 'Tis far too late to ruin my reputation," she said.

But that was not Roman's worry. Tara was his worry. He glanced back through the door, but could see nothing of her.

"Is she the Shadow?"

The shock of her words brought him about full face. "What are ye speaking of?"

"Shh," she said, glancing quickly about. "Father will recognize your brogue."

Hell fire!

"I don't care if she is. I don't care if she's the devil incarnate. Just so long as you get David to safety."

For a moment, Roman concentrated on the girl before him. Or rather, he concentrated on the woman. For surely she was one. She was not at all the flighty flirt he had expected, but a woman, true and loyal. "You love him," he said softly, remembering his French accent.

She said nothing, but looking neither right nor left, she held out her fist. "Take it," she whispered. "I care not what you do with it. Just get him free."

Roman's mind returned with a jolt to their plan. Reaching out, he took the bracelet from her.

She stepped back a pace, her head held high. "I shall never have him," she whispered. "And it would not be safe for him to contact me. But if I know he is well . . ."

"I will get word to you."

She nodded, then drew another steadying breath. "I had best go in. I am on the marriage mart, you know."

Roman let her enter alone. Finally, he could wait no longer. Keeping his strides even and steady, he walked back inside.

Tara stood by a huge silver bowl filled with wine. Dasset dipped a ladle into the liquid, filled a chalice and handed it to her, but as there hands met, the cup was jostled and a few drops splashed onto Tara's hand.

"My apologies," Dagger said, then leaned closer to her ear and whispered something. Roman could not hear the words, but Tara's giggle was clear.

"I'm surprised they let you out in polite public, *monsieur*."

"And I do not think you are quite so innocent as you—"

"You'll excuse me," Roman said. Control! Control was a necessity here. "But I must insist we return to our inn."

"Oh, but—" Tara began.

"Now!" Roman said, then fought his instincts. "I fear we have an early day tomorrow."

Tara's eyes looked exceptionally wide. In a moment she turned them back to Dasset, who still stood too near. Far too near. "I fear he is right, my lord."

"My offer remains to see you home."

"Nay!" Roman said, then loosened his fists and tried again. "I must refuse, Lord Dasset. After all, she is under my protection. You understand."

Their gazes clashed. Deep inside, Roman almost wished Dagger would accuse him of something, anything. Rage, jealousy, and fear were brewing to a fiery potion within him, and he longed to quench the fire with brute action. Didn't she realize she was flirting with death?

"Mayhap we will meet again," Tara was saying.

"Mayhap," said Dasset. Lifting her hand, he kissed it again. "Until then."

Roman stifled the urge to strike out, he quelled the need to pull his dirk and proclaim her his own. He took her arm in his hand. Beneath his fingers, he imagined he felt her tremble, but surely he was wrong, for she thrived on such sport.

She waited until they were well outside the house before she spoke. "You have it?"

Roman kept every muscle tight, lest he lose control. "It?" he asked softly.

"Do not tease me, *mon frère*" she said. "Do you?"

"Do you mean the bracelet?"

"Shh!" For just a moment, she was yanked from her persona. Roman gritted a smile.

"Aye," he said. "While you were busy flirting, I did what we came ta do. But you wouldn't—"

"Shh," she said, and smiled as a man in canary yellow hose passed them. "Joseph," she called, raising one hand. "We are ready to return."

The carriage pulled up. Liam jumped down with a grin and a nod. "I hope you had a lovely time, Mistress Fontaine."

"Oh. Lovely indeed." She sighed. Roman gritted his teeth, and taking her elbow, thrust her inside.

"And Lord Harrington," continued Liam. "He is well?"

"Drive," said Roman, and, following Tara, slammed the door shut in Liam's face.

In a moment, the carriage lurched off, drawn away from the festivities at a steady trot.

"Where is it?" Tara asked.

Roman watched her. Fear was beginning to fade, leaving behind the pungent residue of jealousy and anger. " 'Tis safe."

"Where?" she asked.

"Did Dasset seem familiar ta ye?"

She drew a deep breath and, just for a moment, her eyes closed. "He is Lord Dagger."

Roman said nothing for a moment, then, "I dunna ken what would be worse, ta think ye are so foolish as ta na recognize him, or ta think ye are so foolish as ta try ta . . . seduce him."

She laughed. "I did not try to seduce him."

"Damn ye!" Roman leaned forward, abruptly grabbing her arms. "Think ye that I did not see how ye flirted with him? With him and a score of others? If seduction was not on yer mind, then what?"

"Know this," she said, yanking her arms from his clasp, "had I tried to seduce him, Scotsman, I would have succeeded." She sat absolutely still, the picture of the perfect lady, beautiful, poised, superior.

"And ye would have if the prize was high enough?" he asked.

"Aye." Her tone was steady, her chin raised. "If the prize was high enough, I would have. But you cannot understand that can you, Scotsman? You are far too good to let anything make you sacrifice your morals."

Roman loosened his grip slightly.

"You are far above me, Scotsman," she said quietly. " 'Tis a good thing this will all soon be over so that you can return to those worthy of you. Just a few more details to see to, and you'll be gone. Once Dagger accepts the bracelet—"

"Ye'll na go." He kept his voice very steady.

Hers was the same. "What say you?"

"I'll na have yer death on me conscious. Ye'll na go to Dagger."

"It seems we've discussed this before," she said coolly.

"There will be na need ta discuss it again. Ye willna go."

"And you think *you* are the one to decide that?" she asked. "*You*? I go where I will, and I do what I please. There are not many advantages to being orphaned and destitute," she said. "But there is this one. And I'll keep it. You'll not tell me what to do. I'll go to Dagger."

"Truly?" Roman settled back in the carriage seat. " 'Twill look strange indeed when ye show up with na bracelet. He may be a wee bit disappointed. But mayhap ye can distract him as ye have always distracted me. Ye certainly gave it a good start tanight."

"Where's the bracelet?" she asked, her tone even.

"I'll na tell ye," he said. " 'Tis me own task ta do, and I'll do it alone."

"You've no idea what you're dealing with, Scotsman. Dagger is beyond your ken."

The carriage turned a corner and pulled to a halt. Roman glanced out the window, pushed open the door, and turned to her. "Then I will have trouble. But I tell ye true, lass, I will have trouble alone." He reached for her hand. She did not give it to him. Her face looked pale and her eyes very wide.

"Where is the bracelet, Scotsman?"

"Do ye, mayhap, wish ta announce ta the entire neighborhood that ye be Lady Fontaine? Or are ye about to get away from prying eyes?"

She reached for his hand and he drew her out into the night.

Liam climbed down from his perch behind the team. "When will ya need me?"

Roman held her arm in a tight grip. "She willna be participating in this one, Liam."

"I will—"

"She willna," said Roman, keeping his voice very low as he tightened his grip. "'Twould be far too dangerous, for it seems Lord Dasset is also Lord Dagger."

"Dasset?" Liam whistled low. "God's nuts! Pure evil and nobility, too."

"Aye," Roman said. "And he got far too close a look at Tara. 'Twould be na but suicide for her to go."

She opened her mouth again, but he shook her slightly now and gritted his teeth.

"She'll na go," he repeated, more for her than for Liam. "But I will need yer help tomorrow night, lad. At Cape Hood."

They parted soon after. Roman steered Tara into her room.

She faced him in the darkness. "Why are you doing this?"

Roman watched her. "Christine knows ye are the Shadow."

For a moment Tara stood stunned, but then she

smiled, a small quiet expression. "So she knows," she said softly. "Long ago, I misjudged her. And now I underestimated her."

"Long ago?" Roman eyed her. "When?"

She drew herself from her reverie. "It does not matter, Scotsman. The Shadow is no more. When this deed is done I will not stay in Firthport."

The room was quiet.

"Ye'll na do the deed, Tara."

"Think you that I tolerated Dagger's slimy touch for naught?" she asked.

He remained very still, watching her. "Ye did na enjoy the flirtation?"

"Enjoy it?" Her laugh was shaky. "Aye, I enjoyed it!"

Roman gritted his teeth. "So ye were attracted ta him?"

She narrowed her eyes. "Oh, aye," she crooned, "and what woman would not be? He has power and confidence. Did you not feel it? 'Twas nearly a tangible thing."

"Damnation, woman! Tell me the truth! Did ye desire him?" Roman asked, reaching for her.

She jerked out of his reach. "Desire him!" she railed. "He killed James! Do you think me such a whore that I can forget that?"

The room fell silent.

Roman exhaled and loosened his fists. He had been a fool and he knew it. But his need for her consumed him. "I owe ye an apology, lass," he said quietly. "I am na usually a jealous man. But never before did I know a woman I longed ta make me wife."

Tara's jaw dropped open. "Wife?" She breathed the word.

"Aye."

In a moment, she was in his arms. Her lips were on his, warm, passionate. She felt like heaven there, like drink to a parched man. Her arms were about him, and her hands . . .

Her hands! Reality dawned on Roman with bitter intensity. Her hands could not be trusted.

Kissing her back, he grasped her arms and pushed them up against her chest until she was pressed away from him.

"I said I would wed ye, lass. I did na say I would trust—What the hell is that?" Roman asked.

His eyes were narrowed, and his hands very tight on her wrists.

Tara blinked and shifted her fingers ever so slightly. She must hide the bracelet from him. She must. "What?"

"What have ye got in yer hand?"

"You wish to marry me, Scotsman?" she breathed, leaning closer.

"What have ye got?"

She lowered her head slightly so as to glance at him through her lashes. "I had heard you Scots were not the romantic kind, but surely a proclamation of marriage warrants a kiss."

"Ye have the bracelet, don't ye?"

"The bracelet? How ever—"

But suddenly he had her fist in both hands and was prying it open.

"What are you about? Don't!" she gasped, outraged. Trying to hide the bracelet as quickly as she could, she twisted away. He spun her toward him again. She kept her fist wrapped about the jewelry and glared at him, frustrated and angry.

Roman glared back, holding her wrists in a tight grasp. "How the devil did ye ken where it was?"

"What better place to keep precious jewels than your codpiece?" she snapped.

"Hell fire! Na where is safe from ye. Give it up."

"Nay!" She twisted again and lost her balance.

But before she went down she placed her foot just so.

Roman tripped, toppling with her. They hit the floor together. But while Roman concentrated on softening her blow, Tara concerned herself only with the bracelet.

Her hand dipped swiftly toward her bodice.

Roman took the brunt of their weight on his arm and side, but his head, too, struck the floor. They lay still, breathing hard. Roman groaned and rubbed the side of his skull.

Tara grimaced. "Are you badly hurt?"

"Aye," he said, opening his eyes enough to scowl at her. "I am, so give me the bracelet and cease causing trouble."

He was beautiful, and he was hers, for this moment in time. "The bracelet will not soothe your aches," she said softly.

"Nay?"

"Nay," she murmured, and brushing back the dark hair from above his ear, gently kissed his bruise.

"Ye canna go ta Dagger," he said huskily. "Do na think ta dissuade me."

"Mayhap I only wish to touch you," she said, and kissed his bump again. "Better?"

He grunted noncommittally.

"Is there another place that needs my ministrations?" she asked, drawing away slightly.

He held her with his gaze, then cleared his throat. "Me wrist."

Despite his size and strength, he seemed now like a small boy begging for favors. His hand felt broad and powerful in her own. She lifted it to her lips, turned it, and kissed the underside of his wrist. A fine shiver shook his body. 'Twas forever a mystery how such a man as he could be affected by her touch. It lighted a fire somewhere deep within her.

"Anywhere else?" she asked. Her tone was very quiet.

For a moment he didn't speak, then, "There is me chest."

While she unbuttoned his doublet, she kissed his throat. It seemed strange to her how even his neck could seem so entirely different than her own. Where hers was slim and long, his was broad and thick, heavy with muscle and sinew, and still dark from the walnut stain. She kissed him below his jaw, then between his tendons, and then in the warm hollow where his pulse beat strong and heavy.

His doublet fell open, and then his tunic, baring the broad expanse of his chest. Sweet Mary, it was a beautiful chest, carved muscle covered with warm, velvet flesh, and adorned with the amulet he had once again replaced. She slid her fingers up the leather strip to his collarbone, his shoulder, the hard, seductive slopes of his torso. He shivered when she touched his nipple, and when she kissed it, he jumped.

'Twas all magic. Just the sight of him could make her blood course hot and fast through her veins. But more wondrous still was the fact that he could be what he was and still desire her. Slowly, gently, feeling every inch, every tremor, every ripple of muscle, she slid her hands down his sides. Her fingers trilled over his ribs, brushing his garments aside, memorizing his body, etching each moment indelibly into her mind.

His chest was hard, broad, scarred. She kissed the healing wounds one by one, then ran her kisses soft as Irish rain down his sternum. His belly was flat but for the hillocks of muscle above his hose.

She kissed the muscles, the ribs, the scar that ran along his side.

With utmost tenderness, she kissed his navel. He reverberated beneath her, but now he was no longer content to remain as he was. He rolled her over with ease. Suddenly he was on top and kissing her. And in that moment, every aching need was transported to her kiss. She wrapped her arms around him and pulled him to her.

Roman growled against her mouth, but in a moment he pulled away to kiss her cheek, her throat, the high-pressed, aching orbs of her breasts.

She tightened her grip on his back and arched against him, desperate to have him completely. His hands were everywhere, restless, hot, titillating. She moaned, desire and agony warring in her breast. But now his lips were on hers again, searing away any hope of thought.

"I love ye."

Tara sucked in her breath and lay still. He had uttered the forbidden words. "Don't say that," she whispered.

Holding his weight on his elbows, Roman looked down into her eyes. "'Tis true. I love ye, Tara O'Flynn."

"Nay." She shook her head. Love muddled wits and slowed reflexes. And love between them . . . It could never be. They were worlds apart, just as her parents had been. "Do not say that."

He kissed her again, gently, tenderly. "I must, for it's true. And, therefore, I canna let ye go to Dagger."

"You've little choice, Scotsman, for I have the bracelet," she said.

He eyed her bosom where he had seen her dip her hand "Give it to me, lass."

She shook her head and slipping from his embrace, rose to her feet. "Nay."

"Aye. Ye must," he said, rising too.

She laughed. "And why think ye that I must."

"Because ye love me."

She had known fear before. But this was stronger, deeper—terror for him. She could not afford to love this man, for then she would not be able to bear to let him go. "I do not!"

"Aye, ye do, and because of that love, ye must stay here, for if I lost ye . . ." He lunged for her and suddenly she was wrapped in the steely strength of his arms again. "If I lost ye, life would be without worth." He murmured the words, his breath warm against her face. "Misery would drown me," he whispered. "Please, lass. If I lost ye, I would surely die. I must go alone."

His hand moved up, touching her face, seeming to memorize every feature. Their gazes met, and in them she saw the truth. He *did* love her. No matter what her station in life, no matter what she had done, he still loved her.

She held her breath, letting herself hope. Perhaps she had been wrong. Perhaps they were not like her parents. Perhaps in the Highlands people did not care so whether you were noble or peasant. Maybe, just maybe there was a chance for them.

Roman dropped his fingers into the warm, secret cave of her décolleté. But in a moment, he drew his hand back.

"Where's the bracelet?"

She almost smiled, but she dared not, though her suppressed exitement made her shiver. Perhaps he was right. Perhaps they belonged together. But that only made it all the more important that she not let him endure Dagger's evil alone. She closed her fingers over the amulet that had somehow fallen loose in her hand again. "I'll never tell you, Scotsman."

He gritted his teeth. "Where is it?"

"I'll not see you dead. Not when I just now think I can mayhap keep you alive and still have you for my own."

"You make no sense. Give me the bracelet, lass, so that I may retrieve the necklace and hurry from this city with ye at me side."

"I tell you this, Scotsman—either we go to Dagger together, or I go alone."

For a moment the look in Roman's eyes almost frightened her, but finally he pulled her against his chest, holding her hard in the strength of his arms. "Hell fire, woman," he murmured, "if I did not love ye so, I'd surely throttle ye."

Chapter 24

⌒◯◯⌒

Outside, the night was as dark as pitch. The warehouse at Cape Hood was little different, lit only by a single candle. Still, there were certain things Roman could identify—a small fishing boat, overturned nearby, paddles, nets. The smell of fish and dried salt were tangy in the heavy air.

Roman stood silently beside Tara. They were dressed as gypsies again. She had taken his amulet and hung it about her own neck. It was hidden now beneath her blouse. That knowledge gave him some hope. Mayhap it would give her luck, for surely they would need it. Listening to every noise, he absorbed each nuance of the men around them.

From the darkness, Dagger chuckled. "So ya got the bracelet, Princess."

Tara tossed back her long, black hair. "Did I not say I would get it for you?"

"Aye. Ya did."

Tara smiled. Even in the dimness, Roman could see the gleam of her teeth. They seemed brighter than ever against her walnut-stained skin. She held out her hand. Against her palm, the sapphire bracelet winked. " 'Twill teach ye not to distrust my word."

"I did not distrust it," Dagger said, turning to

pace the room. "Indeed, I think ya could do whatever you set your mind to, Princess. But I did not expect ya to succeed so soon. For ya see, I heard a rumor that the . . . former owner was wearing the piece only last night. Did ya hear such a rumor?"

The warehouse fell silent. Roman tried to quiet his pulse, still it raced out of control, banging against his bare chest like a warning drumroll.

But Salina only shrugged and flipped her hair behind one bare shoulder. "The bracelet is here now. Do you take it and seal our agreement, or do you waste my time questioning my methods?"

"I don't deny that your methods intrigue me," he said. "But then . . ." He sighed. " 'Tis enough to call it mine, for 'tis a pretty bauble and 'twill make a fine match for another piece I have. Mayhap ya would like to see its mate."

She shrugged again. " 'Tis doubtful that the jewels will adorn my own form, so I have little interest in them."

"But ya've such a bonny form," said Dagger. "Angel, bring out the necklace for the princess to see."

Roman's gaze skimmed the darkness as he assessed his enemies on all fronts. Spread in a semicircle behind him, there were at least a half dozen men. But still, the greatest danger stood before him. Angel was to his fore and right, Dagger directly in front of him.

Sapphires and diamonds spun on a fine web of silver tumbled out of a pouch into Angel's hand.

"There it is," Dagger said. "It'd look good on ya, Princess. Mayhap even better than on a French lady or a buxom barmaid."

Dear Jesu! He knew! Roman thought, but Tara cocked her head, looking perfectly relaxed.

"Are you offering me the necklace, Daggerman?"

For a moment, there was absolute silence, then Dagger chuckled. "Sweet Christ, ya are a bright one, Princess. Ya are a bright one, indeed. But who are you? I ask myself. For a time I thought you were the Shadow, himself. Now that seems ridiculous. But I met a woman at . . ." He paused. "She reminded me of you. And yet . . . it couldn't be."

Tara raised her chin. "I do not care to be compared to other women. I think that you will have little chance to get to know me better."

Dagger chuckled again and walked toward the lone candle, letting Tara and Roman see his face. "I fear ya're right," he said. "Because . . ." He lifted his hands as if begging forgiveness, but at the same time he nodded shallowly to the men behind Roman.

A nightmarish memory flashed through Roman's mind. Dagger had nodded to his men before and Scar had died. Roman twisted about. A man lunged toward him, knife outstretched. He died with a gurgling scream.

"Run!" Roman yelled. Tara did. But instead of dashing toward the door, she leapt forward to whisk the necklace from Angel's hand.

The villain's fingers closed a moment too late.

"Kill her!" Dagger shrieked.

Angel yanked a blade from its scabbard. Tara lunged away, but in that instant, Angel grabbed her blouse and reeled her back.

Tara shrieked as she was snapped to a halt. While Angel gloated, Roman leapt with a growl in his throat.

Angel turned toward him. Releasing Tara to defend himself, he swiped with his knife. Roman ducked and stabbed.

There was a rasping gasp of pain. Angel staggered backward, a dirk protruding from his abdomen.

"Run!" Roman shrieked. But Tara was surrounded.

Terror roiled in Roman's stomach. There was nothing he could do but sacrifice his life.

Screaming, he launched himself, bare-handed, into the circle of men. Two of them went down with him.

"Roman! No!" He heard Tara's shriek, but there was no time to think. A blade descended toward him. He rolled to the side and nearly gained his feet. But suddenly pain stabbed through his back.

"No!" Tara screamed again. But he could no longer see her.

He was surrounded by a circle of slavering hounds, drooling as they closed in for the kill.

"What now, Princess?" Dagger crooned.

Tara spun about and Dagger grabbed her arm. There was no time for thought. She snatched the nearby candle and slammed it into her captor's face.

Dagger screamed as the flame bit his cheek. Stumbling backward, he swatted at the sparks in his hair, but the action only fanned the flame. He shrieked for help. Two men turned from Roman and rushed toward him. Tara lunged sideways, not thinking, only reacting.

The oar felt solid and real in her hand. She swung at the nearest man and struck him across his left ear. He yelped, dropping his knife and careening into his companion.

Roman rose from the ground with a growl of fury. A knife flashed in the dim light. A man crumbled. Another backed away. Tara swung again.

"Come on. Come!" Tara yelled.

Roman stumbled toward her. She grabbed his arm, sticky with blood, and dragged him toward the only exit.

"Locked!" he rasped.

But in that moment the door swung open.

"Hurry!" gasped Liam.

They were outside, where darkness swallowed them.

"Kill them!" screamed Dagger.

The guard near their feet moaned.

Liam dragged at Roman's arm, dancing along beside. "Hide," he insisted before darting away.

Tara froze, abandoned, terrified. Roman leaned on her shoulder, heavy and limp.

Footsteps thudded inside the warehouse. Sweet Mary, they were coming. She had to save him. Had to hide.

Gasping for breath, she dragged him along the side of the building. He stumbled and nearly fell, but she pulled him to his feet and hurried on. The warehouse ended abruptly. She pulled him around the corner.

Men careened to a halt as they rushed out after them.

"Where—"

"They're coming. Run!" Liam yelled.

The villains turned as a unit, falling for Liam's ploy and bolting off after him.

Tara allowed herself one moment to rest and pray. "Don't die!" she pleaded quietly.

"The water's our best wager."

"You can speak." Tara hugged Roman's arm to her. Blood smeared across her blouse. His head drooped. "Scotsman." Her voice sounded panicked to her own ears.

His head came up. He lifted his hand and touched her cheek. "Who are ye, Tara O'Flynn?"

"Please." The word came out as a whispered sob. "Please, don't die, Scotsman."

"Sorry," he murmured, and slumped.

"No!" She managed to pull him back up. "The water. I'll get you to the water." But the river was more than twenty rods away, and there would be no cover. Still, they couldn't stay where they were. Dagger's men would surely circle the warehouse once they lost Liam.

Dragging at his arm, Tara toted Roman into the open. Eternity passed with every raspy breath he drew. Terror gnawed at Tara's gut. "Just a little farther. A little—"

"Check by the water!" Dagger growled from the doorway.

Footsteps raced through the darkness toward them.

Tara froze. For the first time in her life, panic consumed her. "I'm sorry." She clung to Roman's arm. "So sorry. Please—" She was babbling.

"Shh," he hissed. Slumping to the ground, he picked up a rock and heaved it with all his remaining might.

"What was that?"

"There! They're over there!"

Footsteps rushed away.

"It willna take them long ta learn they've been tricked," Roman rasped.

"Forgive me," Tara whispered. "Please."

"Get me in the water," Roman ordered.

"Forgive me," she pleaded again.

Roman turned his face to look into her eyes. "I've na wish ta die here, lass." His words were no more than a whimper.

She nodded. Hope was distant thing, far out of her reach. But he had asked her to do it, and she would. From their right, they heard men splash into the water.

"Did ya find 'em?"

"They're 'ere someplace."

A man swore. Their voices were distant, but coming closer.

Tara stepped into the water, dragging Roman

with her. It was shockingly cold, taking her breath as it rose to her chest.

"Tara." Roman's voice was weak. He was half floating now and felt much lighter. "I cannot hold on much longer. Ye must—"

"No! Please."

His hand found her arm and gripped it hard. "Listen ta me, lass."

"Roman," she whimpered.

"Shh. I would have ye know this now, lass, before the darkness takes me. Na matter the circumstances, these days with ye have been the best of me life."

"Roman—"

"Shush now. I am sorry ta have failed ye."

"No. No." She hugged him tighter. "Please—"

"But I must ask ye one more thing." For a moment he went silent. She watched his eyes fall closed. "I am sorry. Very . . ." He shivered. "Cold." He fell silent again. She felt his muscles go lax.

"Roman!" She said it too loudly, but she did not care.

"Shh." He woke with a start. "Ye must leave me."

"Nay!" She sobbed the word.

"Have ye the necklace?"

"I won't leave you. I won't."

He shushed her again. "Ye must get the necklace to Harrington. Tell him I have fulfilled me part of the bargain."

"But—"

"Tell him," Roman begged. "Or me death will be in vain. MacAulay will die with me."

"I'll get you to a healer."

He shook his head, but the motion was weak. "There is na time, lass. The necklace must be in Harrington's hands by tomorrow. It must."

"I know you're here, Princess."

Dagger's raised voice sliced into Tara's thoughts. He was close. Very close.

"I know you're here because this is where I would come." He chuckled. The sound was low and soothing, as if they shared a harmless conspiracy.

"Did y' find the 'ore?" someone gasped, running up.

For a moment there was silence then, "Yes, Wads, I found her," Dagger said.

"I'll kill 'er for y'."

"This one is mine," Dagger said. "Give me your knife."

There was a moment's silence, but suddenly a man's gasp filled the night. Footsteps stumbled. A body fell.

"You should have known she was far too good for the likes of you, Wads," Dagger said.

Tara heard him turn toward her. Terror and cold immobilized her.

"I will not hurt you, Princess," he called. "See, I have killed Wads for you. I'm unarmed, now." He fell silent, pacing closer.

Dear God, he was coming!

"My apologies for the misunderstanding. You saw my face, so I believed you must die. But now I realize your worth."

Tara dared not breathe. Beside her, Roman was silent. Was he dead? She felt a sob rise up her throat, but clasped her hand over her mouth, praying.

"Come out of there, Princess. I can see you, you know. I fear your friend will not live. But perhaps that is best. He seemed the jealous sort. There must be nothing standing between you and me. We were meant to be mated for life. Ahh, the things we could accomplish together."

Tara could see him now. Could he see her?

She heard running footsteps, whispered voices. Someone had joined Dagger.

They were coming. She could wait no longer. She would have to take the final risk. Tara grasped Roman's sleeve. Her fingers were numb. She willed them to tighten, tugging harder. He moved, floating along beside her.

"There! What is that?"

"It's them!"

"Get out there!"

"Get 'em!"

Roman was about to die. He would die, if he weren't already dead. Sweet Mary, please no! The silent lament sang through Tara's heart. "Please no," she whispered, and placing her hands on Roman's shoulders, pushed him under.

He didn't resist as his head sank below the surface. Tara willed herself not to think of that. He was alive. He was merely holding his breath. He had to be. She managed to propel them through the water. Time wavered. Reality dimmed. She could die here with him. What would it matter? Her lungs ached, begging for air, but she moved on, dragging Roman through the dark water, willing him to live.

But finally she could wait no longer. Lungs bursting, she shot to the surface. Air rushed in, sweet, intoxicating, and for a moment she had no strength to worry about Dagger or his men. She was alive for this moment, and that was enough.

Beside her, Roman coughed. Praise God, he was alive. She had to keep moving.

Not bothering to try to distinguish the shadowy forms on the shores, Tara pushed her numb muscles back into motion, dragging Roman along behind her as she trod through the water.

Minutes turned to hours and hours to eternity. The night stretched interminably before her, until finally, exhausted and freezing, Tara dragged Roman to shore.

Shaking, she pulled the amulet from her neck and slipped it over his head with a prayer. When she pressed her ear to his chest, she could hear a pulse, but it would not be there long, not if she didn't get him warm and dry.

Clamping her hands over her freezing arms, Tara glanced around. Dawn was approaching. And with it, additional dangers, or help. She waited for a moment, trying to think.

The sound of a horse's hooves finally penetrated her mind. What should she do? The Shadow, with her precision timing and unflappable bravery was indeed dead. In her place was Tara O'Flynn, terrified and uncertain. But she could not stay there on the bank of the firth forever.

One silent prayer and she was up the slope to the road. A piebald horse was trotting down the lane. It snorted at the sight of her and swerved, rattling the narrow cart behind it.

" 'Oo goes there?'' called a quavering voice.

One quick glance in each direction assured Tara that the road was empty but for this one traveler. " 'Tis just me,'' she said, stepping into the clearing.

The woman on the wagon skimmed her gaze over Tara and then into the brush from which she had stepped. "What be ya doin' out 'ere?''

Tara took another step forward. Her legs wobbled dangerously. "I'm in trouble.''

"I'd like ta 'elp ya, lass,'' said the woman, shifting her nervous gaze sideways again as if searching for villains, "but I needs ta get these fishes ta market 'fore the sun sets 'em ta stinking.''

"Please.'' How rarely had Tara begged before this past week. But pride had abandoned her since Roman's entrance into her life.

The woman chewed her lip. "I got ta go. Mr.

Cobb's been laid up, I'm alls what stands between the babes and hunger." She raised the reins to drive the piebald on. Tara stepped into the middle of the road, trying to think with her senses as she always had. Fear and fatigue weighed her down, but perhaps instinct took over.

"Your husband, will he mend soon?" she asked quickly. Her mind was spinning. She had to think. The sun was rising, pushing a pale, predawn glow over the world.

The woman nodded, settling her rein-bearing hands back on her knees. "'E's been down a bit. But 'e'll be up and givin' little Margaret pig-a-back rides soon enough." A mixture of hope and adoration shone in her eyes, but she shifted them again as if remembering she spoke to a stranger. "Do I know ya, lass?"

Tara shook her head. A scheme was beginning to surface.

"You alone?"

There was no time for mistakes now, and very little time to think. "Nay. I've... I've a friend down by the river."

Mrs. Cobb tensed, ready to flee. Tara took one step closer.

"Please, I need your help. My Rory..." She dropped her face into her cupped palms and felt the sob rise in her throat with no urging. "My Rory! Such a good man is he. 'Tis not our faults he was born to the anvil and I to the manor." She lifted her face to gaze imploring at the fishmonger. "'Tis not our faults."

"'Oly saints," the woman murmured as Tara's words sunk home to her. "'Oo are ya, lass."

Tara bit her lip. Time was fleeting. "My name's Christine," she whispered just loudly enough to be heard. "Christine Harrington."

Chapter 25

～◯◯～

Roman shivered as Mrs. Cobb touched his forehead. "'E's freezin' cold." Her eyes were shrewd and quick as they scanned his scarred chest, his broken nose, his fishhooked ear. Bloody water dripped from various parts of his body into the cold earth beneath him. "What 'append 'ere?"

"It was Dagger," Tara whispered.

"Dagger!" Cobb started, her eyes going wide with fear. "Yer tellin' fibs, lass."

"Nay. I swear 'tis true. 'Twas Dagger and his men what did this to him."

"God's grace! Why ever for?"

"They stole the necklace. My Rory..." She glanced at Roman's unconscious form and sent up a silent prayer. If God would let him live, if he would only grant that one request, she would gladly give up her own life. "He thought mayhap if he could retrieve the necklace, Father might look kindly on him. Might even allow us to marry. He got the necklace back," she whispered. "But Dagger found him. We made it to the river...If he dies..." Her voice betrayed her. Her world crumbled.

"Sweet Mother of God," Mrs. Cobb murmured.

"What a tale ya've got, lass. And no time ta tell it. But where will we take 'im?"

"To Harrington House." Tara barely breathed the words. "Father may be harsh, but he'll not turn his back on my Rory. I will not let him."

Mrs. Cobb watched her eyes for a moment, then nodded brusquely. "'Old on ta love, lass. For sometimes 'tis all we've got. But no time for that. No time." She bent her back, gripping Roman's feet in her capable hands. "Let's get him on the cart."

It was not a simple task carrying Roman up the slope, for he was large and wet. But finally they succeeded.

Dawn was breaking over the eastern horizon when they laid him on the fish in the back of the wagon and covered him with a tarp.

"Will the Daggermen recognize ya, lass?" asked Cobb.

Tara managed a nod and found herself shoved beneath the tarp beside Roman.

It was dark and fetid beneath the canvas. Minutes dragged by like a lifetime in hell. Beside Tara, Roman shivered. She wrapped her arms about him, feeling the beat of his heart and praying.

The wheels were noisy against the road. The piebald's hoofbeats were a steady trot, but suddenly Tara thought she heard another cadence, rapid, galloping, approaching.

"Fishwife! You!"

Sweet Mary! She would recognize Dagger's voice anywhere. Don't stop, please don't stop, she wanted to beg. But the cart slowed and finally rattled to a halt.

"Good morningtide, yer lordship," said Mrs. Cobb. "Were ya wishin' ta buy me fish? I've all sorts, cod, haddock, mackerel, fresh caught this mornin'."

Tara could hear her turn on her seat, felt a light tug on the canvas that covered her.

"Have you seen a man?" The baron's voice had lost its smoothness.

For a moment there was a blank silence, then, "A man, yer lordship?"

"Yes, God damn it," he swore in raspy rage. "A barbarian, half-dressed and wounded."

"Wounded, m' lord?"

"He stole!" The words sounded as if they were issued from between gritted teeth. "Stole what is mine. No one steals from me. No one."

"What . . . what did 'e steal?"

There was another pause as if Dagger was coming to his senses. "Have you seen him?" he growled.

"No. No, m'lord, I was but goin' ta deliver my fresh fishes ta—"

"Get the hell out of my way!" snarled Dagger.

The cart was jostled as he spurred his mount past the piebald, and then he was gone, racing off down the road.

Tara exhaled and closed her eyes in silent prayer.

"Damn dumb aristocrat," muttered Cobb, then, "just a little farther. Hold on, lass."

The cart jolted back into motion.

" 'Tis a wonder ye are ta me lass."

"Roman," Tara gasped, gripping his arm. "You're awake."

But his eyes were already falling closed.

"Roman!" She tightened her grip. "Don't go. Please. Wake up. I need to tell you something."

His eyes opened slowly, found her with some difficulty.

"This is my fault." She whispered the words to him. " 'Tis all my fault."

"Nay, lass, tis—"

"Shh. Nay. Don't talk. Save your strength. You are so strong, so fine," she whispered. "I couldn't resist you, though I knew I should. Now look what I caused," she whispered, then paused, fighting for strength of her own. "I was right all along. You and I . . . we are not meant to be. But I'll get you to safety. I'll take you to Harrington. He will free MacAulay. The two of you will return to your homeland."

For a moment nothing could be heard but the steady clop of the piebald's hooves. Roman's eyes were steady on hers.

"Nay, lass. We will never succeed. Dagger is too powerful. We would be well lucky ta escape past the walls of Firthport. Nay." He breathed deeply. She felt his chest expand beneath her arm. "I will die. But I am ready, so long as I know ye are safe." He touched her face. "Leave, lass. Leave while there is yet time."

"I'll not leave you to die, Scotsman," she said through her teeth.

"But die I will, lass, unless . . ."

"What?" Hope sprang at her from nowhere. "Unless what?"

"Fiona Rose. I have seen her do miracles," he whispered. "If I could only reach Glen Creag, I would have a chance. But . . ." He shook his head again. "I am far gone. Only yer cleverness could get me there. And I willna allow ye ta risk yer life again. Go, lass. Go now."

"Fiona Rose." She breathed the name. "Your mother. The healer. Of course. Hold on, Scotsman. Hold on!" she pleaded. "I will get you to your father's house. And God have mercy on anyone who tries to stop me."

For just a moment, Tara almost thought she saw Roman smile, but then the expression was gone, and his eyes fell closed.

*   *   *

The cart jolted to a halt.

" 'Ere we be, lass. 'Arrington 'ouse.''

Tara pushed the tarp from her head. The world seemed bright now, but no less dangerous. Covering Roman again, she climbed from the dray. The manse loomed above her. Panic swelled within her.

"Yer not really 'is daughter are ya, lass?" Cobb said softly.

Tara swallowed and shook her head absently. "Nay, I am not."

"What do we do now?"

"We go in. Harrington will help us. He *must* help us," Tara said, but for a moment, she couldn't move.

"Come, lass," said Mrs. Cobb, raising her chin. "I'll 'elp ya to the door. Ya must be strong now."

Tara nodded. She tried to slip into a character, but fear and fatigue kept her firmly within herself. Still, she could not fail, for Roman needed her.

She took one step, then another. The house loomed overhead. The animal-shaped shrubbery passed silently, like green gargoyles.

The door felt hard and solid beneath Tara's knuckles. It opened. A face of a servant appeared, seeming strangely disembodied.

"I . . ." She managed that one word before she weakened. "I must see Lord Harrington."

The butler snorted and pushed at the door, but suddenly a hand was pushing it open. It was smeared with blood and drying mud.

Roman's voice was no more than a low rumble from behind her. "Open the door."

Tara turned, wrapping her arm about Roman's waist.

"Leave this house," insisted the servant, pushing at the portal.

Roman kept his hand as it was. "I am na afraid ta die, man. Can ye say the same?"

The doorman stepped smartly back. The door sprang open.

Tara stood on the threshold, unable to move.

"'Tis too late to change the course of things now," Cobb said.

"I am with ye, lass," Roman murmured. Strength. Even now he possessed it like a protective shield. Tara drew a deep breath and stepped forward.

"Harrington." Her voice shook. She drew a breath and yelled again, her voice steadier this time. "Harrington!"

Servants hurried from every direction, only to stop and gawk at the ragtag trio that had breached their home. Tara nearly quelled under their gazes. But she drew herself up. "I've come to see your lord," she said weakly.

"You can't burst in here like this," said one maid. "Get yourself gone now."

For a moment Tara almost backed out. But Roman was wounded. "Harrington!" She screamed the name.

The servants milled nervously.

"Harrington!"

"You can't—"

"What is this racket about?" The old man appeared at the top of the stairs. "What goes on here?"

"I've come," Roman rasped.

"Dear God!" Harrington gripped the rail in gnarled hands. "Is that you, Forbes?"

Roman managed to lift his head, but did not dare leave the support of Tara's arms.

Harrington hurried down the stairs. Tara watched him, breath held, nerves taut. He was an old man, she reminded herself. Old and frail, with a pale face and a bitter heart.

He stopped before them. For a moment there

was something in his eyes, something akin to sympathy, but it was snuffed out in an instant. "Have you the necklace?"

Roman nodded. Tara drew out the pouch with one hand. The leather was slick and wet against her fingers. Slipping it from her neck, she handed it to Harrington.

His gaze held her for a moment, then he tipped the pouch upside down. Two drops of water dripped onto his palm, but nothing else.

The room was silent as a tomb.

"Nay." Tara whispered the word. So luck had finally abandoned her when she needed it most. When she had finally found someone to live for, it had left. She closed her eyes. "I am sorry," she whispered, not daring to face him.

Silence again, heavy and long, then, "It is gone?" Roman asked.

Sweet Mary. She would give her life not to disappoint him. "In the river," she whispered.

Harrington's nostrils flared. He slapped the pouch to the floor. "Then MacAulay dies."

"Nay!" Christine appeared at the top of the stairs. "Please, Father!" She rushed toward them, skimming down the steps.

"I have made my deals," he said, rage showing in his face. "But even the Scotsman did not care enough for his kinsmen to fulfill his end of the bargain. 'Tis all an intricate plan. First MacAulay steals your mother's ring, then Forbes takes the necklace. And now the bracelet, too, is gone."

"Father. I beg you! 'Twas not David that did the deeds."

"The boy dies!" Harrington raged, turning on his daughter.

But in that moment, Tara O'Flynn marshaled all her strength. "He does not die," she said, her voice absolutely steady.

"What's that?" Harrington turned back.

She watched him face her, watched his eyes narrow.

"If you think I will not follow through with my threat, you are sadly mistaken."

"I am not mistaken," Tara said. "You will not do as you threaten, for you owe me."

"You!" He snorted, raising his chin.

She raised hers in unison, meeting his eyes.

"I owe you nothing," he said, but his voice was not so sure now, and his face showed his uncertainty.

"Aye," she said quietly. "You owe me more than you can ever give."

Recognition dawned on Harrington's face. But he pushed the expression away and shook his head as if he had seen a ghost. "Who are you?" he whispered.

Silence echoed in the hall.

"I am your granddaughter," Tara whispered.

Chapter 26

"**D**aughter!" Harrington gasped, falling back on a settle where he clutched his chest. "My little Maude. You've come back." He faltered, breathing hard. "But nay! It couldn't be. Who . . . Who are you?"

Tara said nothing. She stood immobile. Memories rushed around her like a whistling gale.

"Lady Fontaine," he whispered. "I knew your eyes. Your mother's eyes. But I thought 'twas only my guilt twisting the blade in my gut. Dear God." His hands shook.

"Father!" Christine said, crouching beside him. "What is this all about?"

"Tara." Harrington whispered the name. "Your name is Tara."

"Tara?" Christine straightened slowly. "My half sister's daughter? But she died as a babe before I was born."

Harrington's gaze remained on Tara. "I searched for you. Searched. She wrote to me." He squeezed his eyes closed, as if shutting out the memories. "But I did not read her missives. I would have nothing to do with her until I learned of you. I could not bear to think of my grandchild growing up there, so far from home with a penniless father and . . ." He faltered. "My Maude," he whispered. "You are so beautiful."

"Father." Christine dropped to her knees again, gripping the old man's hands. "Maude is gone. Died of the plague long ago. Do you not remember?"

"The plague?" Tara whispered. Unreality threatened to pull her under its swirling tide, but she fought for breath and life.

"You don't remember?" Christine asked, looking up at Tara. "But no, or course you wouldn't." She shook her head. Tears brimmed her sky blue eyes. "You were but a babe when your mother died. Father thought the disease must have taken you as well."

"The plague!" Tara said, her voice stronger. Fire suddenly burned her mind. Her mother's scream torched her soul.

"Please!" Harrington lifted his face. "Please, forgive me. I loved her," he whispered, looking first at Tara, then at Christine. "She was the image of my Mary. So young and fair and vibrant. I would have given my life to make her happy. I did not know . . ." His voice had become fainter still. "I did not know how she loved . . . that Irishman. I was certain she would not be happy with him. Not after all I had given her here. I thought 'twas but a young girl's fancy. I sent them for her. That's all. I but sent them for her." His face fell into his hands again.

" 'Tis not your fault, Father. You could do nothing. The plague takes who it will."

"No!" He shook her hands away, suddenly fretful. "No! 'Tis not true. 'Twas not the plague that took her life. 'Twas a bitter, jealous, old man who could not bear to lose both his wife and his daughter in the same year.

"I sent men for her. I told them to do what they

must to bring her and the child back home. I did not mean for O'Flynn to die. Oh, I hated him!" He gripped his hands into blue-veined fists. "I hated him for taking her from me. But I did not mean for them to kill him. The fire! It was an accident. Why did she go in there when it was ablaze?"

"She loved him," Tara whispered. "More than life."

Silence wrung the place.

"All I had to remember her by was the portrait they brought back. I am sorry." His words were but a whisper. "Dear God, I am so sorry. Please forgive me."

"I can never forgive," Tara said, lost somewhere in a world of broken memories. "But if you set MacAulay free, maybe your daughter will."

Harrington rose shakily. "Edmond, get my carriage."

"No," Tara said, stepping forward. "Dagger will expect Roman to come here. He'll connect him to you. It won't be safe."

"Then . . ."

"Lord 'arrington, your carriage awaits." Liam bowed in the doorway, his tattered clothes in comic difference to his manner.

"Liam," Tara breathed. "How did you get here?"

He grinned. "I never doubted you'd make it through, but 'e don't look so good," he said, nodding to Roman. "Feigning weakness so she'll take care of ya, huh?"

"Just get MacAulay," Roman growled irritably from his seat near the door.

Harrington's mouth had fallen open.

"No time to dawdle," Liam said. "Victor felt a need ta lend me Lady Milan's team again."

"The dowager's team?" Harrington gasped.

"No time for questions," Liam said, grasping the old man's arm and ushering him through the door.

Christine hurried after, but Harrington turned on her, his face pale. "You'll stay here."

"I'll not," she said evenly.

"I'll not take you along."

"Then I'll procure a ride from this fishwife."

Mrs. Cobb swallowed hard, but raised her chin as if in silent defense of young love.

Harrington shook his head, "My own daughter," he mumbled, but Liam was already hurrying him to where the team of bays stood chomping their bits.

Still, Christine paused a moment. "Missus," she said softly, and slipping a gold ring from her finger, pressed it into the woman's rough hand. "I would thank you," she said, and rushed away.

In a moment Liam and the Harringtons were gone. Mrs. Cobb bobbed her head toward Tara. "I don't know who ya are, lass. But you've got heart. Take care of 'im, will ya?" she asked, nodding toward Roman.

"I will," Tara whispered.

Mrs. Cobb turned, hurrying toward her humble cart. The house went quiet, like a tomb awaiting a new arrival.

Tara swallowed. Servants surrounded her, their eyes wide, their jaws slightly ajar.

"I . . . I might fetch you water and bandages . . . for the . . . gentleman . . . Mistress . . . O'Flynn," said a nervous maid.

Tara nodded jerkily and swallowed again. She could creep as silent as a shadow through a darkened house. She could face the Dagger as a gypsy girl, or risk her life in a thousand other ways. But standing here in the hall of her grandfather's mansion frightened her to death.

"Tara," Roman said softly, "are ye well?"

She jerked from her trance. What was wrong with her? Roman had been badly wounded, yet she stood frozen in place like a frightened hare. She hurried to his side. "Roman," she murmured, touching his brow, "I am sorry."

"For saving me life?" he asked. He tilted up one corner of his mouth. Although he did not raise his head from the wall behind him, he looked stronger. Hope surged through her.

"For *endangering* your life," she whispered.

"Ahh," he murmured, touching her face in turn, "but did I na tell ye 'twas worth the trouble ta have known ye."

"Don't talk like that. As if . . ." Her voice failed. Terror gripped her heart. She loved him. Dear God, she loved him. She drew her hand back, frightened by the intensity of her emotions, but in that moment, Roman's eyes fell closed.

"Scotsman. Scotsman!" she said, gripping his arm.

His lids rose, but slowly and only to half-mast. "Lass . . ." His voice was weak. She leaned closer, trying to hear. "Dunna let me die here. Tek me ta the Highlands."

"Roman!" A Scotsman rushed through the door. He was bearded and filthy, but he moved with quick assurance.

Tara rose abruptly to her feet. Roman opened his eyes, but remained on the cot they had set up for him.

"Sweet Jesu," murmured MacAulay, bending over Roman. "What has happened to you?"

The smile again, slowly lifting one corner of Roman's mouth. He raised a hand which was tightly clasped in his countryman's. " 'Tis a long story, me friend. And I have na time for the telling."

Beneath the grime and beard, Tara saw David pale. " 'Tis as bad as that?"

Roman let his smile drop away, shifted his gaze

fretfully to Tara and then back to his friend's. "I dunna wish ta die on English soil," he said simply.

David closed his eyes and tightened his grip, but in a moment he turned to Christine. "I must see me friend safely ta our homeland."

"I know," she whispered.

"And ya'd best 'urry," said Liam from where he looked out the window. "'Is lordship won't stay gone for long."

"His lordship?" Harrington said.

"You've heard of Lord Dagger?" Roman asked, his voice quiet.

"Yes, but—"

"Some call him Lord Dasset."

"Nay." Harrington paled. "It couldn't be."

Roman closed his eyes again. "If you love yer daughter," he said weakly, "dunna let him near her."

"Dear God!"

"It ain't that I want to break up the party," Liam said. "But my 'orses is restless."

"Can you walk?" asked Tara. She had bandaged his wounds and dressed him in one of Harrington's voluminous shirts. Hose had been harder to come by, but finally one of the manservants had given him a serviceable pair.

"I'll make it, lass, if I can lean on ye."

His confidence in her ripped her heart. She had done nothing but wound him since the first moment they'd met. But she wouldn't fail him now.

Roman gritted his teeth as his feet touched the floor, but he rose quickly. They moved in tandem toward the door.

"Tara." Harrington's voice was quiet. She stopped to look over her shoulder at him. "You have her spirit. My Maude would have been proud of you. I but wish I could begin again."

For a moment she held her breath. He had

caused her parents' death, had thrust her into a world of theft and want. But he was her grandfather, old and frail and hurting. Roman's weight lightened on her shoulder, as if he were urging her to go to him. But the memories were too clear. She turned back toward the door, needing air.

Outside, it had begun to rain. They hurried through the weather. The coach leaned as Roman entered it. The seats were red, soft, tufted. Tara eased Roman onto one. He dragged her down beside him. She tried to disengage, to shift toward the window and watch for trouble, but he seemed weaker suddenly, and held her there with a heavy arm.

"Roman?" She breathed his name. "How are you faring?"

"So long as I'm with ye, I dunna feel the pain so sharp."

"But I should watch—"

MacAulay entered. His gaze met Roman's and locked. Understanding flowed between them. "I will watch," he said.

" 'Ere," said Liam, pulling a sheathed sword miraculously from his hose and handing it to David. "Ye may need this."

"Where did you—"

"And one for you, Scotch," Liam said, pulling another from the right leg of his hose.

Tara shook her head and reached for the weapon. "He's too badly wounded," she said.

Liam snorted and opened his mouth, but Roman caught his gaze and took the sword himself.

"Where'd ye get them?" repeated David.

"Folks shouldn't leave such things 'anging carelessly on walls and what not."

"Ye stole them from—" David began, but Liam was already hurrying up to the seat behind the bays. "He stole them?" asked David.

"Watch yer beard," said Roman, glancing out the window, "lest he take a liking ta *that*."

From the seat above, they heard the boy chuckle. Then they lurched into motion.

Again, Tara tried to move to the window, but Roman groaned. "Please dunna move, lass. Ye shelter me from the bumps just as ye are."

Houses skirted both sides of them. Roman watched them rush past as he weighed Tara close to him. They had been relatively safe at Harrington House, but already the city changed. Wealth and prestige was falling behind, replaced by the ragtag end of society. Dagger owned this world. "Are there na routes skirting the slums of Firthport?" Roman asked, and was Liam to be trusted, he wondered, not shifting his watchful gaze from the window.

"There are," Tara said. "But Liam will take the straightest course to the main gate. 'Tis the quickest way out of the city."

"Or to Dagger," Roman murmured.

"What?"

He could feel her gaze on his face and turned to look at her. For a moment, for just one moment in time, his heart stopped. Her hair was still damp and swept away from her face to expose each line with harsh clarity. Her skin was pale, whether from fatigue or worry, he wasn't sure. She was a thief, a ragamuffin. And he loved her so that his soul ached at the sight of her. But he would not tell. He would not frighten her. They were on their way to the Highlands, and that was enough.

They rattled along. Although the motion seemed to jab knives through every part of Roman's body, it also lulled him. Sleep had been too short and too seldom. The blow to his head wore at him, but he could not sleep, could not relax his vigil.

Finally the frenetic pace slowed to something

more sedate. They turned a corner, using all four wheels for the first time, Roman was certain. For several more rods they trotted along, and then they stopped.

"Where are we?" Roman rumbled. Tara tried to see around him, but he held her back. There was no saying who might recognize her.

"We're at the gate," David said.

"Who are you and what's your business?" They could hear the guard's voice clearly from where they sat.

"Me name's Joseph, and me lord's business is none of your concern," said Liam, as cocky as any high-ranking servant.

But Tara gasped suddenly.

Roman jerked his head toward her. "What's amiss?"

"Liam's clothes. He does not have an appropriate costume." She whispered the words.

For a moment the guard was silent, then, "Who is your lord?"

" 'Is name's Lord Argle? P'raps you've 'eard of 'im."

"Nay, I haven't."

Roman could hear Liam fill his chest with air. "Well, 'e'll 'ear bout you if'n ya don't cease wastin' our time."

Tara stood and stepped forward. Roman reeled her back, and drawing a breath for strength, poked his head through the window. "What is the meaning of the delay, *garçon*?" he asked. His French accent was shaky, but he had managed to assume the irritated tone of the upper crust.

There was a moment of silence. The guard moved toward the back of the coach.

"My apologies, m'lord," called Liam. "But this *neminar* says he ain't never 'eard of you. Shall we lippiate 'im?"

Neminar? Lippiate? Roman allowed himself one swift glance over his shoulder at Tara.

She shrugged, looking bewildered.

The guard stopped. "Who you calling a numinar?"

"You," Liam said, effectively drawing the guard away from getting a closer view of the coach's occupants.

"And you think you can . . . What the hell do you think you can do to me?"

"Huh," chortled Liam from his perch behind the bays. "Only a barbarian don't know French."

"*He* doesn't know French," Tara whispered, shifting toward the door once more.

Again Roman pulled her back. Hell fire! He was traveling with a bunch of lunatics. "Keep her inside," he ordered David.

It took all his self-control to open the door and step out without wincing. "What's the meaning of this?" he asked.

The guard shifted his attention from Liam to Roman. His gaze skimmed the man before him, assessing, calculating.

"I'm sorry, m' lord," he said. "But we've had some trouble here this morning. It seems Baron Dasset was robbed. We've orders to stop all coaches and—"

Suddenly, four men sprang out of nowhere. They threw themselves at Roman. But he'd kept Harrington's weapon in his hand. He swiped with it now. A man screamed and fell back. The second lunged at him. Roman dodged behind the door, but even that movement nearly threw him to the ground. A sword twanged against the lacquered wood.

"Roman!" Tara screamed, trying to draw him back.

She was close, far too close to the danger.

"Drive!" he roared, battling to right himself and fend off the next attack.

There was a yell from Liam. The horses lunged against their traces. The carriage was yanked into motion. Roman tried to go with it, to keep his hold on the door, to swing inside, but someone had grabbed his shirt.

"Roman!" Tara screamed, and suddenly she was in the doorway.

Dear Jesu! She was going to jump after him, he realized suddenly. Kicking his assailant aside, he swung on the door toward the carriage. Hands grabbed him, pulled him up. Men yelled. Horses screamed. Roman landed on the red cushion and slammed the door behind him. From up above, he heard Liam laugh with wild triumph.

"He's insane," Roman said, still gripping the sword in one hand.

"Never do that again. Don't ever do that again!" Tara raved. "You could have been killed."

He managed not to smile. "Me apologies," he said, and kissed her. "It seems I forgot to leave all the risk ta ye."

"They're coming," David said, pulling his head inside.

"How many?"

"Four thus far, all mounted."

"How long can we outpace them?"

David shook his head. "I dunna know these horses."

"Ask the lad," Roman ordered.

Tara popped away from his side, levered her body through the window. "How long can we outrun them, Liam?" she yelled into the oncoming wind.

"Sweet Jesu!" Roman swore, grasping her gown near her buttocks. "Get in here."

"These champions will run till they drop," yelled

Liam. "But we can only hold a lead for half a league, maybe less."

Roman reeled Tara in with another curse.

"Half a league," she panted. "Maybe less."

"Don't ever do that again," Roman warned.

"There's a woods ahead," David said.

"We could find cover, unhitch the team, and ride astride," Roman suggested. Poking his head out the window, he glanced behind. Their followers were hidden behind a hill.

"You can't ride," Tara said. " 'Twould never be safe."

"If the steeds have the heart Liam thinks they have, we might yet win the day," Roman reasoned.

"You can't ride."

"If we can unhitch quickly enough," David said, "we might be able to outrun them."

"Outrun them? We could never outrun them. Roman is badly wounded. He cannot ride."

Roman glanced at her. "With ye beside me I could fly, lass."

"But . . ." Tara said.

"David, how far is it to the woods?"

"A quarter league, maybe less."

"But . . ." she said again. "I can't."

Roman turned to her with a scowl, then noticed her pale expression. "Canna what?"

"Cannot ride," she murmured.

"Yer scairt ta ride?" Roman asked.

"Not scared," she corrected. "Never learned."

"Praise the saints," Roman said. "I've found something she's scairt of."

"Not scared," she said again, then bounced as they hit a particularly rough spot in the road. "Untutored."

Roman spared half a grin, then sobered, "Ye could ride with me, but twould slow down the steed and we dunna have enough of a lead for that."

"Then there's little choice but for ye ta jump," David said.

"It appears so," Roman agreed. "At the third rise, slow the team for the count of ten, then push them to the hilt and dunna look back."

"What?" Tara asked.

"We'll hide in the wood," Roman said. "Liam and David will drive on, find a likely spot, unhitch the horses, and lose the guards before returning to us."

"Hide in the woods, and let Liam take the risk?" Tara asked aghast.

" 'Tis the safest thing for ye," David said, then caught Roman's glare and corrected himself. "For *Roman*, I mean. 'Tis the safest thing for Roman. Wounded as he is, he'll not be able ta ride hard enough ta escape."

" 'Tis settled then," Roman said. "Can ye tell Liam of our plans?"

Tara leaned toward the window, ready to do his bidding. Roman caught her arm, pulling her back to his side. " 'Twas speaking ta David," he said.

It was not so difficult a task for David to crawl through the window and up beside Liam.

Roman switched seats to watch the woods approach. Within minutes they entered it. He pulled Tara from her seat, steadying her in front of him. "We'll reach the third rise soon. We'll slow at the curve. When we do, jump."

Their gazes met. "Roman, you're hurt, you can not—"

Leaning forward, he kissed her lightly. "Mayhap ye can catch me."

" 'Tis not a joke."

"I will be fine, lass. Jump far. Then get up and run as if the devil be at yer heels. Can ye do that?"

She nodded once.

Time sped past, then, "Jump!" he ordered.

She did so, propelling herself from the coach. He flung himself after her, but his sense of balance was awry. His skull struck the ground. A thousand daggers stabbed him. His head thundered, threatening darkness. But he fought it off. He could not fail her. He could not.

"Roman!" she gasped, reaching for him.

"I told ye ta run!"

"Come on! Come on!" she urged, pulling him to his feet.

Agony ripped through him, but he gained his balance. The world spun. He was Highlander. He could not fail. She could not die. He managed two steps before falling to his knees. "Run!" he ordered, but she gripped his arm and leaned close.

"Die now, Scotsman, and I'll die right here with you, I swear I will."

"Damn you!" He staggered to his feet, fixed his eyes on the woods and forced himself toward it.

Hoofbeats! He heard them coming.

"Hurry. Hurry, Scotsman."

Roman gritted his teeth, managed a couple of rods, then wrapped his arm tight about Tara's body and dragged her to the ground.

The sound of hoofbeats swelled, exploded in his head, and finally disappeared into oblivion.

"Roman." Tara touched his face, fear unraveling within her. "Roman!"

He did not answer, but lay in pale silence.

"Roman!" She sat up, panic roiling like a brewing storm as she cradled his head in her lap. "Nooo!" She sobbed, but then, beneath her hand, she felt a faint pulse.

"So he is dead already?"

Tara jerked her head up with a gasp.

Not three rods away, Lord Dagger sat upon his

white steed. " 'Tis too bad," he said, dismounting and drawing his sword from its sheath. "I had hoped to kill him myself. I suppose I will have to be content with killing you."

Chapter 27

Panic roiled up within Tara, attempting to consume her. Roman would die, her mind screamed in terror. After all her struggles, he would die here, far from his homeland, far from the people he loved.

Terrible loss ripped through her heart. But years of hardship had taught her to fight to the end. Perhaps he didn't have to die. Not if Dagger believed he was already dead.

"You killed him." Letting Roman's head slip to the earth, Tara grasped the sword he had dropped and rose to her feet. "You killed him," she whispered.

Dagger shook his head as he stepped toward her. "Nay. You deprived me of that pleasure."

He was evil personified, and he was getting closer, closer to Roman. Panic threatened again. Tara pushed it down. Roman must not die. He would not.

She backed away. A fallen branch snagged her skirt. She stepped to the right, praying. True to her pleas, Dagger followed her, veering off the direct course to Roman.

"Tell me, girl," said Dagger, stalking her, "who are you?"

Dagger must die. That was her mission, her reason for being, the culmination of all her years in Firthport. Suddenly, everything seemed so perfectly clear. Everything she had endured had been for this purpose—to give her life for the man she loved. Surely God had ordained it. She would die, but Roman would live.

She stopped, raising her chin and with it, the sword. It was heavy and long, but somehow she would find the strength to use it.

"Who are you?" Dagger asked again, still advancing.

"I am the one sent to kill you," she said.

He stopped for a moment. Then he laughed. Less than a rod separated them. Tara tightened her grip on the sword and waited. "Are you the Shadow?" he asked.

Yes. She was, and that realization sent something akin to pride through her. She lifted the sword another inch and smiled. "Me?" She shook her head. "I am the devil come to claim his own."

He canted his head, moving closer. "Truly."

She stood her ground. God had given her the honor of saving Roman's life. She would not fail.

"You made an intriguing gypsy, and a tempting lady, but I think I like you best as the devil," he said. "Still, I need to know, are you also the Shadow?"

"It matters little."

"Ah, but it matters to me." He slowed his pace and watched her closely. "For if I know I kill the Shadow when I kill you, I will enjoy my work the more, and mayhap I will take my time about it. And I think..." He stopped, studying her from less than a half a rod's distance. "I think you are the Shadow. I think 'twas you that stole the necklace from the Scotsman, the dead Scotsman," he corrected, and chuckled when she paled. " 'Tis strange how life works, is it not? First you steal from him, then you attempt to avenge his death. But I fear I cannot allow that," he said and launched himself toward her.

"Nay!" Tara shrieked. She raised the sword. But Dagger was quick and strong.

Slashing sideways, he knocked her blade aside. She spun away. Her skirts tangled about her ankles and she fell.

He was coming, lunging! She must not die! Not yet. She twisted about, dragging the sword before her. Dagger swung again. His blade struck hers, throwing her to the ground with the strength of his parry. Her head hit a rock. She tried to reel back the blackness and bring her sword to bear, but she could not marshal her senses, could not move.

Dagger stood over her, blade raised.

She had failed her beloved.

Dagger laughed. The sword descended.

"Nay!" Roman shrieked.

Dagger jerked about. Roman swung a branch. The villain ducked, but the bough caught his shoulder, knocking him sideways.

Roman followed, his steps unsteady, his world reeling.

Dagger straightened, watching his opponent with narrowed eyes.

"So you're not yet dead, Scotsman. And the woman knew it all along." He chuckled, bringing his sword to bear. "Ahh, she was a clever one, trying to lead me away from you. In fact, I think she planned to give her life to save yours. As soon as I kill you, I'll finish with her. I rather hope she's still alive."

Weakness and fatigue weighed Roman's arms. Hell yawned before him. He could not die. Not yet.

"How did it feel to fuck a shadow, Scotsman? No need to answer. I'll know soon enough."

Rage screamed through Roman. He lunged, swinging his branch. Dagger parried. Steel met wood, slicing the branch at a sharp angle less than two feet from Roman's hands.

Dagger's laughter filled the air. He advanced and swung again. Roman ducked, barely clearing the blade's path as he backed away. Dagger stalked him, his eyes bright with bloodlust. He swung again. Again, Roman dodged to the right. Dagger's sword sliced his arm, but he was beyond physical pain.

"I'd like to stay and play," Dagger said, advancing again. "But your lady awaits my pleasure, so now . . . you die!" he said and lunged.

Roman tried to twist away. His foot became snared in the bracken. He fell with his branch braced, point up, beside him. Dagger rushed in, sword held before him, ready for the kill. But suddenly, he, too, tripped, and he fell, blade thrust out.

Death roared in upon Roman. He watched it come, helpless to stop it, paralyzed beneath Dagger's sword. He had failed! Dear God, he had failed her.

He felt Dagger's blade slice through his flesh and into the ground below. The blackness swelled around him, and he let it take him.

Unable to stop his fall, Dagger plunged downward onto the branch sharpened by his own sword. It entered below his sternum, ripping into his guts as he shrieked in agony.

"Roman!" Tara stumbled to her feet. "Roman!" She raced toward him, then staggered back as reality grabbed hold of her. Roman was skewered to the ground beside Dagger's lifeless form. "Nay!" Her world ripped apart. She fell to her knees.

Blood ran unchecked from Roman's side.

"You're bleeding," she said softly, as if he could hear her. "Please don't bleed. Don't bleed," she fretted numbly. "I'll help you." Ripping a piece from her skirt, she reached out to press it to the wound. But the sword was still there. She had to remove the blade. She reached toward it, then pulled her hand slowly back. This was her fault.

She stared at the wound. His blood was bright red, still flowing, puddling into the bracken crushed beneath him. She had killed him. But she would not allow him to be defiled. She would remove the sword, bind the wound.

Rising to her feet, Tara reached for the handle. It felt cold and hard beneath her fingers. She closed her eyes and pulled. The sword resisted, clinging to his pierced flesh. Bile rose in Tara's throat, but she tightened her grip and dragged the blade from Roman's body.

The bloodied sword dangled from her fingers.

"Step away," said a voice from behind.

Tara staggered about.

There was another horseman, bigger than Dagger. His sword was drawn and death was in his face.

Sanity was flung aside. "Nay!" Tara screamed. "You will not have him. I will take him to the Highlands."

The huge man dismounted, still watching her. "Step away from him."

"Come on then!" She motioned him toward her. Blood dripped from the sword's tip. "Come if you dare."

Dressed all in black, he approached slowly. "Put down the sword."

"Nay!" she screamed. Hopelessness swallowed her. "Nay! Kill me, too! Kill me, too, and have done with it!"

"Put the sword aside, lass," said the warrior quietly. "And we may yet save your love."

The woods reverberated in the silence. Tara's

mind scrambled as she tried to think, tried to sort the lies from the truth. "Save?" she whispered.

"He yet lives."

"Nay." She shook her head, not daring to hope. "Do not try to fool me."

"The Wolf yet lives, lass," said the warrior, his voice lightly burred. He turned his head, as if having caught the sound of distant danger. "But he willna last much longer if we dunna hide him."

"The Wolf!" The sword drooped in Tara's numbed fingers. "He is the Wolf and you are . . ."

"The Hawk," said the warrior, and, stepping forward, slipped the sword from her hand.

Roman lived, but by the barest of margins. Tara could not touch him, could not hold him. She sat like a doll of rags upon her mount's back. The days passed like nightmares without end, the nights like hell's eternity.

Hawk had carried Roman into hiding. Dagger's men had passed by and finally returned to Firthport. And eventually, after a thousand lifetimes, Liam and David had arrived with the four horses freed from the coach.

Roman's wound had been tightly bound. Hawk believed the sword had missed his vital organs, but Tara did not know whether to believe him. And would it matter in the end? Roman remained unconscious.

For two days they did not stop except for water. The land became rough and rolling, green beyond description.

The third night they stopped some hours past sunset. Tara slipped from her horse. Her legs buckled and she fell to the earth.

The night was cold and endless.

Long before dawn, they were moving again. The night ground away. Morning slid up the horizon.

Tara walked beside Roman, lest he somehow break the bonds that kept him tethered to Hawk's huge mount.

Miles passed beneath them. Tara stumbled and fell. Hands reached for her. She felt herself lifted and set aboard a horse's bare back.

It began to rain, tiny pellets of water.

"How far?" she asked, speaking through exhaustion as heavy as an English fog.

Hawk's eyes were a strange, silver-blue and flat with worry. He turned away. "Dun Ard is near."

Tara braced herself against her mount's withers and lifted her gaze to squint through the rain at Roman's pale face. Mayhap he would yet survive. Mayhap, she thought.

But just then a cry rang through the air and a warrior leapt into their path.

Chapter 28

Tara gasped. No! They were nearly to safety. They could not be stopped now. She would not let them be. Grabbing both her reins and Roman's, she prepared to flee.

Hawk swept his sword from its scabbard, but he held up his opposite hand and stayed perfectly still, facing their attacker. Off to the side, a dozen more men stepped from the woods, mere shadows in the pouring rain.

"So is the Hawk no longer welcome at Dun Ard?" Hawk asked, raising his voice above the pound of the rain.

There was a moment of silence, then, "Haydan, is that ye, lad?"

"Roderic," Hawk breathed.

The leader of the men rushed through the rain toward them. Tara remained poised and ready, but in a moment Hawk was engulfed in a man's embrace.

"Hawk," he said. "Our Hawk has returned to the mews."

Though bigger and broader, Hawk seemed suddenly to droop in the other man's embrace.

Roderic frowned, then lifted his gaze to Tara. "What is this? What's happened?"

" 'Tis Roman," Hawk said. "I came too late to assist him."

"God's wrath! Not Roman."

"Aye. I could not save him, Roddy. 'Tis my fault."

"He is dead?"

"Nay!" Tara said, but the word was a croak of misery. "He will not die. He cannot be."

Roderic's gaze caught hers again, then swept away.

"William!" he yelled.

"Aye, m'lord?" said a young man. He stepped forward, lean and small.

"Ride—nay—take Lochan's Bairn and *fly* ta Glen Creag. Fiona will know what ta do."

William fell back a step, his eyes going wide. "The Flame willna let me take her favorite steed."

"Buck up, man," said Roderic. "She willna bite ye. Bullock, ye'd best go with him, lest I'm wrong."

"Aye, m'lord."

"Adam, run ahead and tell Bethia that the Wolf has been struck."

Within minutes, they crossed a drawbridge. The courtyard was slick beneath Tara's mount's hooves. The keep loomed before her.

Hawk untied Roman and carried him into the hall.

Tara slid to the ground, feeling numb and worn.

"Come, lass," Roderic said, reaching for her hand.

"Nay." She drew back. For a moment of time she had hoped Roman could be hers. For a moment she had dreamed, but no more. When she loved, people died. She could not risk his life.

"He'll die without ye," Roderic said.

"No." She whispered the word. "He will live."

"I know the Wolf well," Roderic said. "He needs ye."

Tara tried to turn away, but she could not. In a moment, she followed Roderic up the stairs to the infirmary.

Tara awoke with a start.

An angel stood in the doorway. "Roman!" she said. Her hair challenged the color of the fire in the hearth, and her eyes were as bright as amethyst.

Another woman rushed forward. She was taller, younger. But her hair was the same bright hue. In Tara's fatigue, it seemed they floated above the floor, ethereal, sent from heaven.

"Help him," she pleaded.

The first angel caught Tara's gaze.

"Do you love him?"

She was not certain if the words were spoken or merely thought, but she was certain she could not risk the truth. Silence ruled the room.

Still, the angel nodded as if she had spoken.

There was no time for denials.

The angels swept forward. They removed Roman's tattered shirt, cut away his bandages.

His wound was swollen and purple, oozing and crusted.

"Noo," moaned the taller woman.

"Flanna," whispered the healer, not taking her gaze from Roman's side. "I need purslane and dogwood leaves."

The younger woman straightened. "I can stay. Let me help."

"Nay," Fiona said, her own face ashen. "I need the leaves."

Flanna nodded and backed away. "What else?"

"Have Bethia bring boiling water and bandages."

Flanna nodded and disappeared.

Tara swallowed hard. "What can I do?" she whispered.

Fiona's gaze caught hers. There was wisdom and healing in the depths of her eyes. But there was more, love so vast it could encompass her even now. "Hold fast and pray, lass," she whispered.

Night fell. Morning dawned. Two days came and went, but Tara was caught forever in darkness. She remained as she was, unspeaking, unmoving. 'Twas her fault he was dying. Therefore, she did not deserve to touch him, but neither could she force herself to leave him.

"David MacAulay is well?" Fiona asked.

Three tawny hounds sat beside Roman's bed. Their long noses rested on his mattress as they gazed at him. Sweet Mary, Tara thought, even the dogs loved him.

There was a small group of people by the door. Tara knew them by name now. Leith was Fiona's husband, dark and solemn. Roderic was Leith's brother, the opposite in both looks and manner, his arm wrapped about his wife Flanna as she pressed close to his side.

Hawk was there, standing apart from the rest as he stared at Roman's pale face.

"Aye." Leith's voice was deep and quiet. "David is well. He has returned to his father."

Fiona nodded. The room fell silent.

Roderic drew a deep breath and absently rubbed his wife's arm. "Is there aught else we can do, Fiona? Are there other herbs that might help?"

Fiona shook her head. "His wounds are grievous, aye, but . . . He has been sorely wounded afore, and always he has fought back to health. But now . . . 'tis almost as if he does not wish to stay amongst us."

Leith tightened his fist. "Mayhap if ye tried more purslane. I could fetch—"

"I have done all I can," Fiona snapped, then stifled a sob with the back of her hand. "I am sorry," she whispered. " 'Tis not your fault. 'Tis only that I . . . I remember him as I first saw him. Brave . . ." Her fingers slipped from her face. Tears washed her cheeks as she gazed at Roman's pale face. "He was so brave," she whispered. "Carrying Dora."

"The hound," Roderic murmured. He cleared his throat, but his eyes were filled with tears. One spilled past his golden lashes. "Sweet Mary, how he loved that hound."

"Enough to give his life," Fiona whispered. "It has always been thus with Roman. So easily could he sacrifice himself for those he cherished. But never could he see the good that is himself. Damn Dermid for the damage he has wrought!" she swore with sudden vehemence.

"Shhh." Leith pulled her into his arms. " 'Tis all past, Fiona. 'Tis yer pure love that saved him. Yer love and none other's."

Fiona pressed her face against his chest. Her fingers gripped his sleeves. "I canna save him now, for he does not wish to be saved."

Tara said nothing. Her world had been ripped in two.

"Mayhap if we move him ta Glen Creag, ta his home, he'll . . ." Leith began, but Fiona shook her head.

"He'll not survive the night," she whispered.

The words yanked Tara from her trance. "Nay!" She shot out of her chair. "Nay!" she screamed. "He'll not die! I do not love him!"

The room went absolutely still. Five pair of eyes watched her.

"He will not die!" she croaked, backing away. "I never said I loved him. I never did."

Fiona drew herself from her husband's arms. "But you do, don't you? And he loves you, but you've not admitted it."

"No!" Tara screamed. She fell to her knees, fists clenched. Tears flooded her eyes. Misery drowned her. "Don't let him die! I'll leave. I'll go and not come back. I swear it."

"And think ye that will heal him?" Fiona asked.

Tara swallowed, swiping the tears away. She had not cried since childhood. "'Tis my fault," she whispered. "He was not for the likes of me. I knew this—and yet I wanted him so. If I love, people die. Da, Mother, Cork. I knew, and yet . . ."

Fiona dropped to her knees. "They died because you loved them?" she asked quietly. Tara tried to avoid her eyes, tried to look away, but she could not. "He is my son," she whispered. "I deserve to know."

Tara nodded. "Make him better." She whimpered the words like a small, broken child. "Make him better, and I'll go away."

Fiona lifted her chin, and gripping Tara's hand, slowly pulled her to her feet. "You'll not go away," she said quietly. "You'll tell him the truth."

Tara gasped and stepped back.

"His spirit's leaving," Fiona rasped, stepping with her. "But love can do miracles. I've seen it afore."

"I do not love. I cannot love. I'm not like you. I have done . . ." She shook her head, clasping her hands close to her chest. "My life has been corrupt. My love could not heal him," she whispered.

Fiona's eyes burned into hers. "So ye have lived with evil, and yet ye long for what is good. Yer soul has not been blackened by that which ye have seen. 'Tis a special gift, Tara O'Flynn. 'Tis the gift that Roman needs. The love of a woman who has seen the darkness and fought for light. We love him, lass, but we cannot understand him, not truly, for he endured that which we shudder to imagine. But ye . . . ye understand him, and yet ye love him. Ye are two hearts destined to be melded. Ye belong together."

"Nay!" Tara gasped, stumbling backward.

"Aye, ye do," Fiona whispered. "Tell him the truth."

"No! No! I'll kill him!" Tara tried to escape, but Fiona held her in a hard grip.

"You are not God," she rasped. "You do not decide who lives and who dies. But love is a gift of God. More powerful, mayhap, than any other force on earth. I'll not stand by and watch my son die while ye deny yers."

The room fell silent. Fire blazed in Fiona's eyes. The truth burned in Tara's soul. Somehow she stumbled forward and fell to her knees.

"Roman." She whispered his name. "I'm sorry. I'm so very sorry. I did not mean to love you. I tried my best to resist but . . ." She laughed. The sound was warbled and painful. "You would not let me." She gripped his hand, leaning over his chest to speak into his face. "I tried to leave you." Tears dripped down her cheek and onto his hand. "Every one of me tried to leave you. Or tried to make you go away," she whispered. "You should have gone while you had a chance, but you were too noble. You had to save MacAulay. You had to save me. Thus, you tricked me into coming. You did not wish to die in England you said. But you would have survived. I see that now. And mayhap I saw it then, but I could not bear to let you go. I told myself I came with you to see you safe to your homeland. I told myself I would leave when you were here. But it was only my weakness." She sniffed and wiped her nose with the back of her hand. Leaning forward, she kissed him. Tears fell on his eyelids, his nose, her hair where it fell upon his cheek. "Please forgive me. But I love you— more than life itself."

* * *

Tara sat in numb silence. Her admission of love had only made her pain more intense. Mayhap that was why she had denied her feelings so long—to save herself from the agony love caused.

Night ground toward morning. He would not survive the night, Fiona had said.

Why had she not been allowed to die under Dagger's sword, Tara wondered. She had lived a life of crime, but surely she did not deserve to watch Roman die. Surely not that.

A glimmer of light appeared at the narrow window of the infirmary. Tara turned toward it.

He would not survive the night!

The words rang in her mind. She tightened her grip on Roman's fingers.

"Please!" She croaked the word. Tears fell on their clasped hands. "Please don't go without me. Please! I'll—"

His fingers twitched in her hand. Tara's breath stopped in her throat.

"Roman?" She barely dared breath the word. "Roman?"

"Lass?" His eyes opened slowly, then lay perfectly immobile, staring at her. "Am I in heaven?" His voice was a hoarse whisper.

Tara shook her head, unable to find her voice.

"Ye are here?" He raised his hand to touch her damp cheek. "Ye are here," he murmured, awe softening his words. "But I thought—I thought I had lost ye. Dagger . . ." He shook his head.

A sob wrenched Tara's chest. She clasped Roman's hand to her chest. "Dagger is dead. You killed him."

"But he killed *you*! I saw him. Ye were lost to

me. I thought to die, too, to follow ye to the hereafter.''

"No,'' she whispered. "I am alive. But I've been a coward, afraid to admit my feelings for you. Afraid of losing you. But I see now that if I do not risk, if I do not admit the truth, I've already lost you.'' She pressed the back of his hand to her tear-drenched cheek. "I am yours, Roman, for as long as the Lord gives us, if you'll have me.''

Chapter 29

❧ ❦ ❧

"**O**h, m'lady, ye look lovely," crooned Fiona's daughter, stepping into the solar. Tara turned. She had met Rachel two days before, when they had first arrived at Glen Creag, Roman's home. It had been only three weeks since Roman had awakened. During that time she had barely left his side. He had mended with miraculous speed. With a Highlander's speed, he had said, and refused to delay their wedding a moment longer.

Their wedding! Tara pressed damp palms against the skirt of her gown. It was mulberry red, shot with threads of silver, and seemed no more real than anything else that had happened in the past few weeks. "Do you think Roman will be pleased?" she murmured.

"Ye jest," Rachel said. At fourteen, she was taller than her mother, but no less exuberant. "Ye look like a flaxen-haired angel."

Guilt twinged Tara. She was far from being an angel. But Roman loved her. And though that knowledge still terrified her, she could not leave him, not for a thousand fears. "Unlike most angelic beings, I wear scarlet instead of white," Tara said.

Fiona rose from her place by the window. "The

color suits ye," she said. " 'Tis rich and alive and—"

"Tara. Oh!" gasped Flame, stepping inside and closing the door quickly behind her. "Ye look as bonny as a rose."

"Roman will swoon," Rachel said.

"When have you ever seen your brother swoon," Fiona asked.

Walking over, Rachel reached out to puff up one of her mother's bright yellow sleeves. "Hawk says Roman swoons every time he sees Tara."

"Hardly that," Tara said, but a thrill of happiness tingled through her at the words. Not since childhood had she had a family. She knew they only accepted her because of Roman. He loved her. And because of that love, she would change. She would become one of this kind, extraordinary family. If she could be the Shadow, she could do that. Couldn't she?

"Hawk says Tara's more dangerous to Roman than a thousand swords, 'cause he forgets to breathe every time she's near," Rachel said, turning her head but still standing close to her mother.

"Hawk needs a wife before..." Fiona began, then, "Rachel, what are ye doing?"

"Oh!" Rachel stomped her foot and dropped her mother's cross back around her neck. It was a simple piece, made of wood and wire. "I can never steal anything proper. Liam said I wouldn't be able to."

"Liam?" Fiona asked.

Tara froze. The breath left her lungs. Who was she fooling? She was a thief and a liar. Love was not a panacea. It could not make her belong here. The truth flashed through her mind like a blazing star.

"Aye, Liam," Rachel said. "He is forever pinching my hair ribbons right off my head. I'm determined to learn his tricks. Tara..." She turned, entreaty in her eyes. "Will ye not teach me the skill. Roman says you're the best thief there is."

Tara couldn't breath. Roman had told his sister that she was a thief, and now his lady mother would know as well. They had known from the start that her background was dubious, but the truth was so much worse.

The room was silent, then, "How could you say such a thing?" Fiona asked. Her tone registered shock.

It would be in her power to refuse this union, Tara knew. She waited, hands formed to fists.

"I but thought . . ." Rachel began.

" 'Tis her wedding day," Fiona reminded. "Mayhap she'll have time to teach you to steal tomorrow. In the meanwhile . . ." She ushered her daughter toward the door. "I can give ye a few pointers. Did I tell ye my uncle Peter could filch your teeth right out of your head. Why, I remember when I was a postulate to the holy order of Mary I lost my cross and . . ." She clasped the necklace that always hung about her neck.

"Oh, 'tis a reminder to me," Flame said suddenly. "I brought ye something." She hurried across the floor to uncurl her hand. A fine string of pearls gleamed with a cool luster. " 'Twas the strand Fiona and Leith gave me when I married Roderic."

Tara's head was swimming. How could they accept her into their perfect lives knowing what she was?

" 'Tis beautiful, Flame, but . . ."

"But I had hoped she would wear something else," Roman said from the doorway.

"Roman!" Rachel said, outraged, "Ye cannot come in here. 'Tis a lady's room."

He stepped inside. Dressed in ceremonial plaid

and a fine, burgundy doublet, he looked like a king. A healthy king, whole and hale and safe, if still a bit stiff from his wounds. Tears sprang into Tara's eyes.

"Roman," she said, a sob in her throat. He rushed across the room to take her in his arms.

"Dunna cry, lass."

"It seems since I've started crying 'tis all I can do."

"All is well, my love."

"All is too good," she murmured.

"Nay, na for ye," he vowed, and kissed her. Lightning struck her lips. Eternity opened its arms.

"Fiona, have ye seen . . ."

Tara remembered they were not alone and managed to pull herself back to reality. From the doorway, Roderic grinned like a golden devil. He held a small blanket-wrapped bundle to his shoulder. "Roman, I'm shocked. Such goings-on before the nuptials."

" 'Twould hate ta think what it would take ta shock ye," rumbled a voice from the hall. Leith entered, squeezing past his brother to stare at the couple wrapped in each other's arms. "Ahh." His brows rose. "Roman ye're—"

"A wise lad," interrupted Roderic.

"Aye," Leith said, looking resplendent, and opening his arms which were soon filled with his wife and daughter. "I taught him everything he knows. Ladies, we be ready ta venture down ta the hall, if our guests be ready for the radiance of yer beauty." They squeezed through the door as one, but in an instant, Leith stuck his head back in. "Ye two, dunna be too long."

Roman nodded, his face characteristically sober before he turned back to Tara and kissed her again. The caress was a hint of paradise, deepening, lengthening.

"Do ye think he'll survive this kiss, me love?" Roderic's voice was very near.

"He'd best survive," Flanna said. " 'Twould hate to think I allowed William to ride Lochan Bairn for nothing."

Roman drew the kiss to an end and turned an irritated scowl on his uncle. "Dunna ye have something better ta do, Roddy?" he asked.

"Better?" Roderic asked, then, "Oh, aye," he said, and pulling Flanna into a one-armed embrace, kissed her.

It was some time before she called an end to it, and when she did, her voice was husky. "I think Roman may have been hinting for privacy, my love."

"The hell with privacy. The lad's old enough ta watch," Roderic growled, and tightened his embrace.

Flanna placed a finger to his lips and laughed. "I meant privacy for them," she said, nodding toward the others.

"Ahh." He turned toward them. "We could teach them how 'tis done."

"Ye've always been generous with yer knowledge, Uncle," Roman said, still scowling.

"Aye, I have, lad."

"Now get the hell out of here."

"He's an ingrate," Roderic said, then turned to the tiny bundle in his arms. "But I'll repay him; I'll save all yer bonny smiles for meself, wee Ramsay. Ahh, Flanna," he sighed, turning to his wife. "Ye are a wonder. Have I thanked ye yet?"

"Many times," Flanna said.

Roderic kissed her again. "Come, I'll thank ye more thoroughly in private."

The door closed. The room fell into silence.

Tears of joy stung Tara's eyes. How had she fallen into such happiness? It seemed to flow over her in warm waves, making her need to do something, to say something, or burst with the emotions.

She cleared her throat. "Your family—" she began, but in an instant, Roman's fingers covered her lips.

" 'Tis too late ta back out now, Tara. Ye vowed ta marry me."

She stared at him.

He scowled. "I know they're strange. But ye'll get used ta them if ye give them a chance."

She couldn't help but laugh. "Compared to my own kinsmen they are saints."

"I'm told David has returned to Firthport. It seems he would disagree where your half sister is concerned."

"He's gone back?" Tara asked, paling.

"Aye," Roman said. "But do na worry, lass. 'Tis said that Harrington has learned the idenity of the thief who first stole his mother's ring. 'Twas his own son, desperate to pay his gambling debts. Lord Harrington has had time to consider his false assumptions, and reassess MacAulay's character."

"Mayhap he will decide the Highlander is na so ignoble as he had thought, for I have surely learned that and much more," she said softly.

"I love ye, Tara O'Flynn," he murmured.

Tara closed her eyes, letting the shiver of euphoria seep to her soul. "And I love you, Roman Forbes," she whispered, a lump catching in her throat.

He drew back slightly, so as to look into her eyes. "Me wife," he whispered. "Forever and always."

"Aye." A tear slipped from her eye, but she did not wipe it away. "And beyond."

"Ye own me heart," he whispered. "Me person is yers. I am na longer just Roman Forbes. Nor am I the Wolf. I am yours—Ye own me, body and soul, the good and the bad. And I thought, mayhap, ye might wear a symbol of who I truly am."

"A symbol?" she whispered.

"Aye, 'tis a strange thing, I suppose, lass," he said. "But I would like ye ta wear . . ."

He lifted his hand to his chest, moved his fingers, and finally sighed before pulling her back against his body and staring over her head into space.

"Me amulet," he said in a monotone, "ye've stolen it again, haven't ye?"

"I like to share," Tara whispered, and smiled against his chest.

Avon Romances—
the best in exceptional authors and unforgettable novels!

WICKED AT HEART   **by Danelle Harmon**
78004-6/ $5.50 US/ $7.50 Can

SOMEONE LIKE YOU   **by Susan Sawyer**
78478-5/ $5.50 US/ $7.50 Can

MINX   **by Julia Quinn**
78562-5/ $5.50 US/ $7.50 Can

SCANDALOUS SUZANNE   **by Glenda Sanders**
77589-1/ $5.50 US/ $7.50 Can

A MAN'S TOUCH   **by Rosalyn West**
78511-0/ $5.50 US/ $7.50 Can

WINTERBURN'S ROSE   **by Kate Moore**
78457-2/ $5.50 US/ $7.50 Can

INDIGO   **by Beverly Jenkins**
78658-3/ $5.50 US/ $7.50 Can

SPRING RAIN   **by Susan Weldon**
78068-2/ $5.50 US/ $7.50 Can

THE MACKENZIES: FLINT   **by Ana Leigh**
78096-8/ $5.50 US/ $7.50 Can

LOVE ME NOT   **by Eve Byron**
77625-1/ $5.50 US/ $7.50 Can